SATURNIUS MONS

Jeremy L. Jones

Cover Design by Nick Martin
Edited By Madison Hansen

This novel is a work of fiction. Names character places and
incidents are either the product of the author's imagination
or are used fictitiously. Any resemblance to actual events
organizations or persons living or dead is purely
coincidental and beyond the interest of either the author or
publisher.

Saturnius Mons
Ruins of Empire #1
Copyright ©2018 by Jeremy L. Jones

ISBN: 978-1-7324709-0-3

ISBN (ePUB) 978-1-7324709-1-0

To Kari

The woman whose beauty and kindness inspired Althea, whose stubborn dedication and tenacity inspired Isra, and who inspires me more every day.

"Gods conceal from men the happiness of death so that they may endure life."

Lucan

PROLOGUE

As I write this, it is exactly ten years since the beginning of the third millennium AD. Five years ago on July 7th, 2999, I, along with millions of others around the world, watched the launch of Corporation Spaceship: Discovery. *The event marked the beginning of a new age of exploration for mankind. It was a testament to the endurance of the human spirit and a symbol of our species' thirst for knowledge. That was the rhetoric used by the leading members of the Corporation, at least.*

Unknown to the cheering crowds that witnessed the launch, Discovery *was a rather ironic name for the vessel. Humankind was not exploring the unknown, but returning to a place they had been forced to abandon centuries ago. When Europeans first set sail for the New World in the eighteenth century, they had no words to describe the act of finding something that nobody knew existed. Here in the third millennium, we shall have to create a word that means 'to discover what was previously known but since forgotten.'*

It's hard to imagine that a space-faring civilization

once thrived on Earth. Its great cities are little more than ruins, its technological advancements lost to time. Even the Ministry and the Corporation are mere shadows of the governments and corporations that once dominated the globe.

There was a time when global civilization spread to every moon and planet in the solar system that could be made adaptable to human life. They established colonies for resource extraction and trade. Distances that seemed insurmountable became crowded thoroughfares. It was a wonder of human creation never before seen nor replicated.

Then came the Fall of Civilization. Deprived of resources and the technical knowledge needed to maintain them, those colonies collapsed. The people, however, continued. On September 05, 3002 the first mission to Mars since the Fall found an entire society still thriving on the vast equatorial plains. The explorers that first met with this long-lost civilization described them as a society of scattered, barely civilized warlords. Some went as far as to describe them as 'savages'. Any memory of their ancestral homeland existed only in myth and legend passed down through the generations.

In spite of that—or because of it—they had survived.

Like the Martian society, our 31st century world is a crude facsimile of an ancient golden age. What caused civilization to collapse into catastrophe only a couple centuries into the second millennium? What happened to the people left behind on those far flung worlds?

I have dedicated my life to finding the answers to these questions and this book is my attempt to share them with the world.

-from The Fall: The Decline and Failure of 21st Century Civilization by
Martin Raffe.

CHAPTER ONE

It could be that civilization is an inherently destructive force. A kind of virus that consumes and destroys everything around it and, when it can no longer sustain itself, commits suicide.

-from The Fall: The Decline and Failure of 21st Century Civilization
by Martin Raffe.

Then, Viekko was awake.

Coming out of hibernation was like waking for the first time. No memories. No pain. No fear. Just darkness and an all-encompassing comfortable stench like that of a well-worn boot.

The darkness turned into a blinding light and Viekko heard a computerized female voice. Some programmer somewhere probably thought that it sounded friendly and comforting. For Viekko it sounded like a woman whispering words of comfort while she looked for a good place to stick a knife.

"Good morning. Your name is Viekko Spade. Today is

April 3rd, 3010. You have been asleep for thirteen months, seven days and sixteen hours. You are aboard the Corporation Resource Transport Ship *Innovation* in a transfer orbit around Saturn en route to the moon, Titan."

Titan. The word echoed in his head like a profanity screamed in church. Memories of exactly who he was and what he was doing here were still fuzzy. They were like pictures in a stranger's photo album. But something about Titan made his guts stir. He knew there was to be some nasty business on Titan, but he couldn't remember why. Only the vague feeling that if there was to be any judgment on the day he died, Titan would be part of the conversation. And possibly the cause.

The voice continued, "The other members of your party, Althea Fallon and Isra Jicarrio, are already reanimated. Althea Fallon requests that you see her in Medical Bay 25 for a post-hibernation physical exam. Some mild muscle discomfort and nausea are a normal part of reanimation."

Whoever wrote this spiel obviously had a twisted sense of humor. It was like saying that jumping out of the airlock 'may cause a slight change in pressure'. Every muscle in his body felt like it had been tied to two horses running in opposite directions and the only thing that kept him from being sick in the hibernation pod was the fact that he couldn't muster the strength. Also, he hadn't eaten anything for over a year.

There was a hiss of rushing air and a drop in pressure that made his ears pop. A small door opened near his feet to a white, glowing beyond. A harness that held him down released and he started to float in a box a little bigger than a coffin.

"The Corporation welcomes you as a guest aboard *Innovation*. Please notify any crew member if there is anything we can do to make your visit more productive. Be careful as extended hibernation may have prolonged effects. Thank you and have a pleasant day."

The last of his memories assembled themselves in his brain and the phrase 'have a pleasant day' seemed like the punchline of a sick joke. He was Viekko Spade, wild man of the Martian steppes. A kind of human ruin from a society caught in the rising tide of civilization. He was here as part of the Human Reconnection Project, a small team of explorers whose aim it was to protect and preserve extra-terrestrial societies and cultures.

But, really, if there was a society left on Titan, he was going to destroy it. Not by choice, but it was inevitable. Civilization was about to descend on Titan and civilization has the same effect on a native culture as a wildfire has on an ancient forest.

But that was his job and it was time he got to it.

The hibernation chamber aboard *Innovation* was little more than two filing cabinets set across from one another. One for personal effects and one for humans.

He pulled himself out of his pod and hung there for a moment hoping the spinning in his head would calm down. Around him, others floated out of their own little holes. Scientists, engineers, and those with no skill except the ability to hold a gun all milled together in this little room. Some looked green and bent over double as they got violently ill inside a black plastic bag. Others didn't seem affected at all.

Trying to keep a low profile, Viekko pushed his way to the other side of the room and found the locker with his own personal effects. He pressed his thumb to a black pad near the locker number. The bolts slid aside and the steel-colored door swung open. He retrieved the few clothes he brought from Earth: a white khaki suit and a wide-brimmed hat with a black stripe. They seemed archaic and frivolous in a spaceship of simple white plastic and Spartan accommodations. Still, the jacket had its uses. For example, it provided a convenient hiding place that the overworked Corporate dock security wasn't as likely to check. Keeping an eye on those around him, he pulled out the suit jacket and started rummaging through the pockets.

If one were to distill all the pleasures of the world and make them into a drug, they would be left with a dose of triple-T. If someone wanted to destroy that world, they would make sure every single person had a dose. It was a drug that made everything feel so good and its victim feel so sharp and alive that the un-enhanced life wasn't worth living anymore.

He plucked a little blue glass container from his pocket. It was shaped like a pill and about as large as the tip of his little finger. The blue gas that swirled inside was so reactive that it had to be contained in glass as it would melt most conventional polymers. Then he placed it between his molars and bit down. There was a sharp sting of glass against his gums. He breathed the gas it released. It tasted like burned plastic and sugar and burned his lungs.

As quick as the flick of a light switch, his world was clear. He tasted the blood from where the shards made tiny cuts in his mouth. He could smell the chemicals they pumped into the ship's air supply to combat the effects of zero gravity on the human body. The hair on his arms stood up at the chill in the air. He felt fear, trepidation, and excitement.

He felt alive.

Next to his suit, there was the standard light blue cotton pants and shirt that was the unofficial uniform of Corporation vessels. He pulled it out of the locker and started to squeeze into it. Whoever was in charge of making these things obviously never planned on a man of Viekko's size. It wasn't just that he was tall, but he was tall and broad. Men had a tendency to call him 'sir' when he was in earshot. Probably to make up for the things whispered about him when he wasn't.

Then there was his hair. Martian warriors traditionally let their hair grow their entire life and braided it into a queue. It was a symbol of respect and masculinity on his home world but here, in zero gravity and unbraided, it was a giant, irritating cloud of hair.

He pulled it back and braided it as well as he could while floating in the hibernation chamber. He briefly considered asking someone to help but the only people on this ship who could braid hair were probably women and they would do it wrong. They'd make him look like a girl. His queue might be a mess, but at least he'd have his dignity.

Dressed and put together, he floated out of the hibernation chamber hatch. The corridors outside were already crammed with people flying toward some important thing or another. Luckily, med bay 25 wasn't far nor terribly hard to find. Viekko knocked on the outside of the hatch a couple of times. He wasn't sure why; it just seemed like a polite thing to do before he went in.

What Viekko saw inside was the most fantastic torture chamber ever dreamed up even by the most diseased mind. Its primary feature was five slabs that hovered in the center of the room, each fitted with a set of straps. Some might say that they were there to keep patients secure in zero gravity and Viekko was sure that was true. However, above the slabs there was a jumble of steel and plastic all set on metal arms and flexible hoses so the medic could select something horrible for every hole the gods drilled into him. Those that wouldn't fill a hole could put a new one in. The sight of the apparatus probably gave more than a few people a powerful urge to make for the nearest exit if not for the straps.

Althea Fallon was waiting for him. She floated near one of the corners touching icons on a hologram projected in front of her. She wore the same blue jumpsuit Viekko did, although she filled it out much better. Of course, Althea would look good in a tarp. She had the kind of fiery too-red hair and piercing green eyes that was only achievable through genetic modification. Floating there, she looked like a kind of angel sent to redeem humanity. Or possibly damn it.

Althea saw Viekko climb through the hatch and hit a switch on a device attached to her arm that made the projection disappear.

"Viekko," said Althea, smiling at him, "How are you feeling?"

In his youth, Viekko heard stories about women so beautiful that armies would fight and die in their name. Any man fighting for Althea would never see battle; she had a smile that would make a convert of anyone.

"Good," said Viekko, "Under the circumstances."

"Any discomfort? Muscle aches, joint pain, nausea, that sort of thing?" said Althea, floating closer.

"No more than usual."

"Lay down," said Althea, patting one of the slabs. "Let's have a look."

'Lay down' was an interesting term for what he had to do. He twisted and arranged his body roughly parallel to the slab. Althea pressed a few more buttons on the metal cuff attached to her arm. Stiff straps unrolled from the side of the slab, around Viekko's body, and bound him to the metal surface and a hologram of Viekko's body materialized above him.

"How's things on Earth?" asked Viekko.

Althea touched the air near the hologram and the projection's skin and muscle disappeared revealing Viekko's inner workings.

"We're not on Earth," said Althea her voice all-business. "You've got mild muscle atrophy. But your cardiovascular system looks good. Blood pressure normal. Heart is strong."

"You seein' anyone?"

Althea floated over Viekko. Her red hair radiated around her face like a halo. She produced a small light from her pocket and waved it over Viekko's eyes. "Reflexes normal. Pupil dilation is a little slow."

"You didn't answer the question," mumbled Viekko squinting into the light.

She turned off the light and turned her attention back to the hologram. "That's because it's none of your business. Take a deep breath please."

Viekko did. "How 'bout the medical consortium? Ain't they any closer to reinstatin' you as a doctor?"

"Another deep breath please."

It wasn't that Viekko wanted to be with Althea again. Well...he did. He'd chop off his queue at the base of his neck for another roll in the hay with Althea Fallon. But that wasn't what he was after now. Viekko found that, when he woke up on the ass-end of the solar system, it was best to focus on the constants of life. Establish a kind of psychic link to those things that proved he was still in the same world that he left when he entered hibernation.

He'd always have his white wide-brimmed hat and khaki suit.

He'd always wear the queue of a Martian warrior.

And Althea Fallon would always treat him like a memory she'd rather forget.

There was a sharp jab in the base of his neck. "Ow!" said Viekko pressing against the restraints, "Ya see, that's your problem. Bedside manner. I'll bet if you were a little nicer—"

Althea pulled something away from his neck. "My mistake. I assumed a tough man such as yourself could handle a simple blood test."

Viekko tried to relax. The good news was that triple-T was hard to detect unless the medic was a good one. Something about the blood brain barrier...he didn't know. But it was always possible. It hadn't happened yet, but it was possible.

Althea floated up to look at the results on a computer screen. "Viekko, are you sure that you are feeling quite all right?"

The problem was Althea was one of the best medics in the Universe despite being banished to the ass-end of it.

Viekko nearly strained a facial muscle trying to look innocent, "Whatcha mean?"

"It's just that...well it's probably nothing, but your plasma endorphins are quite low."

Viekko shrugged as much as the restraints would allow, "It's hibernation. Does all sorts of *sarmagchin baas* to my innards."

Althea floated to another computer terminal. "Low endorphins can be indicative of several problems, but nothing life threatening. It's worth watching in case it materializes into something more severe. Would you take off

10

your shirt please?"

The restraints released and Viekko floated off the slab. "Always tryin' to get me naked."

"Without the sexual innuendo, if you please?"

Viekko grumbled as he pulled the shirt over his head. "I seem to remember a woman with a sense of humor."

Althea opened a compartment and pulled out something that looked like two irregular slabs of metal held together by wires and pocked with lights, ports, and small displays. To say it looked complicated would be to say that the sun looked big. Some engineer had obviously worked out some childhood issues on this piece of equipment.

"You wouldn't believe the amount of data the Corporation demands from crews about to do missions on the surface of a planet. Especially crews they are not keen on having in the first place. If my sense of humor is lacking, it is because we're on a schedule and there's no time slot marked out with your particular brand of ... let's call it charm."

"And just what is that thing?" accused Viekko pointing to the device in Althea's hand.

Althea floated forward. "The RX5 Field Medical Regulator. Something I helped develop before..." she sighed as her voice trailed off. Then she continued, "It will let me monitor your vitals during the mission. Come here and turn around please."

Viekko maneuvered along the wall until he was about a meter away from Althea. As soon as he spun around, she clamped the device on his shoulder. The thing tightened and felt like it was digging into his flesh. He winced as it whirred, whined, and finally settled into place.

They both said nothing for a few moments although he could feel Althea working some controls on the back. Her breathing was slow and came in deep, heaving breaths as if she was trying to focus her mind on the present and away from the more horrific topic of 'could have been.'

"For what it's worth, Althea. I'm glad you'll be here with us," said Viekko with as much sincerity as he could muster.

"If it makes you feel any better, this device is made to be

integrated with the EROS suit. It's probably uncomfortable now, but when they get you fitted for that, you won't even know it's there," Althea said, still working on the controls.

"I know it's been hard for you. Booted out of the medical consortium and all that. But, you know, their loss. Our gain."

Althea finished her calibrations and the device loosened enough for her to pull it off. "That's all I need for now. That will establish some baseline conditions to help it regulate fluids, body temperature and blood chemistry and alert me to possible problems."

Viekko grabbed his shirt out of the air and put it back on. Great—he would have Althea monitoring his body every minute of every day. He thought back to the stash of triple-T still in his jacket pocket. He should be fine sneaking a dose when he needed it. Triple-T was hard to track and Althea would have other things on her mind. Plus, there could be worse things.

Then, one of those worse things happened. Isra Jicarrio opened the hatch and floated into the medical bay. "Is Viekko up and ready yet? We have a meeting with Vince Laban...five minutes ago."

"And nice to see you, Isra," said Viekko. "Out terrorizin' the locals early today?"

Isra glared. No one could drop the temperature in the room with a look alone quite like her. She was a small woman with short black hair, olive skin and dark, almond eyes. She wore the same Corporation blue jumpsuit as everyone else but, in contrast to Viekko, the clothing hung loose over her small, slender frame. At first glance, she was the quiet unassuming type; she could disappear into the crowd if it wasn't for the fact that most of the crowd would be trying to keep their distance from her the minute she spoke. And there was something else about Isra that bothered Viekko.

"What is wrong with him?" said Isra nodding her head at Viekko.

"Nothing to speak of. Just a few anomalies coming out of hibernation," said Althea, putting her equipment away.

Isra examined every inch of Viekko from his hair to his toenails. "Anomalies? He is nervous. Is there something I need to know, Viekko?"

Isra could read people like a book and she had a tendency to flip through the boring parts. Viekko wouldn't go so far as to say she was psychic, but whatever innate skill or talent that psychics needed to convince people they were psychic, Isra had it. A lot of it.

Lying didn't typically work but deflection could if well-timed.

"I need my guns," said Viekko folding his arms.

Isra looked him over again. "They are still in storage. We will ask Laban about them when we see him."

"I ain't setting foot on that *tsosni burkhuleer kuchigdsan baidag* moon unarmed, Isra."

"*Ugsiig khar,*" Isra snapped back. That was the other unsettling thing about Isra, she had a gift with language. Most scholars who studied the Martian languages for years could never get the pronunciation right. Isra spent a week among them and talked like a native when she wanted to.

Isra set her face into a carefully neutral expression. "You will be adequately supplied for this mission; however, I do not anticipate a scenario where violence will become necessary. Now please come with me."

Isra left through the same hatch she entered through and Viekko followed. That was the problem with both Althea and Isra. They were both products of Civilization, a system designed to minimize the amount of violence needed for a productive solution.

Pushing himself after Isra, he passed by a large window. The small orange and blue moon, Titan, was getting closer.

Civilization meant people could meet without violence. But when two civilizations meet, violence was almost a foregone conclusion.

There was going to be blood.

Whose blood and for what reason were still details that would be sorted out in time.

CHAPTER TWO

There are few human emotions as base, vile and creative as greed.
It is a force that changed whole worlds beyond Earth. It is the drive
that pulled people from their terrestrial Eden to far-flung colonies. It is
also what ultimately stranded them.

-from The Fall: The Decline and Failure of 21st Century Civilization
by Martin Raffe.

The tight corridors through *C.R.T.S Innovation* were like some sort of small animal habitat in a madman's laboratory. It was a maze of cramped white plastic and aluminum that twisted and turned around each other so much that any sense of direction was jammed into the tumble drier. Just to make it extra exciting, every corridor and hallway was packed with people. Engineers, soldiers, scientists and crew members damn near had to crawl over each other in the zero-gravity. They all seemed to know where they were going and they were all in a terrible rush to get there.

Viekko could barely make his way through it all. He

found himself inching along the walls trying to escape the press of humanity.

"We are late, Viekko," said Isra, several meters ahead. "Some urgency if you please."

Isra took a ballistic approach to navigating the crowd. She moved with the assumption that people would get out of her way and, not surprising given her normal demeanor, most of them did.

"Did you not hear me? We are late and Laban will use that to his advantage," scolded Isra, nearly barreling into a worried-looking scientist.

She was barely sociable at the best of times, but today she had all the good will and patience of a crocodile with a piece of driftwood crammed up its nethers.

"Who we meetin' again?" asked Viekko, narrowly dodging a couple Corporate executives coming the other way.

"Vince Laban. Mission commander and Energy Consortium executive."

That explained her mood. High ranking Corporate figures tended to be the immovable object to Isra's unstoppable force.

Viekko darted through a hole in the crowd, "So whatchu want me to do?"

"Show up and look tough."

Viekko cursed and flung himself forward. It wasn't that he minded that people viewed him as the embodiment of rage and muscle packed into human form, but he hated being used like he was nothing but a predictable chess piece to be moved around when and where they wanted. But he kept his mouth shut.

And yet, somehow, without even looking back, Isra sensed his annoyance. She stopped and twisted around in the air. "Viekko, you are one of the finest extraterrestrial survival experts in the world as well as a fine military tactician. I am aware and, trust me, I intend to bank on both those skills when we are on Titan. But right now I need a show of force and you are the best visualization I can come up with on short notice."

Viekko grabbed a hand-hold to keep him from plowing into a couple of annoyed Corporation Marines and said, "You think you're gonna needin' a military tactician on Titan?"

"I like to be ready for any number of scenarios, especially with the Corporation involved."

Without another word, Isra pushed back down the corridor and through the crowds. Viekko could only sigh and try to follow. Isra was nervous, and Isra didn't get nervous. The prospects on Titan were getting bleaker by the second.

She continued to lead the way through the white plastic maze until she came to a hatch. At first glance, it was indistinguishable from the dozens they passed between here and the medical bay. Except a small digital sign just above the door release that read, 'Vince Laban: Mission Director'.

Without the slightest hint of hesitation or trepidation, Isra pulled the door release, pushed the hatch open and pulled herself inside.

Now, whoever Vince Laban was, he seemed to be in some sort of denial when it came to space travel. He was a man who wasn't going to let a little setback like zero-gravity keep him from having a well-ordered office. As Viekko pulled himself inside after Isra, he saw a desk complete with an 'In' and 'Out' box and some kind of spinning office knickknack. They were all, presumably, bolted to the top of the desk to keep them all from floating away. The desk, along with a few chairs and a filing cabinet, was bolted to the floor...or ceiling, depending on how one entered the room.

Viekko pushed himself towards the desk and tried to move the spinning thing attached to it. It was one of those toys for those who found themselves creeping towards terminal boredom. It used magnets to spin faster and longer than most things were intended to. That was, as near as Viekko could figure, all it did.

Viekko flicked the spinning part. "What sorta mind does this, you think?"

Isra just surveyed the room with a sense of awe and said,

"The kind that has never been told he cannot have something he wants. In other words, the worst kind."

A man entered from a hatch on the other side of the room. At least it was probably a man. Rats didn't normally grow that big or wear expensive black suits. He had a small scrunched face that radiated from a nose that was several sizes too big for his body. His jet-black hair was combed to mathematical precision and heavily caked with something that could stop a bullet. He plastered a wide amenable smile on his face and pulled himself down to the desk. Even his smile was the kind of fake, toothy grin that never precedes something honest or truthful. He situated himself in a grand, red cushioned chair and gestured to the smaller chairs in front of his desk.

"Please. Have a seat," he said.

The way the man spoke made Viekko want to look behind his chair for an oil-slick.

"How exactly do you expect...?" Viekko started to say. Then he noticed that every red antique chair was fitted with a lap belt.

Once they were both seated and strapped in, Laban steepled his hands and said, "I apologize that we were not able to speak before the entire crew went into hibernation. Your addition to the roster was.... immediate."

He touched the top of his desk and a series of holographic documents appeared. He scrolled through a few pages acting as if he forgot he had people in his office to talk to him. Viekko felt a hot rise of anger but Isra's expression remained perfectly still.

After a few minutes he waved his hand and the documents disappeared. "While Ministry-Corporation treaties allow oversight committees aboard trans-planetary missions, you should inform your superiors that last second additions such as yours disrupt the entire flow of a mission. This has been in the planning stages for months and there was ample time for your people to request passage instead of forcing it on us hours before liftoff."

Isra took a moment and smoothed out some of the

wrinkles in her jumpsuit. This was something Isra did to take control of the situation. There was complicated psychology involved, but it basically meant that the conversation would start when and how Isra wanted it to.

"I apologize, but it could not be helped. And to be perfectly honest, we are not an oversight committee. Not exactly. I am here representing the Ministry's Human Reconnection Project," said Isra after a minute or so. "Are you familiar?"

"I am," said Laban. "I seem to recall you did some excellent work on Mars and some of the Jovian moons, yes? I understand you brought back some very.... entertaining specimens." Laban flashed Viekko a smug smile.

The Martian closed his eyes and imagined caving Laban's skull in with the spinning knickknack. It brought some measure of peace.

Isra brushed a strand of hair out of her face. "Yes. We discover and study lost civilizations stranded on other planets after Earth fell. Which brings us to why we are here. Time is a factor and we could not wait to plan and execute a separate Ministry mission. Signing aboard *Innovation* as an oversight committee is what you might call a... loophole."

Laban's smile grew wider as if being irritated was a pleasant state of mind for the man. "A loophole? Ms. Jicarrio I don't know what game you and the Ministry are playing, but several Ministry officers signed off on the mission specifics and..."

Isra interrupted, "Tell me, Mr. Laban, are you aware of any evidence that Titan might harbor a civilization?"

Viekko couldn't help but look at Isra on that one. It wasn't unusual for her to set people up for a lie, but she was typically a lot more subtle than that. She might as well have opened a bear trap inches from Laban's face.

Laban's expression melted into something resembling concern. "I see. I suppose I should offer my deepest apologies."

"It just so happens," Isra started automatically, "I have documents that prove...wait, what did you say?"

"Yeah, whatchu you say?" asked Viekko.

Laban laid his hands flat down on the table, "Ms. Jicarrio, your reputation within the Ministry is impeccable. Furthermore, delaying a Corporation mission so that you could make it on board is not a minor feat. The Corporation runs on a schedule, I'm sure you know this, and the schedule waits for no one. Which tells me that you have found something. Something I was not aware of, to be sure. This mission was planned in good faith and for the betterment of all humankind. But clearly there has been a... miscalculation. And for that I am sorry."

Incredible, thought Viekko, the man managed a completely sincere apology while accepting exactly zero responsibility. For him or anyone else. Truly the sign of a born leader, at least by Corporation standards.

"I have documents," said Isra unwilling to let a good offensive go to waste, "leaked from Corporate files about the hydrocarbon supply on Titan. May I upload a copy to your SET-path?

The surface of the desk glowed faint blue and a series of icons appeared just above the surface. Laban touched a few. "Please. Go ahead."

Isra touched the screen attached to her forearm. A few seconds later, numbers scrolled above the surface of the desk. Laban watched for a few moments and said, "Ah, yes. This is the hydrocarbon exploration analysis. It lists coordinates on the moon and the level of hydrocarbon deposits that might be available."

"Not might," said Isra folding her arms, "These figures are far too precise to be scanned from orbit. These numbers came from the ground. Pulled from some kind of surface installation settled before the Fall. That means there is still working technology on Titan which proves that someone's there to tend to it. Furthermore, the Corporation knows this."

The numbers disappeared and Laban leaned forward and put his hands together as if pleading. "Like I said. I offer my deepest apologies. I had no idea where those numbers came from. All I knew is that they were good enough to fund a mission."

"You had no idea?" said Isra.

"Miss Jicarrio. I know you view the Corporation as a group of power-hungry sociopaths that would sell their own grandmothers to an organ dealer for a promotion in the Corporate ranks, and your assumption is more accurate than even you know. When our technicians found this information, I will bet their first instinct was to keep its source a secret. But protecting our investment is hardly a crime."

"It is when you withhold information regarding the violation of a Ministry treaty."

"Only if such a violation is known but, as I've tried to explain, Ms. Jicarrio, I had no knowledge regarding the source of the data."

Isra smiled but there wasn't an ounce of friendliness contained in it. It was the smile of a predator who just found its prey cornered, "Ignorance is not a defense. You are in charge of this mission, which means that any and all activity —"

"—Is the responsibility of the managing personnel," interrupted Laban, "Fair enough. How about a show of good faith then? What can I do for the Human Reconnection Project?"

"First of all, your landing zone between the Ligeia Mare and the Kraken Mare has got to change. I have reason to believe that there is a population at that location and the last thing I need is for you to drop landers right on top of them."

Laban took a deep breath and Isra braced herself for a fight. It was a confrontation that was expected and necessary. There was no way that Laban would give up his landing zone, but it would give Isra a starting point to compromise.

"Very well. We have a backup landing zone on a peninsula approximately sixty kilometers to the East. We will begin operations there if that is your wish."

Or there was the possibility that he would just roll over

and give Isra whatever she wanted. It was not a contingency that Viekko had anticipated and, from the look on Isra's face, neither had she.

"Wait...you are willing to move the landing zone?" said Isra.

"As a show of good faith," said Laban spreading his hands, "I can move it farther east if you would like, but if I go much farther away it will be harder for you to get to that population. You are going to visit them while you are there, yes?"

"Uh... yes, of course," said Isra.

"Then I will arrange a crawler for you and your team. I can also arrange a military escort if you would like."

"No," said Isra dropping the word like a steel weight. "I do not want anyone Corporate anywhere near that city. Do I make myself clear?"

"Crystal," said Laban again spreading his hands in a gesture of surrender. "I will see to it personally that no member of my team gets within twenty-five kilometers of the city."

Isra leaned back again confused. It was like getting into a boxing match with a waterfall.

"Is there anything else me or my team can do for you?" said Laban.

Isra sat and stared for a moment. Every part of Laban's face practically radiated sincere helpfulness. Viekko wondered if Isra saw anything else. If she did, she didn't say anything.

"My guns," said Viekko, "I had 'em surrendered when I boarded the shuttle on Earth. I'm gonna need them once we hit dirt." Isra flashed him a glare and he added, "What? He asked if there was anythin' else he could do."

"Of course," said Laban with his voice like engine grease, "All weapons confiscated before hibernation are stored in the armory. I'll make sure they are delivered to our military depot on Titan. You may pick them up there, good enough?"

Viekko nodded.

"I have to admit," said Isra suspiciously, "I did not

expect you to be this helpful. You are aware if we find a lost civilization on Titan, the Ministry will force you to halt your hydrocarbon extraction operation?"

"Delay," said Laban abruptly, "Temporarily. *If* you find something."

Viekko folded his arms, "Whaddya mean 'if'?"

Laban reached out to touch the holographic documents in front of him. The pages cycled to the left with every flick of his wrist, "Well your only real proof that there is anyone on Titan the fact that our orbital scans were too accurate."

Isra pushed against the restraints that held her in her seat, "They *are* too accurate. Nobody can get that level of detail from orbit."

Laban waved his hand and the document disappeared, "The Ministry can't. I think you will find that, within the Corporation, all things are possible if they are profitable enough. But that's not the point. I am willing to help you because I have nothing to hide. And if, by some miracle, you are correct and there is a civilization on Titan that has been lost to us then we will gladly cooperate to ensure their safety and prosperity. The Corporation is on Titan to make a profit but I would like to believe we are building something bigger than that. We are on the precipice of a new age. We must move forward as a civilization without repeating the mistakes of our past."

He held out his hand toward Isra.

She shook it and said, "It does my heart good to hear you say that."

"We are currently in a transfer orbit," Laban said, releasing Isra's hand. "We'll be firing the engines that will put us in a stable orbit above Titan very soon. It would be wise to find a safe place for you and your crew."

"Thank you, I will do that," said Isra unstrapping herself from the seat.

Viekko followed her as she pulled herself back into the hallway.

"There ain't no way he's not up to something," Viekko said after they were far enough away.

"I am aware," said Isra. Her voice had a sub-zero quality to it.

"If he don't got somethin' rollin' 'round his noggin, he'da fought you on some of that. He just rolled over like a broke-dick dog."

"I am aware."

"So whatchu wanna do about it?" asked Viekko, losing his patience at Isra's constant monotone.

"Nothing."

"Nothin'?"

Isra grabbed a hand-hold that brought her to a quick stop and flipped around. "If we do anything to cause trouble now he can go the Ministry and rightfully claim that he cooperated fully to the best of his ability. He has got us right where he wants us."

"Is there any chance that he was being truthful in there?"

Isra scowled, "The only time the Corporation is ever truthful is when they are sliding a knife between your ribs. But for now, play nice. When Laban makes his move, we react. But not before."

Isra turned and pulled herself down the corridor.

The worst thing about the crew decks was the stench. It was the sweat and shit of five-hundred marines and engineers recirculated in the same confined space for over fourteen months. It even made the bare aluminum walls feel greasy as Laban floated through the crowd.

And there were people everywhere. Ever since he left the executive deck, Vince Laban felt crushed against the walls by the constant flow of humanity. And even though people took one look at his pressed black suit and gave him extra room, there was still something claustrophobic about the place.

In truth, he would never be found outside the executive decks, but Laban was a pragmatic man above all else. Isra Jicarrio seemed satisfied for the time being, but that was temporary. She would start to cause trouble soon enough and it would be best to have an agent in play.

Laban found the marine barracks just as a recorded message played through the speakers, "Orbital thrusters engaging in one minute. All personnel and cargo must be secured immediately. Repeat, orbital thrusters in one minute..."

Corporate soldiers in dark-blue uniforms and grey body armor scrambled to find a place to strap in as the recorded message continued.

Places to sit were filling up, but there were a group of seats around one marine in particular that were noticeably vacant. He had a large scar etched down the side of his face and short, blonde hair cut to exact Corporate standards. He sat alone sharpening a knife with a leather strap held between one hand and his foot. The blade looked long enough to run through two or three people if he put enough effort into it. And he looked like the type who would give it a try.

Laban pulled himself into a seat next to the soldier and buckled the seatbelt. "It is my understanding that weapons are not allowed aboard Corporation spacecraft."

The man slid the blade up and examined the edge. "They made an exception for me. Because I'm such a nice guy. Can I help you, sir?"

Vince detected an air of sarcasm in the marine's voice. Bordering on defiant. "Sergeant Carr, am I right?"

"You'd be right." He ran the knife back down the strap and said, "And just what can I do for you?"

The speakers clicked on again, "forty-five seconds until orbital thrusters..."

"I have a problem. I am told that you have a gift for solving problems. Problems that need to be taken care of... discretely."

The soldier continued to sharpen his knife. When it became clear that Carr had no intention to react, Laban continued, "You are aware that we have some... guests on this mission, Sergeant?"

Carr shook his head, "We are not to engage, hinder,

molest or interact with Ministry personnel in any way without express permission from command. That would be you. Sir."

"And, of course, I would never give an order contrary to the wishes of the Great Corporation. The CEO himself expressed his wish that no action will be taken against the Ministry or the Human Reconnection Project."

"Well that saves us some time," said Carr, returning his attention to his knife.

"I need someone to watch and report back to me. Someone to make sure that they are following the treaties between the Ministry and the Corporation."

"Sir. You are in the wrong compartment, sir. Agents are farther up. You probably passed them on your way here."

Laban smiled. "Agents require paperwork. I need some work done... off the books."

"Fifteen seconds," said the computerized voice, "All personnel..."

"Work like that is highly illegal, sir."

"You will be compensated, of course."

"Why, if I may ask, are you so eager to keep this off the books?"

"I was put in charge of this mission to ensure that the Corporation has control of the hydrocarbon fields of Titan and I intend to do that. The Corporation may be bound by the treaties with the Ministry, but I am not. I may be punished for my actions if they are ever found out, but it is a risk I can assume."

"Kind of a human sacrifice thing? Suffer for the greater good?"

"Something like that."

Carr sheathed the knife, "I want 600 million in Corporation Fiat. 300 million paid in full to an account in my wife's name before we land on Titan. And I want to verify that she received it. The other 300 million is due on my return to *Innovation*."

The voice started the countdown, "Ten, nine, eight..."

"That is a lot of money, but it can be arranged."

"Then I believe we have a deal."

The countdown ended and the ship jolted forward as the nuclear engines fired all at once to slow the ship into a stable orbit around the moon.

CHAPTER THREE

History has a strange sense of the ironic.

In the beginning of the twenty-first century, global corporations emerged on the world stage as a power that rivaled the traditional nation-state. Their lust for money and power drove them to, at first, undermine and, later, utterly destroy the governments whose job it was to keep them in check. After the collapse of the great nations—the United States, China, the European Union, India, and the Russian Federation—there was only one entity that could possibly fill the power vacuum.

Hence, the global corporations were forced, over time, to unite and form The Corporation, a governing body to provide the oversight and regulation that they fought so hard to destroy. In essence, becoming exactly what they so despised.

-from The Fall: The Decline and Failure of 21st Century Civilization

by Martin Raffe.

Titan was tidally locked to Saturn which meant that it stayed in the same spot above the horizon. Every day throughout Titan's year the ringed planet remained perfectly still while the icy moons and stars drifted across the sky. During the seven-day-long night it bathed the moon in a soft glow that rivaled the light from the sun during the day. It cast deep shadows through the towering trees and rocky outcropping that dominated the skyline.

The moon was silent except for the wind through the trees and the muted sound of laughter and mayhem that came from a certain clearing. There, the remains of a massive tanker ship lay where it crashed nearly a millennium ago. It was almost part of the forest now; only small parts of steel and aluminum underneath the vines, ferns and trees gleamed in the soft glow. The flicker of firelight could be seen through the windows that were still open to the sky. There was a rare sense of warmth on a moon coming out of another frigid night.

A solitary man opened one of the hatches. He wrapped thick, heavy furs around his body as he stepped out onto the hard, frozen ground. It was cold, dreadfully cold. It stung any piece of exposed skin. The man spat and it snapped as it froze in mid-air. It was always the coldest in the long, final hours before the sun returned to warm the moon again.

He stopped walking and turned his gaze upward. Only Saturn, Rhea, two or three icy moons, and a few of the brightest stars could cut through the constant cloud cover of Titan. The rest of the sky was like a choking black sheet. The man reflected on the tales from ancient times; stories of men who jumped from far away stars and brought the people to Titan. Tonight, it felt like whoever brought them here covered the moon in clouds so they could never escape.

Well, it was official. On this night, after hours of

argument in the Great Hall, the Elders finally made their decision and another generation of his people would grow up as slaves. Most would die but a few would come back, become old men and sell another generation into slavery. Titan was place where everything remained constant, even the sky dominated by the great ringed planet.

The man bowed his head and recited a prayer. It was the quiet sort meant to be heard only by the man and any deity that cared to listen. He spoke in the language of his people. A language that, legend said, was also a gift from the ancients who came before. *"Great Kompanio. I still believe you care about all the people of Titan. I still believe you will come for us someday. Please, give me some sign. Show me that my faith is not misplaced. Let me know that I am doing the right thing."*

Saturn didn't move nor did any of the icy moons or stars. Nothing ever changes on Titan.

Just as the man turned to go back to the warmth of the ship, a light filled the entire sky. Brighter than Saturn. Brighter than the sun during the day. It lit the entire horizon with a blinding flash. When the light dimmed and he could see again, there was a new star flying across the sky at amazing speed.

The flash was bright enough to draw more people from the ship. They gasped at the white point of light speeding toward the horizon. There were descriptions of stars like this in the ancient writings but nothing like it had been seen in a thousand years. The people knew what they were seeing even if they couldn't put words to it.

The man turned to the assembled crowd and screamed in their native tongue, *"They have returned. They have returned! They have come to free us at last! I called for them and they have come! We must gather offerings. We meet at the landing place! Kompanio has returned! Returned to free us all!"*

Inside one of the shuttle's staging areas, Viekko struggled to pull on the shirt-piece of his EROS suit in a room with ten or fifteen other Corporate personnel. He privately wondered if someone purposely gave him a suit that was a size or two too small for him so the others could enjoy watching a man of Viekko's size turn himself into a sausage.

The material was a strange sort: flexible in some places, stiff and pokey in others. The way it felt reminded Viekko of the plate-male armor used by some tribes on the Martian steppes. Except this suit was thin, lightweight, black, and had a slight shine to it. As he pulled the top half into place the whole thing adjusted. Bits of metal, wire, and fabric pulled and pinched him in some very awkward and, at times, very personal places.

Then there was Althea's RX5 Medical Regulator. It was waiting for him in the supply locker having made its way to him from the medical bay through all sorts of Corporate channels. He clamped the device on his right shoulder and clenched his teeth while metal plates and probes spread out across his chest to his heart and to the middle of his spine on the other side.

Once he felt he was through the worst of the discomfort, he put the white khaki pants and a white jacket checking the inside pocket to make sure his stash of Triple-T was still there. He slipped a sleeve-shaped device on his forearm that covered it from wrist to elbow. He removed the earbud charging in a matchbox-sized compartment in the locker, placed it in his ear, and touched the screen on the inside of his forearm to activate it.

The same infuriating computerized woman's voice sounded in his ear: "Welcome to the Body-Mod Consortium version 8 Environmental Reorientation and Operations Suit. Our goal is to make your work outside the confines of Earth gravity and atmosphere as safe and as comfortable as possible."

That was the Corporation, thought Viekko, always trying to make everyone safe and comfortable. Like a big, suffocating blanket around all of society. He grabbed his hat and followed a few others out of staging area and into a hallway leading to the cargo bay.

"Your EROS suit is equipped with nano-actuators built into the polycarbonate weave that will help compensate for microgravity conditions. Oxide-based conductors use the suit's motion and your own heat to keep your body at a comfortable temperature while working in harsh, extra-planetary environments."

Lights flashed through the corridors and the same woman's voice announced that the main bay doors were opening. Even though the hallways were choked with engineers, scientists and soldiers, he increased his pace through the crowd. He reached one of the airlocks leading to the cargo bay already packed full with people and, despite the protests of a few, crammed himself inside before the door slammed shut.

"Your EROS suit is also equipped with an interface pad attached to your arm. This provides an uplink to the Corporation satellite network for location and communication services. Welcome to Titan and have a safe and productive visit."

The airlock door slid open and a flood of completely new, heavy, choking air filled his lungs. It was like sticking his face in a bag of noxious gases. At the same time there was something invigorating about it. There was much more oxygen here; Viekko could feel it in every cell of his body.

The cargo bay was a mass of carefully controlled chaos as a thousand different people tried to accomplish a thousand different tasks at the exact same time. Soldiers in formation marched double-time into the blinding light outside to secure the parameter. Teams of workers tried to keep spools of hose as large as a tractor tire from rolling uncontrolled down the ramp. Closer to the open doors, he could make out a landscape of towering trees already being obscured by tall metal scaffolds, inflatable domed structures, and drilling rigs. Civilization had arrived on Titan and it was already making a mess of the place.

Viekko rammed his wide-brimmed hat in place and activated the communications application through the screen on his arm and selected Isra's channel. There was a series of tones through his earpiece as the computer connected.

Isra's voice came through, "Where are you, Viekko?"

Viekko looked around. "Cargo bay. Just gonna take a walk outside and see 'bout getting my guns back."

"We will meet at the weapons depot," said Isra, ending the comm.

Viekko took his first steps onto the alien world. The ground was soft, granular, and his boots sank into it like wet sand on a beach when the waves came in. The landing zone was surrounded on three sides by a green-blue ocean that stretched beyond the horizon. Ahead, the land disappeared into a dense, green forest. The trees were so impossibly tall that the tops disappeared into the orange mist that covered the sky of Titan. From his position it looked like a solid green wall between Civilization and the rest of the planet. The sun, peeking through the perpetual clouds was just above the sea and, above it, the planet Saturn twice the size as the moon as viewed from Earth.

Even with the EROS suit, it was cold here. Not a harsh freeze, but an invigorating chill that encouraged a man to keep active to stay warm. Viekko buttoned up his jacket and went looking for the marine supply depot.

It turned out it wasn't terribly hard to find. Just about every hard-faced, dull-eyed goon wearing Corporation Blue armor was headed in the same direction and soon he found a whole mess of them lined up single-file in front of a collection of crates where a few ranking officers were handing out standard-issue gear and weapons.

Viekko got into one of the lines and, before he knew it, found himself at the front. There weren't many good things one could say about Corporation marines, but they were efficient which, depending on what they were trying to accomplish, might be another strike against them.

A corporal near the supply crates was entering

something into his own EROS computer when Viekko walked up. He gave Viekko a look of barely contained disgust and continued to key in commands on the arm computer, "Name and rank...soldier." The word 'soldier' had a distinct sarcastic tone to it.

"Viekko Spade and I'm with the Human Reconnection Project. Special assignment with the Ministry."

The corporal tapped a few icons on the screen. "Supplies for Corporation military only. Next."

A marine behind him started to push forward but Viekko didn't move. "'Scuse me, sir. I don't wanna bother you, but I got a job to do, same as you. You should have two Old-Earth style handguns..."

Another man, a sergeant, approached the line of marines and surveyed the situation for a moment. His Corporation Blue breastplate had black carbon scoring in several areas and he bore a large, jagged scar down the side of his face that just missed his left eye. Apart from that, the man's every physical characteristic was straight out of the Corporation marine guidelines from the shine on his boots to the short, blond crew cut. His gaze settled on Viekko. It was a smug, bemused look. The same look that a man like him might give to a yapping puppy right before he shot it.

"What exactly is the problem here?" he asked wearily.

Before the corporal could answer, Viekko looked the sergeant in the eye and said, "No problem. I just gonna collect my guns and then I'll be on my way. Vince Laban told me they'd be here, Sergeant."

The man activated the screen on his arm. "Carr. Sergeant Carr. Name and rank?"

"Viekko Spade. Special assignment from the Ministry."

Something flashed on the sergeant's screen that made him smile then he looked Viekko up and down as if sizing him up, "Viekko Spade? Interesting. I do see an entry in the ship manifest for a pair of antique guns, but I'm afraid I am not authorized to release any non-standard equipment to any personnel. And certainly not to... non Corporate entities."

"The hell is that supposed to mean?"

"It means that the Corporation is not in the habit of handing out unapproved weapons to civilians and letting them run rampant through the operation." The way Carr pronounced the word 'civilians' told Viekko that he was a man who divided the Universe into two groups: military and nonmilitary. Non-military belonged to the same group as cockroaches.

Viekko stood fast. "Listen, Vince Laban said this is where I could pick up my guns and I aim to stay here 'til that happens."

"Then I suggest you take it up with Laban. We've got a whole platoon to equip and we don't have time to bend over for every Ministry brat with a false sense of entitlement. Come back when you have the proper authorization. Move along."

The man behind Viekko tried to push his way in front but Viekko shot him a glare and stood his ground. He took a step forward until he was eye to eye with Sergeant Carr. The two sized each other up for a moment before Carr added, "You got something to say?"

The wisest thing would be to just walk away. On the other hand, there were few things in the Universe better than slapping down some testosterone-torqued imbecile. It was the most satisfying thing one could accomplish fully clothed.

"Just some advice," said Viekko, "I don't know what aftershave you are using but it smells like a dog's *gurgaldai*. You know you can just spray a little 'round, right? You're not supposed to bathe in the stuff."

Carr chuckled slightly. "What do you wanna do about it?"

Viekko shrugged, "Might take you out and toss you in the ocean there. Wash some of the stink off ya."

Carr paused for a moment with the smug smile still on his face then he looked at the man behind Viekko. "Get this guy out of here and keep the line moving. I'm on assignment so I will be briefing my unit early. I suggest you all be ready..."

A hand tried to pull Viekko away from the front of the line. Without thinking, the Martian spun around and punched. With luck he caught a soldier just below the jaw and the marine fell like a sack of grain in a stupid blue uniform. Another rushed forward and swung for Viekko's head. He covered himself with his left arm while his right landed a punch in the man's kidneys. The marine groaned, staggered back and Viekko took the opportunity to land a punch directly on the man's face.

Viekko put up his hands and waited for another fighter but the rest of the marines in line kept their distance. Behind him, there was the whine and click of several Corporation sidearms being cocked. Viekko put his hands on the back of his head. He turned to find that he had an excellent view of the inside of at least nine gun barrels.

Isra strolled into this scene as if Viekko being held at gunpoint by several angry Corporation officers was as normal as a sunrise in the morning. "Calm down. Everybody, just calm down for a moment. What exactly is happening here?"

Carr lowered his gun but the others around him didn't. "This man assaulted my soldiers."

Isra looked up at Viekko accusingly. "Is this true?"

"There was a disagreement," said Viekko mildly.

"What kind of disagreement?"

"I wanted my guns, they felt the exact opposite."

Isra sighed and pulled up the sleeve on her jacket. Isra had thrown some clothes on over her Eros suit as well, but only a pair of tan pants and a thick brown jacket both of which had seen more than a few off-world missions and would likely see a few more. She activated the EROS computer and started to work.

Carr bared his teeth and turned to his own soldiers, "Put this man in bonds and escort him to the brig."

Isra didn't look up, "As you were, marines. Sergeant, I see you put a hold on Viekko's guns. Now, I have authorization from two Ministry officials and one

Consortium officer to secure all equipment needed for this mission, and that overrides such a petty procedural tactic."

Carr straightened up as if pressing a point that overrides everything else. "He assaulted my men."

Viekko balled up his fist. "Damn right. I'll take out every last one of you *yamaany khairlagchid—*"

Isra looked up, "Viekko! Stand down or I'll slap the bonds on you myself."

Viekko seethed but stepped back.

Isra went back to her EROS computer, "A copy of the order should be on its way to your SET-com as we speak. Now, if you want to press the issue I can request an emergency tribunal in accordance with Corporation law. It will take hours, put this whole operation behind and you will still lose. How do you feel about that?"

Something beeped at Carr and he checked his own computer then shrugged, "It checks out. Go get him what he wants."

A few seconds later a marine brought a small steel case from the supply depot and placed it on top of a crate. Viekko opened it and produced two handguns. They were both modeled after the ancient Remington M1911 design and cast in a dull, tarnished bronze. They might look like something that belonged in a museum but these were built by the finest gunsmith on Mars, which put him in contention for the best gunsmith in the Known Universe. The gunmaker's sign, +Ulfbert+, was engraved into each of their handles.

Carr watched and sniffed, "I knew you people went looking for ancient civilizations. Didn't think you still used the same weapons as them."

Viekko slid a clip into the chamber and peered through the sights, "They are the most effective weapons in the world provided you have an attack strategy more complex than 'spray bullets and hope for the best.'"

Isra snapped at him, "Enough. Sergeant, are we good here?"

Carr shook his head. "We got rules here. Make sure that they are followed." Carr looked around at the audience that had amassed. "What are you all staring at? Get back to work!" Then he stomped off.

Isra grabbed Viekko's arm as he slid his guns into a pair of shoulder holsters. "We must go."

They walked toward the shuttle for a few moments before Isra spoke. "Really, Viekko. Can you even be on Titan a whole hour before picking a fight?"

"To be fair," said Viekko, adjusting his hat, "They were doin' checks for ninety minutes when we landed so I've been on Titan almost two hours before picking a fight. You have any idea what that was all about?"

Isra shrugged. "Carr orchestrated that meeting. That is why he put that block on your weapons. He wanted to meet you, size you up and see how you handle conflict."

"Wait, the computer said all that?"

"No," said Isra walking a touch faster, "The system just indicated a block on those items. It did not indicate who. But it was him."

Isra's ability to read minds at work. It made the hairs on Viekko's neck bristle, "Why would he do that?"

"Because you are going to fight him soon. He wanted to see who would win."

"Yeah, and who's gonna win?"

"Well, considering how you were faring when I walked up, I would say your prospects do not look good without a change of venue. Now please hurry. Carr is not our problem right now. There is someone even more disagreeable."

Viekko thought about this. "More disagreeable than Carr? Did ya run into a cougar with a stick up its *iljig*?"

Isra shook her head, "Something like that. I need your help."

"What do you want me to do?"

"You ever heard of the Gordian Knot?"

Viekko thought for a moment. "Thinkin' I might have been doin' that with a girl in old Hong Kong. It was thrillin' but bruised my back somethin' fierce."

"Not what I was talking about, but similar themes might apply. And, also, you are disgusting."

They walked back to the shuttle where Althea was standing near a Corporation crawler. It was a six-wheeled all-terrain vehicle with two seats and a large cargo bed capable of carrying two standard Corporation crates side-by side. There were several stacks of those crates nearby and Althea was in the middle of a deep, philosophical debate with a cargo officer about them. Over her own EROS suit, she wore a white medical coat as if she wanted the entire world to know that she was still a doctor even if the Medical Consortiums on Earth disagreed. It didn't seem to have any positive influence on the current conversation either.

"...for the last time, I don't have the code to unlock them but there's nothing inside but food, equipment and other supplies. What could we possibly bring..."

The Corporation officer, who looked like he could have been a boxer twenty years ago, touched some icons on his EROS computer, "Sorry, orders from up top. All cargo not assembled by Corporation personnel needs to be inspected. "

Isra walked up with Viekko and pointed to four crates in a pile by the crawler. They stood out from the others being slightly smaller, green instead of blue, marked with the Ministry globe and olive branch and secured with an electronic lock on the front which Viekko assumed was the original point of contention.

"Those, Viekko," said Isra. "If you would be so kind as to load them onto the crawler?"

Viekko paused, looked at the crates and then at the Corporation worker. Viekko had a few inches and a decade or two on the man, but there would still be a considerable scrap if the two men got into it. And, unlike the previous situation, Viekko guessed that Corporation law wasn't on their side. So Isra was playing a game of chicken using Viekko as the front bumper.

Viekko stepped toward the stack. Each crate was about two meters long and a half a meter wide meter wide and deep with handles on either side. It was far too long for Viekko to get his arms around and, even in the fractional gravity of Titan, carried considerable weight. He grabbed the handle on one and pulled it off the pile. It fell and embedded itself in the soft ground.

"I'll get dock security..." the official tried.

Viekko started dragging the crate across the ground leaving a little trail as he went. Isra watched pleased with herself. "Please do. I would hurry, though. Despite what it looks like, the Martian works fast."

Viekko set the side he was carrying on the back of the crawler. He walked around the other side, shot Isra the quickest of dirty looks and lifted and pushed the other end so that the crate was fully loaded onto the back of the six-wheeled vehicle.

Isra continued, "And when they do come, there will be paperwork. They will want to take your statement and file reports. Then, of course, there is your schedule. But I am sure you will make up for lost time. You may even be commended for stopping such an egregious act. You know how the Corporation rewards its people."

Viekko lumbered back to pull another case over.

The officer scowled and waved his finger in Isra's face, "I'm going to get security and if I find out that you people took off..."

"A world of trouble that we cannot fathom. Thank you, sir."

The officer cast one look at all three of them and stomped off.

Viekko pulled the second crate off and started dragging, "He ain't coming back is he?"

Althea rushed over and took the other side. She strained a little but managed to get the end off the ground. "Or he will, but he will make bloody sure that we are already gone. That way he's done his duty but without mucking up his day."

Isra stood still watching the man leave. "Most likely. We should still move as fast as possible. He does not have a high sense of duty or loyalty to the Corporation, but just enough that he does not wish to be seen as ineffective.

When they placed the fourth and final crate, Althea checked the serial numbers against a list on her EROS computer. "That's all of them. Everything in the register."

"Seems like a lot," muttered Viekko looking up at the pile and wiping his forehead with his hat in the other hand.

Isra patted the crates. "It is adequate."

Viekko put his hat back on his head, "What's with all the friction from the Corporation? They are a bunch of *aryn talyn orgostei* but they ain't usually this stirred up. They're more the 'path of least resistance' types."

Isra walked toward the front of the crawler, "Titan is their last best hope."

Althea turned off her screen. "Hope for what exactly?"

Isra sighed and turned to address the two, "Titan is not just another land grab for them or another group of people to exploit. One thousand years ago, the various corporations managed to hold Earth hostage and they used energy to do it. They lost their grip because that energy disappeared. It is one of the things that contributed to the Fall."

"But Earth got plenty of energy," said Viekko folding his arms, "Got new solar tech, fusion, hell I read somethin' recently about some anti...whatsit."

"The anti-matter reactor field," said Althea patiently.

"Yeah, that. So what do they need Titan for?" he concluded waving dismissively in the direction of the camp.

"The problem is," said Isra stressing her words, "those energies cannot be controlled by any one person or entity. The sun is always up, hydrogen for fusion is ubiquitous and, once you can isolate it, antimatter just pops into existence. You cannot control them, not entirely. You can, perhaps control the necessary equipment for a time, but it is a temporary monopoly at best. Petrochemicals, on the other hand, are easier. And we are standing on the largest single source in the solar system."

"In other words," said Althea placing her medical bag in the back seat of the crawler, "If the Corporation controls

40

Titan, they're well on their way to controlling the rest of the solar system."

Isra nodded slightly, "Exactly. The Human Reconnection Project was formed to study and protect lost civilizations, but our mission here has repercussions that extend well beyond Titan. I do not exaggerate when I say the fate of all of human civilization in all its forms hinges on this mission."

Viekko pulled one of his guns and checked the chamber, "Well then we best get to movin'."

"We are still waiting for one more person," said Isra reviewing some data on the screen attached to her arm.

Viekko let the slide of his gun snap back in place, "One more person? Since when?"

Isra touched a few icons, "The Ministry suggested that we include an Old-Earth computing and communications expert. He should be arriving shortly, I have sent our location to his EROS suit."

"Who is this guy?"

Isra shut off her EROS computer. "I am unfamiliar with him. He goes by a cryptic code name."

"What code name?" asked Viekko.

"I am Cronus." answered a voice.

Viekko looked around for a moment but didn't see the source. It was like the words came from nowhere until Viekko risked a glance downward. He saw a round face almost completely hidden by a huge set of dark goggles staring up at him. The odd-looking little ma was dressed in a dark-green vest and dark-green pants over his own EROS suit. Both looked too new as if he'd purchased them specifically for this trip. He also wore a backpack large enough for him to climb into if the occasion came up.

The man gave Viekko a wide, borderline insane grin and stuck out his hand. "Pleased to meet you, Viekko Spade."

Viekko reached out to shake his hand. Cronus's small bony appendage practically disappeared in his fist. "You know me?"

"When conducting a symphony, one must know every instrument. One must read the notes in order to play the music. You are Viekko Spade the first man born on another planet to return to Earth since the Fall."

Cronus pulled his hand out of Viekko's grip and moved to take Althea's.

"Althea Fallon," said Cronus, "A great shining star of the medical world that unexpectedly disappeared without a trace. She resurfaces now on Titan using her brilliance and beauty to light the darkest regions of the Solar System."

Althea gave Cronus a nervous little smile. "Thank you... I think," she said.

"And Isra Jicarrio," said Cronus moving down the line, "... I have to admit a certain amount of ignorance here. I could not find any records of you before you were appointed as an ambassador in the Ministry four years ago."

Isra grumbled but shook his hand. "And you, Cronus? What is your real name and what are you doing here?"

"My real name? At birth I was given a name, but it is not one that I chose. I chose Cronus and it is by Cronus that I am known. If all of the world calls me Cronus- well, that is my real name."

Cronus peeled the goggles off of his face and grinned at the three of them. He looked like a person who considered sleep a thing that other people wasted their time with among other silly ideas like direct sunlight. It was impossible to tell his age, but a balding patch suggested somewhere in the thirties or possibly forties. Still, Cronus had a kind of pure exuberance in the way he moved and talked that only came from youth or maybe some heavy medication.

Cronus continued, "There is a civilization on Titan-"

Isra interrupted, "We got reports from a leak somewhere in the Corporation but we do not know for a fact—"

"It is there," said Cronus firmly, "And with it, an ancient computer system. I came here to find it and see what secrets it has. Old data from the ancients, very valuable."

"If you say so," muttered Isra, walking toward the crawler.

She grabbed a small data chip from the seat and inserted it into a slot in her EROS suit just below the elbow. She beckoned everyone closer as a holographic map of the area appeared in the air.

"We are here," said Isra indicating a blinking dot near the South coast of the Ligeia Mare. "We believe the city is located somewhere here." A large piece of land on the Western side of the ocean, several dozen kilometers away, started blinking.

"We will follow the coast around the Ligeia Mare. Satellite images pick up some sort of structure along the Western coast. Moving at a steady pace, we should be able to reach it in approximately twelve hours. Our mission is to stall for time. We make contact, send word back to the Ministry proving that there is a civilization here and, thus, force the Corporation to stand down operations until the civilization can be studied and protected. Is everyone prepared?"

Viekko did one more visual check of his guns and replaced them in his shoulder holsters. While he did he cupped the capsules of triple-T he had stashed in his inside jacket pocket for reassurance. "Ready."

Althea patted her black medical bag in the back as if to assure herself that it was there and took a seat in the driver's side. "Good to go."

Cronus unpacked a device that looked like two silver vines wrapped around each other. He slipped his arm through the twisting silver coils. Each finger moved into an intricate series of interconnected rings. With that, he pulled his goggles back over his eyes and climbed on top of the crates. Lights came from the strange metal glove and his goggles started glowing a pale green as he laid down. "I am prepared. To a new world."

"Viekko, you take point," said Isra.

Althea turned on the crawler's electric engine and Viekko started walking over the soft sand toward the West.

CHAPTER FOUR

Ostensibly, the Corporation was formed to manage the planet's resources but its structure has always been and remains self-serving in nature. Individuals and organizations at the top reap the greatest benefits while the rest are meant to scramble for the remains. In times of plenty, people are willing to forgive the excesses of a small portion of the population.

But when thousands are starving in the streets, the winds of change blow strong and it is the top that sways the most.

-from The Fall: The Decline and Failure of 21st Century Civilization *by Martin Raffe.*

Viekko walked in silence ahead of the crawler. He felt the thick, stinking breeze blowing off the Ligeia Mare and watched as the waves rolled onto a beach made of marble-sized pebbles. Each time the waves receded it sounded like a thousand bubbles popping at the same time. It was enough to drown out the mechanical whine of the crawler behind him. Father away from the water, the pebbles became sand

and then soil and disappeared into thick ferns, bushes and towering trees, the tops of which disappeared into the clouds.

Cronus, laying on top of the crates, reached out and touched invisible things with the metal device wrapped around his arm. He was lost and content in a world of his own while Althea drove the crawler with all the speed its name would imply.

"Viekko. Progress report, please," said Isra, walking beside the all-terrain vehicle.

Isra seemed to be in a good mood. She didn't normally use the word 'please' outside of diplomatic talks. She probably supposed that it was a waste of time.

Viekko pressed a button on his arm and read the data on the screen. "We're clearing ground at a decent rate. Maintaining a steady pace of about 5.5 kilometers per hour. If we keep this up we could be knocking on someone's door in time for dinner."

Isra nodded, satisfied. "It will take Laban and his men several hours to set up for hydrocarbon extraction. At this pace it is possible to get to the location, find proof of civilization and put a halt to his operation before it even gets started."

On top of the stack of cargo crates, Cronus sneezed.

A rustling sound in the trees overhead caught Viekko's attention and he looked up to see a bird with a wingspan as large as a condor leap from the canopy and glide out over the Ligeia Mare. Farther down the coast, one of the trees was in full bloom. The flowers added an explosion of color to the bleak, orange sky. Viekko smiled at the serene beauty of this place. It was like a massive wildcat dozing in the afternoon sun. Beautiful, majestic and likely to leave you bleeding out on the ground if the situation goes wrong.

The breeze coming off the water died down. Viekko stopped in his tracks and sniffed the air.

Althea parked the crawler next to him.

"Viekko," said Isra, "Why did you stop?"

Viekko stuck his nose in the air and took a long breath

in. "Somethin's wrong."

From on top of the crates, Cronus launched into a minor coughing fit.

Isra looked from the forests to the sea but nothing moved except the leaves in the wind. "What is it?"

"Somethin' don't belong. I smell the sea, the leaves, the flowers and... somethin' else. Somethin' that ain't natural. It's faint, though. Can't quite nail it down."

"Is it dangerous?"

Viekko watched the coast behind them but nothing moved. "It's still a ways away. Could be nothing. Still, best thing to do is try and put some distance between it and us."

Cronus launched into another coughing fit. This one was not so minor. He sounded like his guts were planning a quick and violent escape.

Althea looked over her shoulder. "Cronus, are you alright?"

Cronus wheezed, coughed for a few more seconds, and rolled off the top of the crates. He landed on the pebbly ground with a heavy crunch.

Althea jumped out of the driver's seat, grabbed her black medical bag out of the back and rushed to where he lay on the ground gasping for air.

Isra and Viekko both knelt down beside him as well. Somehow, in the couple of hours since they left the landing zone, Cronus's head had swelled to the point that he now looked like a pale, distressed pumpkin. He clawed at his throat with fat hands that used to have much longer fingers.

"Cronus," said Althea with practiced calm, "Cronus! Look at me, can you speak?"

Cronus wheezed and started weakly coughing again, gasping for air as if choking to death.

"What is wrong with him?" said Isra.

Althea opened her bag and started rooting around. "I think he's having some kind of allergic reaction."

"To what?" asked, Viekko leaning close. "He ain't touched nothin' since he got here. Just laid on top of them crates."

"He could be reacting to pollen, spores, microorganisms or something else in the air." said Althea, producing syringe from her medical bag. It wasn't the type that ended in a needle, but one made to be inserted into the RX5's delivery system through an external port. "One of those crates should have medical supplies. I'll need a breather."

Viekko got up and rushed to the bed of the crawler. He pulled one of the crates down and tried to open it when he saw the electronic lock in front. "Isra, what's the damn code to these locks?"

Isra pushed him out of the way. "I will get it. You help Althea."

The tone of Isra's voice along with the fact that she shoved him out of the way gave him a twist in his gut. There was a touch of fear there and Isra was never afraid. Even if she was, she would never show it and give another person that edge.

"Cronus," said Althea, holding the syringe front of his face, "I'm going to give you a shot of adrenaline. It should open your airways enough to breathe."

Viekko's head swiveled around to watch Cronus struggling under Althea's grasp and then back to Isra who was staring Viekko down with raw determination.

"Cronus!" said Althea trying to access his RX5, "I need you to relax. I can't help you if you don't relax!"

"Go help Althea" said Isra, "You do not even know which crate to open. Or where the breathers are. I do."

At that moment, Viekko was compelled to ask what was in the crates. Isra went to such lengths to avoid Corporation inspections. And she was afraid. What could possibly...

Cronus bucked and flailed under Althea's grasp. She could barely hold him in place, much less insert the syringe.

Isra motioned toward them. "Go. Help them. I will find the breathers."

Viekko grumbled but arguing the point at a time like this was poor form. Viekko went over and knelt by Cronus who was clawing at his own chest and breathing in short, shallow bursts.

"What's happenin'?" said Viekko.

"I think he's having a panic attack," said Althea still struggling with him.

Viekko held one of Cronus's arms down and pressed down on his chest. Cronus fought but Viekko was able to hold him steady enough for Althea to pull his green vest aside enough to reveal the ports on the medical regulator on his shoulder. She jammed the syringe in one of the ports and twisted, locking it into place. She leaned back and touched an icon on her EROS computer and the plunger of the syringe started to descend. As soon as the medicine was in, Cronus took his first full breath in several minutes.

Viekko let go and said, "You all right?"

Cronus took a few more deep breaths before he could answer. "I can breathe. What is happening to me?"

"I don't know," said Althea.

"Am I going to die out here?"

Althea grabbed a hand-held laser retinal scanner from her bag, "No, you're not going to die. We'll turn back if necessary." She used her fingers to open one of Cronus's eyes, waited for the green laser to scan across the retina, did the same on the other, and said, "Some swelling in the sclera. No infection detected in the blood vessels. Nothing to indicate anything more than a common allergen."

Isra returned with a small, clear plastic mask. Althea took it, slipped the strap over Cronus's head and fit the mask over his mouth and nose.

"Try this for now," said Althea. "It will keep your lungs clear and allow you to breathe."

"How long?" asked Cronus, his voice partially muffled by the mask.

"Until we can determine the cause and, even then, only if we can find a way eliminate or minimize the symptoms."

Viekko and Althea helped Cronus to his feet and walked him to the passenger side of the crawler. As they got him settled again, Viekko caught another hint of the odd smell. It was spicy and floral but like nothing really found in nature. And it was stronger.

"Is everything alright?" said Isra.

"No," Viekko said in a low tone, "We need to get moving. Now."

The next hour had an anxious feel to it. Cronus rode in the passenger side of the crawler next to Althea. His breathing through the mask was labored and, even though he had barely moved since he fell off the crates, his face was flushed with sweat. Althea paused every once in a while for a quick examination. Retinal, blood and swab tests all came back inconclusive. Althea didn't know what was happening, but she seemed to know that it wasn't good.

As a result, their pace had dropped considerably. The beach was gradually getting rockier and the dark forest seemed to be looming closer and closer providing precious little space to maneuver the crawler between the dense forest and the sub-zero sea.

Add to that, the triple T was starting to wear off and the Haze was setting in. Triple T made everything sharper, it made colors more vivid, smells more potent and feelings more intense. But when the 'T' started to wear off, it left the mind worse than it found it. The sounds of the waves churning the rocks was less distinct. The vivid colors of the forest started to dull. After the Shard, his mind focused on every sight, sound, smell and texture. Everything was in the now. Already, just a few hours later, it started to slip.

Isra growled and pulled Viekko from his thoughts. "Progress report."

Viekko pulled up his sleeve and activated the screen. "Three point four five kilometers over the last hour. Looks like we won't get there until..." Viekko stopped and sniffed the air again.

Isra walked up behind him, "What is it? The same thing you were talking about earlier?"

Viekko couldn't identify the smell before. It was too distant and the breeze from the sea blew it away before he could concentrate on it. But the way the coast curved and the

49

breeze moved meant that the source was downwind. He could smell it even through the beginning of the Haze. Him and his terrible aftershave. Sergeant Carr.

"I think we're bein' followed," said Viekko.

Isra spun in the direction they came. "Who? Where?"

"Carr. I ain't seen him but his scent stands out like a priest at a *gaarsan*. He's keeping to the forest to stay out of sight," said Viekko.

"Then we move faster," said Isra with added force in her voice. "We must outrun him. Lose him somewhere."

"Isra, we're four people and a crawler. One of them is laid up and another has to stop and make sure that he keeps to breathin'. The man out there is just one guy who moves as he likes. There ain't no outrunnin' him and there ain't no hidin' from him as long as we're out in the open."

Isra looked back at the beach and the forest that bordered it. The way her face moved, Viekko could feel terrible ideas whipping around her head. "Through the forest then," she said. "The direct route. It will be more challenging terrain but he may lose us in the underbrush."

Viekko paused for a moment. "That's crazy, Isra. It might slow him down a touch but it's going to stop us near complete. Who knows what Laban will get up to if we're trudgin' through the forest for three days?"

"But staying out here will do nothing but lead him directly to the city. If Laban learns that there is a civilization here before we can contact the Ministry, he will find some way to keep it from them." Isra looked at the dark forest that stretched along the beach back the way they came, "Our only hope is to lose him in the trees."

Viekko stepped close to her. He was a head taller than most men and it was hard to argue with someone when looking up their nostrils. Isra stood just shy of his sternum.

"You wanna lead this team into unknown and possibly dangerous conditions so you can lose a Corporate marine who don't pose much of a threat to us. A guy who's likely under orders not to mess with us?"

Isra's gaze didn't move an inch. "Those are your orders,

Viekko."

"Then you best be tellin' me why. What the hell are you so afraid of? What are you plannin' that is so bad that the Corporation can't find out about it? What's in those crates?"

"They are supplies. Enough for us for the duration of the mission and some extra in case humanitarian efforts are required. Nothing more. I told you what is at stake here and I intend to take no chances. The forest is riskier, but I made sure this mission had, in its ranks, maybe the finest interplanetary survival expert available. A man who I had to fight to include on this mission because he spent most of his time looking for gutters to pass out it."

Isra shifted. She looked at him as if she might disassemble his brain with her look alone, "But I did it. I did it because he, unlike anyone on Earth, actually grew up on another planet and faced the challenges associated with that. Did I make a mistake, Viekko?"

Somehow Viekko's righteous indignation just slammed into the brick wall of Isra's rhetoric. He hated her a little bit at that moment.

Viekko turned to Althea who was checking Cronus's vitals again. "What 'bout him?"

Althea settled back into the driver's seat, "It's progressing, but I still don't see anything life threatening. It's her call."

Viekko glanced back at Isra. Her gaze felt even harder. Viekko sighed. "You heard her. Make a hard left into the forest."

With that Viekko headed for the tree line. Out of the corner of his eye, he saw leaves rustling in the brush back the way they came. They weren't going to lose Carr in the forest any more than they were on the beach. The best he could hope for was that Carr would stumble across something hungry and that thing would be too full to come after the rest of them.

CHAPTER FIVE

Nature provides our species with everything it needs. Civilization provides it with everything it wants. History shows us that it is important while we develop the latter, we do not destroy the former. That way leads to inevitable ruin.

-from The Fall: The Decline and Failure of 21st Century Civilization by Martin Raffe.

Moving through the forest was proving to be every bit the nightmare that Viekko assumed it would be. It had been four hours with most of it spent pulling the crawler out of the mud or clearing enough space through fallen trees and brush to get through. If it weren't for the crates of supplies, they would have been better off leaving the damned crawler behind.

"Viekko." said Isra, "Progress report."

Isra's requests were curt, demanding, and getting more so, but they carried an amount of weariness with them now. Plus, they were getting a tad ridiculous.

Viekko didn't look at his computer but pointed to a tree a hundred meters behind them, "There. That's where we were when you last asked. We were there. Now we're here. That's your progress."

Isra grumbled and kept walking. She must have been more exhausted than she let on. Her breathing was labored, she was caked in dirt and sweat and, if Isra Jicarrio didn't have enough energy for a retort, she was about ready to drop.

Althea didn't look much better. She was driving the crawler but she had spent her fair share of time on the end of a tow cable trying to dislodge it from whatever unpleasant situation it found itself in at that particular minute. The only one of them that escaped mostly unscathed was Cronus, still breathing through a plastic mask.

The pain forming in his muscles kept his mind focused on the world around him. Maybe it was his tolerance or maybe it had something to do with the amount of oxygen on Titan, but the Haze was hitting faster. He found himself forcing his mind to concentrate on the situation in front of him. The trees, ferns and undergrowth were all blending together. He'd lost Carr's scent and he wasn't sure if it was because they'd shaken him or if Viekko just wasn't sharp enough now.

Viekko shook his head and forced himself to focus on his surroundings. The forest really was beautiful. Everywhere he looked, Viekko saw and felt nature. Not the fenced-in, domesticated nature that he sometimes found on Earth. And not the harsh, unforgiving bitch that was the wilds of the Martian steppes. Up above, a tree practically exploded with red and blue flowers and buzzed with insects. There were vines heavy with deep red fruits. Here, the flowers almost masked the petroleum stench near the Ligeia Mare. There was something nurturing about this place. Innocent. Primeval.

As they continued, the largest trees disappeared and were replaced by smaller, younger ones that were still as high as a two or three story building. A few minutes later, Viekko emerged into a narrow clearing. For the first time since they walked into the thick of the forest, Viekko could see the sky, the sun hanging close to the eastern horizon and Saturn in its spot almost directly overhead. Seeing the wide open space, Viekko felt his own fatigue kick in.

Isra paused to lean against a tree. "Progress report," she demanded but in a tone that suggested that she, like the rest of them, was ready to collapse.

Viekko sat on a rock near the edge of the clearing, "Isra, it don't do no good to be shoutin' for a progress report every fifteen minutes. I take no pleasure in saying it, but I was right. We weren't in no shape to cross through the forest. We'll get it done, but it ain't gonna happen quick."

Isra's eyes narrowed, "We need to keep moving then. Come on."

Isra started a determined march across the clearing but Althea, in a stunning display of protest, shut down the electric engine.

Isra stopped and turned around. "Althea. What are you doing?"

Althea stepped out of the crawler. "Isra, we should rest. Take a minute, maybe eat something. It won't do us any good if we stagger into harm's way totally spent and starving."

Isra was about to say something but Cronus moved the mask to the side, gave several good coughs and followed it up with a pathetic little wheeze.

"And I should check his blood again," Althea added. "See if anything particularly nasty is happening to him."

Isra flashed a look at Viekko maybe hoping for a bit of solidarity or maybe just expecting one more person to let her down.

Either way Viekko went with the latter.

"She's right," said Viekko, reclining on the rock, "We ain't had anything since we left the LZ. And, like you said, the sun ain't setting on this rock any time soon."

"What about the soldier? The one tailing us?" Isra insisted.

"Hard tellin'. I haven't picked up any signs of him lately. Probably he's keeping his distance and following our tracks. Or maybe he's given up and gone back to camp."

Not likely, thought Viekko, but if Isra bought it, all the better.

All Isra did was slowly blink and say, "Fine." Viekko heard a whole encyclopedia of annoyance expressed in that one word, but that was it. Isra walked back to the crawler and said, "I will pull some rations for us."

Althea ran her hand through a bush and pulled a fruit that looked like a strawberry except it was longer, bright orange, and the size of Althea's palm, "I'd like to take a moment and analyze some of the fruit, nuts and seeds I've seen along the way. This planet is full of them and I'd like to see if any of it happens to be edible."

Viekko nodded and said, "I'll scout ahead. See how big this clearing is and if I can find an easy way for the crawler."

"You do know what a rest is, right Viekko?" asked Althea, pulling a handful of berries off a vine.

Viekko shoved his hand in his pocket and felt the little glass capsules of triple-T. "It won't take long," he said.

The clearing was about fifty meters wide and curved to the left. He followed it, keeping close to the trees, until he was well out of sight of the crawler. As he walked, he noticed the clearing getting wider and that the grass had a distinctly traveled look it. From the broken branches and scratches on the trees, it was fair to say whatever came through this way last was both big and vicious.

He found a tree with a convenient root and sat leaning back against it. He closed his eyes and just enjoyed the silence for a moment. His hand slid into his coat pocket and selected a shard of 'T.

In a moment, the world would be even clearer and sharper. He would feel as good as he did when they first landed. It was for the good of the group, after all. He couldn't protect the others if the Haze started to hit. Hell, he couldn't protect himself.

He slid the glass capsule in between his molars and bit down.

Once again, the world became sharp. He could parse out the cacophony of the forest and pick out the individual sounds; the buzz of a large dragonfly-like insect in a flowering bush, the call of a bird high in the trees, a strange trumpeting sound like an elephant's call in the distance. The individual odors of the forest each became prominent and, at the same time, distinct. There was the sweetness of the fruit hanging in the trees, the earthy musk of animal sweat in the distance and the echoes of Carr's aftershave still casting an unnatural shadow over the place. Even the less tangible feelings became as sharp as broken glass. For example, the feeling that Althea was closing in on his position.

He jumped back to his feet, spat out the shard and wiped the blood from his mouth just as Althea appeared.

"Viekko!" shouted Althea at a full sprint with her medical bag in hand. "What happened?"

Viekko tipped his hat back and, with a voice as nonchalant as he could physically manage, said, "Hiked up a-ways. Looks to be easier goin' this way, although..."

Althea damn near tackled Viekko to the ground when she got to him. "Sit down before you bloody well collapse."

He sat down hard on the tree root and, a few moments later, he was squinting into the bright light of Althea's retinal scanner. "Jaysus, Althea. What in *tam-iin khaalga* is wrong?"

Althea turned off the retinal scanner and just looked at him in the eye as if she expected to find something not-quite-human behind them. "Were you stung or bitten by anything? Or did you eat or touch a strange plant just now?"

"No stranger than anything here, I suppose. What exactly are you getting at, Althea?"

She searched her bag for something, "Did you fall or cut yourself? Sprain an ankle... anything?"

"Damn it, Althea, ain't nothin' happened. What exactly are you gettin' riled up about?"

Althea produced a syringe containing a beige liquid, "Just a few minutes after you were out of sight, I got an alert from your medical regulator. Your brain chemistry went totally bonkers. Your endorphin levels went off the charts, your dopamine shot up, your serotonin tanked...take off your jacket."

A surge of fear crossed Viekko's mind as he eyed the syringe. "Just hang on a moment, I don't know what's got your horses all reared up, but I ain't takin what's in that syringe. Ain't nothin wrong with me."

Althea leaned close, "We can't know that. A change this drastic in your body could mean anything. You might well be poisoned by the same thing that's affecting Cronus, but there's no way to tell until I can sort through all the other noise. This will help regulate your brain chemistry so, hopefully I can see what's wrong. Now take off your jacket and turn around."

He found himself doing exactly as she said even though he knew that he should just come clean, dig the capsules out of his pocket and show her.

"Are you sure there's nothing you want to tell me?" said Althea approaching his medical regulator with a syringe.

"Why do you ask?" said Viekko.

"Because this is going feel a little weird."

Althea plugged the syringe into a port in the back of his regulator and twisted. She touched a few icons on her EROS computer. Then it felt like the entire world spiraled right out from underneath him. His whole body felt dizzy and nauseous like he might try to purge all his guts in one go. At the same time all his skin tingled the way his arm or legs did when they went to sleep. Then he wasn't. For a moment he was standing. He saw Althea kneeling over a body helping them lie down. The body wore white khaki pants and a suit jacket. Then the world faded to white and black.

The next thing he knew he was looking up at Althea's retinal scanner again. She leaned back and checked the data being downloaded to her EROS computer. A look of growing concern spread across her face every moment she spent working on it. Finally she turned off her screen and said, "Your brain chemistry isn't leveling out. Your endorphins are still dropping. I don't understand this at all. Tell me again what you were doing?"

Viekko swallowed hard as he tried to think of a lie. There was nothing out here besides more trees, bushes and...just then, he heard a sound like a low moaning trumpet. Althea heard it too and stared off in the same direction.

"I was scoutin' ahead," said Viekko sitting up.

Althea put her hand on his chest and gently tried to get him to lay back down, "Viekko. Be careful."

Viekko pushed past her light resistance until he was sitting upright. Somewhere in the distance he heard an animal trumpet. "I was scoutin' ahead and I was just about to investigate whatever the hell that sound is."

Before Althea could say anything, Viekko got to his feet. He wobbled a moment and then started walking with Althea tailing behind. The path went up a small rolling hill. The calls got louder and more frequent as he got closer. The low, barely audible moans and higher trumpets made Viekko picture a large herbivore. Something like a buffalo or an ox or possibly an elephant.

Viekko reached the top of the hill first and knelt down. Partially because his brain still hadn't cleared from whatever hellish serum Althea shot him up with. And also because he wasn't sure how to process what he just saw on the other side of the hill.

Althea caught up, knelt down next to him and gasped, "Oh my God. Viekko."

The valley on the other side of the hill was filled with animals. They were basically elephants except much larger, much hairier, and they hadn't been seen outside of a museum for tens of thousands of years.

"Mammoths," whispered Althea, watching the herd of approximately thirty animals. "How is that even possible?"

"Not sure," said Viekko. "I suspect that when they was colonizing the planets, they brought a few useful animals with them. In particular, those that would best survive the climate. Those that didn't exist, they created. Or recreated, as it were."

A high, nasally, mucus-coated voice made Viekko jump. "Isra wants to know what you two are doing."

Ta nar bogood ergu teneg, bi chamain kharaah," said Viekko cursing in his native Martian tongue, "What the hell are you doing here?"

Cronus took a few deep breaths from the plastic mask

and pulled it away. "I am not here to be carried. Isra is busy so I came to help. I can walk. I can—" Cronus's words were cut short by another coughing fit. He slapped the mask back over his mouth and nose.

"Yeah but you can't breathe, now can ya?" berated Viekko. "Be quiet now. No tellin' what those things are capable of."

"What are they?" said Cronus.

"Mammoths," said Viekko, "That's as near as I can figure, at least. I'm open to suggestions."

Cronus looked for a moment and, given the situation, gave the most unimpressed "oh," imaginable.

"Oh?" said Viekko, "That's all you got? You're lookin' at animals that should, by all reason, be extinct and the best you got is, 'oh'?"

Cronus took a few deep breaths from his breather and pulled it away, "It makes sense to me. It's cold here and they would thrive and humans thrive from them. Life consumes life. When programming a system, you write the code that serves the function, not the function to the code. What is Althea doing?"

Viekko looked down the hill. Somehow, Althea was already halfway down and heading directly for the largest bull mammoth a couple hundred meters away.

"*Teneg okhin!*" Viekko activated the radio on his arm and, fighting to keep his voice below a whisper, said, "Althea what the... what are you doin'?"

The grass was well trampled by the animals but Althea crouched and moved slowly through the remaining strands. She paused to activate her own radio and whispered, "I want to get a closer look."

"You'll be lookin' at it from the end of its tusk if you ain't careful!" said Viekko forcing a whisper.

"You said yourself that they were bred here. If they were raised that would require a lot of human interaction."

"You're gonna go and base your survival on the *baas* that comes out of my mouth?"

Althea didn't respond. Viekko could only watch as she

crept down the hill. At the bottom, she caught the eye of the large bull. He stopped lazily picking leaves off a fern tree and looked at her. Althea remained motionless for a moment. Viekko's mind worked frantically to figure out what to do if the massive animal charged. There wasn't any cover for quite a distance and they'd be staring down four meters of ivory moving at high velocity. His survival would be a sheer matter of chance and there was nothing he could do for Althea.

She stood up. Viekko watched the mammoth's reaction and it seemed totally disinterested. It regarded Althea for a moment and, deciding she was no more a threat than your basic insect, went back to the fern tree. And Althea, being the type who couldn't leave things alone, moved closer. She stopped less than a meter away, reached out and ran her hand through the mammoth's fur. He looked back at her a moment, let out a low moan and went back to his meal.

"It's okay," said Althea over the radio, "They are quite tame."

"Great," whispered Viekko to himself more than anyone else, "Just peachy. Now get back up here before somethin' terrible happens."

There was another trumpet sound, this time from the northwest, the direction they were traveling. This one had a loud, piercing quality to it. It didn't sound like it came from another mammoth; it was fake and electronic, as if it was made to sound like it came from the mammoths. Only louder. So loud that it echoed off the mountains in the distance.

"That sound" said Cronus peeking up his head, "From the direction of the city. A call. The city calls to them."

The herd started moving. It was slow at first like a lazy river that was just hitting a patch of whitewater.

"Althea!" Viekko yelled.

Althea became aware something was wrong. She started by backing away from the bull and back up the hill to where Cronus and Viekko were watching. But as the herd became more and more agitated, Althea pivoted right and sprinted.

But it was already too late. Before she could get out of the way, the mammoths were in full stampede.

"Uh, Viekko..." said Cronus with rising concern.

Viekko could only see her in short bursts in between the mammoths stomping past.

"Viekko..." Cronus said with a touch of panic.

And then Althea was gone. She dove to the ground just as another mammoth ran by or, Viekko felt a little sick at the thought, over her. And that seemed to be it. She was lost in the dirt and dust as the whole herd ran behind the big bull male.

"Viekko!"

Right up the hill where they were standing.

"Don't go and wait on my account!" yelled Viekko. "Run! Damn it! Run!"

Viekko and Cronus turned and bolted down the other side of the hill back in the direction they came and away from the stampeding animals. With every step, he could feel the EROS suit resisting his movements. He couldn't run as fast as he knew he could. The Corporation wanted Titan to feel more like Earth. For a moment, Viekko imagined dropping whatever idiot designed this hellish contraption right in front of the stampede.

Viekko pushed harder. He took longer strides taking extra advantage of Titan's gravity.

He had a good turn of speed by the time he was at the bottom. He could feel the EROS suit tearing as it fought against his muscles. He sprinted a few meters and angled left for the tree line. The herd would keep to the clearing. At very least the trees would slow them down and give him a fighting chance to escape. At that moment, just a few meters from the safety of the dense forest, he heard Cronus.

"Viekko!" Cronus wheezed. "I can't breathe! I can't run!"

Viekko spun around. Sure enough Cronus was clutching his chest at the bottom of the hill just as the first mammoths were cresting it.

Viekko sprinted back, grabbed Cronus by the arm and pulled him toward the tree line. The deafening drum roll of mammoth feet got louder with each passing second. A momentary glance to his left told him that he was out of time. A medium-sized but imposing cow was close enough that he could see the determined look in her eye.

He stopped running, grabbed Cronus by the collar of his green vest with one hand and his pants with the other. Viekko stepped forward, spun and launched Cronus like a very large, screaming, crying shot put.

Viekko had an instant to see Cronus hit the branches of a tree before he had to leap out of the way of the mammoth. He tucked, rolled and got to his feet. He had a moment to gather his situation before he had to leap out of the way of a smallish-bull. The animal just missed him, his tusk made a small tear in Viekko's jacket as it ran past. There were more coming and there was nothing he could do. In an instant of panic he lunged for the treeline. Several more mammoths missed him but more out of luck than any skill.

He reached the forest and ran directly toward the first tree he could find. His whole body slammed against the rough bark. He found grips for his hands and pulled himself up. He got another grip at the height of his arc and pulled up again.

This time he managed to grab a thick branch. Below, something brushed against his boot. His muscles were screaming in protest. His EROS suit let out a barely audible whine as it worked hard against him. Still, he managed to pull himself fully onto the branch. There, he wrapped his body around it and stayed there until the ground stopped moving.

CHAPTER SIX

Scholars have long debated the causes of the Fall. Most have come to the conclusion that a complete collapse at the height of human civilization was inevitable; all it needed was the right trigger. Still, centuries later, we don't know what that trigger was. The records just do not exist. It is like a whole chapter was ripped out of the Book of History and we turn the page only to find a world on fire.

-from The Fall: The Decline and Failure of 21st Century Civilization
by Martin Raffe.

Viekko held on to the branch until the last mammoth, a relatively small calf that was still big enough to trample him to death, ran underneath his feet. After that, the forest was strangely quiet. As if the small animals, birds, and insects also beat it for higher ground. Or maybe the constant humming background of the forest was simply no match for the all-encompassing roar or the stampede.

The Martian dropped to the ground. The clearing was wider than it was a few minutes ago. The smaller trees were snapped at the base and the brush and ferns were trampled into the mud. The ground was littered with broken branches, crushed fruit, and leaves, but nothing squishy and red which meant the balding little hacker was probably alive somewhere.

"Cronus!" called Viekko.

Nothing besides the faint rustle of leaves in the canopy.

"Cronus! You okay?"

Cronus's voice answered from somewhere in the foliage. "My body is intact. My resolve is somewhat broken."

Viekko walked in the direction of the voice. "You hurt?"

Cronus wheezed and sounded like he was trying to cough up a raw oyster. He croaked out, "I dropped the breather."

"Well come on down and we'll get you another."

"I am curious on how you would like to accomplish that."

Viekko spotted the little man overhead draped over a high branch like a naughty child over his daddy's knee. His frantically kicking legs was all that kept him from falling through the canopy.

"Drop, Cronus. Titan's gravity's weak, you won't fall near as hard."

"I'm supposed to take your word for that?" asked Cronus, struggling.

"Cronus!"

"You will catch me, right?"

Viekko rolled his eyes. "Yeah. I'll catch you. Just drop."

Cronus stopped kicking and let his body go limp. He lost his grip and fell through the lower tree branches like a big, screaming, pasty lump of stone. Viekko repositioned himself as Cronus careened off several branches until he finally landed in Viekko's arms. Titan's lower gravity made it feel like catching a large, awkward baby.

Viekko set Cronus on his feet. The hacker clutched his chest and sucked in few frantic gasps of air. "You did as you promised. Even though it was you who threw me up there to begin with, I thank you."

"It was either that or we'd be scraping you off a

mammoth's foot," said Viekko surveying the new landscape. "We should find Althea."

Or what's left of her, he added in his mind.

They didn't have to go far. By the time they got back to the hill, he saw Althea coming over the crest. She was covered in mud and leaves and had a few twigs poking out of her bright red hair, but she was walking.

"Althea!" yelled Viekko, "You alright?"

Althea pulled a tangle of brambles from her hair. "Bloody fantastic."

She was sassy. That was a good sign. "Not hurt or nothin'?" said Viekko.

Althea shook her head and a couple of twigs fell out. "No. I fell down when the mammoths charged but I cozied myself next to a fallen log. They just ran over me. A bit lucky, I guess." Althea flushed red. "I guess that was a stupid thing to do."

Viekko looked back in the direction of the stampede. "Somethin' else set 'em off. The noise called to 'em like a dog whistle. Only with much bigger dogs. We just happened to be in the wrong clearing... oh Hell."

Althea seemed to realize the same thing. "Oh no. Isra?"

"Ain't heard from her. Come on."

They hurried back to the crawler as fast as Cronus, in his state, could manage. The vehicle was where they left it, beaten, battered and tossed upside-down. The four crates that had been stacked onto the cargo bed were scattered across the forest floor in the direction of the carnage. There was no sign of the expedition's leader.

Viekko ran up to the vehicle. "Isra! You there?"

An annoyed voice echoed from under the crawler. "Yes."

Viekko knelt down beside it. "You hurt?"

"I am fine. Just help me out of here," said Isra.

Viekko grabbed the side of the crawler and lifted. It would have been an impossible feat on Earth but in Titan's fractional gravity he was able to lift one side of the vehicle over his head. Isra was balled up under the cargo bed. As Viekko held it, Isra slid out, got to her feet and helped

Viekko push. After some straining, the crawler fell back on its wheels. There was some ominous metal clanking inside followed by a pathetic electric whine. The front windshield was crushed and broken off and there were a couple of large tusk punctures in the door and in a wheel well.

Isra looked at the crawler as if making a mental log of all the damage it sustained. She turned to Viekko. "What. The Hell. Was that?" Every word felt like an accusation pointed directly at his head.

"Local wildlife?" Viekko hazarded.

"It was my fault," said Althea approaching the crawler, "We found the mammoths in a nearby field. They looked domesticated and...I guess I...I'm sorry."

Viekko tilted his hat back. "It weren't that. You mighta heard a loud trumpet call come from the northwest, 'bout where we think the city might be if I'm any judge. Those animals, there were domesticated, and they responded to the master's call. That there is proof of civilization, right?"

Isra glared at Viekko. "No, it is my fault. I thought I could let you out of my sight for a moment. I want both of you to stay close from here on out. Understand?"

Althea nodded. Viekko shrugged and said, "Fine."

Isra took a deep breath and looked back at the crawler and the crates thrown to the forest floor in the stampede. Her calm voice returned, "This is good evidence for a civilization remaining on this moon. We should cover more ground while we still have the energy. Help me with these crates."

They walked for several more hours all the time heading toward the same blinking dot on a satellite map in between the Ligeia Mare and the Kraken Mare.

Every moment of the way, Viekko felt his mind slipping deeper and deeper into the Haze. The scenery, for all its beauty, became a muted green blur with little accents of color here and there. The sounds all ran together until he felt like he was walking in the middle of a wildlife echo chamber.

He had long since lost Carr's scent although he knew the marine was watching them from somewhere in the forest.

That being said, they couldn't go much longer. Isra wasn't so much walking as lurching forward propelled by her own stubbornness and looked as if a strong breeze could blow her over. Althea and Cronus were in a better state riding in the crawler, but even then, Viekko caught Althea's head nod as she tried to prevent herself from falling asleep behind the wheel, and Cronus was wheezing hard even through the breather.

And the Universe, being an entity that enjoyed a sick joke as much, if not more than most, played its part. Driving at the edge of a steep embankment, the strange, granular sand seemed to turn to liquid beneath their feet. The hill became a river of wet mud carrying the crawler and everyone else down with it before anyone could react. The wave swept them toward the bottom of the hill, leaving Viekko and Isra buried up to their knees and the crawler up to its hood. And just as fast as it moved out from under their feet, the land was solid, hard-packed dirt.

"*Tam garig.*" Viekko muttered pulling himself out of wet earth, "Everyone okay?"

Althea shut off the engine and sat back in her chair, "We're fine. Shall I get the tow cables again?"

Isra laid flat on the ground in order to pull her legs out of the hole, "No. This is pointless. Not without some rest." She freed her legs and rolled over to get a look at their surroundings, "We may as well stop here. Help me set up the shelters."

Althea grabbed her bag from the back of the crawler. "I would like to check up on Cronus and Viekko while we do that."

While Althea gave Cronus a check-up, Viekko helped Isra with the shelters. They weren't much, just a heat-reflective material pulled over carbon alloy frames. Useful for protection from both extreme heat and cold and, despite its appearance, could withstand some heavy weather events.

They just finished the fourth shelter when Althea called

67

him over. He sat down on the crawler's passenger seat and Althea began her examination, starting with the retinal scanner. "Feel any different than the last time I looked?"

"Not 'specially," he said. He added in his own mind, *If you don't count that every moment my mind is slipping farther and farther away from me, I'm peachy.*

Althea sat back and checked the readout on her screen. "Are you sure? Your endorphin levels are tanking even worse than earlier. I'd imagine you'd be seeing some mental effects by now. Do you have any sense that the world around you is dream-like or not real? Do you feel like your actions and your thoughts are actually yours?"

"Only every day of my life," said Viekko. Then, aware that the sarcasm was not helping him, added, "But nothin' more than normal."

"Are you sure? You needn't play the tough guy act for me."

Viekko jumped up. "I'm sure. *Ta zondoo*, I'm sure. What are you accusin' me of?" Viekko stopped. He wasn't sure why he had an outburst like that.

A flash of fear crossed Althea's face then her expression hardened, "I'm not accusing you, Viekko. I'm just trying to make sense of this. I've got two patients exhibiting two wildly different reactions to the same environmental agent. If I'm to make any sense of it, I have to know what's happening. Now. Sit down."

Her voice contained all the warmth and caring of a rattlesnake rattle. Viekko decided to just do as she asked.

Althea continued her examination. While she took his blood, Viekko found himself saying, "What makes you think what me and what Cronus have are related?"

Althea shook her head as she inserted the blood sample into a black, palm-sized device with a small screen across the front, "Honestly, can't be sure of that either. But I've got to start somewhere. You both have symptoms that started around the same time. If they are not related, then I have literally nothing to go on."

Part of his brain found itself willing her to check his

pockets but he forced the thought back before he could say anything.

Cronus, meanwhile, had settled back on top of the crates and used his immersion goggles and glove to manipulate objects in a world that only he could see. Something gave him quite a start and he sat bolt upright and pulled the goggles off his head. "Isra, Althea. Something strange is happening."

Isra, securing the shelter, stopped and approached the crawler, "What is it, Cronus?"

"I tapped the air. Listened to the light. A place that still has old Earth tech would use both, but I found something strange."

Althea got up to listen to him as well. Viekko just grumbled. "Yeah we found somethin' strange too. He's sitting on our supplies spouting nonsense."

Isra flashed him a quick glare and turned back to Cronus, "Radio frequencies?"

Cronus cracked that weird sadistic grin of his, "Exactly right. Light and air. It's mostly Corporation military, but I found a blank spot in the middle."

Isra cocked her head, "Interference from the city?"

"No. Interference would sound different, like two sounds competing for the attention of the ear. This is blocked out. Nothing there..."

As Cronus continued to talk, something foul in the air caught Viekko's attention. It was light, far way and strangely familiar.

"Gonna go check something out," muttered Viekko to the others, and he started tracking the source of the smell.

He stumbled through the forest and became aware that the Haze was hitting him harder and more acutely than he had anticipated. He tried to focus on the scent and on his situation but the more he tried to focus on it, the more the rest of the world slipped away.

Then everything around him changed. He could have sworn he was on Titan, but all he could see around him was the scrub plains and rocky outcroppings of the Martian

Steppes. He held a rifle and walked up a steep slope toward a set of rocky peaks. There were other men around him and he felt as if he knew who they were, but whenever he tried to look them in the face they always turned away at the last moment. But he was sure that he knew them. Familiar voices chattering in his native language proved that. They talked of victory, triumph and vengeance. They joked about death and boasted about future battles.

He followed his comrades in between towers of red rock. The stench, light and faint just a few moments, ago grew stronger. He reached the summit of the hill and looked down on a nomadic village. He remembered these people. They were raiders: thieves, murderers, and rapists. They plagued his colony for years before the security force discovered their hidden campsite...this hidden campsite, come to think of it.

As soon as the thought occurred to him, the entire village caught fire before his eyes. He knelt down and watched his comrades moving in the village below and shooting fleeing families.

"Viekko?"

He breathed the air. The stench overwhelmed his senses, but it smelled good. Justified. Vindicated. It smelled as if the gods themselves rained fire upon his enemies.

"Viekko!"

Now he was in the village among the ashes. He walked in between burned tent poles and smoldering piles of ash. He found a body lying face down on the ground. Its blackened skin peeled away revealing charred red and brown muscle and blood. The body curled around something Viekko couldn't see until he knelt.

"Viekko! Talk to me!"

Viekko moved the body and saw a tiny hand peeking out from underneath. A baby crushed by its mother trying to save it from the flames. He jumped back in horror and had to set his jaw to keep from being violently ill.

"Viekko! Can you hear me? Isra. Help me get him to lie down."

He continued to walk through the smoke and the flames.

70

Compelled forward by some figure moving between the tents. A shadow that seemed always ahead but moved out of sight at the last moment before he could see it. The faster he moved, the faster it ran out of sight.

"What is wrong with him?" said Isra's voice somewhere in the distance.

"I think it's a depersonalization episode. Help me get his coat off so I can get this in his medical regulator."

The figure stopped with her back to Viekko. He could see it was a woman with long, black hair and a simple homemade dress. He approached slowly and felt, without seeing her face, close to her somehow. He stopped just a few meters away and reached out to touch her, "Mother?"

As fast as it appeared, Mars was gone. In its place was Althea's retinal scanner and, behind it, her concerned face. He blinked at the light and covered his eyes, "Jaysus, Althea. That ain't nothing to wake up to! 'Specially twice in one day!"

Althea leaned back, "It looks like he is cognizant again. Viekko, can you sit up?"

He did. Isra and Cronus were both there and watching him with deep concern on their faces. Something about that caused a wave of annoyance in Viekko. Almost as an act of defiance, he moved to get to his feet.

Althea tried to steady him. "Careful, Viekko. You just had a major episode."

Viekko shook his head "What happened?"

"It was like you were sleepwalking. At the end I think you called me 'Mother'. Do you remember what you saw?"

Already the vision was disappearing like a dream in the first few minutes after being awake, but one part of it remained as strong if not more powerful than ever. That smell was overwhelming, sickening. He became aware that Isra was shielding her nose from it. Cronus, still breathing through the mask, held it tighter than normal.

"That smell," said Viekko walking towards its source, "I smelled it in that dream."

"What is it?" asked Isra her voice muffled by her own

hand.

Viekko didn't answer, but continued to walk through the forest. Given the overpowering strength of the odor, its source couldn't be far away. And true to his instincts, he only walked a few meters through the forest until he emerged onto the crumbled remains of tarmac. The forest was starting the process of reclaiming this land; small trees and bushes pushed their way through breaks in the asphalt. He could see a few small groves exploiting larger holes. Still, there was a strange sense of stepping back in time as his boots touched hard, paved ground.

A few meters from the forest, he came across a body. It was probably human, although it was burned so badly that Viekko had some doubts. The face was an incomprehensible mess of charred flesh and the hands and feet were burned all the way to the bone. The body was oddly proportioned as well. The legs and arms were longer than a typical human, the torso was slim and the head appeared more oblong. It was as if the entire body was put on a rack and pulled longer like a piece of clay. The only clothing was a pelt of animal skin as badly burned as its owner.

Viekko knelt down and held his hand over the body. Heat radiated off of it and the skin crackled as it split. Whatever happened here happened only a few hours ago. A large plume of smoke from some still-smoldering inferno a couple hundred meters away supported that idea.

He swallowed hard. They had caused this. Just by coming here, maybe just by landing on the planet, they caused this to happen. Viekko didn't know how, but he knew it was true.

He turned back toward the forest where Althea, Isra and Cronus were themselves coming to grips with what they were seeing. There were other bodies scattered around that patch of asphalt all as badly burned, if not worse, than the one at Viekko's feet.

Oddly, Viekko didn't feel much of anything. Maybe it was the drugs or maybe it was a defense mechanism born out of a lifetime of horrific sights. But Viekko wondered if he was preparing himself for a string of human atrocities that would be worse than this.

In the distance, just beyond the largest plume of smoke, there was a grandiose building that stretched across the entire length of the tarmac. It gleamed white and curved inward, encompassing a fraction of it within a crescent.

Isra took a step forward and nodded in the distance, "We should check out that building. Survivors, if there are any still around, would have likely sought shelter there."

Isra led the way and Viekko grudgingly followed.

Civilization had arrived, and Titan would burn before it retreated again.

CHAPTER SEVEN

Ultimately, the secrets of The Fall may forever lie with the dead. But, if we listen close, we can still hear their voices echoing through the centuries.

-*from* The Fall: The Decline and Failure of 21st Century Civilization
by Martin Raffe.

It was a massacre. It was genocide in its cruelest, most horrific form. The few randomly scattered bodies like the one at Viekko's feet were just the start. The real horror was clustered around the largest plume of smoke in between the crescent-shaped building and the tree line. Hundreds of bodies smoldered there in a pile of charred flesh and bone.

There was a Spartan simplicity about these people that somehow made their slaughter worse. Those with clothing intact wore long lengths of fur in the form of cloaks or dresses belted around their narrow frames. The men looked as if they let their hair and beards grow their entire lives without so much as a comb to pull through it. The women, by contrast, hacked their tangled, matted hair off at the shoulder. The only marks of vanity or luxury were bowl-shaped fur hats and leather straps or belts. Their entire culture, as seen from their remains, was one of harsh utility, a means of survival against the elements.

When the group was only a couple hundred meters away from the pile of bodies, Cronus fell to his knees, moved his breather to the side and gagged, "I... feel... I've never... I've seen the words and heard the voices of human cruelty. But I've never seen so much of it so... clearly."

Althea knelt down, helped him take his mask off and held it over his nose. "Deep breath, Cronus. It's okay. Be sick if you need to."

Isra, on the other hand, was strangely compelled toward wretched horrors. She approached the edge walking carefully as if not to step in anything or anyone. She knelt down. "Viekko take a look at this."

Viekko knelt down beside her. It was a woman, or at least the half-burned skeleton seemed vaguely shaped like a woman. Her hands clutched what looked to be the remains of a shallow woven basket. She held it up to her face as if trying to use it to shield herself from the terrible forces that did this.

"I think she was carrying a basket of fruit," said Isra, noting some of the native foods scattered around the area where the woman fell.

Near the woman, Viekko saw a man carrying a makeshift wooden torch burned down to the stick. There were similar torches scattered among the bodies including more food, musical instruments, and wooden figurines carved in rough animal shapes.

Viekko stood back. "Looks like one hell of a party."

Isra closed her eyes and clenched her teeth, "Yes. But what happened? Who... what could do this?"

Viekko tilted his hat back. "I would venture that there was some kind of gatherin' and somebody went and played crowd control with a flamethrower. Whoever did it didn't leave much of a trace though. It's all just fire and death."

Isra tensed, "Are we safe here?"

The Martian surveyed the area, "Nothing movin'

anymore. Looks to be whatever done the killin' finished the deed and left. Ain't nothing out there but a stack of corpses. But they couldn't have got far, that pile's still smokin'.'"

Althea helped Cronus to his feet. Cronus's tissue-paper-like skin was even paler than before and his breath came in short, erratic bursts, but he could stand and walk for now.

Isra watched the sprawling building looming less than a hundred meters away. "I don't like this."

"Can't say I'm giddy about the prospect myself," said Viekko. "Still feel like makin' for that building there?"

Isra said nothing, and just gave him a single solemn nod.

Viekko unholstered both his guns and handed one to Isra. "I'll take point. Isra, watch our path back to the camp. If we get ourselves surrounded, we're cooked... literally. Althea, Cronus, stay close. And if I say 'run' you haul it as fast as you can for cover. Understand?"

He started to lead the way toward the white building and felt a wave of dizziness run over him. He stumbled forward and, for a moment, had that far-away, uneasy feeling that he would get when the Haze took hold. At least it was probably only a moment. Could have been an hour as far as Viekko was concerned.

Althea touched his arm. "Viekko are you okay?"

He looked at Althea and then at Cronus who was staying close to her side. The idea that he might fail them both sent waves of terror running through his mind which turned into shame which morphed into anger.

He tried to will his mind back, make it sharper through sheer stubbornness. He snapped, "I'm fine. Just...I think the smell is gettin' to me. Let's go."

The space in between the worse of the massacre and the white building was empty. That meant that the culprits came from this direction and drove the people toward the forest. His grip on his pistol tightened as he scanned the dirty windows for any sign of life but nothing moved.

Viekko flashed on something the preacher used to recite back home on the Meridani Colony on Mars. He always said it when it came time to bury someone. He could almost hear the holy man's voice in his head, "Though I walk through the valley of the shadow of death, I will fear no evil...for you are with me...something...something."

"Did you say something?" said Althea. She was still walking beside him with a look of concern that irritated every nerve that wasn't numbed by withdrawals.

"Nothin'," said Viekko, "Just divine protection."

"There is no divinity here," said Cronus watching the sky as he walked, "No protection, no safety, no limits. Only people. Animals. Free to do as they will with no chance of retribution."

Viekko tightened his grip on his gun, "Cronus, this place is creepy enough as it is. Don't go losin' your head and makin' it worse."

He quickened his steps and left Althea a few paces behind him. It didn't matter. Whether he was standing over the body of a fallen comrade on Mars or trudging through the burned-out remains on his hell, there was no Earth god that gave a *galt baas* about what happened on other planets.

Viekko stopped walking and shook his head to try and clear it. His mind was wandering. The Haze was setting in faster and harder than it ever had in the past. Whatever Althea had given him was causing him to crash hard.

Althea caught up and put her hand on his arm again. "Viekko, are you sure you're all right?"

Cronus, tailing at Viekko's heel, was still fixated on the sky when he murmured, "They came from above. They had to. We will never escape them here."

Viekko brushed Althea's hand away. "How about instead of worryin' about me, you calm that kid the *khayakh* down? Can't focus with him yammerin' on like that."

Viekko quickened his pace but Althea and Cronus kept right behind him, "Cronus is acting exactly as one should given the circumstances. It's you I'm worried about."

Some motion, some smell back toward the trees caught Viekko's attention. Taking up the rear of the formation, Isra raised her gun, "What is it Viekko? What do you see?"

Viekko sniffed. He must be imagining things, there was

no way he could smell anything over the metallic, charcoal scent of burning flesh. The Haze was getting to him.

He turned back around, "Nothin'. Come on. Best we keep movin'"

A few minutes later, the crescent building loomed large in front of them. It wasn't as white as it appeared from a distance; the paint was tarnished, dirty and it had flaked off in several places revealing a dull, grey metal. The windows that stood from the floor to the ceiling were so filthy as to be nearly opaque.

Isra and Viekko rushed toward a sliding metal door. She stood off to the side holding one of his handguns at ready while he put his ear to it for a moment and, hearing nothing, tried to open it.

"*Novch Gej!* Locked. Althea, looks like it's your show."

Althea flashed Viekko a look of mild contempt but walked up to the door anyway. She tried pulling on the handle as well and knelt down to examine a keypad next to the door. "The lock and door are both electric. It might not even be secured, it just doesn't have any power. Cronus, do you have a screwdriver?"

Cronus lurched forward still looking sickly. "I think so."

As he dropped his backpack to root through it, Althea added, "And a battery. A strong one for preference, but any spare battery will do."

Cronus cocked his head at the request but continued looking. He produced both items from the recesses of his bag and handed them to Althea.

In one quick motion, she jammed the screwdriver into a space just behind the keypad and levered it out of the socket. It fell and hung suspended by several wires. Althea ran her fingers down the individual metal strands, muttering something to herself before she pulled two away from the keypad.

She held up red and white wires and the battery and looked at Viekko, "When I say go, pull on that handle as hard as you can."

Viekko grabbed the door and got ready to throw all his

weight behind him.

Althea waited a moment, shouted "Now!" and touched the wires to the battery contacts. There was a flash and crack of electricity and Viekko pulled as hard as he could. It barely moved at first but, after a moment, it opened so fast that he nearly fell backwards.

Althea stood and handed the battery and screwdriver back to Cronus. He took them and pulled the breather away for a moment, "Why does a medical doctor know how to spark-boot a lock? It is a subject not routinely covered in medical schools."

Althea looked away embarrassed, "I wasn't always a doctor, and we shall leave it at that."

Viekko checked his gun, "Don't go bein' modest, Althea. Why don't you tell the man about..."

Viekko's voice trailed off under Althea's withering glare. Although Cronus had a wide-eyed look of curiosity plastered all over, self-preservation dictated a swift change of subject. "Never mind, keep your eyes movin' in your head, everyone. Every dark corner, every doorway."

Viekko entered first with his gun raised but everything inside was still quiet.

Standing at the doorway, Viekko felt as if he were about to step a thousand years back in time. He stared down a carpeted hallway with a dizzying red and blue diamond design that curved around until it disappeared in the distance. This was punctuated on the right by wooden kiosks, rows of uncomfortable chairs, banks of monitors and all the other trappings of what was once a bustling transport hub. Somewhere in Viekko's mind he could almost hear the dull roar and bustle of the hundreds of travelers from a millennia ago. He could feel his spine tense as if he just walked over the graves of every single one of them.

Isra tucked his other gun into her waistband and walked in behind him. She cupped her hands to her mouth and yelled, "Hello! *Nin hao! Zdravstvuyte! Hola!*" She tried several other variants, pausing briefly between each one, but nobody answered back.

Cronus and Althea followed them into the ancient spaceport and then started down the hallway together. It was all remarkably well-preserved. The windows were cracked and so dirty as to be opaque, the carpet was faded and the fake wood peeled off the kiosks but it all looked like it had been abandoned for years, not centuries. Viekko had seen ruins both on Earth and beyond and they were nothing like this. They always felt like a vague representation of what it used to be. There, he had to close his eyes and imagine what the walls would have looked like still standing or what paint might have been on the walls. What the joint might have looked like when it still had a roof. But this place was pristine, quiet and empty as if the gods themselves lifted it from its own time and dropped it here.

The faint roar of turbines and a breath of air through the vents told Viekko that this place still had some small auxiliary power source, solar or geothermal energy most likely. The air purifiers were still working and scrubbed the thick chemical smog of Titan until it smelled bad in the same way pure, distilled water tasted bad.

As they walked, Isra continued to shout greetings in every language she knew. Viekko wanted to tell her to shut up. There was obviously something on this planet and, judging from the killing field outside, they weren't much for visitors. Instead Viekko strained his senses through the Haze to pick up the soft patter of feet on carpet or the salty-musk of sweat. Anything to try and detect another soul before it was too late. But there was nothing but that too-clean air and silence.

They all paused near one of the wooden kiosks. It was identical to the others: fake wood with two monitors built into a desk on one side and a golden company logo on the other where travelers would line up. The logo was three initials, TPE, partially enclosed in a circle with a tiny rocket leaving a trail through the letters. Most of the gold had flaked off or was covered in grime but, where it wasn't, it gleamed in the dim light.

Cronus looked at the logo and cocked his head. "'TPE':

Transplanetary Energy Corporation. A smaller piece of the whole. A large chunk of what was to be the Corporation. They were a powerful influence on Earth and around Sol before the Fall."

Isra ran her fingers across the face of two monitors on the other side of the kiosk, "Cronus, can you do anything with these computers?"

Cronus crossed around back, knelt down and opened a set of doors near the bottom of the kiosk. There was an impossible tangled mess but Cronus looked at it all for a moment as if reading a perfect set of instructions. He removed his breath mask, "Possible. Connections are miraculously intact. Fiber to micro-filament to quantum-state servers. There is power, but not enough. I will need time."

Cronus pulled his pack full of equipment off his back and dove into the wires like it was the only home he'd ever known.

"Viekko, Isra, take a look at this," said Althea several meters away.

She had wandered farther down the hallway and looked in awe at an indent in the wall near a flight of stairs. Viekko and Isra left Cronus to his work and went to see what Althea was going on about. Someone had painted in very neat black lettering:

Ni faris tion por ni.
Ni faris por la Urbo.
Ni faris por la Kompanio.

Viekko cocked his head, "Language you recognize, Isra?"

Isra leaned forward and squinted at the words, "No... well yes. It is strange. I see some structure and vocabulary similar to several Earth languages but it is different somehow."

"A completely new language?" asked Althea.

"Possibly. But there is something familiar about it."

Viekko stepped close to the words, sniffed and touched one of the letters. The paint left a black smear on his finger. The sight sent a surge of fear through his gut.

"It's fresh," he whispered, "A few hours old, if that."

Something drew his attention and his gaze snapped up the stairs. It was nothing he could sense as much as something instinctual. He took a step back. Every survival instinct in his body wanted to bolt for the door. Both of his hands wrapped around the grip of the gun. They were shaking.

Isra without a trace of fear or anxiety pulled the gun from her waistband and shouted a few more greetings up the stairs but, again, nobody answered. She walked up with Althea close at her heel. Viekko, pushing aside everything he felt, followed.

The stairs went to some kind of lounge area with larger, more comfortable chairs and sofas littered around. One side was entirely made of up glass as dirty as it was downstairs. Isra and Althea both paused at the top to take in the scene. The carpet was replaced with a wood floor that still showed hints of gloss. Viekko found himself compelled toward a door in the glass wall. He walked up, tried the knob, and it opened to the outside.

He walked out onto the roof of the spaceport and stopped near the edge. From here, he could see the paved area in its entirety all the way to the edges where the Titanian forests reclaimed it inch by inch. Isra and Althea joined him to look out over the landscape.

Althea wrapped her arms around herself, "There's nothing moving out there, is there?"

Isra sighed, "Not a thing. I do not understand it."

"It looks like they all just gathered in a circle," said Althea mournfully, "Just stood around and let themselves be killed."

Isra gestured in the direction of the forest where a few bodies fell, "A few tried to run, but you are right. Most just... stayed. Why would they just stand there while..."

Isra's voice faded away like smoke in the wind. The sky

turned dark and the whole world with it until the only light came from the ringed planet hovering about forty-five degrees above the Eastern horizon.

The circle was alive now. Dark figures and light danced in a circle around a growing pile in the center. Then Viekko was in the middle of it all. Everywhere he looked there were figures like ghosts, visible but not tangible. They carried torches and baskets of food while they lifted their heads to the skies and sang.

And then there was awful, pained screaming everywhere. Viekko found himself surrounded by fire and the figures, light and wispy before turned black. Viekko screamed and jumped backward to avoid being consumed by the flames.

One of the dark figures turned toward him. "Viekko?"

He raised his gun and one of the figures yelled in Isra's voice, "Jaysus, Viekko. Put that away. What is the matter with you?"

The flames closed in and so did the dark figures. He waved his gun at all of them and growled, "Stay away from me, ya hear! Just back away!"

Another figure in Althea's voice said, "Oh no. He's having another episode. Viekko, calm down, listen to my voice. You are fine. Everything is fine."

Still, the flames got closer. Viekko kept backing up until he tripped over something and fell. His head slammed against the concrete roof of the building. The darkness went away and was replaced by the light orange clouds of Titan.

Isra rushed over to him. "Althea, grab his gun."

He realized that he dropped it when he fell. Althea scooped it up and held it close to her chest.

Isra helped Viekko to a sitting position, "Viekko? What happened?"

Viekko realized he was panting and soaked with sweat. His voice cracked and quaked with fear. "The food, the figurines, the tools... all offerings. And the torches and the circle. It was a ritual. And then... *burkhad namaig alakh bolno*, they were killed."

Althea took a step backward. Her face was white with fear. Even Isra leaned away from Viekko. There was a twitch near her eye that betrayed her carefully neutral expression.

"You see don't you?" said Viekko. "We've got to get out of here. Get back to the shuttles and hit sky. We can't be here!"

Althea swallowed hard, "Viekko, you're scaring me."

"You damn well should be scared! Can't you see what's in front of your face? We've stumbled into a damned holy war."

CHAPTER EIGHT

The digital records are sparse from that time. Most were either destroyed in the global wars or scrubbed by governmental or corporate entities in an attempt to write their own version of history. Much from that time has been forgotten and what is known has been passed to us through the tradition of oral history. It is not the most reliable source but, when it comes to the pain of watching one's loved ones massacred in the killing fields or the anguish of fleeing one's home for a far-flung colony, our species has a very long memory.

-from The Fall: The Decline and Failure of 21st Century Civilization *by Martin Raffe.*

Cronus blinked a few times. Numbers projected on a screen looked so still, so... two-dimensional. Maybe that's why they didn't make sense. He was used to the way the numbers moved around him. They weren't just numbers then, they were smells, colors, emotions. They were alive.

He searched through his pack until he found a gleaming silver board about the size of his hand. Hundreds of black lines were etched into every millimeter and those contained thousands of transistors. With this, he could make the numbers dance.

He crawled back into the mass of wires to install the board. The technology inside the kiosk was ancient but, with a few adapters and encoding lines, he was able to integrate the board into the computer system. Once he had it plugged in, he stood up and pulled his goggles back over his eyes. The world filled with digits streaming past him in every direction. It made him smile.

He reached out to touch a scrolling matrix. When he saw it earlier it didn't make any sense. It was the wrong sort of programming language. It was primitive, even for an ancient computer system such as this. Now in context, dancing and singing with the other numbers, Cronus understood. It was a security protocol but nothing installed when the system was in use on Titan. This was something written much later by somebody who had a rough understanding of the technology and the language but failed to grasp the elegant nuance of the system.

It was like somebody with basic knowledge of space travel trying to lock the hatch of a starship by nailing a length of wood across it.

It was a simple security protocol to circumvent. Cronus set a simple breach algorithm on it and waited for the program to chew through the tangles of logic.

Some commotion in the outside world caught Cronus's attention. He pulled up his goggles in time to see Althea and Isra leading Viekko down the stairs and setting him down on a bench near the kiosk.

The huge warrior was in an agitated state. He was panting, sweating and yelling out that, "They were going to die here," and, "we have to get out."

Althea placed her bag on the ground and retrieved a needle. It wasn't the typical syringe that plugged into the RX5, but an actual needle. The type that went into skin. Cronus's gut twisted at the thought.

"Viekko," said Althea with forced calm, "I need you to relax. Isra, you might need to hold him down and open his jacket. Viekko, I'm going to give you a shot. It will calm you."

Viekko was fighting, but it was a weak, desperate fight. Not against Isra in particular but against something... everything. Isra was able to pull one side of his jacket down over his shoulder while Althea jabbed the needle right through the EROS suit. Viekko's eyes widened for a moment and then his whole body relaxed.

Althea withdrew the needle and placed it into a mylar sack she retrieved from her medical bag. "We can do without medical transport, but I would like to send a beacon out on the emergency channel."

Isra stood up. "We cannot. There is a civilization out here and we should not risk any Corporate influence until we have some basic protections for the people."

Althea helped Viekko lean back and checked his vitals on the screen mounted to her arm. "All the more reason we should leave now. He's stable. He'll make it back to base. But we shouldn't delay..."

"We are not leaving," said Isra firmly.

"Isra, it's madness here. Viekko is right—we've walked into something we can't understand and certainly not control. We're not prepared for anything like this and certainly not with two people incapacitated."

Isra shook her head, "Not now. Now when we are this close. The city has got to be only a few kilometers away."

"Jaysus, Isra. We'll come back! Properly rested and at full strength."

"These people might not have that kind of time. You remember the gap in the radio band. The Corporation is on the move. If we abandon the mission now, there is no telling what Laban will do."

Althea stood up, becoming equally exasperated. "Then call your people. Tell them we've found a Civilization. We clearly have! We can get protection for these people."

"We do not have evidence."

"Don't have evidence?" said Althea motioning toward the massacre outside, "Are you honestly suggesting that those people out there set themselves on fire?"

A series of high-pitch beeps from the computer pulled Cronus's attention from the argument and back to the kiosk computer. He slid the goggles back over his face and looked at the numbers again.

Isra took a deep breath and spoke in the same calm, emotionless tone. "Of course not. But we are looking for civilization, Althea. There is no civilization out there. It might be the opposite of it."

Althea sat back down and reached into her bag for the silver retinal scanner. "I'm sorry Isra. But as your medical officer, I can't sign off on this. Viekko needs medical attention. So does Cronus..."

"Isra, Althea," Cronus said, his high-pitched voice straining to be heard over the argument, "I think you should see something."

Isra put her hands on her hips, "Will he die?"

Althea shook her head wearily, "What do you mean, 'will he die?'"

"Will he die in the next six hours?"

Cronus watched the numbers scatter erratically around him. "Something is happening. I cannot tell if it is automatic or human-monitored, but something senses my presence and it is reacting."

Althea went back to the retinal scanner. "No," she conceded, "No he won't"

"Will he die in the next eight hours?" Isra pushed.

Althea jerked her head back. "Just what are you asking?"

Isra maintained her calm. "Time. Just long enough to get the proof we need for the Ministry to set protections..."

Lights all over the spaceport flickered and Isra's voice trailed off. An ear-piercing screech signaled an ancient sound system coming to life and all around them screens flickered. They were so old that many only displayed distorted colors and lines if they displayed anything at all.

Cronus unplugged the silver board from under the kiosk along with the adapters and stashed it in his bag.

Althea and Isra watched the flickering screens in shock. They all showed a table of Earth city names, dates, times and a status column. The last of which flashed a few times and showed 'delayed' for every row.

Althea stood up. "What is this?'

"A time table," said Isra. "The comings and goings of transport ships from a thousand years ago."

The picture on the screen flickered to black and then displayed an unsettling face. It was an old man with deep wrinkles, a hard frown and a general look of miserable authority. The picture showed him only from the tops of the shoulders to the forehead and he looked through the screen like a displeased school master.

Cronus jumped and pulled on his backpack. "I think... someone knows that we are here."

The man spoke, "*Malamikoj de la Kompanio. Lasi tiun lokon. Forlasi antau la eklipso...*"

Althea whispered, "Do you understand any of it?"

Isra closed her eyes, "Some of the words are familiar. Some of the syntax as well but not enough to translate."

Althea and Isra listened as the man finished his speech in the strange language. Then he began again, "Enemies of the *Kompanio*. Leave this place. *Venganto* appear at the eclipse. Leave or you will burn. Leave and never return to Titan. Our people resist you. Our city repels you. *Venganto* will destroy you. *Saluton la Kompanio!*"

The screens went blank, the lights flickered off, and the whole spaceport was sucked into a dark silence.

Althea swallowed. "I understood that."

Isra breathed hard. "So did I."

Althea picked up her medical bag. "Can we leave now?"

Isra led the way across the tarmac, clutching Viekko's gun and scanning the open landscape and the forest ahead for any sign of danger. Cronus followed so close behind that his high, nasally wheezing through the mask grated on her nerves. A few meters back, Althea and Viekko struggled to keep up. As the sedative Althea gave him took hold, he slipped into an incoherent, semi-conscious state. He stumbled forward while Althea, under his arm, braced his enormous body with her relatively small frame.

The silence and stillness of the area was still only interrupted by wafting smoke and the crackle of still-smoldering bodies. Isra's eyes darted in her head and she kept her gun raised as she pushed the group forward toward the relative safety of the forest.

Back within the trees and under the canopy, Isra felt she could relax to some degree. She released a breath of air that she felt she had been holding since they left the spaceport. Out of immediate danger, her mind went back to the old man's warning on the screens.

"Leave this place. *La Venganto* appear at the eclipse. Leave or you will burn. Leave and never return to Titan."

Isra looked at the sun peeking through the canopy and creeping toward Saturn above the Eastern horizon. The fourteen-day rotation of Titan made for long days but, even then, she estimated they only had about twelve hours before the sun disappeared behind Saturn.

They all stumbled into the clearing where Isra set up camp less than an hour ago, but it was not as they left it. The domed tents were still standing, but everything she had stashed inside was thrown out and scattered on the forest floor. In a flash of panic she sprinted to the camp. The two crates she stashed inside her tent were gone. The two left on the back of the crawler were missing as well. Everything was gone.

Isra paced back and forth between the crawler and her tent. Her normally cool, composed demeanor crumbled like a castle in an earthquake. "No...no...this cannot be happening."

Althea strained under Viekko's weight, "What's wrong, Isra?"

Isra pulled her short black hair back. "It is all gone. The food, the supplies, the.... it is all gone."

Althea limped with Viekko to the crawler and helped him sit down, "It will be okay, Isra. We'll get as far as we can, then we can call for assistance."

Isra paced back and forth. "We cannot leave now."

Both Althea and Cronus were stunned. Cronus took a couple deep breaths through the mask, "Can't leave? Can't stay? Doomed either way?"

"It's okay, Cronus," Althea reassured. "Isra, we already agreed. And you saw the screens in the spaceport..."

Isra marched to Althea and put her hand on her shoulder so that the two women were face to face and only centimeters apart. "Althea, do you trust me?"

The medial officer blinked at the question. "Of course."

Isra continued, "And you know I would never put us at great risk. Not unless it was absolutely necessary?"

"I don't understand, Isra. What's going on?"

"There is something I cannot tell you about this mission. Something about what was in a couple of the crates. We must not leave without them. I need Viekko to track them down."

Althea stepped back and glanced down at Viekko slumped in the seat of the crawler with his eyelids half-closed and twitching. "Are you mad? He's in no state..."

"Can you bring him out of it?"

"Well, not directly... the sedative needs time to work its way through his body. And his endorphins are still shot, I can't..."

Isra touched her shoulder again. "Please. It is important."

Isra watched Althea's face. Althea was loyal and she did trust Isra, almost to a fault. But she could see the waves of conflict in her eyes as she wrestled with the notion.

"I would not ask," Isra added, "not unless it was important. I will tell you why very soon, and I promise that you will understand."

Althea took a deep quivering breath and looked back down at Viekko, "It will take a cocktail of drugs. I'm not quite sure how they will interact, what he will be like or for how long."

Isra turned Althea so that she could look her in the eyes

again. "It is that important. Please. Trust me."

Althea nodded and knelt down to sort through her medical bag. One-by-one she pulled out three syringes and an electronic cylinder with several ports on the side. She put each of the syringes in one of the ports, set the cylinder aside, and worked on the screen attached to her arm. After a few moments the plungers on the three syringes dropped in varying degrees. Althea pulled a fresh syringe from her bag, plugged it into the cylinder, and pulled out the new mixture.

Althea opened Viekko's jacket to expose his medical regulator. Just before she locked the new drug combination into place, she glanced at Isra.

Isra nodded. "We need him."

Althea placed the syringe into the port and touched the button on top. The plunger slowly descended.

There were at least ten people and they were moving through the forest at quite a clip. They didn't act overly concerned about where and how they walked. That was good. It left a trail that Viekko could follow; a good number of broken branches, crushed bushes, and footprints in the soft, muddy ground.

Viekko paused, sniffed the air and took in the sounds of the forest.

"Well, where did they go?" asked Isra, kneeling beside him.

"Quiet!" Viekko snapped.

He closed his eyes and tried to listen again. He couldn't detect anything but the ambient sound of the forest along with Cronus's perpetual wheeze through the breather.

Viekko looked back to where Cronus and Althea were standing behind him. "Could you shut him up too?"

Althea glared. "What would you have me do, Viekko? Ask him to stop breathing?"

Viekko shrugged. They could only be so lucky. But the truth was, it didn't matter if he did or not. The shot Althea gave him helped. It made him more alert and focused his mind, but he could still feel the Haze clouding his senses. It was like a cup of strong coffee after being awake for seventy-two hours.

Viekko stood. "They're headin' south. Stay close and try to keep quiet."

They started walking again and Viekko had to fight to keep his mind present. The triple-T withdrawal was in full force and made worse by the sedative Althea had given him. It threatened to take away whatever part of him was still there. At one point, the forest of Titan disappeared and it was replaced by the Martian steppes and Viekko was tracking a wildcat through the waist-high scrub grass. Later he was wandering through the neon-lit club district of Rio de Janeiro looking for a hit of the 'T. Visions hit one after the other and fantasy blurred with reality and again into fantasy until it was hard to tell one from the other.

Behind him Isra's voice snapped him back to reality. "Viekko. Focus."

His world snapped back. He was on Titan. Deep in a lush, green forest. There were footprints on the ground. Bare, and larger than average, but human. Next to that, a tree with a scratch in the bark.

He turned to Isra. "They're headin' west."

And again they were moving, Isra right beside him trying to read the same trail marks that he saw. Althea and Cronus struggled to keep up.

The Haze hit again. This time he was strolling through the slums of Rome looking for a shard of 'T. Then, flash, he was a child running through tall fields of barley away from the raiders attacking his village.

All hallucinations. More frequent. More vivid. He needed a shard of 'T'. Now, before he lost himself completely.

But that was impossible. If Althea saw him, if Isra saw him, it would be over. They would kick him back to Earth where he would die in some gutter.

He forced himself to focus. They were heading east now and there was a trail of footprints in the soft ground.

The forest started looking the same. The trees, the shrubs, the rocks and lay of the land all seemed familiar, like a memory replayed in his mind. Even the trail signs he followed started to repeat themselves.

Then he stopped and looked at a set of bare footprints. Next to that, a tree with a scratch in the bark.

Behind him, Isra snapped, "Viekko! What is wrong? We need to keep..."

Viekko had a moment of clarity. Things didn't look the same because his mind was turning into mush. Things were really the same. Whatever, whoever they were tracking was aware and leading them in a circle.

"We have to stop," Viekko slurred.

Isra walked in front. "Why exactly?"

Viekko raised his head and scanned the canopy. "We've been here before. They're swinging back around taking us the way we came."

Isra started to say something when Althea walked up. "He's right." She pointed at a set of boot prints in the mud; Viekko's prints. "We just came this way not too long ago."

"They know we're followin' 'em," said Viekko desperately. "They're lettin' us know that they know. This is a message. 'Back off'."

Isra put her hands on her hips. "And if we do not?"

"Followin' 'em will do us no good. They know we're here and know these forests. There ain't no reason they won't jump out of the trees right now and slit our throats. We have to go now. It's over."

Isra looked around the forest, taking full stock of their situation. It should have been an easy decision, but she hesitated. Why? What was so damned important? Then she spoke in a strange, resigned tone, "Fall back to camp. We need to regroup and come up with another plan."

Sergeant Carr crouched in the dense underbrush and watched the members of the Human Reconnection Project. They were just standing in the middle of the forest and...

talking. He remained as still as he could. His knees and lower back throbbed in pain from being stuck in the same position for so long. But, he waited.

For a moment, he wondered if Viekko hadn't picked up his scent again. Something was wrong. For the last hour, they had been wandering the forest like blind dogs in a squirrel enclosure. They weaved and zig-zagged and then did a giant three-sixty turn. It made not a lick of sense and he couldn't get close enough to hear what, if anything, their reasoning was.

He set his rifle down as slow and gently as he could so as to barely disturb the foliage around him. He fished a transmitter Laban gave him out of his pocket, lifted it to his mouth, and whispered, "This is Carr. Subjects are engaging in some kind of reconnaissance action in the woods near the city. No contact with native civilizations yet. There's a possibility my position has been compromised. I'm falling back for now. Next report in two hours."

He replaced the transmitter and picked up his gun with the same precise, paranoid care he used before. At that moment, the whole group turned around and started heading in his direction. Shit! Had they heard him or were they just lost?

He picked a direction and started to ease himself out of their path. He had to put some distance between himself and them and, hopefully, get behind them. Once he felt he was safely out of their way, he started moving faster. He planned to move in a wide arch around their position and come up from behind. Even if they had detected him, they might get to a certain point, find no evidence, and assume they were hearing things.

He came to a narrow clearing where a stream ran down a short, rocky cliff and formed a little waterfall. He set his rifle down next to it and examined the water. It looked clear but reeked of ammonia. Carr grimaced and retrieved his own canteen.

He sat on a rock near the stream, sipped water, and relaxed for a moment. He would let them get a ways away before he picked up the trail again. For now, he found himself enjoying this peaceful little place.

He screwed the cap back on his canteen and replaced it on his belt. Leaves and branches rustled around him as something or someone moved through them. He grabbed his gun and looked up to find his position covered on all sides by men. Long, gangly-looking men completely covered in thick animal skins. They didn't speak, but they all pointed rifles in his direction. Rifles more advanced than the weapon he carried and far too advanced for this moon.

Carr grinned, placed his gun on the ground, raised his hands and clasped his palms behind his head. One by one they started to converge on his position, keeping their guns pointed directly at him.

Carr laughed, "Come on there, little fellas, no need to be afraid. You caught me fair and square."

CHAPTER NINE

*For those stranded far from Earth, the first years of the Fall must
have been a supernova. Bright and all-encompassing for a short while
and then like nothing ever existed. Far from the influence of a global
culture, I often wonder what we will find as we return to worlds we left
behind so long ago. Will we find long-lost friends and family
welcoming us with joy and celebration? Or will we find ourselves
looking at each other as strangers with all the distrust and animosity
that comes with it?*

-from The Fall: The Decline and Failure of 21st Century Civilization *by
Martin Raffe.*

Isra used the satellite uplink on her EROS suit to
navigate back to the makeshift camp where they left the
crawler. It took time, too much time for a crew that was on
the brink of total exhaustion. It was up to Isra to lead the
way again as Althea's drug cocktail was already wearing off.
She would look back every once in a while and, every time
she did, she saw more and more lucidity drain from Viekko's
eyes.

By the time they arrived, Isra and Althea led Viekko with his arms over both their shoulders to the crawler where they set him down. If anything, Viekko was worse off now than ever before. His eyes were glazed over and he stared off in the distance not really focusing on any one thing. His mouth moved in some silent conversation.

Cronus walked beside them and set himself down on the back of the now-empty crawler bed. Even through the breather, he struggled to catch every breath in between fits of coughing.

Althea went to work downloading the readout from both of the men's medical regulators while Isra watched. "Any idea what is happening to them?"

Althea shook her head, "Whatever they have, it's not related. Cronus got better inside the spaceport where the air was filtered. Viekko has been getting progressively worse since before we landed on Titan."

Isra stopped. "Before we landed?"

Althea turned off her screen. "His endorphin production was a little low during his post-hibernation checkup."

Isra felt a swell of rage flash inside her. "Are you telling me you knew about this the entire time and you did not inform me?"

Althea held out her hands. "There was no way of knowing it would progress this far or this fast. Hibernation has vast and unpredictable side effects some of which are not completely understood, but they tend work themselves out—"

"Tend to work themselves out? The best medial mind the Ministry could find and all you have is 'tend to work themselves out?" Isra paused and gathered herself. "I am sorry. It is not your fault. I am afraid my feelings are getting the best of me. The mission is over. We need to go back to the base and persuade Laban to form a reconnaissance team."

"A reconnaissance team? A...Corporate reconnaissance team? Isra, you've spent the entire time trying to prevent the Corporation getting anywhere near the city."

Isra started taking down one of the shelters. "The situation has changed, Althea."

Althea got out of the crawler and slowly approached. "This has something to do with the crates, doesn't it? Isra, what were we carrying?"

Isra set a collapsed shelter next to Cronus. "You are mistaken. My rapid change of approach is in response to our current situation and resources. Viekko, even in peak condition, would not be sufficient to provide security for this mission. What we saw at the spaceport proves that. We will need armed mediation if we are going ensure the survival of any civilization on Titan...what's left of it at any rate."

Isra felt a twinge of guilt lying to Althea. It was a lie of omission, but a lie. But if Althea knew what she did—what the Ministry forced on her, she corrected herself—what would Althea think then?

"But what about the Corporation?" asked Althea. "You said yourself that without Ministry protection, they will move in and enslave the entire population. We've seen it before."

Isra paused, then activated the satellite map on her EROS computer. "It is best if we follow the coastline back to the base. If we head approximately east-northeast, we should pass right by the area where the assumed city is. Maybe we will get lucky and find solid proof of civilization, or at least enough to get Ministry protection before we hand the whole thing over to the Corporation."

Althea sat back down at the driver's side of the crawler. The tension in her body told Isra that she had serious reservations about the whole idea, but her downcast eyes said that she didn't have a solid argument against it, either. "If you think it's best."

Isra grabbed the tow cables from the back. "I am afraid all other options have been exhausted. Help me pull out the crawler. There is not much time before the eclipse."

Twenty hours, maybe twenty-four...Isra was starting to

lose track of how long she'd been awake. By keeping to the less densely wooded area near the edge of the tarmac and following the tree line into a relatively open plain, the travel itself was far less grueling than cutting straight through the forest. Now, it was pure exhaustion that proved to be the hardest obstacle and, at the same time, a force that propelled her forward.

Isra glanced at Cronus who passed in and out of sleep, awakened in between by fits of coughing and wheezing. Whatever Viekko was doing, it wasn't sleeping. He slumped in his seat, breathed in short, sporadic bursts while his eyes darted wildly in all directions. But Althea kept driving and Isra kept moving at a steady pace at the edge of the forest.

Until the constantly shifting ground of Titan played its part.

Isra kept trudging along until the high-pitched whine of the electrical engine straining made her turn around. The left-back wheels of the crawler fell into a mini-sink hole and, as much as Althea gunned the throttle, the wheels sunk deeper and deeper into the ground until they were buried and the opposite corner raised up several centimeters.

Althea released the throttle and banged the wheel with both fists. "Damn....damn this bloody moon and its bloody useless ground. We'd be better off driving on a bloody lake."

Isra raised an eyebrow. The fact that Althea still had the energy to be frustrated surprised her.

"Get the tow cable," Isra half-mumbled. "I will find an easier route."

Isra stepped over some fallen logs and through a patch of dense ferns. They had been avoiding the wide open plains nearby fearing that it would leave them too exposed. But there had been no sign of another human since the spaceport and keeping themselves hidden was taking its toll.

Isra stepped out of the forest and found herself face to face with a towering grey wall and a wooden gate both larger than anything seen on Earth. Neither were ornate or complex but utilitarian to an intimidating degree. The gate was as high as the wall and made with several planks of wood held by a series of ten crossbeams. Each vertical plank looked like it was made from a single piece of wood. The sheer size made that an impossibility on Earth. Even the now-extinct California redwood would barely grow large enough for such a project.

Behind the wall, just beyond the perpetual haze of Titan, she could make out the remains of an ancient city complete with skyscrapers that extended into the clouds. At one time, this little plot of land was likely a glowing jewel in the rugged wilderness of the extraterrestrial colonies. Now, several of the larger buildings ended in jagged ruins, suggesting that the upper floors had long since collapsed in on themselves. There were no lights in the windows, no gleam of polished metal or glass. It all felt like a cold, dark reminder of what existed a millennium ago.

Isra turned back toward the crawler. "Althea, come look at this."

Althea reluctantly moved out of the forest to join Isra and marveled at the sight in front of her. "Oh my...we found it. The City. It's still here."

"Was," said Isra, activating her EROS screen. "Was here. It does not prove anything we did not know before. Ruins are not proof of civilization."

"Isra, the gate is moving."

Isra stopped and watched as the wooden gate large enough to accommodate a shuttle slid open a few meters. A small group of about ten emerged from the crack. At that distance, Isra could only make out the fact that they wore long brown coats and they were human-shaped.

Isra opened the bionic applications in her EROS suit. She selected the optical recorder and felt a slight tingle behind her right eye. Now, what she saw would be recorded to the computer memory so it could be sent to the Ministry.

She watched the people leaving the city closely.

"Isra," said Althea nervously, "is it quite safe to stay here?"

Keeping close to the forest, it would be hard to pick her and Althea out at this distance unless they were looking for them. All the same, they were getting closer.

Isra stopped the recording. "You are right. We should get back to the crawler and avoid contact until we know for sure that it is safe."

They turned to go back. Cronus was still fitfully laying on the empty bed but Viekko was conspicuously missing.

Althea looked around and, with a hint of panic in her voice, said, "Where's Viekko?"

Isra had a feeling. A sick, twisting in her gut that said that she already knew the answer and she didn't like it. She cursed under her breath and bolted back toward the clearing and, to her horror, found she was right.

Althea wasn't far behind. She stopped next to Isra and gasped, "Oh no! Viekko! What they bloody hell are you doing?"

Isra watched that damned fool walk out into the open field toward the small group of natives alone and completely exposed.

Viekko was too far gone now. He could see that. All he could do was just sit in that crawler and stare off into space. How pathetic. There was once a time he was a fearless, near invincible warrior. Now he saw himself like his mind was outside his body looking back at it. Looking back at that worthless fool in the off-white khaki suit and wide-brimmed white hat. That waste of flesh that still dishonored his heritage by wearing his long, black hair in a warrior's queue.

When the crawler got stuck and Isra and Althea left, there was a powerful fear that became the only focus of his mind. Fear that they were wandering into danger. He should be there to help them, to protect them. If he couldn't do that, he should do the right thing and stop being a burden.

Get up, you worthless zondin. Get up and do something. Anything.

He saw his body start to move.

That's it...On yer feet. Now move. Walk, you bastard.

He watched his body lurch forward like a drunk who'd

just been dragged from the bar stool and shoved down the street. He stumbled out of the grove of trees and into the open field. He could see the city gate in the distance and the people emerging from it.

A few meters away, he saw Isra and Althea retreat back into forest. He wanted to call out to them. He wanted to ask why they were running away. Everything they worked so hard to find was right in front of them. Why wouldn't they go out and meet them?

He looked back at his own body barely standing on its feet, looking bleary-eyed into the distance.

They're retreatin' because they have no protection, you idiot, he thought. *That was your job. Your one* kharasaasan *job and you can't even do that.* Well, he might as well do something useful.

Somebody had to be first. Somebody had to walk out there with their head held high and let their presence be known. Yeah it was dangerous, of course it was. There were hundreds of people lying dead in front of the spaceport that would attest to that. That's why he had to do it. So what if he got killed? It would be a goddamned *yallagdakh* blessing. At least he wouldn't be stuck in that useless body.

He started to walk toward the small group.

Somewhere behind him he heard Althea cry, "Viekko! What the bloody hell are you doing?"

It's okay, Althea. I'm sorry. I'm so sorry. I promised to protect you. I can do this.

Althea was back at the tree line and, for a moment, it looked like she was ready to run after that stupid idiot. Thankfully Isra held her back.

Don't go, Althea. Leave me to die. I can't do anythin' else for you, but I can do this. I can sacrifice myself.

There were shouts from the group in the distance and they started running toward him. They were wearing some sort of heavy brown coat that extended all the way to their ankles and had collars that extended as high as the top of their heads. They brandished batons and snares as they ran at him.

That stupid idiot with the white hat just stopped and looked at them. Damn it! He should do something. Anything! He should speak, draw his guns. Do a dance! Anything would be better than nothing. Instead he just stood there while the people from the city gathered around. He just stood there as one of the men hit him right below the ribcage with a baton.

Althea came running with her black medical bag in hand as Viekko sank to his knees. *Damn it, Althea. Stay back where it's safe. Leave me.*

Viekko felt a jolt of pain across his head. He couldn't see from where he stood, but one of the men must have clubbed him across the temple, right where it would do that imbecile the least amount of damage.

Isra and Cronus came running out now.

He wanted to call out, *Stay back. Let 'em take me. Let 'em do whatever the* khaykh *they want to me.*

He felt another crack of a baton, this time across his shoulder blades.

There was another flash of pain and he was back in his own body and lying face down in the grass. Some of the men grabbed him by his arms and pulled him to his knees. There was a painful bite of cords being tightened around his wrists to bind them together.

Althea's voice came from somewhere behind him. "Please! Please! Don't hurt him!"

The men lifted him to his feet and he could see Althea, Isra and Cronus running to where he was. One of the men stepped forward and raised his baton as if to strike.

Althea dropped to her knees and put her hands in the air. "Don't hurt us. We are not here to harm any of you."

Isra stopped and did the same thing. "We are members of the Human Reconnection Project. We are from Earth. We want to talk."

The men spoke among themselves. It sounded similar to the language the old man used in the spaceport.

"Cronus!" said Isra impatiently, "Do as we do. On your knees. Hands up."

Cronus was so far out of his element now that he couldn't walk without step-by-step instructions. He fell to his knees like a puppet whose strings were cut and hyperventilated behind his mask as he put his hands in the air.

The men spoke among themselves again. Two of the men went to Althea, took the bag from her, lifted her to her feet and tied her hands. They did the same to the others, confiscating Cronus's backpack and Viekko's other gun that Isra still had on her. One of the men searched Viekko's coat and relieved him of his weapon as well. Once they were all secured, the men started leading them through the gates and into the city.

At least I was able to do something useful, thought Viekko. *At least I wasn't totally worthless.*

And with that thought, his mind drifted away for good.

CHAPTER TEN

In a sense, scholars should be generous when looking at the failures of the Corporation. They were no more suited to rule the Earth than the Catholic Church was to rule the remains of the Roman Empire. Looking at the two, the similarities are striking. The Corporation, like The Church believed in a purpose that superseded the well-being of the people under its charge. Their true loyalty was to the institution itself which would, in turn, lead the world to true enlightenment. Thus, the institution, not the people, was to be nurtured and defended above all else.

The difference, of course, was that the Catholic Church believed in the spiritual whereas the Corporation believed in economics. But neither were worth the cost the world paid in human life.

-from The Fall: The Decline and Failure of 21st Century Civilization *by Martin Raffe.*

It's true, Althea thought as they were paraded through the city. *They are people.* Just like the people who walked the market streets of London every day of the week. Just like the doctors and nurses who worked the hospitals of Johannesburg and the patients who came in seeking aid. The people here were stockier on average with finer features. Compared to the people outside the walls, they looked more...well, like humans on Earth. It was as if the city preserved a little more of what the original settlers arrived with. The men dressed in leather belted tunics with a heavy fur cloaks wrapped around their shoulders. The women and children wore long coats and hoods made of thick felt with simple, colorful designs kitted into the fabric.

The men who captured them outside the gates led them through the streets. Althea tried to look at their faces for any clue as to what might be in store for them, but the collar of the coat kept their faces hidden most of the time. The occasional glimpses revealed nothing but blank, stony expressions. Her arms bound behind her back made her feel exposed and caused every little hair on her body to stand upright.

The city looked ancient, old and forgotten like the ruins of Perth, Phoenix, or Kuwait City on Earth. But, whereas those cities had long been abandoned, people here lived inside the remains of the once great outpost. They made their homes in the crumbling skyscrapers and lived their lives on the cracked, decaying streets. It made Althea think of sea creatures swimming inside the remains of an old shipwreck or rodents and small mammals scurrying around in small ecosystems within bare, forsaken concrete walls. The people here inhabited a shell of something greater than them; something they couldn't fully understand.

Everywhere Althea looked, people came out of their houses and shops to see them walk by. Children stopped playing their little games in the street and gawked. People came out of skyscrapers, they leaned out of windows and stopped in their tracks to watch mystified. The road they marched down was wide enough for at least three cars on Earth, but there were none here. Most people on the street were on foot although a few rode push scooters and a few of the children played with wooden bicycles or tricycles. Men and women pulled carts stacked high with food, cloth or other goods but there were no pack animals to be seen.

As they walked, there was an eerie silence all around them. Nobody cheered, or hissed, or anything. They didn't seem afraid, but just watched with curious eyes as the men lead the shackled team through the streets. There were screens just about everywhere Althea looked, attached to light poles, the sides of buildings—even a few in the dark recesses of the old buildings. They were all dark and silent; relics of a long forgotten past.

Isra looked as if she was taking in the sights of the city with a certain air of polite interest. As if she might be on a diplomatic tour if it wasn't for the ropes binding her hands. Viekko...well, he was so out of his mind he probably didn't know where he was. Even Cronus didn't look particularly worried but that was because his mind had taken him far past fear into paralyzing horror. He looked down as he walked as if acknowledging the world around him would make it real. Every once in a while, one of their soldiers would prod him with their baton to make him hurry.

The men lead them to a building near the center of town. Althea imagined that, at one time, it was the tallest building in the city with two towers ascending into the thick, misty Titanian air. Now, one of them was nothing more than a pile of twisted metal and concrete. The other was mostly standing, although it looked like a good stiff breeze could finish the job someday.

The men led them up a steep set of stairs into a building that connected the two towers on the ground floor. It was a much smaller, squat structure that could have served as the lobby for whatever was happening in the towers. At the top of the stairs, the men said a few words to each other and opened a set of wooden doors. They weren't original—sliding glass doors would have fit the building much better—but those were likely destroyed and replaced long ago. Still, someone went to the trouble of carving small, elegant symbols into them. Even though none of the team gave the slightest hint of resisting, the men in the brown coats grabbed them roughly one-by-one and shoved them inside.

It felt like a completely different world in there. The city outside was drab, grey and crumbling as if all the color had faded over the years with the city. But in here, every surface was adorned with color. They walked through a wide hall on rich, red carpeting. Paintings and sculptures decorated every available space along the walls. And there were lights, real electric lights. They looked poorly made and cast a sickly orange glow over the hall, but it was electricity. Somehow its presence made the place feel less alien.

Isra looked impressed even if she didn't say anything.

Here in this palace, Althea felt they had crossed into another social caste. Unlike the women outside, the hooded cloaks the women wore here were covered from the collar to the floor in vibrant colors and intricate designs. As they walked through the building, Althea saw some women wearing something closer to dresses in bright reds and yellows. A few wore jewelry in the form of gold and silver necklaces, rings, and brooches, although it looked restricted to a select group.

The people formed small clusters of five or less and were deep in conversation until the men led Althea and the rest of the team past them, at which point they would stop and watch them go by with an air of smug amusement. Althea's sick, twisting feeling of foreboding grew.

More soldiers opened a set of double doors for the group. One of their captors shoved Althea through the doorway so hard that she lost her balance and fell face first into the rich, soft carpeting. As she got to her feet her eyes met Cronus's eyes for a moment and Althea saw a fear that had lapsed into sadness. The idea of the condemned being marched to their execution popped again into Althea's mind.

There was music when they first entered. A strange kind of metallic lilting like from a harpsichord or a hurdy-gurdy. There was also conversations between the fifty or so people clustered in the chamber, both of which ceased when they got a look at what had just been shoved through the door.

The room was immense and extravagantly decorated. Descriptions in Althea's mind shot way past 'lavish' and planted firmly on 'gaudy'. The walls were angled so that her eyes were naturally drawn to a large, curved indent in the wall opposite the doors. There was a man on a throne but he didn't look like he was sitting as much as he been set and encased in gold like a diamond in a ring. The decorations around him were intricately designed to the point that it would take years to note them all. On a cursory glance, Althea could see that Saturn was a motif, along with other celestial symbols. The most striking thing sat just above the man's head, the same Transplanetary Energy Corporation logo they saw on the kiosk at the spaceport.

She identified the man sitting in the throne immediately as the same face that warned them to leave back in the spaceport. If the people here equated power with how tall a person's hat was and how many pointy claw-like things were sticking out of it, then this person was bordering on a god. It looked like someone poked a dozen or more boar tusks through an incredibly long beehive and set it on this man's head.

The men in the long brown coats fell to their hands and knees to kowtow before the man in the ridiculous hat. They held that position for a few moments and lifted their heads to speak.

Althea leaned over to Isra. "Is anything they are saying making any sense?"

Isra cocked her head. "Yes and no. There are a lot of words with Latin and Germanic roots. I think they referred to us as the 'people who fell from the sky'."

The men in the long brown coats stepped back to stand close to their prisoners. The ruler looked over those assembled in front of him for a moment as if assigning a grade to each individual. Then he spoke. "You speak the... ancient language?"

His English was slow and deliberate as if translating on the fly but even this level of fluency shocked Isra. Finally, she stepped forward. "Yes. We do. My name is Isra Jicarrio. This is Althea Fallon, Viekko Spade, and Cronus. We have come from Earth.

The man nodded. "I am the Houston of *Urbo Ligeia*. You are lucky with the *Kompanio*. The *Perfiduloi*, the people who exist outside the walls, they would kill you and eat of

110

your flesh if they see you. What is your business here?"

Isra stood up as straight as she could with her arms bound, "It is good to meet you Houston. You and your people. We have come to learn from you. To learn of your ways and culture. To find out how your society has developed in the many years since our peoples were one. We have also come to protect you. Something is happening that will be hard for you to understand. There are those who would take your land from you. They are here. On this planet."

The Houston chuckled slightly and spoke to the assembled crowd in their own language. Whatever he said caused a wave of self-satisfied snickers throughout the crowd.

The Houston held his hand out toward the members of the Human Reconnection Project assembled in front of him, "You speak the language of the *Kompanio*. You arrive on boats of fire like the *Kompanio*, but you are not from Earth."

Isra paused. "I am sure this must seem incredible. I cannot imagine what it must feel like to find people who claim to be from another planet. But you must believe..."

"If you were from Earth, the *Kompanio* would tell me. The *Kompanio* still talks to me. They did not speak of you."

"*Kompanio*?" said Isra, rolling the word over her tongue. "I do not understand. What is *Kompanio*?"

Isra maintained a fixed neutral expression. If she was worried at all it didn't reflect in her demeanor or her voice. Althea was a different story, however. Something dangerous was happening. She could see it in her quick glances around the room in the eyes of the nobles watching. Something in their eyes condemned them. She shivered as if a chill filled the room.

"Of course you do not understand," the Houston answered. "You know nothing of *Kompanio*. You are *Perfidulo*. I see that. You may have come from the stars but you have not come to save us. You have come to destroy us. Again."

The word '*Perfidulo*' caused some frantic and hushed

discussions among the nobles gathered around. They understood that word and it carried some hefty baggage judging from the reaction.

Even Isra started shifting uncomfortably at the sudden commotion around her. "Forgive me, Houston, I am confused. *Kompanio. Perfidulo.* I do not know what any of those mean. Believe that we did come from Earth. I would talk with you more about us if you would let me."

The Houston grinned and said something to the rest of the crowd. He waved his right hand in a graceful flourish as he spoke as if trying to emphasize some grand point. When he stopped speaking everyone in the room gave the ruler a kind of muted laugh. Not a full belly laugh that comes when someone says something actually funny. More the kind of half-hearted laugh that happens when someone in power says something that was supposed to be taken as funny.

The Houston raised his hand and the laughter, such as it was, died down. "If you are from Earth, if you are *Kompanio*, then answer a question for me. When is the next departure for Earth? When will the ships return to carry our people back home?"

Isra sighed. "There is no such mission as of now. Your people, this city, it has been forgotten by the people of Earth. Something terrible happened many years ago. It is what caused the ships to stop coming to Titan. You are remembering a long forgotten past, but let us talk with you. We will listen and maybe we can discuss a transportation mission in time."

The Houston sat back. "You are not *Kompanio*. You are not from Earth. The *Kompanio* would never forget its people. Earth is a paradise of perfection. Nothing bad could happen there. *Ilin Forporti Al la malliberejon.* You will be punished for your lies, *Perfidulo*."

Before Isra or Althea could say another word, the men with the batons and the long brown coats grabbed them by their bound wrists and started hauling them back toward the door.

Isra struggled briefly against the men. "Houston! You

must believe us. Something terrible is coming to Titan. Your people are not safe! You need..."

Her words were cut short when one of the men hit her in the stomach with a baton. She crumpled to her knees before one of the men hauled her back to her feet. No one resisted after that but let the men lead them away. The music started up again as did the chatter of the nobles as the doors clicked closed behind them.

This wasn't the first time Viekko woke up in some dark, stinking pit. In fact, laying on a hard, concrete floor with the smell of urine wafting in the air was vaguely familiar. He could just as well be lying in a gutter behind some Rio club. He might have been just coming to in his shitty apartment having failed to make it to bed. Then the memory of Titan flashed across his mind and he sat bolt upright.

"Oh good, you're awake," said Althea.

Viekko squinted in the dark. At first he couldn't make out much of anything. As his eyes adjusted, however, he saw Althea curled up in a little ball in the corner. He took in the rest of his surroundings, such as they were. It was a jail, no doubt about that. The walls and floor were made of damp concrete and a barred door with a lock separated them from the outside world. He'd been in enough of them to recognize the tell-tale signs. Cronus and Isra were there as well. The group leader was laying on her side near the opposite wall while Cronus lie curled in a fetal position in the far corner wheezing through his breath mask. Both seemed to be asleep.

At that point, he realized that his mind was clear. No haze, no disconnect, no sign of triple-T withdrawal at all. Either he had been here so long that he'd completely recovered from the addiction, or...

"You lied to me Viekko."

Or the jig was up and Althea finally figured out what he had been doing up to this point.

Viekko checked his pockets and found them all empty.

He wasn't surprised, but that didn't stop him from swearing under his breath. "How did you find out?"

"Besides checking your pockets? Depersonalization disorder has few causes and all of them tied to endorphins. While hibernation can muddy up brain chemistry, it doesn't last as long or hit as hard as your levels indicated. Short of a chronic problem, there is only one factor that can destroy endorphin production as completely. Trihydroxide-thiosulfate-tetraoxide. What in the hell is the matter with you, Viekko?"

"Althea, I can explain."

"You can explain, can you? Well, this ought to be jolly good fun. Go ahead, then. Explain. I can't wait to hear why you are charging all over Titan hopped up on the worst bloody drug created by humankind. Ooh, and I can't wait for the part where you talk about how you put everyone on this mission in mortal danger while you detox. This will be fantastic."

Viekko leaned his head back until it bumped against the wall. "I could've managed it, okay? I had plenty to get me through this whole mission. But you had to go and shoot me up with some ugly thing. And I knew if you saw me, you'd throw a fit. Thank you, by the way, for provin' me right."

Althea spread herself out and glared at him. "Don't you dare blame this on me. You're the bloody junky. You're the one who smuggled that awful stuff here to begin with. You did all of this; don't you dare try to put it on me."

"I did what I had to do, Althea. Like you said, I'm an addict. I don't do what I do because it's smart. I do it because I ain't in control. The triple-T is and you saw what happens if I don't do what it says. You of all people should know what that's like. You got your own demons."

Althea paused and looked down at the floor. For a moment, he felt a twinge of guilt that he had gone too far. But screw her—she brought it up.

Althea took a deep breath. "It's different and you know it."

"Really? How's that?"

"I stopped."

"Yeah, only after you lost your career, your family and your entire life. The only reason you ain't in some detention pit now is because the Ministry struck a deal with the Corporation so you could slum it around the solar system and hand out bandages. You lost everything and that's sad but don't go and act like you are so much better than me." Viekko clenched his teeth. Okay, that was over the line. Even before Althea responded he felt a wave of remorse.

Althea shook her head. "You're a real bastard, Viekko."

Viekko rubbed his right temple. "Listen, I'm sorry. That was uncalled for, but..."

Althea turned her body away from him. "I think I am quite done talking with you for tonight."

"Fine. Just answer me this. What happens between us?" said Viekko.

"Us?" asked Althea with a certain icy tone. "There is no us. Not anymore."

"That's not what I meant. I mean what do you want me to do? What happens next?"

Althea reached into her coat pocket, pulled the little capsules out and looked at them for a moment. "When we get out of here... if we get out of here. You have to leave. You need to go back to the base camp and tell them about your condition. Declare yourself unfit for service and wait for the ship to go back to Earth."

"Come on, Althea. You saw the scene outside the spaceport. That didn't happen years, months, or even days ago. It happened a few hours before we arrived. There's somethin' bad happenin' here. You can't do this without me."

Althea looked at him. "Well, we bloody well can't do it with you, now can we?"

Viekko stood up. "You're right. I screwed up. I screwed up somethin' terrible. And when I get back to Earth, I'm done. I'll check myself into some triple-T program. I'll fight through the Haze and the Disconnect until I come out the other side. I'll never touch the stuff again. But right now, just let me get through this."

Althea saw him on his feet and recoiled. "What exactly are you suggesting? I give you your drugs back? You want me to look the other way while you continue to dose yourself?"

"See, when you say it like that, it sounds wrong. I'm askin' you to let me continue to do the job that I came here to do."

"While blazing on triple-T?"

Viekko shushed her and looked back at Cronus and Isra. They were both still asleep. "Just say that a little louder, why don't you?"

Althea cupped her hand around the pills and held them away from Viekko. "It doesn't matter. It's going to be out soon enough because you are not getting your drugs back. So you can either admit what you did, go back to the base camp and get some help, or you can keep it a secret until the Haze hits again. At that point, I'll tell Isra that you've caught something incurable and suggest a medical evacuation. Or you can wander off and just die. I don't particularly care which."

Viekko stopped. He'd never heard Althea talk like this. It was like the friendly family dog rearing back and biting his hand when he went to pet it. "You... you don't mean that."

Althea replaced the capsules in her pocket. "Yes, Viekko, I do. We're not just talking about what happens if you lose your fix or don't get a regular dose. What about an overdose? Do you have any idea what somebody with too much triple-T is capable of?"

Of course he was. He'd seen and heard all the stories about triple-T rage. It made all the news wires almost every day.

So had Althea. "Because I do. I see the women and children caught in the wrong place with the wrong person during an overdose. They come into trauma centers raped or beaten nearly to death. I will not put myself or Isra in that position. Not now, not ever."

Viekko sat down next to Althea. She was right. Well, she

wasn't; Viekko could manage himself fine. But she had the high ground and it was a tough argument to win. She was a doctor after all. She would have seen the worst of triple-T.

She's seen the worst... so she'll be able to treat it, thought Viekko. "Okay, you're right. I'm an addict and can't be trusted. But I trust you."

Althea shrank into the corner. "What do you mean 'you trust me'?"

"I mean you can keep up on how much I've been takin'. You can watch my withdrawal levels and my tolerance. You keep all the shards. Give me, say three a day, don't let me near the rest of 'em. That should be enough to keep me sharp but not enough to overdose."

Althea's mouth gaped open. "Are you insane! You want me to give you drugs?"

Viekko shrugged. "That's your job, right? You give people medicine, make sure they get the correct dosage, they get better..."

"Triple-T isn't medicine. It's the most destructive drug ever created and I will have no part in making sure you continue to kill yourself on it."

"It is medicine. For me, right now, it's medicine. I need the stuff to function."

"Why on Earth would I ever consider that?"

Viekko nearly shouted. "Because you need me!" He winced and, when he was sure Isra and Cronus were still sleeping, he continued. "Think about that slaughter outside the spaceport. Think about those people who went and raided our supplies. Jaysus, Althea, take a look at where we are now. It ain't a matter of if there's gonna to be a fight, but when and how bad. Now you know medicine better than anyone I know. Isra could talk a preacher into heresy and convince him that it was his idea. Cronus... well, I'm pretty sure he's good at somethin'. Me? I know how to fight. I can lead people into a fight. If I'm not here Titan will burn and take you, Isra, and Cronus with it."

Althea slid her hand back into her pocket. "This is madness, Viekko. You are asking me to keep you dosed on a highly illegal drug and keep quiet about it."

"You already did it once."

"I did it so we could talk. And... I guess part of me thought if I snapped you out of it, you could figure a way out of here." She cupped her face in her hands. "You will get one a day, no more, no less."

"One a day? That's barely enough to..."

"Are you seriously going to argue with me about the dosage right now? Because I think it's bonkers to be considering it in the first place, but you are right. We are in a bad situation and we need you functional."

"I'll need more than one a day to be functional."

"Well, that's all you're getting, so I suggest you adjust your tolerance. That's my offer. Take it or go back to the basecamp."

Viekko sighed. "Fine. But if the Haze gets real bad, we can talk right?"

"You'll get what I prescribe and that is all. And you're going to rehab when we get to Earth."

It was a terrible deal, but it was as good as he was going to get. He nodded. "Fine."

"Good, then we have a deal."

"Great...er, what do we do now?"

Althea stretched out to lay prone on the floor. "We're in prison Viekko. We wait."

CHAPTER ELEVEN

There is no religion that punishes unbelievers quite like Economics.

-from The Fall: The Decline and Failure of 21st Century Civilization *by Martin Raffe.*

Viekko woke to a screeching metal hinge and a blast of white light. There were no windows, lights or candles in this dank pit, so the sudden brightness was like the arrival of a god. Out of reflex, he pulled his hat over his eyes and pressed himself into the corner of the cell.

A silhouette appeared in the open door that some tattered scrap of Viekko's mind identified as the leader of this city. Either that or some other idiot got his head stuck in a giant, spiky beehive. The man descended the stairs with a slow deliberateness as if trying to make a point with each step. Two soldiers followed in his wake. The light woke Althea, Isra, and Cronus as well. One by one, they blinked at the brightness and stood.

The Houston stopped a few feet from the cell door. Viekko got to his feet and approached. When he got close, he could see the details in the Houston's eyes. His thin, wrinkled face bore the wild-eyed look of a man who'd seen a lot in the last few hours and very little of it had been pleasant. His mouth pulled into the defiant sneer of a man being forced into a last resort that was only slightly better than death.

"I take it somethin' bad has happened," said Viekko flatly.

Isra came to the same conclusion. She approached, placed her hands on the bars, and read the old man's face. "There is something wrong with the city. No, larger than that. The existence of every person on this moon is in danger and you need our help."

The old man touched the bars just a few inches from Isra's face. "Titan is dying." He turned and shouted orders in another language to the soldiers behind him.   They scrambled to unlock the door while the Houston turned back to Isra. "You must come with me to talk to the *Kompanio*. Ask them what we have done wrong."

Isra cocked her head. "So you believe we are *Kompanio* now? That we are from Earth?"

The cell door swung open and the Houston backed away from the bars, "I do not know what you are. If you are *Kompanio*, you will speak to Earth and save my people. If not, *Venganto* will add your ashes to the dead. Please. Come with me."

The Houston led them back up the stairs and into the palace. As soon as they were back in the lavishly decorated halls, they were flanked by two sets of guards in the long brown military uniforms. It all had the feel of security detail, although Viekko had to wonder what they were protecting and from whom.

They walked out the front doors of the palace and the Houston stopped at the top of the stairs.   A crowd was gathered on the street outside and filled a street wide enough for two vehicles on earth to pass each other. And yet they stood in eerie silence. Somewhere above them a bird with a wingspan that would embarrass an albatross flapped its wings and flew off the top of the ruined tower and soared over the city. The beat of the wings in the air was louder than anything on the street.

The people of the city, dressed in dull browns and greys and looked at them with expressions that contained varying mixtures of curiosity, confusion, horror and awe. A soft murmur went through as the Houston led the team down the stairs. Viekko got an uneasy feeling like he was looking into the eyes of a people drained of life. Robots would have at least beeped in a meaningful way.

The Houston made a slight gesture as he walked, just a flick of the wrist and a flourish of the fingers, and several soldiers marched down the stairs ahead of them to clear a path. The crowd spread revealing a cracked asphalt road that seemed just barely able to contain the plant life struggling to grow out of it. At the bottom of the stairs, the Houston turned and led the Human Reconnection Project down the road while the soldiers hurried into a box formation around them.

Althea stayed close to Viekko and eyed the people they passed. "They're just looking at us. No talking, shouting... just staring."

Viekko sniffed. "Say...Houston...sir? Looks like you've got a big turn-out here. What's the occasion?"

The Houston didn't look back or even adjust his brisk pace, "They have been here since you arrived. They are... curious, about our new visitors."

"Ahh," Viekko nodded. "You'd think they'd have mustered a might more enthusiasm."

As they walked, the crowd moved with them as if being pulled by a strong source of gravity. The more they walked, the more the crowd started chattering in their own language. Just whispers between each other at first, but gradually louder and more constant. A few started shouting things at the group. One young man pointed at Viekko and shouted something.

"What did that boy say?" asked Viekko, walking close to the Houston.

"He asked why you wear your hair like a girl," said the Houston, smiling slightly.

Viekko made a rude gesture in the boy's direction.

As they continued to walk, Viekko became interested in the number and condition of the screens that lined the streets. Unlike many parts of the city that were on the brink of collapse from disrepair, the monitors, for the most part, looked clean and functioning. A few displayed large cracks across their faces but most looked like they could flicker to life at any moment.

Isra must have been thinking the same thing. She caught up to the Houston and said, "I must say, I am impressed by the level of preservation in this city. Your public communications platform," she pointed to a couple of the larger screens mounted onto the side of a building, "looks remarkably intact."

The Houston bowed his head slightly. "By order of the *Kompanio*. It was the method they used to speak to the people of the city. We have maintained them through their long silence."

Isra glanced up at the dark screens. "And does the *Kompanio* still speak to the people?"

"The *Kompanio* speaks to me. I speak to the people."

"Funny," said Viekko, "If *Kompanio* and you are such great friends, you'd think they'd mention us."

"I think what my friend means," said Isra shooting Viekko a lightning-fast glare, "if the *Kompanio* speaks to you, then why do you need our help?"

The Houston walked in silence for several steps before answering. "It is the will of the *Kompanio* that I speak of. The instructions that we must all live by."

"Ah, so one of them metaphorical things," said, Viekko glancing upward.

Through the grey decay of crumbling buildings, a gleaming pyramid ahead stood out in stark contrast like a small jewel in a gravel pit. It wasn't as tall as most of the buildings around it—Viekko estimated it was around a hundred meters high—but it added a touch of dazzling brilliance to a city that was otherwise fading to black.

After a kilometer or so, they emerged from the narrow streets into a grand courtyard. The pyramid, surrounded by grass, trees, and small stone monuments, took on an even more august atmosphere. The sides, probably made of some long-forgotten polymer, looked like polished bronze and reflected the sun's light in such a way that gave the courtyard and surrounding buildings a golden hue.

They approached an entrance set into the base of the pyramid where two guards stood at attention. They didn't so much as blink as the Houston walked past them and keyed in some numbers on a steel keypad. Two steel doors thick enough to withstand a nuclear blast slid open. Viekko started to realize that whoever designed this place did so intending the structure to remain long after the last human died away.

Inside, they walked down a narrow, dark hallway for a few meters and emerged in an immense, open space. The walls all emitted a gentle white glow and there was a shiny steel catwalk polished to a mirror finish that led to a horseshoe-shaped control area. The catwalk hung above rows and rows of whirring black boxes with a few figures in full-body white robes drifting among them. They stopped to attend to some part of the vast machine but otherwise moved like ghosts in white bedsheets in a strange, black electronic maze.

Isra peered over the side at the men working in the servers below, "They are like acolytes to a cult of the machine. Do you think they understand the tasks they perform?"

"I don't even understand what I'm lookin' at. Nothin' but lights and buttons and far too many wires for my likin'. They couldn't have built this out here, not before the Fall. So why is it still here?" said Viekko

Cronus, however, seemed to know exactly what they were looking at. He shoved his way to the front of the group. "It's...it's A Markee 8700 supercomputer. I've read about these."

Viekko folded his arms. "A Markee... what?"

Cronus practically snarled at Viekko as if he had just blasphemed in this holy place. "It was the last great transistor-powered supercomputer. Before quantum computing became the norm. Before The Fall all but destroyed it all. Even when it was built, it was considered a dinosaur. But it worked. Quantum computing, at the time, was unpredictable and prone to failures. But this...this was all solid state memory, half-life capacitors and graphene conductors. The right crew with the right training could keep a Markee going for...well, a millennium."

Viekko watched as Cronus walked up the catwalk running his hand along the railing as if he were caressing the entire apparatus. The most blessed relic or a patch of ground tread on by the most holy person never received such reverence. He sat down at a chair in the middle of the horseshoe shaped control area like a god returning to his throne.

"Physical keyboards!" Cronus exclaimed laughing maniacally, "They still used physical keyboards. Amazing! I haven't seen one since the excavation of Old Seattle. It was half-buried inside the caved-in skull of some office worker. Before the wars."

To be fair, it was the kind of crazed god that fertilized the earth with his father's genitals and threw thunderbolts around like rice at a wedding.

Viekko glanced at the Houston who had an impatient air about him. Viekko called out across the room, "That's great, Cronus. I'm happy for you, I really am. Listen, we look to be still on parole and they might be itching to throw us back in that hole if you don't find somethin'."

Cronus reached out and slowly pressed a single key as if he were afraid the slightest touch might cause the whole thing to fall apart. When it didn't his other hand touched another. As if remembering a skill long since forgotten, Cronus started typing. It was slow at first but, by the time Viekko, Isra, Althea and the Houston crossed the catwalk and stood behind him, he was typing at a furious pace. Images and numbers flashed across the five screens in front of him at a pace that could bring on epilepsy. Viekko wondered how Cronus's fingers didn't get tangled at the pace they were moving.

Then, Cronus stopped. Isra leaned forward and squinted at the screens. "What did you find?"

Cronus sat back. "Nothing."

"Nothin'?" said Viekko.

"Nothing," repeated Isra with a touch more force.

"I tried several different paths into the data servers, but I'm afraid the majority of the system is locked out and encrypted. All I've found is that the system is experiencing something called a 'general shutdown protocol'."

Isra sneered. "Nothing more?"

Cronus went back to work on the keyboard. "Well, there is something else. I can use a backdoor into one of the security systems. It's somehow connected to the shutdown protocol. I thought it was just a hardware artifact, but let's take a look."

The screens changed so that each one showed a complicated black and white diagram. To Viekko's eye it looked like an impossibly intricate tangle of geometric shapes. A lot of those shapes, to Viekko's dismay, were flashing red. In his, albeit limited engineering experience, that was not a good sign. "What the hell are we lookin' at?"

"System overview," said Cronus, still typing. "There is some kind of complex to the east of the city, near the banks of the Ligeia Mare. The computer is reporting the shutdown or failure of multiple systems and more are failing as we speak. The system wants us to fix this first. It has locked down every other application. No data until we fix this. It must be extremely important."

Both Isra and Viekko turned to face the Houston. A good deal of blood seemed to have drained from his face. Isra pointed to the diagram on the screens. "Do you know what this is?"

The Houston tried to compose himself, although beads of sweat were still forming on his brow. "Extractors and refineries left to us by the *Kompanio*. The last time they spoke to the people, we were ordered to keep them running no matter what the cost. We have workers there. *Perfidulo*.

125

People we rescued from the forest. They must have deserted us."

Viekko examined the Houston for a moment. Something about the way he talked about the forest people made him suspicious, "Whaddya mean 'rescued'?"

The Houston straightened up, "*Perfidulo.* They live savage lives. They kill without thinking. They have lived without the light of the *Kompanio* for too long. We do what we can to help but it is difficult. They fight us at every opportunity."

Viekko's mind went back to the spaceport and the piles of bodies burning. Was that their massacre or some kind of human sacrifice? Was the Houston genuine or just covering up the sins of his people?

Cronus interrupted his train of thought, "Three more sections just shut down. I don't think this is neglect. It's all happening too fast and the systems are not shutting down in random order. This is not entropy, this is deliberate. Someone is doing this."

The Houston went even whiter. He opened his mouth a few times as if to speak and then turned and started walking back down the catwalk, "*Malbono perfiduloj, mi mortigos ilin ciujin.* I must go assemble warriors."

Viekko watched the screens for a moment. With all the activity, he'd all but forgotten that they weren't alone on this planet. Laban was still at the base camp, probably fuming about being kept from the city. And then there was Carr; Viekko didn't know when or if he stopped following them. If something strange was happening, it was a sure bet that they were both in the center of it all.

He turned to catch up with the Houston. "Sir...uh, Houston. A moment."

The Houston stopped and turned. "*Jes?*"

"We ain't the only people from Earth running around this rock. I wonder, did you see bright lights or fire in the sky several hours ago? Before the sun rose."

The Houston paused. "*Jes.* I'm afraid a great many saw it. It was... unsettling for my people."

"Well, that ain't the half of it. Those were shuttles. A couple of them. Packed to the top with people from Earth. They are here to do some harm to you and your world. We're here to stop that from happenin'."

The Houston shook his head. "The *Kompanio* protects us. Nothing bad can come from the Earth."

Viekko threw his hands up, "Then they came from elsewhere. Point is, they are here now and they mean to do you harm."

"What would you have me do?"

Viekko glanced back at Isra, not for his benefit, but for hers. Isra always had a strange way of knowing things. Just by looking at his face, she would know what he was planning. She examined him for a moment, closed her eyes and gave him a slight nod.

Viekko turned back. "Let me go with them. Your warriors, I mean. Give me my guns back and the things you took when you locked us away. Also, get some of your men to go with me. I'll get to the bottom of this."

The Houston looked back at the screens. He had a far-away stare that suggested that he would never consider a request like this in a million years. Of course, he'd never considered a threat like this in that time frame.

He looked back at Viekko. "Very well. Come with me."

CHAPTER TWELVE

The domination by the Corporation was so complete by the twenty-second century that the CEO and his staff never foresaw war, even as a remote possibility. But looking back through the lens of history, it was inevitable. People cannot be oppressed forever. Anger, resentment and hatred mix with a longing for freedom and self-determination to create a volatile solution. The longer a society tries to keep it contained, the more it builds. Then, all it needs is the right spark.

-from The Fall: The Decline and Failure of 21st Century Civilization *by Martin Raffe.*

Viekko lead five of the Houston's soldiers through the forest outside the city. It was unsettling at first, trudging back into the unknown of the dense forest with the Houston's men. He couldn't recall much about how he was brought into the city, but the pieces and parts he did remember flashed in his brain like moments of a nightmarish memory long repressed. They still wore the brown coats with collars that went up almost to their eyes. His muscles tightened whenever he looked at them.

But, in practice, they were agreeable enough folk. With enough pointing and hand signals he was able to give orders and they followed. He even managed to learn their names in the process. Lucjo was in charge. He spoke some rudimentary English and was able to relay commands to the rest of the squad. There was Mikelo; he looked to be in his late forties and was the oldest of the bunch. More than a few scars crisscrossed his wrinkled face and he walked with a slight limp. Viekko reckoned he commanded a great deal of respect among the group by the way the others talked to him. He was a quiet sort but when he spoke, the others listened. By contrast, the youngest, Vilcelo, could barely get a word in. He carried himself like a man who had, up to now, landed the worst jobs in any position and was looking forward to several more. Then there was Jocjo. Viekko couldn't tell if it was a quirk with the language, but Jocjo always sounded angry when he spoke. Viekko imagined that if he translated the world's most beautiful poem into the man's native tongue, it would come out like a declaration of war. Finally there was Alisa, the squad's lone female member. Viekko didn't know how many women served in the Houston's army—the uniform made it hard to tell sexes apart—but he guessed that they were few. Alisa had the force of personality and bravado that comes from having to constantly prove one's worth in a military boy's club. She was shorter than the others, but Viekko suspected that, if it came to a scrap, she would use that to her advantage.

They carried the same weapons that Viekko vaguely remembered from his last encounter: long batons and bola snares weighted with four smooth, white stones. Effective, no doubt, but not lethal. Not that Viekko wanted anyone dead; the killing field by the spaceport was quite enough death for one mission. Still, other people always wanted *him* dead. So it was best to go into this conflict ready to kill if need be.

But when Viekko asked the Houston for lethal arms, the leader was opposed. He said something cryptic about how his people fight *Perfidulo* but do not kill them. It made Viekko feel better about the conflict between the two peoples although it didn't explain the carnage at the spaceport. And it also meant that Viekko was effectively on his own.

Trudging through the forest underbrush, Viekko

remembered an old saying that said, "You go to war with the army you have, not the army you want." Right now, Viekko had five soldiers who were armed to capture stray cattle, not face the enemy. And up ahead was Sergeant Carr and whatever hell he managed to raise just for this occasion.

As they walked through the forest, Viekko saw several smokestacks in the distance towering over the canopy. Most were belching thick clouds of some noxious looking yellow gas. A few weren't, however, and it caused some anxiety among Viekko's companions. They pointed to the empty sky above them and chattered excitedly. Viekko got the impression, just from the tone of their voices, that they were witnessing the harbinger of cataclysm.

They emerged from the forest and came to a grey, stone wall about three meters high. One by one, Viekko helped them up and then scaled the wall himself using Titan's lighter gravity to scramble up the side. Beyond that, there was another grassy open space pockmarked with boulder-sized chunks of broken concrete.

The refineries were approximately four hundred yards away across the grassy, ruinous landscape. As Viekko walked closer, it looked like a huge, steaming tangle of metal pipes, scaffolds, and towers. One could hide entire armies in its twisting folds and any hapless fool approaching would be completely unaware.

As they walked, the gas from another smokestack thinned out and disappeared. The five Titanian soldiers watched with their hands around the batons attached to their belts and a look of terror in their eyes. A gust of wind rippled through the grass that gave the area a false sense of peace. Faint hisses and clanks echoed from the refinery, regular like the beat of a heart. The refinery itself was still, nothing ducking for cover, nothing darting around the corner or lurking under pipes, just the regular timing of the machines. For a moment, Viekko dared wonder if the refinery problems were just that: refinery problems, unrelated mechanical glitches that were making everyone extra tense given the circumstances.

He knelt down behind a rock and signaled for the others to do the same. He peeked his head up and watched the complex. When he was sure that it was clear, he crawled over the slab of concrete and motioned for the rest to follow.

Once inside, the smell overwhelmed his senses. Not just the flatulent stench of petrochemicals that leaked and burst out of every pipe they passed, but the tangy, metallic scent of blood and the sweet rot of decay. A few dark stains on the concrete proved to Viekko that the horrors of this world weren't confined to the spaceport; this place had seen more than a few.

Walking through a narrow passage with thick pipes on either side, he stopped to listen. Somewhere metal strained and moaned like a predator defending its territory. The groan got louder and closer until it felt like it was only a few centimeters from his head. Before he could react, Lucjo pulled him back by the collar of his coat. Viekko spun around to yell but was cut off by a sharp crack as the pipe burst and sprayed seething-hot gas right where he was standing.

Another moment in that spot, and his face would have melted off.

He looked at the native soldiers under his command. "People work in these conditions?"

Lucjo shrugged. *"Jes. Nur Perfiduloi."*

Viekko shook his head. "Whatever that means. Best find another way 'round."

They climbed over a bundle of pipes and found a new path through the twisting metal and steam, all the while keeping a heightened appreciation for the unusual sounds and smells around him. For a moment, he was worried about his recent charges, but he noticed that they were faster to react then he was. Faster to jump out of the way when metal screamed in protest, faster to stop and determine if a particular path was safe and generally more aware of the hazards around them. They knew full well what existed here but he wasn't sure why.

Then he heard something that wasn't mechanical. At

first, it was nearly indistinguishable from the rhythmic hisses and impacts of the machinery. But as it grew, Viekko could make out stray voices along with a series of rapid footsteps on metal. He crouched behind a concrete pylon and listened.

There was frantic discussion in the distance. He peeked over the concrete to see three of the forest people, *Perfiduloi* as the Houston called them, making for the open ground outside the refineries. They were the first of their kind Viekko had seen alive and he immediately wondered what they were doing here. Of all the places on this *karaasan* moon, why this slice of hell? Others followed fast. They had the same long face and gangly build but they were all dressed in loose, brown clothing. The type that only had two functions: to cover up any parts of the body considered indecent and to make everyone look like everybody else.

From the way they ran and scrambled over the banks of metal pipe, they looked tired and thin. So much so that Viekko was shocked that they didn't collapse.

The Houston's soldiers began talking among themselves. Something in their tone suggested a debate that was heating up. Viekko glanced around them and, satisfied that nobody heard them yet, shushed them. "Quiet! What's this about?"

Lucjo whispered, "*Perfiduloi*. Job not done. Never see Earth. But too much danger to rescue."

Viekko watched the last of the *Perfiduloi* run away. There was something sinister in the way the term 'rescue' was thrown around. The people he saw were fleeing and Viekko got the distinct impression that they were running from whatever 'help' the people of the city were providing. He didn't have much time to work out the situation in his mind before the wind shifted and Viekko spun around. There was an added component to the air now. Aside from the chemicals and death he picked up something else: Carr's awful aftershave.

Viekko leapt over the concrete divider and yelled, "On our six! Take cover!" Before any of the five soldiers could react, the first shot split the air like a whip crack. The youngest, Vilcelo, grabbed his throat just as a torrent of blood began to pour from between his hands.

The others followed Viekko's example and crouched on the other side of the divider before machine gun fire followed. Viekko pressed his back against the slab even as bullets whizzed overhead, ricocheted off metal pipes, and slammed against concrete and stone. Gas hissed through the new holes.

In the distance, someone yelled, "Stop! Stop! *Cesigi! Cesigi!* Damn it all, I told you guys to hold your damned fire!"

Viekko recognized the voice as surely as he recognized the smell in the air.

"Viekko Spade!" yelled Carr when the bullets stopped, "Was that you I saw out there?"

"Sergeant Carr!" Viekko called out. "Funny seeing you out here. Especially since, according to the treaties, you and your kind ain't supposed to be anywhere near us."

Viekko took a quick consensus of their situation. Four of the five—Alisa, Lucjo, Mikelo and Jocjo—were crouching nearby. Viekko put his finger to his lips then waved his hand down to indicate they should be quiet and stay low.

"The funny thing about treaties is that once you break 'em they do not exist," said Carr in the distance.

Viekko risked a glance toward the voice. There were ten more *Perfiduloi* among the pipes, vats, and twisted metal. They all were waving some kind of gun that couldn't possibly exist on this world. Viekko had never seen a weapon like it and, judging from the way they were being handled, neither had the people holding them. They were different from the people he just saw fleeing. These men were lean, muscular and had a fire in their eyes. Given how they spaced themselves out through the complex, they weren't the most organized militia that ever existed, but they were far from the lawless rabble the Houston described.

Viekko ducked back down behind the concrete divider. So, they were outnumbered by a factor of two and spectacularly out-gunned. Never mind winning this encounter; if he got out alive at all it would be a victory. Viekko gulped. "You ain't wrong, Carr. But when word of what you did gets back to Earth, it will cause no end of trouble for the Corporation. You'll probably lose Titan in the process."

"That may have been true had we been the one to break the treaty. But we didn't. This is a defense action. This is us protecting ourselves from the actions of a rogue organization."

Viekko stole a glance again. He couldn't see Carr but he was likely behind his own piece of cover. "I dunno, I'm looking at some pretty spectacular weaponry out there. You trying to tell me they came up with those guns all by their lonesome?"

Carr laughed. "Really? Is that what you think? Maybe you should go ask that girl Isra. Send her my thanks, by the way."

Viekko clenched his teeth while he muttered a torrent of profanity. Those guns... Isra brought them. Viekko wanted to believe that Carr was lying but then he remembered the extra crates, the secrecy, and how tense she got when Viekko discovered Carr following them. Damn Isra. What was she thinking?

Jocjo groaned and slumped against the concrete divider. Viekko hadn't noticed before, but the man had an expanding red wet spot in his coat. One man dead. One injured. And Viekko had the only two guns. Viekko glanced at the forest people holding the assault rifles in their long, bony arms. He hoped they were as inept as they looked.

"Okay, Carr. You got us. No need for killin'. We can talk about this. I'm alive and you got the upper hand. I'm sure Laban don't want this to be any bloodier than it needs to be."

Carr laughed again. "Well, the boss does like to keep it clean. You and your people surrender to us right now and we talk."

"Carr, I want assurances that I don't get my head blasted off if I stand. Your guys look like they got itchy trigger fingers. You tell 'em I'm gonna stand up. I'm gonna stand

and they ain't to shoot me. Make sure they know it."

Carr shouted orders in the same strange language that the natives spoke. How the hell did he learn it?

Viekko leaned toward Lucjo and whispered, "When I say 'go' you all run. Tell them."

Lucjo nodded. While the other side was still conversing, he passed word to Alisa, Mikelo, and Jocjo.

When the conversation ended Carr said, "Okay, we're all set. Now you just come out now."

Viekko turned and put his hands up over the divider first. Satisfied that he didn't get his hand blown off, he started to stand.

Carr stood up as well from behind a cluster of pipes. He held one of those strange guns while the forest people spread out around him. Now that Viekko got a good look, there were closer to fifteen men all armed with this rifle. He started wondering how many of those damn things Isra brought and how she could have been stupid enough to think that it was a good idea.

Carr aimed his gun at Viekko. "You alone?"

"No. There are others here with me. Soldiers from the city."

Carr's eyes surveyed the area. "Are they armed?"

"Only with blunt weapons and snares."

"What about you?"

"I'm packing two guns in my shoulder holster."

Carr motioned with his gun. "Take 'em out and throw them here."

Viekko glanced around and found himself looking at a whole mess of gun barrels all being held by folk with some terrible shakes. All it would take was one bad move and they would snap up their guns and spray the area with bullets.

Viekko shook his head. "If it's all the same to you, I'd rather someone come here and disarm me. Your guys are lookin' twitchy and if I go reachin' for my gun, I might end up fulla holes."

Carr considered this. He turned to a couple of the men and said something. They hesitated for a moment and

135

started in Viekko's direction. Viekko remained as still as he could to avoid spooking them. He didn't move when they both got close. He didn't twitch as one, holding the rifle with one hand, went to go for Viekko's gun with the other.

Viekko smiled. At least they were as inexperienced as they looked. A professional would never get that close.

In one swift movement, Viekko grabbed the barrel of the rifle with one hand and pushed it to the side. With the other, he pulled one of his handguns and fired two shots. The first one went into the head of the other gunman standing nearby, the other into the head of the man frisking him. Then he fell back behind the concrete as every other man with a gun unleashed a storm of bullets.

Viekko turned and yelled at Lucjo, "Go! Now! Go! Go!" Then he stood just enough to see over the barricade shouldered the rifle and fired full automatic on Carr's position.

His goal was just to spray bullets downfield and create enough violence of action to give the rest of his men a moment to escape. The gun was remarkable though. In the initial few fractions of a second the gun locked on to several targets and augmented the barrel to hit them. He managed to hit and kill five...no, six of them. Seven with another shot from his handgun.

But he only had a moment, and he was pushing the limits of that unit of time. The men he hadn't killed scrambled for their own cover, so he turned and sprinted as hard and as fast as he could out of the refinery complex.

Viekko jumped and scrambled his way through the obstacle course of steel and concrete. Once he hit open ground, he surged forward as fast as his legs and the EROS suit would allow. Lucjo was out ahead followed by Mikelo and Alisa helping Jocjo run. A few hundred feet into open ground, it felt like the gates of Hell opened from behind them. Viekko kept running, focusing on nothing but the refinery wall and the forest looming in the distance.

Lucjo paused for a moment and turned to see if the rest of his people were behind him. It was a mistake. As soon as he stopped, his body erupted into a hundred little red geysers and he fell backward into the grass.

Seeing their leader fall caused Alisa and Jocjo to pause either in shock, or just at a loss of what to do next.

Viekko had a realization. Those tracking systems were amazing but they could only do so much. In the hands of an untrained person who couldn't hit the ground if it wasn't for gravity, even the auto-track would have a time shooting a moving target. They were safe...well, safer if they kept moving.

Viekko headed right for Alisa and Jocjo. He barreled into the two of them and sent them both tumbling into the grass. Viekko rolled until he found a broken slab of concrete for cover. He raised the rifle and returned fire.

Viekko watched the forest people streaming out of the refinery through the gun sights. Unlike the blind attack earlier, Viekko focused on precision. He aimed, squeezed off a few bullets, and an enemy fell. He went to the next, squeezed off a few rounds and moved on. He managed to pick off another five before Carr screamed orders and the others sought cover. It was a shame he couldn't get Carr into his sights.

Viekko took a moment to check on Alisa and Jocjo. Alisa knelt over her fellow soldier's body and watched in horror as Jocjo took his last breath.

One of Carr's men showed himself. Viekko squeezed off a few more rounds before he turned, grabbed Alisa, and ran for it.

Mikelo never stopped running. One doesn't become an old soldier without knowing when the time is right to flee. He waited at the wall and helped Alisa over. Viekko helped him next and got over himself just as a few bullets slammed into the stone.

Once over the wall, they charged through the forests toward the safety of the city. There was still the occasional crack of rifle fire as they sprinted through the forest, but they didn't seem to be giving chase. After a few moments, Viekko felt they were safe.

More people were dead and Laban now had control of the refineries. And, frankly, he could have them. There wasn't anything on Titan worth dying over as far as Viekko was concerned, and he wasn't going to try.

CHAPTER THIRTEEN

Before the war, Earth glowed with the lights of a hundred mega-cities. After the war, the only light came from the fires of a world ignited. The light of Civilization would not be seen for many generations.

-from The Fall: The Decline and Failure of 21st Century Civilization *by Martin Raffe.*

Despite her better instincts, Althea established an uplink to Viekko's medical regulator. She told herself it was to look for any adverse reactions to the triple-T. It was a dangerous drug, after all, not produced in any reputable lab but in small, clandestine operations with no regard to purity or sanitation. Using it in this way was a risky treatment, if you could call it that, and she had to be extra vigilant during this time.

But in reality, she needed to know that Viekko was alive out there.

She touched her EROS computer and scrolled through the data. His pulse was racing, his blood pressure and adrenaline were lower than before but still high for...

She shut off the screen on her EROS computer and closed her eyes. All of the readings were perfectly normal for a man in his situation. She hoped that the lower readings meant that he was out of danger and on his way back. Or, at very least, somewhere safe. Even if every single reading flatlined at once, there was nothing she could do from here.

Althea needed a distraction. Isra and the Houston were conversing and mostly in the native language now. She couldn't understand a word, so that left Cronus who was typing away at the supercomputer's keyboards, oblivious to the world around him.

She leaned against the console near him, smiled, and said, "Have you found anything?"

Cronus didn't look away. "Almost. I am trying to bypass the lockdown protocol on the rest of the computer's systems. I am almost there, but I have found something else. Something important. Something that continues even while the whole system is in lockdown. It is the Signal."

Althea leaned closer to the screen. To her eyes it didn't look like anything but a blur of symbols scrolling endlessly top to bottom, moving so fast that it didn't register as anything with meaning.

"I don't understand," said Althea. "What do you see here?"

"It is a code," said Cronus looking at her with a manic grin, "A constant string of data being transmitted. Terabytes of data. Generated constantly requiring the bulk of this machine's processing power. And this machine was designed to perfectly simulate evolution of all life on Earth."

"What is it for? What does it say?"

Cronus's grin faded slightly and he turned back to the screens. "No idea. But there is so much. One does not dedicate a piece of art like this to a task if it's not important." He leaned close and whispered conspiratorially, "And one does not elevate system maintenance to a religious practice without cause." He motioned with his head to the acolytes in the white robes wandering between the server towers.

Althea watched an acolyte open a panel and pull out a keyboard on a rolling slide. He or she -Althea couldn't tell with the hood- methodically typed a few commands, pushed the keyboard back into its place and closed the panel.

"It's all ritualistic," Cronus explained. "No thought payed to the process and no understanding of the science. The wires, the code, transmission protocols and data management; they understand none of it. They only know what to do, not why."

Althea watched the acolytes at work. A religion based around the computers. It made a strange sort of sense. Althea considered herself reasonably proficient with computer technology. Above average, at any rate. But she had to admit a level of ignorance when it came to how it all worked. And what was magic if not a catch-all explanation for things beyond most people's understanding? And what was religion if not a way to control that which one does not understand?

The sound of the main door sliding open and several loud footsteps on the steel catwalk made Althea jump. She wasn't expecting anyone quite so soon. Viekko entered with a fire in his eyes that suggested that he was bringing the demons of hell with him. Two of the Houston's soldiers tailed him. They too had a certain look in their eyes and the front of one of their coats was covered in blood. Viekko cradled a rifle in his arms more advanced than anything Althea had ever seen. Corporation Marines didn't even have such equipment. He stopped just inside the temple and, without a word, dropped the gun. It hit the catwalk with a resounding clang like the toll of a funeral bell.

The Houston approached with his mouth twisted in a sneer. "Has the problem been resolved?"

Viekko stared back defiantly. "Not as such, no."

The Houston inspected his soldiers paying particular attention to the bloodstain that covered the front of the woman's coat. "And what of my other soldiers?"

Viekko's eyes hardened into a glare that could shatter steel. "The enemy is entrenched in the refineries. Our small force suffered heavy casualties in the encounter and we were lucky to leave without a total loss. Mikelo and Alisa here were the only survivors."

The Houston bowed his head and clasped his hands together as if he were saying a prayer. He spoke a few words to his solders who immediately bowed their head and turned to leave the building. The Houston watched them leave for a moment before he shook his head, "I trusted you. The *Urbanoi* trusted you. What has happened?"

Viekko motioned to Isra. "That's what I aim to ask her."

Althea looked hard at Isra's face to see any trace of fear or confusion. Repulsion or guilt. Something that would let Althea know what, if anything, Isra had to do with this. But her face was blank.

Viekko looked for it too. When he couldn't find it he said, "What? You don't got nothin' to say about that? Nothin' at all?"

Isra sighed through her nose as if the whole matter were a trivial annoyance. "What would you like me to say?"

Viekko looked down at the gun at his feet. His voice was cold and mournful. "Any damn thing. Lie to me. Tell me this *tengeriin nokhoi baas* ain't what it looks like! Tell me that it looks bad but you've got an explanation. Tell me that *mich* Laban set you up and you didn't do what I think you did."

Althea didn't want to believe what she was looking at could be real. She wanted to believe that, against all reason, the rifle had always been there. But her eyes drifted over the tiny targeting screen built into the upper receiver which housed sophisticated components built out of centuries of arms research. This couldn't have been created here, not on a planet that could barely maintain the computer equipment of the fallen civilization. She remembered the locked supply crates and how Isra changed when they were stolen, and she understood. She didn't want to. She wanted there to be a different explanation, but there was only one that made any sense. Isra brought those guns to Titan.

The room fell into an uncomfortable silence. Even Cronus stopped his incessant typing to turn and wait for a response. Althea desperately hoped the mission leader would have something, anything that could justify such a reckless action.

But Isra was monotone and calculating, like she was going to describe her own death with total medical accuracy. "As I mentioned before, if we lose Titan, they will have everything they need to keep humanity under the Corporate boot."

"The guns!" yelled Viekko, "Tell me about the *ta zondoo* guns! I ain't seen nothin' as sophisticated as them."

Isra, as calm as ever, glanced back at the Houston. "I am getting to that. Suffice it to say the Ministry's orders were to succeed at all costs. What you found was a weapon that could be given to literally any person anywhere and the technology could compensate for their lack of training. Dubbed the 'Peasant Gun,' it was developed by the Ministry to instantly turn citizens into soldiers as deadly as the most highly trained marines. It was meant to give us the edge. A way to apply sufficient force against the Corporation if they decided to violate interplanetary law, which is clearly what they have done."

Viekko folded his arms. "With your own guns I might add."

"Your people," said the Houston as if trying to wrap his mind around something, "They have come to Titan to destroy us? It was them who killed my soldiers?"

Viekko stepped back, "It weren't people from Earth. Well, it was one man from Earth, but the rest, they were people from this planet, the forest people, the *Perfiduloi* as you say. The same ones we found dead outside the city walls. If you ask me somethin don't make sense."

"Viekko—" Isra started.

"No! No more lies or secrets. Everyone's cards on the table right now. Houston, is anything you told us about the forest people true? What happens to the people you 'rescue'? What the hell happened at the spaceport?"

The Houston closed his eyes. "I did not want that. My people, the *Urbanoi*, want to help them. To rescue their souls and bring them into the light of the *Kompanio*. But when the new star flashed in the sky, the *Perfiduloi* gathered against the *Kompanio*. They came to welcome those who would destroy us. I tried to convince them to leave but in the end... The judgment of the *Venganto* was complete. There was nothing we could do."

"What is the *Venganto*?" said Isra.

The Houston regarded Isra and Viekko with a look of slight contempt, "The *Venganto* were left to us by the *Kompanio*. When the ships first stopped coming, there were others. Rivals of the *Kompanio* that came to take our city and destroy the *Urbanoi*. The *Venganto* protected us then. They protect us now."

Viekko kicked the gun across the catwalk to the Houston's feet. "Well I don't suppose these *Venganto* want to fix this situation then?"

The Houston shook his head, "They only come in darkness. That is why you and your people must leave before the eclipse. The *Venganto* will cleanse this world."

Isra started to say something when three of the City's soldiers ran across the catwalk to the Houston. One of them whispered something in the Houston's ear. His face remained unchanged.

He dismissed the soldiers and turned to Isra, "I'm afraid your failure is complete and we must put our faith in the *Kompanio*. It was foolish to do otherwise. You must leave now."

The Houston made a slight gesture and the soldiers surged forward. A couple took Viekko by the arms, a brave action since Viekko was nearly a third taller than either of them and outweighed them by a factor of two.

The other went to escort Althea out and Isra yelled, "Houston! This is not over. From what Cronus told me, you will need help using the computer to restore the refineries once we reclaim them. We just need time."

The Houston turned his head toward the sky. "I have heard the *Kompanio*. They are clear. Remove all Outsiders from the city."

"You want to hear the *Kompanio*?" asked Cronus, turning back to the keyboard. "All you had to do was ask. I have found their voice. Hear it now."

144

The pyramid filled with an unholy screech. Althea covered her ears and winced. It was like the sound of a nail on chalkboard recorded and then sent through a feedback loop. The noise lasted for a few seconds and ended with a pop. When Althea uncovered her ears there was a pleasant female voice instead: "...those left behind, it is imperative to the continuation of Transplanetary Energy's work on Titan that you follow these procedures. The refinery complex must never be allowed to fail."

All around her the soldiers and even the Houston repeated the words, "The refinery complex must never be allowed to fail." She realized that all of the soldiers were on their knees.

The Houston, still standing, stepped toward Cronus, "You... you have found the voice of the *Kompanio?*"

Cronus tapped a few keys and the voice ceased. "This and much more. Files locked away for many hundreds of years."

The Houston's face screwed up into some combination of pain and anger. For a brief moment, Althea worried that Cronus had committed a sin far greater than anything else up to now. Then the Houston turned and started walking toward the exit. "The *Kompanio* must have chosen you. You must be here to bring their message back to the people." He paused and turned around. "You may stay here for the time being. Finish your work. I believe it would still be wise to leave this place before the eclipse. *Soldatoi, venu!*"

With those words, the soldiers rose from their knees and scurried after the Houston.

Viekko folded his arms as he watched the entourage leave. "Nice work, Cronus."

Cronus raised his goggles and grinned at the group, "Deus ex machina! God from the machine!"

Viekko turned back to Isra, "It's about the guns you know. And if it ain't, it's only a matter of time. Whatever murderous little system existed here is done fer. Now it's just murder and death for whoever ain't lucky enough to be packin'."

Isra sighed. For the first time, a flash of remorse crossed her face. "Those guns were never meant to be removed from their containers. There were only there in case of emergency."

Viekko leaned against the rail. "Well, guess what, Isra? They're out now. What's worse is Sergeant Carr is leading the men that got 'em."

"Carr? That is...unfortunate."

Althea couldn't believe what she was hearing. "Unfortunate? Is that all this is to you,'unfortunate'?"

In a rare display of emotion, Isra started pacing the catwalk. "You are right. That was a poor choice of words. This is what we must do. We know where they are and who they are. We should talk to the Houston and have him assemble a larger army. Every person he can get. We force Carr and Laban out of the area by sheer force of numbers..."

Viekko stood still with his mouth open. Althea couldn't quite wrap her mind around it either. Isra was always irritatingly methodical and logical, but this? This was madness bordering on delusion.

Viekko took off his hat and rubbed his head. "Isra, would you listen to what you're saying? I lost three men in a matter of minutes. Now you wanna grab everyone in the city and march them in front of machine guns? What's the matter, does Laban not work fast enough for your liking?"

Althea stepped forward. "He's right, Isra. We can't in good conscious keep leading people to their death."

Isra closed her eyes. "They are dead anyway. If Carr has those guns, then it is only a matter of time. The only thing we can do, the only chance we have—that these people have —is to try and recover those guns."

Viekko replaced his hat. "Listen to me carefully. There ain't no fixin' it. It's over. Laban's got the people, the guns, and a fortified position. A coordinated military operation would be hard pressed to force them out, never mind a bunch of people waving sticks! I'm sorry, Isra, but it's time to negotiate."

Isra closed her eyes. "There will be no negotiation. We

have nothing to negotiate with. The only thing we could offer would be our complete and unconditional withdrawal.

Viekko spun around and headed for the main entrance. "Let's do that then! Seems we've done enough damage. What we don't kill, Laban can finish."

Althea went after him. "Viekko, where are you going?"

Viekko didn't even pause or slow down. "Going for a walk, Althea. Need to get my mind right."

Being outside the pyramid and away from Isra didn't help near enough in Viekko's estimation. He tore down the street kicking the odd bit of trash and scaring onlooking children. There was static in his ear followed by Althea's voice for a split second before he switched it off.

An ear-piercing trumpet call reverberated through the city. It was the same he heard earlier while he was watching the mammoths, only now it was so near that it made his teeth vibrate. For reasons he didn't completely understand, he started walking in the direction of the noise. Maybe it was just his body running on autopilot while his mind worked or maybe it was to satisfy some curiosity about the city. He didn't know nor did he give it much consideration.

He found himself near the city gates. The space around them was an open, grassy courtyard. Perhaps the only spot like it in the city except for the space around the pyramid. But while that space looked immaculately kept, this lawn was overgrown and neglected. As if it were kept up just enough so they would have space for what came next.

The gate opened and five huge mammoths charged through and formed a circle in the courtyard, corralled by twenty or so *Urbanoi* people. Through a series of yelled commands and complicated movements, the wranglers managed to cut two mammoths from the herd and drive them into two huge metal cages. Then came several men carrying sharpened spears each twice as long as a single person.

Viekko's eyes narrowed as he watched the slaughter. It

was simple, quick, and brutally efficient, and it all happened under the disinterested eyes of the rest of the herd. There was something irritatingly poignant about the scene. Each animal had enough power contained within it to bust out. It could trample its captors, ram through the city walls and be free, but it didn't. There was a routine and, even if they knew or cared how it ended, they followed through with almost mechanical precision.

The city would end the same way. Even the Houston had to see that, but he couldn't bring himself to change it. Same with Isra. They were all going to follow the same script and dance the same routine right until the end.

And it's the same with me, Viekko thought as his hand groped inside his pocket feeling for the little glass capsules of triple-T that weren't there. All of them, every single person on this moon and probably in the Universe, all stuck in cycles that will ultimately destroy them. And all because they lacked the will or the courage to make the change.

A group of four city soldiers ran by at a full sprint and several more followed. The citizens, still corralling the mammoths or butchering the meat, dropped what they were doing and ran toward the city gate. They climbed up narrow stairways that led to the top of the wall where they could see over.

In a few short minutes, the area around the gates was crowded with people running in every conceivable direction. Soldiers arrived carrying huge logs on their shoulders. The city gate rode on wheels that moved on metal rails like a train track. Soldiers jammed the logs in between the wheels and braced them with even more logs. Soon it would have taken a jet engine to move that door.

Viekko had the urge to grab one of the soldiers and ask what was going on. That was stupid, of course; even if they understood him, he wouldn't understand the answer.

More soldiers ran up a long, narrow stairway that ran along the wall all the way to the top. There they gathered in a line along the edge, pointing and talking among themselves with obvious excitement and fear.

148

Viekko charged up the stairs as fast as he could. He jostled other soldiers in the process who yelled something as he passed. He got to the top and looked out over the city walls.

There was an army massing, there was no mistaking it. Judging from their animal skin clothing, long hair and lanky build, it was the forest people. There were hundreds and they looked eager to take their revenge.

That, in and of itself, didn't bother Viekko. There was no way Isra could have brought enough guns to arm every single one of them and, even if she did, the city wall would provide ample protection.

What worried him was what an object he watched the Corporation marines pushing through the forest just beyond the open grassland. It was a machine with two long, square metal bars that jutted out from a rough dome-shaped structure. This, in turn, was mounted to a platform carried by three wheels, two large in front and a smaller one in back. All in all, it didn't look unlike the ancient cannons humans used when they first invented gunpowder.

It was a compact version of an artillery railgun. The two square beams charged with electricity would accelerate a projectile to a velocity approaching light speed. The result was a weapon that could do incalculable damage.

Well, that was the idea. The railgun Viekko could see in the breaks in the foliage could only get a tiny projectile up to a fraction of that. On Earth, small versions like these would be a joke. It would be like showing up to a gunfight with an air rifle. But on Titan, there was no weapon that could compare. Besides, it didn't need much power. All it had to do was blast through a wall. Even this small version could do that easily.

Another glint in the forest caught his eye and he saw another railgun being wheeled through the trees toward the city. Then another and another. Four in total. Laban wasn't going to be satisfied with tearing down the wall. He intended to level the whole city.

Viekko activated his EROS computer. "Isra, are you

there?"

There was a crackle of radio static and Isra's annoyed voice was in his ear, "Viekko? Where are you?"

"I'm sittin' on the city wall. We've got a whole lotta badness rolling in on us."

"It is no better here. The Houston has lost his mind. Make your way to my position. Follow my beacon and be careful."

Viekko sprinted back down the stairs. When he got to the bottom, he turned and headed toward Isra's blip on the satellite radar. It looked like Isra was going to have her war. Whether she wanted it or not, or whether there was any means of fighting it or not, she was going to have it.

CHAPTER FOURTEEN

Could the Corporation have prevented the war? It is a question that has been asked by students and scholars for a thousand years. It certainly had the power. What it lacked was political wisdom.

The initial attack on Corporation outposts drove its leaders to cry for revenge. Nothing short of complete victory would be acceptable. The Corporation could not have prevented the war because it did everything in its power to start it.

-from The Fall: The Decline and Failure of 21st Century Civilization *by Martin Raffe.*

The people of the city assembled at a particular spot just a few blocks from the courtyard with the gleaming pyramid. Isra and Althea followed the people to a metal platform beneath a huge black screen. There were monitors all over this city, but this was grander than anything they had yet come across. It was mounted on the brick wall of a building that towered over a grassy triangular space in between where two roads came together.

That space was already filling up when Isra and Althea arrived. People crowded shoulder to shoulder in front of the platform just a few meters from the base of the giant screen. Isra and Althea elbowed their way through the crowd already watching the platform with unshakable attention.

There were few soldiers around, a small division assembled on the outskirts to keep the crowd civil, Isra reasoned. But everyone was armed. Men and women idly stroked clubs as they watched the stage. A few swung bolo snares where they had space to do so.

Isra and Althea found a spot near the stage and stopped. Althea glanced around with a measure of discretion and leaned close. "You don't think these people mean to fight do you?"

"I think that is the most likely scenario," said Isra. "Although their choice of weapons is interesting."

"It's the same with the soldiers," Althea added. "Guess we should be thankful that they don't carry anything lethal."

Isra stopped in front of the stage and risked one more glance around. "Yes. If I were outside the gates ready to sack this place, I would be thankful."

Then Isra saw some disturbance in the crowd, like some kind of animal charging through. A big, dumb, angry animal in a white hat, to be specific.

Viekko pushed and shoved his way through the throng, eliciting several complaints and shouts from the people he dislocated in the process. A few gave him some dirty looks, but none showed any urge to stop him or confront him in any way. Of course, most of the population was shouting at the space just above his navel.

"It looks to be getting a touch out of hand here," said Viekko, sauntering up.

"It is," said Isra. "What is causing it?"

Viekko tilted back his hat. "Laban's went and got himself an army. Along with a few toys from Earth."

Isra's eyes narrowed while she waited for him to explain what he meant.

"They have mini-railguns. Nothin' big, but enough," said Viekko, responding to her glare.

There was an appreciative roar from the crowd and Isra turned back to the stage. The Houston strode up one set of stairs just to the right with a number of other officiants in bright garments and jewelry. He raised his hands to quiet the crowd and began a speech in the native language. *"My fellow Urbanoi, servants of the Kompanio and rightful rulers of Titan!"*

The crowd erupted in approval and the Houston waited for it to die down, then continued, *"Long we have existed in peace, preserved from the enemies of the Kompanio by our faith and our diligence to duty. But the Kompanio warned of a time when the rivals would come back and claim Titan for their own. The Kompanio tells us that it is our duty now to stand and fight against their enemies."*

Viekko tilted his hat back. "The hell is he goin' on about? I hear the word 'Kompanio' a lot. Don't suppose these 'Kompanio' fellas are tellin' them to do the smart thing when it comes to those railguns?"

"No," Isra said in emotionless monotone, "The *Kompanio* are like gods to them. Gods rarely if ever tell people to do the smart thing. Especially when it comes to war." Isra activated the radio on her EROS computer. "Cronus, are you there?"

"Standing by," he said through her earpiece.

"Cronus, can you activate the screens in the city?"

"It is possible. Why?"

"I need to convince these people to listen to me. Having some technological backup might help."

"I will try."

"You will not be alone," the Houston continued, *"Look! Look to the East. The sun will disappear behind Saturn at any moment. The Venganto slumber, but soon they will arise to purge this world of the outsiders. Keep faith in the Kompanio. Keep duty in your hearts and we will all be rewarded-"*

A jubilant roar from the crowd cut off the Houston's words. In some pockets, the roar was punctuated by the rhythmic slap of clubs against palms, in others with chants that Isra couldn't quite pick out among the din.

"The crowd is getting a tad unruly, don't you think?" said Viekko.

Isra activated her radio again. "Cronus? Any progress?"

"Some," replied Cronus with the staccato tap of a keyboard in the background, "It doesn't appear I can access them directly. They are connected to an external relay-"

"Cronus, I do not have time for the specifics. Can you do it now?"

"Not without some modifications to the City's power grid."

The crowd calmed enough so that the Houston could get a few more words in. *"Go to the city gates and wait for the Venganto. They will lead you to victory!"*

So there was nothing left to try except something brash. There was only one chance and that was to appeal to the sanity of the people, if there was any left. She charged forward shoving her way to the metal platform. Somewhere behind her Althea yelled, "Isra, what are you doing?"

Isra shouted back, "I am going to try to stop this!"

If that was even possible. There was enough momentum in this crowd to stop a starship.

Isra charged out of the crowd and bolted up the steps to where the Houston stood. He was more surprised to see her than anything. There was, perhaps, a tiny twitch of suspicion in his eye and a slight upturn of the mouth to suggest bemusement. She turned to the crowd, half of which were already starting to disperse for the gates, the other half watched her with the same mix of surprise.

Isra took a deep breath and spoke as loud as she could in the Titianian language, *"Listen, you cannot fight them."*

There was a pause and then calls from the crowd. Isra could only pick out fragments from the people shouting back at her:

"It is our duty."

"The Kompanio will protect us."

"We must purge the outsiders."

Isra tried to speak above the crowd. *"Please, please listen. I know the people that gather outside the gates. They have brought weapons. Weapons that you cannot fight against. Weapons that will easily destroy this city."*

The response from the crowd got louder and angrier. The Houston raised his hand in the air calling for the people to settle down. Once they had, he smiled at Isra. *"Please, forgive our dear guest. She has yet to experience the power of the Venganto."*

"I have seen it!" Isra snapped. *"I saw what they did to unarmed people outside the city. This is different. These people carry weapons like nothing you have ever seen."*

The Houston took a step forward so that he stood inches from the edge of the stage. *"The Venganto are invincible. They are the wrath of the Kompanio!"*

"They are people!" countered Isra, partially addressing the Houston and part the crowd. *"Just like you and me. They can bleed. They can be killed and they will fall. Just like—"*

Several soldiers marched up the stairs on either side of the stage and surrounded her. They closed in, took her by the arm and shoulders and led her toward the stairs. They were not forceful or aggressive in this, but something in the way they moved told Isra that they were prepared to carry her off the stage if she resisted.

She struggled, but the soldiers held her firm and kept walking her away. Behind her, The Houston smiled.

"Let me help you!" Isra cried in English, "I can negotiate a truce. I can save your city."

The Houston didn't pay the slightest attention. He turned back to the crowd and raised his arms. The frenzy of the crowd reached a crescendo and he spoke again in the people's language, *"Go now! Meet the enemies of the Kompanio on the field of battle! Rejoice as the Venganto strike our enemies! Honor the Kompanio with the spoils of battle!"*

With those words, he pivoted and marched off the stage with the cadre of dignitaries following close behind. The crowd started to disperse. The speech had accomplished what it was meant to, the air practically buzzed with the elation of the crowd as they marched to their deaths.

Isra stepped off the stage and away from the soldiers.

Althea and Viekko pushed their way to where she stood.

"Didn't go as well as expected, huh?" asked Viekko.

Isra brushed her hair back. "I would say it went exactly as well as I expected. One does not rise to the top of the Ministry by being an optimist. You mentioned some artillery being wheeled out, Viekko?"

He nodded. "Yes, ma'am. Four mini railguns. Course' mini is a relative term. One of them could level a city like this given enough time."

"And what are the chances of stopping them before that?"

Viekko glanced in the direction of the wall. "Assuming I can get behind 'em, pretty good."

Isra nodded. "Do that then. Althea, go with him to the city gates. There will be wounded coming in by the hundreds. I want you to see what you can do for these people."

Althea stammered, "I'll do what I can."

"Good," said Isra. "I am going to keep an eye on the Houston. On the off-chance we can stop this war, I need to know what he plans to do."

CHAPTER FIFTEEN

The initial attacks against the Corporation were little more than terrorist actions; guerrilla warfare perpetrated by a handful of radicals in order to lure the mercenary stormtroopers into an unwinnable war.

All great civilizations fear being seen as weak in the eyes of their enemy. Hundreds of great empires throughout human history have ripped themselves apart just to avoid being seen as weak.

-from The Fall: The Decline and Failure of 21st Century Civilization *by Martin Raffe.*

Viekko stood atop the wall again, looking out over the grassy plains. In the sky over the trees, the sun crept behind the rings of Saturn. The refracting light caused a kind of surreal shimmering effect across the field below. A whole army gathered there now, at least a thousand marines and *Perfiduloi* warriors by Viekko's estimation, standing in formation in the open field. The *Perfiduloi* units were easy to pick out. Their rough, brown clothing and loose formations stood in stark contrast to the tight lines of marines in the Corporation blues that surrounded the railguns. The *Perfiduloi* warriors made up the front lines and were organized in groups of a hundred or more. They lined up in several formations twenty wide and three or four deep. Viekko saw the glint of metal from the peasant guns in the formation that stood front and center. The rest had spears and bow and arrows, the same types of weapons Viekko saw on the dead outside the spaceport.

Looking at the way the army amassed outside the gates filled Viekko with a kind of sadness. Whatever they had done to the people of the city over the years, whatever needless slaughter occurred over the centuries between these two people, nobody deserved this. The marines were using these people as sacrificial animals. To them they were just hunks of raw meat to be thrown into the grinder of war so that a handful of people sitting in gleaming towers of metal and glass could reap the rewards. He was quickly taken with the urge to protect the *Perfiduloi* armies along with the City.

But with what army, exactly? He glanced back on the city side of the wall. The Houston's people gathered behind the gates. Not just soldiers, but ordinary citizens arrived in droves to wait anxiously. Viekko had seen them on his way to the wall. The deadliest thing any of them carried were short blades and clubs. Most carried bola snares and nets. This wasn't even bringing a knife to a gunfight; this was showing up at the gunfight with a sack and hoping somebody falls into it.

Viekko was on his own out there and that meant he needed to focus on the biggest threat and work down. The relatively small platoon armed with the Peasant Gun wasn't the problem right now. With the right show of force, the untrained warriors would likely panic and flee. The railguns were another issue. He could clearly see four of them now, just a few hundred meters from the trees. They were well behind the lines of native soldiers and guarded by tight groups of Corporation marines. They wouldn't expect the battle to break past the front lines which, to Viekko's mind, made them vulnerable.

Viekko became aware that someone was climbing the stairs to the top of the city walls. He turned around to see Althea approach with a downcast, solemn expression as if she were walking up to view his corpse at his funeral. She gave Viekko a soft little smile that made his heart beat just a little faster. "You come up with a plan, then?"

Viekko turned back to the armies gathered out front. "Yep, charge out, single-handedly route the army, save the day and be back in time for pie. There will be pie, right?"

Althea approached the parapet. Her brow furrowed when she saw the army massed outside. "They are just lined up out in the open?"

Viekko adjusted his hat. "Carr must be in charge. Laban strikes me as the type that would wait and shoot an unarmed man in the back. But Sergeant Carr? If he's got strength in numbers, he damn well wants to show it."

Some commotion within the *Perfiduloi* army caught Viekko's eye. A few runners sprinted from formation to formation and, wherever they went, the ranks of warriors tightened. From this vantage, it was like watching the muscles of a predator tense as it readied itself to pounce.

Viekko knew that his body should be flooding with adrenalin, his muscles should be tensing, and he should be basking in the rush of fear and anticipation. Instead, he felt nothing.

"Althea, you should go," said Viekko, surprised at the monotone in his own voice. "But before you do, I need to ask you a favor."

"Sure," said Althea in a low, comforting tone.

"I need another shard of triple-T"

Althea rolled her eyes. "Really? Is that all you can think about right now? More drugs?"

"Triple-T makes me sharp. It makes me fast; how I move, how I react and how I think. Everything happens at a lightnin' pace. When I'm on the 'T, it's like the rest of the world waits for me. I ain't going to survive down there without it."

Althea grabbed Viekko by his broad shoulders and turned him around so she could look into his eyes. "You will be fine, you hear me? This is the first step. Once you realize that you don't need that horrible stuff anymore, you can start getting better."

Viekko started to protest, but he heard a distinct sound in the distance. Those rail guns took a few minutes to heat up and build enough charge to fire. During that time, the gun made a high-pitched whine that was almost beyond the range of human perception. The attack was going to happen at any moment.

Viekko grabbed Althea by the arms and started to lead her to the stairs. "It's too late. Get down now. Run back to the pyramid. If this goes bad, you will need to get Isra and Cronus somewhere safe and get them out of this city. Go now!"

Althea looked like she wanted to argue, but she glanced at the army outside the gates and did as she was told. Viekko watched her descend the steps out of sight.

Viekko stretched his arms. He could feel the EROS suit underneath his clothing pulling on his muscles with every movement. It was a device made to make it feel like he was still on Earth, but it had its limits.

Viekko backed up on the platform as far as he could. Hopefully, Althea was right about him and the triple-T. He took a running leap off the edge of the wall.

He sailed through the air in a wide arc. That was the first limitation of the EROS suit. It could compensate for Titan's lack of gravity, but it couldn't change it. On this planet he could still move like a superhuman.

He landed and rolled on the soft ground. He didn't pause, but ended back on his feet and started sprinting as hard as he could. The suit tore at his muscles trying to resist them. It felt like sandpaper being run underneath his skin, but he pressed forward as hard as he physically could.

That was the second limitation of the EROS suit. It could keep a person born on Earth in check on Titan, but Viekko wasn't born on Earth. He had grown up on a planet that had a fraction of the atmosphere that Earth had, and Titan had twice the oxygen of Earth. His muscles worked harder and more efficient than they ever had in his life. The suit could compensate for your average sedentary engineer, but not for a Martian warrior.

He saw a rock poking up among the grass and ran towards it. He sprinted to the top, pushed off and caught incredible altitude. He realized, at the height of his arc, that he had miscalculated his jump. He had hoped to get high and far enough to clear a group of *Perfiduloi* warriors. He could land, roll, sprint and jump again. The third jump would get him close to the first rail gun. Instead, he realized he was about to land right in the middle of those warriors.

He fell into the middle of the group, knocking over a few warriors as he rolled. He used the momentum to get to his feet and found himself face to face with a visibly surprised *Perfiduloi* man. For just a split second, the two men looked into each other's faces. The warrior had a scraggly beard and long, unkempt hair. If Viekko imagined what humans looked like before cities, agriculture and civilization domesticated them, this is what he would have pictured.

Before either could act, a deafening boom drew both men's attention. Viekko glanced back at the city to see a projectile from one of the rail guns rip through the high, grey city walls like a bullet through tissue paper. In an instant, a whole section of wall disintegrated into a spray of dust and rock. Behind that, a crumbling building shuddered and collapsed. Viekko could only imagine the chaos behind the walls now. Those weapons really could level the entire city in a matter of minutes.

He turned and slugged the *Perfiduloi* man in the face. The native warrior fell to the ground and Viekko started to run for the rail guns. A couple of warriors tried to stop him, but Viekko moved with a quick graceful ease that didn't even break his momentum. He hit the first man with a right jab in the sternum. He stepped forward with his left foot, rotated his body and threw his right elbow into the next man's throat. A third made a motion towards him and Viekko simply lowered his shoulder and ran at full speed. Viekko easily plowed through the warrior who rolled off into the grass. It was only a few seconds since the rail gun fired and Viekko was sprinting in open ground.

161

He reached a rounded rock and used it as another launch point. This jump was much more accurate and would bring him just a few meters away from ten marines clustered around the artillery weapon. At the height of his jump, he drew his guns. The marines were so focused on the weapon and the walls ahead of them that they didn't see Viekko flying in the air toward their position. He only had a few moments before they did.

Viekko started firing. The first few shots were well-aimed and hit at least four of the marines, two of them fatally. After that, Viekko just started emptying the clips. These shots were not intended to injure as much as they were to cause confusion and fear and to keep the marines off balance until Viekko landed. Still, he managed to wound a couple in the process.

His guns clicked empty just moments before he landed. He rolled and holstered them. He saw a marine running in a blind panic a few meters ahead. At the same time, the soldier saw Viekko and raised his assault weapon to fire. Viekko was on him before he managed to get a shot off. He grabbed the barrel of the gun and landed a right jab on the man's throat with enough force to collapse his windpipe. The marine staggered backward and released his grip on the gun. Viekko followed up by clubbing the man across the head with the butt of the rifle.

Viekko shouldered the weapon and moved forward. The marines around the rail gun were just starting to recover from the attack and swarmed around with their own rifles raised. Viekko saw them first and had time to aim and fire his weapon. Three bursts of automatic fire took down one, two, and then a third marine.

Viekko crouched in the grass and watched the rail gun. The immediate area was clear, although he did see a few marines retreating into the distance. Corporation military was famously easy to break. They looked tough but, when bullets started flying and blood was shed, they ran. The Corporation paid them enough to walk around with a big-ass gun looking tough; it didn't pay enough for people to put their lives on the line.

Still, there was the occasional misplaced hero. When Viekko approached the back of the rail gun, he found a young man cowering behind it. Viekko figured he had pinned him down and the soldier was still there out of fear. When Viekko got close, however, the man pulled his field knife and lunged at him. The blade clanged against the barrel of the gun and Viekko jumped back. The man pressed his advantage and slashed for Viekko's chest. The Martian used his assault rifle to block the attack, but the force caused him to lose his grip on it. The man went to slash again but, this time, Viekko was ready. Before the soldier could lunge, Viekko grabbed his wrist and broke the man's arm above the elbow with his other hand.

The marine yelled in pain and Viekko snatched the knife away and plunged it through the man's rib cage. The soldier looked shocked, then his eyes rolled back into his head and he fell.

There was nobody around the rail gun anymore but it was hot and ready to fire. All it needed was a target. Viekko pulled the gun around, pointed it at the next railgun over and fired. The sonic boom was louder than a shuttle launch. The artillery kicked so hard that it pushed Viekko to the ground and knocked the wind out of him.

The shot was a direct hit. Viekko got up and smiled as the second rail gun disappeared in a plume of dirt and debris. Pieces of the weapon rained down around the field along with some pieces of the soldiers around it.

There was no time to celebrate his victory. He got this far by element of surprise alone. That had just been blown apart as spectacularly as the rail gun. He picked up the assault rifle and emptied the rest of the bullets into the electrical components. They exploded in a shower of white-hot sparks. It was unlikely that this gun could be repaired with the limited resources available on Titan. That was enough. Two guns down, two left.

He grabbed some clips from one of the dead soldiers, reloaded the rifle, and stuck a couple more in his jacket pocket. It was safer to move through the forest now. There was a lot more cover plus the chance to sneak up on someone. He sprinted for safety and heard bullets thunk against tree trunks. From there, he moved toward the next objective. Most of the marines were focused on the events in front of them.

There were two holes in the city wall now. Somehow, in the haze of battle, they managed to get a shot off without him noticing. Already, the front formations of *Perfiduloi* advanced into the breaks. Screams and gunfire were becoming apparent even where he was standing.

Viekko moved as quickly as he could through the dense foliage using the cover to his advantage. He killed marines looking for him and, when he could, he also picked off those too distracted by the events near the city wall.

He paused just behind the third rail gun to collect himself and reload. The forest around him grew darker as the sun started to disappear behind the ringed planet. Just a few minutes left of daylight before the eclipse plunged the battlefield into darkness. And only a few minutes before they'd find out if the Houston's predictions carried anything but hot air.

He paused for a moment. He still didn't feel the rush of pure adrenaline that he usually associated with battle. There was something cold and distant about the way he fought. There was no thrill, no sense of honor and glory. Just the cold, bloody reality of systematic murder. Still, it seemed to be effective. Maybe Althea was right. Maybe he didn't need the drugs to fight; he just needed them to enjoy the bloodshed.

He emerged from the forest firing full automatic at the marines clustered around the third rail gun. Most were oblivious to him and fell down dead under the rain of bullets. Those who didn't ran from their post. By the time Viekko emptied this clip, this railgun was abandoned as well.

Viekko examined the weapon. This one was recently fired and just beginning to charge again. He saw some movement out of the corner of his eye. He turned to see the last rail gun pointing in his direction. The distant, piercing screech told him that it was fully charged. He swore and bolted for the trees again but it was too late. There was a roar like Hell itself erupting from the ground. Then, for a few moments, there was nothing.

They were standing there.   Why were they just standing there? The whole city held their ground in front of the gates that were still closed. Even when the shells from the railguns burst through the towering walls like a bullet through a watermelon. Even as the buildings around them collapsed and showered the crowd with chunks of concrete and steel. Even as the first of the *Perfinduloi* warriors ascended the rubble and began firing into the crowd, they just stood.

Althea rushed into the crowd gripped with a need to save just a few. Maybe even one. Gunfire echoed between the buildings as she pushed her way through the waiting crowd.

It wasn't long before she came upon a man lying on the ground. His face was streaked with blood where something, maybe a chunk of debris or a bullet, had hit him.

She knelt beside him, "Can you stand?"

More gun shots. Althea looked up and saw five *Perfinduloi* warriors standing on the top of the rubble that used to be part of the wall. They fired shots into the crowd while they threw rocks, bolo snares and anything they could at them. One gunman, hit in the head with a rock, fell back, but the rest kept firing.

She took the man by the arm, "I'm going to get you out of here."

The man pulled his arm out of her grasp.   "*No! Mi Atendas!*"

Althea tried again but the man pulled away and said, with a certain finality, "*Mi Atendas!*"

Althea stood and backed away. Everyone around her just stood watching the sky. Over the wall, a sliver of the sun still showed from behind Saturn.

Viekko woke up looking at the orange clouds of Titan. The disk of the sun was almost completely hidden behind Saturn. Gunshots rang in the air all around him. The events of the last few seconds flashed in his brain. He had been knocked out but, thankfully, only for a matter of seconds.

He rolled onto his stomach and felt an agonizing, fiery pain in his side. He lifted his body just enough to see a blood stain spreading in his clothes and dripping into the grass. He must have been hit by a piece of shrapnel. He wiggled his toes and realized, with some relief, that they were still there. He looked for the assault rifle but couldn't find it.

His attention focused to the gunfire around him. Bullets whizzed in all directions, but no one fired directly at him. In the deep grass, Viekko was invisible and presumed dead. Where the third rail gun had been a moment ago, there was a deep, smoldering crater. It was better cover than he had now. He started crawling on his stomach towards it. Every movement felt like he was tearing the wound in his side deeper.

He reached the crater and tumbled in. He slid in the wet, muddy ground about halfway into the hole. He flipped onto his back and unholstered one of his handguns and replaced the spent clip. As it snapped into place, a couple of marines appeared over the lip of the crater. Viekko calmly aimed his gun and fired. He hit both in the head and they were dead before their bodies slid to the muddy bottom.

Viekko maneuvered his way to the other side of the hole so he could peek over at the fourth rail gun and its crew. As soon as his head appeared over the top, several marines fired. He quickly ducked back into the hole, but he continued to hear gunfire from the direction of the rail gun.

He pulled up his sleeve to look at the display on his EROS suit. By some miracle, it was not damaged.

He raised his wrist to his mouth and said, "Call Althea."

He waited a moment and then heard Althea's voice in his ear. "Viekko! Are you okay?"

Viekko gulped. "I'm hurt. I'm hurt bad. They got me

pinned down and I don't think I'm getting out of here."

He heard the whine of the rail gun charging.

Before Althea could respond, he continued. "You and Isra gotta find a way to disable that last gun. If you can't, evacuate the area. Go back to the base camp."

"Where are you?" said Althea.

Viekko winced. "Just do as I say! Forget about me, you gotta take care of yourself."

The fading light dimmed to black as the last sliver of sun disappeared behind Saturn. The rings brilliantly lit the sky while the gas giant itself appeared as black as a sphere of flint.

Another pause and Althea said, "Viekko...there's something...happening."

Something was happening. Cronus scanned the matrices as, row by row, the numbers changed and then whole programs shut down. Cronus closed out that part of the program and tried to access new parts of the system, but as fast as he could pull new data up from the servers below, they froze and stopped transmitting.

Was there something physically wrong with the server farms? Cronus got up and walked over to the edge of the catwalk. He had gotten used to the soft steps of the acolytes below along with the small sounds of their work. But now it was completely silent. The acolytes, who seemed a constant fixture wandering the space in between the servers, were absent.

Cronus sat back down. It was strange. The maintenance of this computer system was, as near as he could figure, the entire purpose of those people's existence. They were priests tending to the God of the Machine. If something was wrong, why would they leave? The simple answer was that nothing was wrong.

Cronus gripped the edge of the chair as the entire building started vibrating.

Viekko peaked over the lip of the crater again. The battle just stopped. Dead. As if somebody had gone out there and called a timeout on account of the darkness. The marines nearest him pointed at the city, specifically the golden pyramid that glowed even in the darkness. Four panels that formed the cap spread apart and slid down the side of the pyramid and several dark figures jumped up from the now exposed top. They shot into the clouds one or two at a time just seconds apart.

He knew immediately what he was seeing, although he was not sure he could or wanted to believe it. It was the *Venganto*, the avenging angels that the Houston talked about in his speech. Viekko figured it to be a myth or a story. Something to tell the kiddies while tucking them into bed. 'Don't be afraid, little one, the *Venganto* watch over us.' That sort of thing.

The forest people attacking the city seemed to know it too. As fast as they charged the holes, they turned and ran back toward Viekko, back toward the safety of the forest. As they did, he saw the dark figures in the skies overhead moving so fast that he could only make out flashes of movement against the clouds. They started diving towards the fleeing soldiers and everywhere they did flashes of light and fountains of flame erupted.

Viekko started to crawl out of the hole still holding the spot in his guts where the piece of shrapnel hit him. He got up and started stumbling forward toward the city, keeping a low profile so one of those things in the sky didn't mark him as a hostile.

The *Perfiduloi* were running past him in desperation. He shielded his eyes from two bursts of flame and ignored the agonized screams from the poor bastards caught in the blast. It was brutal, but it was war. Nobody should ever feel bad about going home after a war, no matter what happened to those who didn't. That's what he told himself as he staggered forward thinking fond thoughts about a soft bed, Althea's face, and some drugs that would make reality feel a whole lot better.

One of the forest people ran at him but stumbled and fell hard in the mud. Viekko was going to walk right on by until he noticed a bolo snare around the man's legs. He got out of the way just as three *Urbanoi* people—not soldiers, just citizens by the look of them—pulled the man to his feet. One took a club and gave the *Perfiduloi* man a blow to the gut that Viekko could almost feel where he stood.

He turned his head away and kept staggering forward. He tried to focus his mind on rest for his sore muscles, medication for his wound, and maybe a touch of triple-T for his mind.

Nearby, he watched one of the forest people take a blow to the head so hard he swore he could hear the crack of bone splintering. The man had his hands tied behind him and he crumbled to the ground like someone just let the air out of him. An *Urbanoi* soldier grabbed the man by the arm and started dragging him back to the city.

Viekko pushed himself forward, toward the gates. Isra could fix this. That was her job. His job was to kill things. That was what he was good at. Isra's job was to get people to link arms and sing happy songs. And if everywhere he looked on this bloody field, he saw a people who had fought a brave and noble battle beaten down and put in a slaver's chains...well, that was just the way things were going to be. A jolt in his side reminded him that he was in no state to do anything about it anyway.

A young *Perfiduloi* man, just barely old enough to grow the scraggly beginnings of a beard, came running up at him, chased by a small pack of *Urbanoi* citizens. He was wild-eyed with fear and he seemed to call out to Viekko.

He wanted to say to the kid, 'Sorry. This is war. I can't help you.'

The citizens caught up to him. One threw his arm around the boy's neck while another hit in the sternum with his club. Even through the wails and din of battle, Viekko heard the boy scream.

Viekko limped forward thinking, *Ain't no good gonna come from me gettin' in the middle of this. I'll find a way to help you and yours later.*

The boy fell down in the mud. The citizens went to pick him up.

Sorry kid. I want to help but-

The citizens pulled the kid to his feet and he locked eyes with Viekko for one heartbreaking moment. Viekko's mind flashed back to the refinery. The blood-stained concrete, the bursts of scalding steam and emaciated forest people running for freedom.

Viekko realized why the term 'rescued' had such an unsettling tone.   He also realized what the future had in store for this kid if Viekko didn't do anything.

Damn it...fine.

Viekko pulled one of his guns from his shoulder holster. If the citizens even knew Viekko was standing where he was, they didn't show it. The just started dragging the *Perfiduloi* youth away when Viekko fired off a shot. Then another, then another.

Three city people slumped to the ground dead and a fourth gasped in horror and ran. Viekko took the kid by the arm and bolted for the tree line. The pain in his side was so intense that it made him dizzy and every bone and muscle screamed in protest as they worked against the EROS suit, but Viekko kept running.

It was an old cliché. There's no way he could stop the *Urbanoi* taking who they liked and throwing them in that hell of a refinery to die. But if he could save one, just one... well, maybe he'd quiet the guilt twisting in his gut enough to get himself fixed up.

Out past the immediate vicinity of the walls, the *Venganto* mopped up the few pockets of resistance that remained in the field, mostly clusters of *Perfiduloi* who hadn't made it to the safety of the forest yet. The dark field was lit up by bursts of flame as Viekko dragged the kid to safety.

Under the forest canopy felt like a different world. The darkness and quiet were all-enveloping. The thunderous roar of the *Venganto* attacks, the screams and war cries

170

seemed a long way off. Viekko stopped to catch his breath and looked at the kid.

Even though he couldn't understand a word, Viekko said, "You're safe. Now get goin'."

The boy got real scared all of a sudden. He backed away and shouted something at Viekko.

"Damn it boy! Keep quiet. Keep low and—"

Something crashed down on Viekko's head and rattled his brain inside his skull like a bell clapper. The next thing he was aware of, he was face down in the thick Titanian mud. Someone was sitting on his legs pulling his arms behind him and tying them with some sort of rope.

There was arguing in the native language. He couldn't make it out, but the tempo and volume of the back-and-forth discussion held all the marks of a heated debate.

Two more people, older forest men it turned out, pulled Viekko to his knees and started to lift him to his feet. One *Perfiduloi* with a spear prodded Viekko's chest with the butt and hit one of his guns in a shoulder holster. "*Viaj armiloj! Guto!*"

Two other men reached inside Viekko's jacket and relieved him of his weapons. After that, they all continued to pat him down while the kid he saved just looked at him on the verge of tears.

So, that was the way it was going to be. Viekko was a prisoner. He contemplated making a run for it; getting a good sprint, and a long jump. Chances were he could do it fast enough that they wouldn't follow. Then the throbbing pain and lightheadedness came back to him. He was badly injured and was losing blood.

When they were finished, the one with the spear prodded Viekko in the back of the leg with the point. Viekko started walking into the darkness of the forest, escorted by the men as their prisoner.

CHAPTER SIXTEEN

*Every Corporation assault that destroyed a village persuaded
hundreds to join the revolution. Every airstrike that leveled a training
area was better than a hundred recruiting events. Pictures of rebel
soldiers and their families executed and thrown into mass graves was
the greatest propaganda available.*

*The Corporation's early campaigns were famously successful and
every victory brought them closer to their own demise.*

-from The Fall: The Decline and Failure of 21st Century Civilization *by
Martin Raffe.*

The sun appeared once again from behind Saturn. Isra
watched with wonder as the *Venganto* darted across the sky
and disappeared into tip of the pyramid like bats fleeing the
daylight.

Inside the City, victory was more brutal than defeat. The
ecstasy of triumph ripped off the mask off the city and
exposed the true face of the *Urbanoi*. By disabling the
railguns, Viekko kept the city from being torn apart, and
now Isra watched people stream out of the broken walls and
swarm over their fallen opponent like wild dogs.

She walked in step with the Houston. He wore a beatific
grin complete with a serenity to his movements as he

watched the skies. "It is as I described," said the Houston startling her, "The enemies of the *Kompanio* are driven away. *Urbano Ligeia* is safe again."

Isra watched the first of the city's warriors drag their prizes, bound in rope and shackles, inside the walls. The people cheered as they pushed and prodded the captured *Perfiduloi* to the grassy spot near the gates. A whole processing apparatus had been set up so fast that Isra didn't even notice it being put together. People hauled out cages as large as a house and filled them with prisoners. Even then, there was so little space that many *Perfiduloi* were tied to lamp posts, railings, and any other easily accessible fixture. In a sick way, there was something comical about the short, squat *Urbanoi* forcing the tall, slender *Perfiduloi* to kneel in a line. Isra thought the forest people's size alone would prevent them from being taken and held. But, there they were, kneeling while citizens hacked off their long hair and beards with finger-length blades. When they were done, the men's facial hair was cut to stubble on their chin and both sexes were left with a patch of short, rough hair on their heads.

From there, they were hosed down with cold water fed by hands pumps, given plain brown clothing, strapped together chain-gang-style at their ankles, and led away in teams of five to ten. The efficiency by which dozens of people were stripped of their humanity was both impressive and terrifying.

As they walked, Isra occasionally caught the eye of one of the *Urbanoi* herding prisoners to be processed or performing some dehumanizing task. There was nothing there except cold, mechanical resolve. As if every person in the city snuffed out their spark of human compassion long enough to complete the task.

When her eyes met those of the *Perfiduloi*, Isra felt her heart being wrenched out of her body. A man bloodied from so many beatings hauled to his feet to have his hands bound, a woman crying as her hair was cut down to her scalp, a whole group strapped together at the ankles and beaten as they were driven away; each left an indelible scar on Isra's soul when she looked at them. She closed her eyes and forced her feelings down. There would be a time to grieve for these people. There would be a time to raise her voice and, if necessary, arms in opposition to this brutal oppression. But one failed attempt would not discourage Laban and the Corporation. They would try again and it would require a united resistance to stop them. The Corporate chains were not as tangible but no less real and much harder to break.

The Houston observed the work as if the people being dragged into the city were nothing but livestock. "The *Kompanio* has surely blessed us. With these prisoners of war, we will be able to restore the refineries and bring order to the world." He glanced over at Isra and added, "You do not approve."

Isra sucked a bit of air through her teeth. She let the scene affect her and it showed. She'd have to watch herself. "The *Venganto* did drive away the outsiders, but it is only temporary. This attack was a fraction of their potential force and, next time, they will not hesitate to use it all. These people that you are subjugating, you will need to fight alongside them if you have any hope of surviving."

"They are enemies of the *Kompanio*. They have shown this by allying with its enemies, just as they did so long ago. This is why they are forced to live in the forest away from the blessed presence of the *Kompanio*. This is why they must purify their souls in the refineries.

Isra shook her head but her voice remained cool and impassive. "I am afraid you do not understand the threat these outsiders pose. It is unlike—"

The Houston cut her off. "I am aware of the danger. It is greater than even you know. I have felt an imbalance. Titan is suffering."

Isra looked away as several citizens threw a resisting *Perfiduloi* man to the ground and beat him with clubs. "I do not understand. What imbalance?"

The Houston sniffed the air, "Can you not sense it? There is a change. A sickness. What we do here may seem cruel, but the *Kompanio* demands it to restore balance. Without the *Kompanio*, Titan dies."

Isra had been avoiding the subject until now, but it couldn't be ignored anymore. It was on display, brazenly. Proudly, even. Isra looked up at the Houston. "Is that why you killed all those people outside the city gates? Did you burn those *Perfiduloi* to maintain balance?"

To her surprise, the Houston stiffened. "That was not me or my people. The *Perfiduloi* were in direct confrontation with the *Kompanio* and were judged by the *Venganto*. I wept for those souls, for they will never see Earth."

Isra found it strange that the Houston could watch people dragged into the city, beaten, stripped of their individuality and sent to be worked as slaves without a single shred of remorse. But remembering the death of hundreds in the spaceport made him defensive.

"And these people will?" said Isra motioning to the grizzly scene that surrounded them.

The Houston bowed his head, "Yes. If they serve the *Kompanio* well, they will return to our home. They will be reunited with friends and family long since departed and waiting for us on that perfect world."

Isra ran up and stood in the Houston's path, forcing him to stop. "Please, I do not understand. What balance? What happened?"

The Houston smiled almost amused. "Why, you arrived of course." He sniffed the air one more time and continued, "Even as we speak, Titan dies. Balance cannot exist here when enemies of the *Kompanio* are present. Take what you see here as a warning. The will of the *Kompanio* will be done. Balance will be restored. You and the rest of your people have until the sun sets. Once that happens, the *Venganto* will finish the job they began today. Hear my warning. Leave this place."

The Houston walked around Isra and continued his inspection. This time, Isra didn't follow. She wandered back to the gate where, besides the makeshift prison camp, they also set up a rudimentary field hospital. There, wounded

Urbanoi and *Perfiduloi* soldiers lay on cots, each faction on opposite sides of each other. A few soldiers tended to the *Urbanoi* wounded and, among them, Althea Fallon. She applied an antibiotic spray to a bloody laceration that ran down the side of a soldier's body and finished up with gauze and bandages when Isra walked up.

"They won't let me treat the others," said Althea mournfully. "Not until I finish with these people."

Isra glanced over at the *Perfiduloi* on the opposite side of the field. There was not a single person tending to them and, from what Isra could see, the wounds were more severe.

"Not that I could do much," said Althea standing, "Without proper facilities and advanced technology, the most I could do is make their death a little more comfortable."

"There is no way to save this society as it is now," said Isra, watching the *Perfiduloi* suffer alone. "As long as the divide exists, the Corporation will exploit that and play one against the other. Eventually, they will bring the whole civilization to heel."

Althea pulled off the bloody latex gloves she was wearing. "Seems like such a trivial concern—our Ministry-Corporation bickering—what with the cost of humanity we are seeing."

"That too." Isra sighed, "Do what you need to do out here. I will go back to the pyramid to see Cronus."

"What do you intend to do?"

Isra paused and surveyed the wounded. "The Houston spoke of balance. I do not know how or why but that 'balance' he seeks is somehow connected with the refineries. Maybe Cronus has found something that will explain it and help me figure out a way to end this war between the *Urbanoi* and the *Perfiduloi*."

Whatever small benefit the battle brought to Viekko's mind was wearing off along with the last dose of Triple-T.

Once again, he found himself marching through the dense forests as his mind slipped away from him. Only the occasional prods by the man who held the ropes around his wrists along with the stabbing pain in his side kept Viekko aware enough to maintain any situational awareness. One of the arms tied behind him vibrated just slightly; the signal for an incoming message. Isra and Althea were trying to get ahold of him. They'd have to wait for now, until he completely understood the situation. Having them charge in with no intel would just lead to more death.

The shrapnel in his side would be a problem soon. So long as he didn't pull it out, he wouldn't bleed to death immediately, but it wasn't doing his internal plumbing any good. At least he could walk for the moment. If he could keep his mind focused on his present surroundings, he could find a way to escape.

After a couple hours, and a few kilometers, he noticed that he was no longer alone with his captor. Others dragged themselves through the freezing jungle having just escaped the battle themselves. Men and women emerged from the trees with their animal skin clothing still smoldering. Many had burns on their arms, legs and face; a mark of the *Venganto* attacks. He noticed the stench of burnt hair and skin as the path they were traveling became more crowded.

They emerged into a clearing around a large, irregularly shaped hill. Unlike the gentle, rounded slopes that were fairly common in the area, this was a sharp rise like a sudden cliff in the forest. It was, at least, hundred meters long. It was covered in moss, grass and a few small trees, but there was something geometric and man-made about it. As he got closer, he saw the glint of something shiny underneath the plant life. Soon, silver metal peeked out among the browns and greens. He realized he was looking at the remains of a spacecraft. It had been there a while, maybe even a millennium. The way the forest people clustered around it, told him that this wasn't just another forgotten relic, but a home.

He noticed a familiar voice as he was being dragged

toward the ancient ship. He didn't recognize what was said—it was in the native language—but he knew the person it came from. Sergeant Carr was about twenty meters away walking with a certain *Perfiduloi* man. He was about a head taller than most of the others, which was rather impressive for these people, with broad shoulders and a long, braided beard. Along with the fur cloak that everyone else here wore, he also had a sash around his waist made of bright, white animal fur. That, and the fact that several warriors followed in his wake, gave the man an air of authority or, at the very least, influence. At the moment, he listened to Carr talk, but his expression suggested that he didn't like what he was hearing at all.

What happened next was a reflex more than anything else. Viekko bolted forward, yanking his rope from his surprised captor's hands, and charged at the tall man and his entourage as fast as the wound in his side would allow. He screamed Carr's name like the marine had personally murdered his family. It was a desperate act brought on by equal parts fear, rage, and withdrawal-induced confusion.

The entourage assembled in a line with their spears raised before Viekko could get anywhere close. He stopped just out of reach and screamed Carr's name again.

"Viekko! Is that you?" he said with false warmth as he walked through the line of soldiers, "I thought you were dead." He walked up to Viekko until they were standing less than a meter apart. "Maybe I just hoped you were considering what you did to my artillery batteries."

As quick as a shot, Carr punched Viekko under the jaw with a right cross. Viekko fell to the ground groaning and spitting blood.

The man in charge approached. "*Kiu estas ci tiu?*"

"*Li estas neniu. Estus pli bone de vi mortigis lin,*" said Carr.

Viekko spat and got to his knees. He looked up at Carr, the leader, and several spear heads just a few centimeters from his face. "Ain't nobody tell you that it's rude to talk in a language not everyone understands?"

Carr looked like he was going to say something but the other man beat him to it. "I apologize. We were discussing if we should kill you or not."

It was awkward getting to his feet with his hands bound and a pain in his side like someone taking a hot knife and jiggling it around his innards, but Viekko managed it. "You speak English?"

The man smiled slightly. "The Houston and his pets are not the only ones to speak the language of the *Kompanio*, no matter how hard they try to keep it to themselves. But as you say, I am being rude. Call me Halifaco. You know Sergeant Carr?"

Viekko snarled at the marine. "We've met. The man is as low-down and slimy as they come. He'll destroy you and everyone around you."

Carr clenched and made like he was going to punch Viekko again, but Halifaco held up his hand. "*Cesu!* I must say that I don't disagree with you. We have suffered greatly by allowing this man to tempt us into battle."

The marine reeled back. "The assault was working! It's not my fault that your men run at the first sign of trouble!"

Halifaco glared at Carr. "You assured me that you, your men, and your weapons could defeat the *Venganto*. You failed."

"Well, you failed to mention that the *Venganto* were a legion of black flying...things shooting fire out of their asses. And we could have brought them down if your men didn't run like cowards."

The two men were clearly in the middle an extended argument. Even now, Viekko had the presence of mind to realize that it could work to his advantage. "If I may, Halifaco, I saw the toys he brought. They ain't good for nothin' 'sept blowing holes in the ground and keeping mechanics in business. He should know that. Hell, I'd say he was trying to get you into a battle you couldn't win."

The look Carr gave him was red-hot. If Carr had a gun, he wouldn't bother to shoot Viekko, he'd just beat him with the blunt end until he was a creamy, red paste. "That's some pretty bold words coming from somebody smuggling guns to those heathens in the city."

Viekko slurred. "It wasn't our intention to arm anyone. We brought those in case we had to keep the peace. We was protectin' people. What did you do besides take the refineries for your own uses and get more folk dead in the process?"

Up to this point, Halifaco watched like a spectator at a tennis match. But on mention of the refineries he shot Carr a look of pure hatred. "What does this man speak of? You told me you shut down the refineries."

Carr waved his hand dismissively. "We did, we did. Don't listen to him. We had an agreement. Those refineries are down and they are never coming back."

Even through the Haze, Viekko snorted trying to suppress a laugh.

Halifaco glared at him. "Is there something funny?"

Viekko shook his head. "Nothin' at all sir. I'm sure he's tellin' the truth. Even though he and his people traveled billions of kilometers just to get at those refineries, I'm sure they had a change of heart."

Carr squared up to Viekko. "You just shut your damn lyin' face."

This time Viekko laughed out loud. "I'm a liar. Sure, why not? What did you come here for then? Sun and beach? A little sightseein' expedition? Drinks that change color and girls in tight clothin'?"

Carr snarled. "What about you, Viekko, why are you here?"

Viekko's head rolled toward the sky. "It don't matter what my intentions are. Even if I came here to do some really, really bad things, my weapons got stolen, I had to retreat from a tactically advantageous point and, in case you missed it, I've been captured. If evil intentions I had, they ain't goin' so well. Meanwhile, you captured the refineries on the pretext that you would be shuttin' them down. 'Course, I bet as soon as the place was secure, you told Halifaco here that his men weren't needed."

Halifaco's head snapped toward Carr and he gave him another withering look.

Carr clenched his teeth. "Shut up, Viekko, or I'll be wiping the remains of your face off my boot."

"I'll bet if you go back right now, you'd see a thousand marines stealing every bit of fuel that machinery produces."

"I said shut your—"

"He'll use you and your people until the last one drops dead, be sure of it. And the whole time he will promise that the refineries will be shut down forever while he steals right from underneath you."

Carr swung again and, this time, Viekko rolled with it. He felt a sharp stinging pain on his cheek and found himself face down in the dirt. He laid there until a few men picked him back up.

Carr turned to Halifaco, "Sir, you must not listen to this man. He is a spy and an enemy. He will only do you harm while he is alive."

Halifaco looked like a man on the tail end of his patience. He considered this for a moment before he pointed to Carr and spoke to his men. "*Ligu lin.*"

Two men came from behind Carr and pulled his hands behind him. He tried to resist yelling, "Get away from me! Sir, you can't..."

Halifaco pulled a knife and held it to Carr's throat. "I have listened to you once and more of my people have been slaughtered by the demons that hold the city. Before I consider listening to you again, I will put it to the people who will have to fight and die. We celebrate our battle with a feast and we will decide which of you lives and which dies. *Prenu lin!*"

The two men pulled Carr's hands behind him again. This time he didn't resist. Once his hands were bound, Halifaco shouted more orders.

Carr, bound and walking next to Viekko, leaned close and whispered, "Brilliant work you maniac. Now you're going to get us both killed."

True, it wasn't exactly what Viekko hoped for, but it was

a start. Somehow, getting Carr on the same execution block as himself was a minor victory.

CHAPTER SEVENTEEN

*It is tempting to think of every leader and soldier in the early
rebellions as brave freedom fighters rallying against oppression, but
that's as inaccurate as the idea that the Corporation was a benign
social entity that existed only for the allocation of resources. Many
rebels were bloodthirsty warlords and as willing to murder an entire
population as set them free.*

*Not every soulless butcher was born into the highest ranks of the
Corporation. Many were born poor, oppressed, and desperate for a
piece of the prosperity they saw around them, and they had few
scruples when it came to grabbing some.*

-from The Fall: The Decline and Failure of 21st Century Civilization *by
Martin Raffe.*

Viekko found himself locked in a dark, dank prison cell
for the second time in as many days. He was somewhere in
the bowels of the ancient ship far away from any source of
light apart from a small hole in the ceiling that let in just
enough to give definition to the darkness. The cell was little
more than a nine-by-six box with a metal shelf big enough to
lay on. This could have been sleeping quarters for the crew
when the ship was space-worthy. There was just enough
room to sleep and store a few personal effects.

He laid on the metal shelf and listened. The hollow

interior amplified everything so that every step, door slam, and conversation existed just on the edge of hearing. It was like a hallucination where hundreds of disembodied voices talked at once.

He was aware enough to know that, if he could hear everything going on in the ship, they could hear him too. But he didn't have much choice. Devoid of triple-T since the previous night, he felt his brain slipping deeper and deeper into the Haze. He had to call for rescue while he was still aware enough to be worth rescuing.

He pulled up his sleeve and activated the display on the arm of his EROS suit. It flashed on and proceeded to find the nearest signal. It took a while since Isra, Althea, and Cronus were still in the city nearly five kilometers away.

The computer locked and Viekko sent a call to Isra. Moments later he could hear her voice in his ear. "Viekko, are you okay? We have been trying to contact you. Where are you?"

Viekko coughed and tasted blood. "Sorry, went and got myself tied up. I'm alive for now. I'm the special guest of a local chieftain named Halifaco. He's got me put up in our normal Titanian accommodations. How about you?"

Isra sniffed. "At the pyramid with Cronus trying to find a way to stop this fight between the *Perfiduloi* and the *Urbanoi*. Our time may be limited, though. The Houston's patience for 'outsiders' is growing short. I do not know how much longer he will tolerate our presence here."

Viekko coughed up another smattering of blood. "Well, then my being captured has put us into a fortuitous position. Halifaco is none too pleased with the way the last attack went down. Carr's went and lost favor and is languishing in similar conditions. I figure if we've got dirt on the Corporation, now's the time to use it and turn Halifaco to our side."

There was a long pause then Isra said, "Cronus is looking into the refineries. They have a central connection to Titan and the Titanian culture. Everything they do, every belief they hold dear, and every cultural construct functions

184

to keep the refineries operational either directly or indirectly."

"I will say, Halifaco has a pretty big grudge against those refineries. Apparently, when his people are captured they go and work there until they manage to escape or die."

Isra paused again. Her voice sounded strained. "I... I know. I saw them process prisoners of war and prepare them for work."

"Well, it seems that Carr promised Halifaco that the refineries were offline so long as the Corporation is in the area. Now I don't know about you but I don't think the Corporation is capable of sitting on top of a pile of refined fuels and not doin' somethin' about it. It's like asking a jewel thief to guard the diamond store."

Isra's voice perked up, "You think the Corporation could be running the refineries in direct violation of a deal with the *Perfiduloi?*"

"I wouldn't put it past them and, if they were, it would rile the Houston up as well."

"I will have Cronus look into it."

"Ain't gotta be much, just somethin' to prove that the refineries are not shut down as promised. Find that and have him bring it to me. From the sounds of things, he's got about six hours."

Isra paused. "Six hours? What happens in six hours?"

"There's to be some kind of feast and they are going to decide as a group what to do with me and Sergeant Carr."

"That is not a lot of time. Is there another way out?"

"Could be, could be. They are definitely short-handed since the battle. But there are still a lot of people here and they ain't the negotiating type. You'll have to rampage your way in just to get to me. There'll be lot of blood, Isra, a lot of blood."

"Can you find a way to escape?"

Viekko sat up and winced. "I took a hunk of metal to the guts during the battle. I'll live... for now. But I can't move terribly fast for a time."

"You think we can get this Halifaco on board with the

right evidence?"

"I think it's the best chance we got."

"I will see what I can do."

"Good, I'll wait here."

Viekko turned off his arm computer, laid back down and let himself slip into unconsciousness.

The numbers were too flat on the screen. Always too flat. Cronus could see them, but he could not feel and, thus, could not understand them. He disconnected a plug from the back of the supercomputer's dual monitors and the screens flashed to black. He reached into his pack sitting on the desk, just off the side to the keyboard, and selected the silver box and the adapters he would need to make it work.

He pulled his goggles over his eyes and the world sprang to life once more. He saw the Code once again. A constant stream of numbers sent from the supercomputer to the refineries. Only four numbers: different combinations of zero, one, two and three. On the flat screen they merely scrolled down. So flat. So boring. Now he could see them for what they really were. They cascaded all around him, spiraling as they went.

Four numbers. A spiral. A constant Code. It meant something, Cronus knew this for a fact but he still couldn't put it together in his mind.

"Cronus!"

Isra's sharp voice jolted him out of his world. He pulled the goggles back off his eyes and the numbers vanished. There was only this world. And Isra looking impatient. She must have been trying to get his attention for some time.

"What are you working on?" she continued with her preternatural calm.

"The Code. The signal between the refineries and this place. There's something we are missing. Something fundamental. This place, these people, they revolve around the Code the way Titan revolves around Saturn. It is everything and it is only four numbers repeated in a

186

seemingly random fashion."

"Interesting," said Isra, without looking remotely interested. "I need you to put that on hold for a minute. What can you tell me about the refineries?"

Cronus touched an icon on top of the silver box and the dual monitors flashed back to life. The code was gone now and replaced with detailed schematics of the refinery complex. "Everything. I found the original plans for the refineries and adapted an algorithm to update its structures and current functions. The System controls everything and now I see the System."

Isra leaned close. "Is there anything odd going on?"

Cronus scrolled through the complex diagrams. "The Corporation shut down most of the systems. They remain inactive. Extraction pumps, transfer pipes, distillers, condensers, all of it is—"

Cronus stopped. There was some activity at one of the mid-process chemical tanks. He typed a few commands and the diagram zoomed in on three conical tanks. There was a set of numbers showing how much of what chemicals they contained and they were falling.

"What? What do you see?" asked Isra.

Cronus zoomed back out to look at the schematic as a whole again. "Holding tanks for hydrocarbon chemical compounds. They were full but the level is dropping. They contained refined hydrocarbons but they are not being transferred. Not in the system. Which means..." Cronus spun around in the chair and activated the screen on his EROS suit. He linked to the satellite view and zoomed in close to the Ligeia Mare.

"There! Do you see it?" he said holding his arm out so Isra could look at the screen.

She bent down. "The Ligeia Mare?"

"Look close. Do you see something strange on the surface?"

Isra looked closer. "I do...what are those?"

Cronus pulled his arm back. "Do you recall the spools they unloaded? Hundreds of meters of carbon-reinforced synthetic tubing."

Isra thought for a moment. "The giant spools of hose. Enough to stretch across the Legia Mare?"

"Several times," added Cronus, looking at his EROS computer again. "They planned this. They knew about this city and the refineries all along. That's far too much weight to ship a billion miles from Earth, even for the Corporation. There's no other reason to be prepared for a situation like this unless that was their plan from the start." Cronus turned back to the monitors. "There's your evidence."

"What evidence do you speak of?"

Cronus tapped his ear. "I've kept the channel open. Listened to the lies and the secrets. If you humans insist on destroying this City, then it is up to me to protect this place and its secrets. I know about Viekko and I know you need evidence to present against the Corporation. You have it now."

Isra sighed. "Then you know that Viekko is injured and in danger. We need to make that evidence portable and show it to the forest people holding him. Can you do that?"

Cronus turned and blinked a few times, "Well...yes, it is possible. I have devices that can store and replay complicated systems like this. But it is not easy to transfer and use. It will take time to show you how—"

Isra straightened up. "No need. You will be going. Althea is still tending to the wounded but, as soon as she can get away, I want you and her on the crawler and moving toward Viekko's signal. Understand?"

Cronus looked back at the Code, those flat numbers on the screen. "I need...time. I'm so close. I can almost see it."

Isra started walking toward the main door. "You will have plenty of time to come back to that. Viekko needs help now and I need every team member in play to make sure he is safe. So do what you need to do and be ready to leave in about thirty minutes. I'll be back after I talk to Althea."

That was it. No discussion. Just Isra's footsteps on the steel catwalk as she walked out of the pyramid. Cronus pulled the goggles over his head, hit the icon on the box and watched the numbers dance in their beautiful spiral patterns for a few minutes.

He needed time. He could see it, but he didn't perceive it yet. He needed time.

CHAPTER EIGHTEEN

At any other time and place, these regional warlords would have been happy to kill each other for scraps from the Corporation's table. But this was a time when nearly every person living in the outlying provinces could point to a friend or family member that had been killed or tortured by Corporate soldiers.

The Global Corporation was indeed strong, but it became the perfect common enemy for many population groups that normally would have been quite happy killing each other.

-from The Fall: The Decline and Failure of 21st Century Civilization *by Martin Raffe.*

Althea loosened her coat as she drove the crawler through the forest. The sun was high in the sky now and, despite being a fraction of the size it was as seen from Earth, it warmed Titan surprisingly well. All around, a thin mist rose from the ground as if the whole moon was thawing. She drove on a path of packed earth just wide enough for the crawler. The trees and shrubs on either side were trampled or had branches broken implying some constant traffic.

As they traveled, Althea noticed something wrong with the forests. The huge ferns, massive trees, and other diverse plant life were not as vibrant and green as she remembered them just hours ago. Maybe it was a characteristic of the area she traveled through, but the flora looked like houseplants that someone forgot to water.

Cronus looked better now sitting in the passenger side, even if he clearly wanted to be anywhere else. He didn't speak or move or even busy himself with his holographic computers. He just sat holding the breath mask over his mouth and nose and stared out at the passing landscape like a petulant child.

Althea stopped the crawler and pulled up the sleeve on her coat to check the EROS display. A flashing icon indicated Viekko's signal a little over ten kilos from their position, almost due South. She pressed another icon on the screen to talk to Isra.

"Status?" said Isra's voice in Althea's ear.

"Ten kilos away now. The crawler isn't running particularly well. It will need some more work when I get back, but everything else is just lovely."

Not running well was an understatement. Going faster than a few kilometers per hour caused the engine to whine and belch smoke from under the hood. She was sure there was a fluid leak in the transmission and occasional clunking from the engine sometimes threatened to shake the machine apart, but it was moving for the moment and that was what was important.

Isra responded over Althea's earpiece. "Keep me posted. Out."

Althea pulled her sleeve back down and continued driving. She glanced at Cronus again. "Sorry to pull you from your work, Cronus, but this is quite important. Isra says that Viekko didn't sound terribly well."

Cronus just glanced at her while holding the breath mask to his face.

Althea, the type to make polite conversation in any circumstance, continued, "Were you making any headway? Did you find something interesting?"

Cronus pulled the mask away from his face. "I don't know. There is something about that place. And the refineries. Something bigger than both of them. I can't read the code yet, but it is important. Not like normal computer code. It is a strange quaternary system, nothing like it in any known computer coding."

"Quaternary system?"

Cronus held up four fingers. "Most computing uses two base numbers. Each corresponding to a different argument. Yes and no. Some use three. Yes, no and maybe. Then there are four base numbers. Yes, no, maybe, who the hell knows? It makes no sense, but it's there. It's everywhere in that system."

Althea smiled pleasantly. "Well I'm sure you will figure it out. You look well. Are the allergies getting better?"

Cronus pulled the mask away again. "Yes, which is strange. They went away inside the pyramid. The effect out here is mild."

"Maybe it was just a temporary reaction. We're not entirely sure what effects alien plant life will have on terrestrial systems. Your body might have just been adjusting to the new environment."

Cronus put the breathing mask back over his face and looked away.

Petulance was one thing, but Cronus acted genuinely afraid of something. Well, Cronus was more or less permanently afraid since they landed, but this was different. He wasn't just afraid for his life at the moment.

"What's wrong, Cronus?" said Althea.

Cronus took a couple deep breaths from the breather and pulled it away. "I can't quite pinpoint it. It's like a flash of light beyond the peripheral. There's something important about the mainframe and the refineries. If it gets out, it will be destroyed."

"What will be destroyed?"

Cronus put the breather back up to his mouth and took a several deep breaths. He did this for several seconds before he pulled the breather down and said, "Everything."

Althea was about to ask him to explain that cryptic remark when she heard a hollow thump from the woods. Something flew out of the brush and fell to the right side of the crawler. Before Althea could swerve, there was a deafening blast and the feeling that the whole world was just stashed in a tumble drier. There was a sensation of falling and then pain as her body smashed into the hard, wet ground.

When the world stopped spinning, she was lying face down in the mud. At first, there was no sound but the ringing in her ears. But, as it died away, she became aware of rapid gunfire. The crawler, what was left of it anyway, was upside down not far from where she was lying on the ground.

Where was Cronus?

She took a quick look around and found him sprawled a couple meters away.

She crawled on her belly, keeping as low to the ground as possible. When she got to

Cronus, she put her fingers to the artery in his neck.

He was breathing and he had a pulse. Aside from some minor scratches, she couldn't see any wounds.

Bullets ricocheted off the crawler and a nearby rock. She had to get Cronus to safety, but he had just been thrown from the crawler. Moving him could be as dangerous as leaving him there until she knew he didn't have a spinal injury.

Still lying flat on the ground, she placed her hands on her head and yelled, "We surrender! Please! Stop shooting! We surrender."

The gunshots died away and were replaced by someone shouting orders. Althea laid there trembling until she heard boot steps a few meters away and a gruff voice yell, "On your feet!"

Keeping her hands on her head, she maneuvered herself into a kneeling position and then stood up. She found herself face to face with two Corporation marines in full body armor.

One of the two men stepped forward, pointing the barrel of his rifle directly at Althea's head. "Drop any weapons you have, slowly. Then turn around and put your hands behind your back."

The Corporation marines—basically a highly organized mercenary battalion—tended to attract people who divided up the world into two groups: enemies and civilians. And to the marines, 'civilian' was a word said with the same tone as 'cockroach'. It was a useful trait if played right.

Althea turned her head away and sucked in a few irregular breaths as if desperately trying to keep from breaking down completely. The trick was to appear powerless. She took another deep breath and whimpered, "Cronus?"

Cronus let out a pathetic little whimper.

Althea turned back to the marine. "He's injured. Badly. He will die if you don't let me save him."

Cronus groaned again and moved his arms as if to push himself up.

The marine motioned with his gun. "He's alive. Now you do as I say before I change that."

Althea snapped back around, "Cronus! Listen to me. Don't move. You have a severe spinal laceration. If you move, you risk paralysis. It will be a bloody miracle if I can save your feet, so don't move!"

Cronus froze.

Althea turned back to the marine and managed to work up some tears. "He needs lorazepam right now or I can't even begin to save his life." She motioned to the crawler. "My bag is in there. If you will just let me..."

The marine pressed the rifle closer to her face. "Sorry. Can't let you do that."

"We are representatives of the Ministry!" said Althea letting more hysteria creep into every word, "What do you think will happen if I tell them that Corporation marines just stood by and watched one of their people die?"

Althea saw a slight twitch of fear cross the marine's face. Marines responded to power and, as much as they enjoyed lording over people, they also understood what it meant to be on the wrong end of the Chain of Command.

There was a click as the marine switched off the rifle's safety. "And what do you think will happen if I just kill you both?"

Althea gulped. "A lot of paperwork, I should think."

It was a joke, but only just barely. The marine clicked the safety back into place.

"Please, let me help him. Don't..." Althea gulped and let herself cry, "Don't let me watch him die."

The marine looked toward the crawler, then at Cronus, then back to the crawler, then Cronus. "Henderson!" shouted the Marine, "Get in there and find...whatever she was talking about."

"It will be in a black leather bag," said Althea, wiping her eyes. "I had it in the back before..."

The second marine pulled the bag from under the wrecked crawler and started rooting through it. "What the hell am I looking for?"

"Lorazepam," said Althea, forgetting her feigned hysteria for a moment. "It will be a proper syringe with a needle with a yellow label."

The soldier rooted around a while and produced a disposable syringe filled with medication. He threw it to his partner who examined it for a moment. "This the stuff?"

Althea nodded and the marine handed it to her.

Still under the watchful eye of the marines, she went and knelt beside Cronus. She pulled the cap off the syringe. "Try not to move, this will all be over soon." Then she gave him a quick wink.

She turned back and looked up at the marine, "Come kneel down beside him here."

"What?" said the marine still holding the assault rifle on her.

"Kneel down. I need you to hold him while I give him the injection."

His hands holding the assault weapon trembled. "I can't..."

Althea glared at him right in the eye. "If I give him this and he has a reaction he can spasm so hard he breaks his own back. It's not good for any of us if he dies. Not me, not you, and definitely not him. You are in this now, so get down

195

here and hold him." She turned to the second marine. "And you, if this goes terribly wrong, I'll need the portable defibrillator. It's in the bag as well."

The second marine went back to rooting in the bag. The one standing nearby swore under his breath and slung his rifle behind him. "What do you want me to do?"

"Put your hand here and here," said Althea indicating Cronus's shoulder and stomach. "On the count of three."

In one quick and effortless motion, she jabbed the needle into the marine's neck and pressed all the way down on the plunger. "One."

The dose was so high that the marine didn't even have time to get a word out before his eyes rolled back into his head. He fell down and Althea pulled the rifle strap over his head. "Two."

Cradling the weapon in her arms she stood to face the second marine. "And three."

The second marine stood up with a pair of palm-sized silver paddles in his hand. "Is this what you are looking..." His voice trailed off.

Althea now spoke in a flat, even tone. "Now remove the clip from your rifle, empty the rounds from the chambers, and throw it away. After that, do the same with your sidearm. Then throw away your combat knife."

The soldier hesitated so Althea fired a short burst a meter or so from the man's head. "That was just in case you had any doubts as to whether I could use a gun. Now, do as I say."

The marine grimaced as if he'd just eaten something foul but did as he was instructed. As he threw his knife away Althea asked, "Who else is out here? Are you alone?"

"Lady, in this forest you can't move a dozen steps without someone watching through a sniper scope."

Althea nodded. "I see. Well if that's the case, then it seems we are in a stalemate. So why don't you go fetch someone with rank. We'll stay here and watch your friend." she indicated the man now sleeping soundly on the ground near Cronus. "And, if I were you, I'd hurry. If the wind so much as blows the leaves in a way I don't like, well, it won't end well for him."

The man started walking away. "You know that you are basically both dead now, right? It's just a matter of time. We're going to bring fire and pain down on you."

"I'm quite sure that is true," said Althea. "And you wouldn't want to delay that, would you? Run along now."

The marine turned and ran into the forest. Althea watched with her gun aimed at him until she was sure he was gone.

"Um...shouldn't you give me that injection?" said Cronus still laying as motionless as possible.

"Relax. You are okay," said Althea, lowering the gun.

"I can move?"

"Can you feel your toes?"

Cronus hesitated a moment. "Yes."

"Then you're fine." She went to pick up her medical bag by the crawler. "Come on, we should get moving."

Cronus stood up. "Moving? What about all the soldiers?"

Althea shook her head. "We're dealing with someone who's just smart enough to follow orders and not shoot himself in the foot. That doesn't leave a lot of room for analytical thinking. If there were soldiers out there, he would have told us he was alone. Now come on, Viekko is still several kilometers away."

Cronus went to the crawler and pulled his backpack out of the wreckage. It was scorched but looked mostly unharmed. "What was that, Althea? Why did they attack us?"

Althea looked around her. "I don't know. Obviously someone didn't want us to get to Viekko. I should call Isra."

She pulled up her sleeve to activate the display on her EROS suit. Cronus, moving at a speed Althea had hitherto thought him incapable, jumped to his feet and grabbed her arm.

He looked down at the EROS computer as if he had just temporarily disarmed a bomb. "Those soldiers knew our path. They knew where we were and where we were going to be. This forest is huge. How did they know that?"

Althea pulled her arm away and looked at the blank display on her arm. "The tracking signal on our EROS suit?"

"They have hacked into our signal. It's the only way they would know our position with that level of accuracy."

"If we disable the tracking signal, Viekko and Isra will have no idea if we are alive or dead. With no relay, we can't contact anyone."

Cronus looked at the drugged marine. "Neither will they."

"With no relay, we can't contact anyone. And how would we find Viekko?"

Cronus activated the display on his arm. "I can disable the transceiver in the suit. We can still use Viekko's last known position."

Althea looked up at the ringed planet in the sky. "And Saturn doesn't move which will make it easy to walk in a straight line." She looked down at the display screen. "We'll need to move fast. Viekko will think we are dead or in trouble if he can't see our signal. There's no telling what horrors he will get up to then."

Viekko sat at a wooden banquet table almost twenty meters long, staring at a hunk of charred meat on a stick while his mind drifted farther away. This room inside the ship was cavernous. It was possibly the cargo hold or even a stripped-out engine room. It was large enough to house five long tables each seating upwards of twenty to thirty Perfiduloi with room to spare all eating meat from skewers and drinking some black fermented fruit drink. Light streamed in through a series of windows high above their heads.

Viekko closed his eyes and tried to focus on the here and now. A few moments ago, he thought he was sitting at the family table just after his mother's funeral on Mars. Before that, he pictured himself in the Colony Defense Force mess hall looking at something unidentifiable on a metal platter.

Before that, a small round table in a Rio club looking at a drink changing colors right in front of his eyes.

Each time he had to force his mind back to the present. He was here on Titan. Surrounded by a hundred *Perfiduloi* warriors all tearing big chunks of mammoth meat from the sticks with their teeth. After that was done, there was going to be some kind of trial. At which point they were probably going to kill Carr, Viekko or both of them.

He pulled up his sleeve to contact Isra again. He whispered just under his breath, "Anything yet?"

There was a long pause before he heard Isra's voice over the earpiece. "Nothing. I have made some inquiries with Laban's people but that is not likely to get us anywhere. The Houston is not willing to send any of his people outside the walls. I hate to say it, but you are on your own."

Viekko swallowed hard. "Is she dead?"

"We do not know anything yet. It could be an equipment malfunction or her signal dropped or is somewhere out of satellite line-of-sight. Viekko, listen carefully. You need to think about yourself now. Get yourself to safety and then, we will worry about Althea and Cronus."

Viekko sighed. "Understood."

Carr, sitting next to him, took a big bite of meat. "S'matter Viekko? Not hungry?"

Viekko looked at the hunk of meat again. Somewhere he felt vague pangs of hunger poking out through the Haze, but they were too far away. What little grasp he had on reality at the moment was entirely focused on Althea.

Carr took another bite. "I wouldn't worry about your friends. They got rerouted."

Viekko slowly turned his head. "Say that again."

Carr gave Viekko a smug, grease-covered grin. "I said they got rerouted. We managed to isolate your private signal before you even left base camp. You didn't think we'd just let you traipse all over this moon unsupervised, did you? They are safe. I just needed to make sure they didn't interfere. Are you going to eat that?"

The world around Viekko got sharper. It wasn't as good

as a shard of triple-T, but the thought of pulling the hunk of meat from his skewer and stabbing Carr in the eye sharpened him up enough to appreciate his surroundings.

Halifaco sat at a table nearby and at the head of the room with two older men on either side. These elders clearly commanded some respect and reverence from the rest of the society. While the rest of the hall sat closely packed, conversed and joked as they ate, these five ate in silence. When one of them finished the meat in front of them, someone appeared with a fresh skewer. When they finished their mug, somebody arrived to fill it from their own.

Every once in a while, Halifaco raised his head as if judging the mood of the crowd. Then, once he judged the time right, he drained his ceramic mug and banged it hard on the table. The room went silent; more silent than before.

Halifaco launched into a speech in his native language. From the inflection and tone it sounded like the man was calling down fire and brimstone. The wrath of the gods, blood of infidels; the entirety of religious righteousness and wrath distilled into pure speech.

When he was done, he motioned to Carr and Viekko. "You will both be allowed to speak. Since you do not speak our language, I will tell them all what you are saying. Which of you will speak first?"

Carr looked sideways at Viekko and smiled. "Well, since my friend here is a little reluctant, I will start."

Carr stood up. As he began speaking, Halifaco translated for the assembled crowd. "My friends. I just want you all to know that I'm as shocked and saddened as you are that this whole thing went as terribly as it did. I mourn those who lost their lives in the service of the *Kompanio* as much as you do. I underestimated the enemy, I will admit to that. And, for what it is worth, I am sorry."

This was not good, thought Viekko. Most Corporation marines were a group of barely-functioning, monosyllabic sociopaths. But the one time he needed a man to live down to that ideal, he turned into a damned orator.

Carr paused for a moment to let Halifaco catch up and

continued. "Now, you all are suspicious and rightly so. If you weren't, you'd be damn fools. I've been accused by this man," he gestured to Viekko, "of purposefully misleading you all gathered here today. I've been accused of knowingly leading brave warriors to death or enslavement. Furthermore, I've been accused of breaking my promise regarding the refineries. But, where was this man while this was going on? He was in The City working with the Houston and all the others to destroy the *Kompanio*. He was seen on the battlefield killing your warriors. He gets captured, so what does he do? He lies." Carr turned to Viekko and smiled. It was a smug, knowing expression. "He lies to save himself. He lies to further cripple your efforts to free yourself from the tyranny of the Houston."

He turned back to the crowd, "We all know what side he is on. So the only real question is about me. I've brought you tools to help free yourselves. Since me and my people have taken the refineries, not one wisp of smoke has risen from them."

Carr sat down clearly satisfied. There was an expectant silence as the five elders at the front of the room talked among themselves. Then Viekko realized everyone was looking at him. He stood up and stared into the silent crowd. The rage helped sharpen his brain, but it was still hard to put coherent thoughts together. He stood there for so long a few began whispering.

Halifaco cocked his head. "Do you have something to say?"

Viekko started slurring, "This...thing. This fight, you think it's still between you and the *Urbanoi*. But it ain't. Not anymore. You've got something new to fight, and it ain't like anything you've ever seen. The people that have come to this moon, they intend to take everything from you. Maybe not at first, but they will. First they will come as friends and allies. They will offer to help you defeat your enemies. And they will. By the time those men are done, the city will be rubble and every last soul either dead or enslaved. And, once they finish with them, you will lose your usefulness and will become a threat. Then it is too late, you will share the fate of your enemy."

As Halifaco finished translating, the people at the table stirred and talked among themselves with urgency in their voices.

Carr saw it too and he stood up. "More outrageous lies! Do you have any proof of this?"

Viekko pulled up his jacket sleeve and activated the display on the arm of his Eros suit. There was still no sign of Althea or Cronus.

He gritted his teeth and looked up at the crowd again. "Proof? Yeah, I had proof. I had proof from the City itself but that man didn't want you to see it. So he went and made sure of that."

Carr raised his arms in the air. "This is ridiculous! He doesn't have any proof. It's all just lies and—"

"You had your chance to speak," said Halifaco. "It is time for you to be silent." He turned to Viekko. "Do you have any proof of what you claim?"

Viekko fought through the Haze to grasp onto something, anything to convince these people. He had nothing tangible, so he had to appeal to something else. Something these people would accept without proof.

"*The Kompanio!*" Viekko exclaimed.

The elders whispered among themselves and one at the end said, "What did you say?"

"You are right, I have no proof. But I speak the truth and the *Kompanio* knows it. So let me prove it. Let me fight him," said Viekko, nodding toward Sergeant Carr.

As Halifaco translated this to the crowd, Carr laughed. "You are not serious. You're injured. I'd kill you in a second."

Viekko looked at the crowd. They became more and more excited as Halifaco finished the translation. He smiled, "You're right, I can't possibly defeat you in battle." He turned back to Halifaco. "Not without help from the *Kompanio.*"

Halifaco paused for a moment and, again, the five elders talked among themselves. While they did, excitement built in the hall until Viekko could feel it vibrating his bones.

Halifaco stood up and spoke to the crowd. Whatever he said was exactly what they wanted to hear. A cheer went up along with the clatter of the ceramic mugs beaten against the wooden tables. Viekko looked at Carr who had a self-satisfied grin on his face.

When the commotion died down, Halifaco spoke to Viekko and Carr at the table. "Judgment has been made. You are wise to put your trust in *Kompanio*, Viekko. The Elders agree that, if you speak true, the *Kompanio* will give you strength."

Viekko grinned and leaned back. Through the rage and the Haze it all made a strange kind of sense. It was a win-win. If he could fight and triumph, he could make his escape and rescue Althea. If she was still alive. If he died, Althea and Cronus would be useless to the Corporation. Carr was a bastard, but he didn't kill for fun. He'd let them go if they had no further value to him. Either way, Althea would be safe and Viekko could die honorably in battle.

He watched the crowd get up and start to file outside to watch the fight.

It was a perfect win-win.

CHAPTER NINETEEN

*Any person or government that attacks everyone out of fear of
being surrounded by enemies, soon finds their suspicions correct.*

-from The Fall: The Decline and Failure of 21st Century Civilization *by
Martin Raffe.*

Viekko found himself back in the wide clearing outside
the ancient derelict ship, surrounded by a circle of yelling,
chanting, and cheering *Perfiduloi* people.

Viekko focused on the chants and yells in the Titanian
language. It sounded like a thousand people speaking in
tongues. They shook their fists and danced in little circles
while their furs whirled around them. It was as if he and
Sergeant Carr were surrounded by a pack of tall, hairy
demons crying for their damnation.

Carr was on the opposite side of the circle. He took off
his blue Corporation-issued coat, stripped down to the tight-
fitting black EROS suit, and boxed the air to warm up his
muscles. Every once in a while he'd flash a menacing grin at
Viekko like a cat sizing up a three-legged mouse.

Viekko followed suit, taking off his white coat and
shoulder holster and placing them in a pile just beyond the
edge of the circle. There was a ruddy stain of mostly dried

blood about the size of a softball where the shrapnel hit him. The Haze dulled the pain but, as he stretched, he could feel a tugging or pulling on the wound. It was useful in a way. He could focus on that to keep his mind grounded.

Halifaco stepped into the middle of the circle and gave some kind of grand speech. Something with big inflections and wild hand gestures. The crowd worked themselves up getting more and more manic with every word. Viekko got the impression that the *Perfiduloi* leader spent a decent portion of his life haranguing the masses. When he was done, he walked over to Viekko and pressed his palm to the Martian's forehead. "May *Kompanio* grant you strength, Viekko."

He crossed the circle and did the same to Carr. After that, he joined the rest of the spectators gathered in the circle. Just like that, the fight was on. Carr walked to the middle of the circle and Viekko went to meet him.

As soon as Viekko raised his fists, Carr launched forward with a jab. Viekko stepped back and slapped it away. Carr repeated the jab and, again, Viekko slapped it away and followed with a right cross. Carr staggered back a moment and launched forward with a flurry of punches. Viekko barely had time to react before a punch connected with his cheek and sent him sprawling to the mud.

Somewhere just beyond the Haze, he felt his jaw throbbing. The crowd yelled, clapped, and danced even more as Viekko got to his feet. He locked eyes with Sergeant Carr and put up his hands.

During that first volley, Carr might have been sizing him up. Or maybe he was just playing to the crowd. This time he went for Viekko's weakest point. He got close enough for Viekko to throw a couple short jabs. As soon as he did, Carr stepped to the right and landed a firm punch right in his shrapnel wound.

Viekko felt something sharp scrape and tear against something soft somewhere in his guts. Lights flashed in his head. He dropped his hands to cover his wound and screamed like a man unhinged. Carr landed three more punches, two to the gut and one to the face, and Viekko fell back into the mud.

Maybe the punch pushed the little piece of metal farther in. Maybe something vital was ripped to shreds and he was going to bleed out right here. Either way, the pain was excruciating. It kept his mind on this world before, but now it was like focusing on the sun at the height of noon, too intense to manage for long. So he let his mind slide away.

Then he was standing outside his own body. He watched Sergeant Carr raise his fists and parade around the ring in victory while the crowd cheered. Halifaco ran into the circle and knelt beside Viekko's body.

Viekko tried to will his body to get up and fight. He screamed curses inside his own head. *Get up, you* mori omkhii baas kheregtie, *get up and fight!*

His body pushed itself off the ground, got its feet underneath him, and stood. Carr waved his fists and shouted at the crowd. He didn't notice that Viekko was up and staggering toward him.

Viekko's body lurched into such a wild, clumsy attack—it was somewhere between a roundhouse and a windmill punch—that the soldier would have seen it coming had he been paying attention. As it was, Viekko's fist managed to connect with the back of Carr's neck.

The punch did little more than make Carr angry. He turned and threw a series of punches at Viekko's body. In this state, Viekko didn't have fine muscle control, not enough to defend himself. Carr might as well have been tenderizing a huge slab of meat in a butcher shop. When Viekko's body finally fell, it just crumpled backwards as if some unseen force holding it up ceased to exist.

Viekko tried to will his body up again and managed to get into a sitting position. But Carr kicked Viekko back to the ground, put his knee on his chest and started pummeling his head.

When he was done, Viekko's face looked like it had been sucked into a plasma jet engine. As Carr got up and walked away, he tried to will his body up one more time, but it

206

wouldn't budge. He felt his mind slipping into a deeper Haze. The yells and chants of the crowd, the dark green foliage, and the black mud all faded into white.

Then, he was back in his apartment in Rio. Everything around him was fuzzy shades of white and grey but he somehow knew where he was as if in a dream. He was laying down naked while another body, just a different colored blur among the rest, rode on top of him.

Then he heard a voice. It was sweet, lilting and screaming in ecstasy. It was Althea and she was screaming his name: "Viekko!"

Pieces of the memory started to come into focus. The bright city lights streaming in through the window, the creaking of old bed springs and Althea in all her glory, tossing her fiery red hair back as she closed her eyes.

"Oh...Viekko!"

As far as memories go, this was a good one to end his life on. It was the last perfect night Viekko could remember. After that, everything went so horribly wrong that his death on some God forsaken planet was inevitable.

Althea's voice changed from the breathy squeal of sexual ecstasy to something harsh and urgent. "Viekko!"

The memory started to fade even as he tried to hold on to it. The fine details he managed to pick out faded away.

"Viekko!"

New sounds filled his surroundings, like a hundred people all talking and shouting at once. It was as if he'd been dropped into the middle of an angry mob.

"Viekko! Damn it, come back to me!"

He opened his eye—the other was swelled shut—to see Althea looking down at him. Her expression bordered on panic, but it softened when he met her eyes.

Althea helped him into a sitting position. "Jaysus, Viekko. What the hell were you thinking?"

"I was waiting for you," Viekko slurred. "I was just stalling for time."

"With your face? Come on, let's get you up."

Viekko winced as Althea pulled him to his feet. "In the

battle. I got...in the side..."

"I saw it. It's not life-threatening, but you risk bleeding out and sepsis if I try to do anything here. We'll get you somewhere safe first."

Once Viekko was on his feet, he saw what all the commotion was. The *Perfiduloi* gathered around while Cronus held a black disk-shaped device in his hand. Lights shot from all angles and created a holographic map of the refineries hovering over the heads of the entire crowd.

"As you can see," Cronus explained to Halifaco standing nearby, "Refining operations are still in progress. If anything, they are larger than ever. But storage tanks are not filling up. I will show you why."

Carr was on his knees with his hands bound behind him. Two *Perfiduloi* men stood on either side, holding him there. He struggled and yelled, "This is insane! Halifaco! Don't tell me you buy this nonsense."

The map overhead fell to the ground, causing some of the forest people to duck and cover like there was a mountain coming down on them. But, instead, they found themselves surrounded by translucent images of tanks and pipes and pumping equipment.

"These tanks here," said Cronus, pointing at a set of conical tanks that towered over the assembled crowd, "They hold intermediate products. Ethane. Methane. Propane. Carr and his people have bypassed the system. They are stealing from these tanks as we speak."

Carr tried to stand up. "Lies! I'm tellin' you. This is all a cheap light show to make you all slaves to these people!"

Viekko stood up with Althea's help. "Slaves, huh? Rich. Halifaco, why don't you ask this upstanding man right here, if these visions are not true, why don't we all go look? I'm sure Carr here could arrange a tour to prove the honorable intentions of his people."

Halifaco regarded Viekko for a moment and marched up to Carr. "Speak then. Show us what your people are doing there."

Carr looked panicked. His eyes darted from Halifaco to

Viekko to Cronus and back again. "I can't do that. There's security concerns and threats of sabotage. We can't allow—"

Carr's words were cut short by Halifaco's blow to the side of the head. "I have heard enough. Withdraw your people now."

Carr just looked up at Halifaco at a complete loss.

"Let me just help you out here," slurred Viekko. "You want the refineries? You want them shut down for good, then they ain't the ones to do it."

"The Houston and the *Urbanoi* are ready to talk," added Althea, "They now understand the danger of the outsiders. They want to help you expel them."

Halifaco nodded, "We will go then. Bring that one with us," he said motioning to Carr. "He may yet be useful in the negotiations."

They were back trudging through that cursed forest. Cronus took a few deep breaths from the breather. He didn't need it as much; that was good. He could breathe the air now with limited assistance.

Still, the forest unnerved him. It was a place of strange sounds and things always moving just beyond sight. In his imagination, it was a place where life was in a constant battle for survival. It was a place where everything could be divided into two categories: predators or prey, and being in one category didn't necessarily negate being in the other.

The company he kept didn't help his anxiety at all. There was Viekko, of course, but there was something wrong. Just like when they first approached the city walls, he seemed completely unaware of where he was. He hardly spoke and, when he did, most of it was slurred and disjointed to the point of incomprehension. Lucid moments were infrequent and brief. Most of the time, he stared off into space as if his mind was somewhere else. Althea had his arm around her and helped him walk.

Then there was the rest of the group: Halifaco and his pack of savages. They were like something out of a strange, neolithic nightmare. Most had scars and many were still wounded from whatever horrors this world put them through. They all marched straight ahead with a look of pure murder in their eyes. They were all just another item on the list of predators and prey and they looked determinedly predatory.

His thoughts went back the pyramid and the treasure trove of information stored within. Never mind the strange correlation between the refineries, the computer, and the indecipherable code between them; there were records from the colony before The Fall. Business reports, personal communications, ship manifests—he'd just begun to scratch the surface of the priceless knowledge that was hidden there.

"Cronus," said Althea, straining under Viekko's weight, "I don't think the Corporation will bother us at the moment. Call Isra and tell her to get the Houston and bring him to the city gates. Tell her the *Perfiduloi* leader is ready to make an alliance against the outsiders."

An alliance, thought Cronus. Great. An alliance meant another war. And another war put the precious data in danger yet again.

During the original battle, Cronus heard the roar of what he later learned were small rail guns. The sound of projectiles screaming at near-light speed and collapsing buildings echoed through the pyramid. He started downloading what he could at that point. He didn't know what it was, but he would preserve it. But there were terabytes, maybe even petabytes of data on those ancient drives. It could take years to download and store it all. But all it would take was one stray projectile and another piece of human history would disappear forever.

"Cronus? Did you hear me?" asked Althea.

"Of course. I'm sorry," said Cronus, pulling up his sleeve to activate the EROS display.

There was static and Isra's voice came over the earpiece: "Cronus? What happened? You disappeared from my tracker."

"It was an ambush. Corporation marines. We survived

210

and got away, and we rescued Viekko. He's hurt, but he will live."

"That is good. What about the *Perfiduloi*? How did they react to the information we brought them?"

Cronus stole a glance at Carr. He had his hands bound and two ropes tied around his neck. A pair of soldiers carried the other ends like a leash.

"I suppose that depends on your perspective. The leader of the *Perfiduloi* wants to talk to the Houston. He's ready to make peace at The City Gates."

"I will make sure he is there. Be careful."

Cronus took a couple deep breaths from the breather. *Be careful.* The words seemed like the punchline of a cruel joke. Careful wouldn't have them at the mercy of sociopaths in some disease-ridden forest. Careful wouldn't have them on this moon in the first place. Of course, nobody forced him to come to Titan. That was his decision and one that he was regretting.

They arrived at the tree line in front of the gates after about thirty minutes. The plains in between them and the massive wooden doors still bore all the scars of war. Colorful birds circled over the bodies of *Perfiduloi*, Corporation Marines and *Urbanoi*. Smoke rose from two sizable craters near the trees. Besides the scavengers taking what they wanted from the field, the whole scene had an unreal stillness and silence to it.

Across the field, a group of around twenty people waited outside the gate.

Althea tried to shake Viekko awake, but he just stared ahead, glassy-eyed and unresponsive. "Cronus. See if Isra is with them. Try to organize a meeting that won't get anyone killed."

Cronus activated the communicator on the EROS suit. "Isra, are you standing by the gates of the city?"

"I am. Is that you I see near the tree line?"

"Yes."

"I have spoken to the Houston. He and I will meet you, Althea, Viekko, and the *Perfiduloi* leader near the center of the field. Our respective forces will keep their distance to ensure security on both sides."

Cronus relayed the message to Althea who told Halifaco. He consulted with his men and agreed. They marched onto that battlefield alone with Althea still helping Viekko walk and Halifaco leading the way with a kind of eager rage.

The Houston was in full ceremonial dress when they met. His short, thin frame almost dripped with colorful cloth and brilliant jewels. He was surrounded by a group of his soldiers. One, in particular, Cronus vaguely recognized, a squat woman with a hard, stone-like expression. There was a large ruddy stain on the front of her coat, the mark of yet more killing in the past. There was never going to be an end to this cycle, Cronus realized. People would be wounded or see friends or family killed only to come back and exact revenge on the perceived perpetrators.

The Houston bowed toward Halifaco and Isra spoke first. "We would ask that these proceeding be carried out in the language of the *Kompanio* if that is all right."

Halifaco nodded solemnly. "I will agree to that."

The Houston pulled up the sleeves of his robe so that his hands were visible and held them out to Halifaco. "Your people have been lost to us for many years, *Perfidulo*. Are you and your people ready to repent for your many transgressions?"

Halifaco's eyes burned hotter. "False leader, it is you who betray *Kompanio* by carrying on in this holy place. You dishonor their memory by trying to replace them."

The Houston started to retort but Isra cut in, "Gentlemen. This is not productive. There is clearly a long history between your respective peoples with wrongs on both sides. You must put them aside for now and work for the good of both your peoples. Can you do that?"

The Houston stiffened. "Your most recent transgression: you allied with outsiders who attacked out city. Will you repent for that at least?"

Halifaco calmed down. "That was a mistake, I will admit. I will repent for that."

The Houston closed his eyes. "Your words are wise, but I fear they are not genuine. Give me a sign that your relationship with those people is finished."

Halifaco nodded. "That is fair. I would like to bring some people forward, with your permission."

The Houston nodded and Halifaco signaled his men back at the tree line. A moment later, two Perfiduloi men walked forward with Sergeant Carr still bound and being led by the neck. When they arrived, they set him on his knees and undid the leashes around his throat.

Halifaco walked behind Carr and addressed the Houston. "Do you know this man? He is the one that came to us after we found the weapons. He was the one who provided the weapons that damaged the city walls."

The Houston eyed the soldier kneeling in the mud in his Corporation blues. "Is this true? Are you that man?"

Carr looked the Houston right in the eye. If there was any fear in him it was hidden behind a thick wall of defiance. "I am. What do you want to do about that?"

Before anyone could speak, Halifaco pulled a long knife from his fur cloak. With one quick motion as impersonal as cutting a slab of meat, Halifaco brought the knife to Sergeant Carr's throat and sliced it open.

Blood poured from the wound. It spurted on the grass near where the Houston and Isra stood watching with stony impassiveness. Carr grabbed his neck in a desperate attempt to stop the bleeding. The look of horror on his face burned itself into Cronus's mind. This man who, moments before, seemed to hold no fear of anything, suddenly looked more terrified than anything Cronus had ever seen.

He fell forward gurgling blood. Nobody, not even Althea, moved to help him. She just turned her head and muttered something under her breath.

"...heee wasch a baschtard anywaysss...," Viekko slurred. It was the most he said or did since they left the camp.

A few moments later, Sergeant Carr was dead. Cronus knew he wasn't a good person. The specifics were fuzzy but he didn't deserve this. Not in this place. Not like that.

213

The Houston watched and clapped his hands together. "I accept your demonstration. Let us talk."

Halifaco sheathed his knife inside his cloak. "Jes, let us talk."

The group turned and walked toward the city. Cronus turned around one last time. One of the large birds that had been circling overhead landed on Carr's head and started nibbling on his ear.

CHAPTER TWENTY

The Corporation military effort during the height of Global Revolution was nothing short of astounding. Students of military strategy could spend a lifetime studying its complexity and still not completely understand its nuances.

And yet, The Corporation may as well have been pushing back a glacier. Their paid mercenaries were no match against the passion of the men and women in the grips of revolutionary fervor. The mercs fought for paychecks. The rebels fought for their very existence.

-from The Fall: The Decline and Failure of 21st Century Civilization *by Martin Raffe.*

Isra got up from her chair and paced around the room where the negotiations had been going steady for nearly three hours; negotiations being a loose term for what was going on. She'd seen better cooperation in a bar fight.

The room was beautiful like most of the rooms in the Houston's palace. The walls were decorated with ornate carved wooden murals depicting humankind's assent to the heavens, the colonization of Titan and, of course, the glory and supremacy of the Transplanetary Energy Corporation that made it all possible. The carvings were faded and cracked with time as were the ornately patterned red carpet and the dark wooden table in the center. The Houston and Halifaco sat on opposite sides of the three-meter-long table, staring each other down in icy contempt.

Isra stopped roughly in between the two men, placed her hands face down on the table, and closed her eyes. "Houston, please. In order for these negotiations—"

"There is no negotiation," the Houston sneered. "If *Perfiduloi* wish to atone for their sin against *Kompanio*, it will require five-hundred of their people to bring themselves to the refineries."

Halifaco snapped, "I will agree to nothing until you release all my people and destroy those cursed refineries!"

The Houston shook his head. "Why can you not see? Titan suffers because of the sins you have committed. The forest you love dies even while you argue with me, the one man who can save it."

"Titan suffers because of you. Because the time of our freedom is here. *Kompanio* has shown us this and you deny it. You saw the light in the skies and you killed the people who come out to greet them. The forest morns my people and *Kompanio* will avenge them."

The Houston folded his arms and a slight smile crossed his face. "Five-hundred. That is what I require to ensure *Kompanio* is pleased and Titan survives. I will not discuss anything else."

Halifaco jumped up and headed toward the door. "I have heard enough as well."

Isra hurried to stop him. "Halifaco, please..."

Halifaco paused at the door and pointed at the Houston. "This man wants nothing but death for my people."

The Houston remained maddeningly serene. He looked straight ahead when he spoke as if not even acknowledging Halifaco in the room. "I offer atonement. A chance for your people to be forgiven for their many sins against *Kompanio*. In truth, I am in envy of you for you will see Earth long before I ever will."

Halifaco drew a knife from somewhere in his cloak. It was smaller than the one he used to kill Carr and about the size and shape of a letter opener. The warrior meant to conceal it, but Isra noted the glint in the light. As he rounded the table to lunge at the Houston, Isra stepped in front of him with her body in between the two and grabbed his wrist in a firm, bruise-inducing hold.

Holding his arm with the miniature dagger still she leaned forward and whispered, "That is not the way."

"This man cares nothing for us. He will kill my people."

"And how will your people fare if you die in this room today? Give me the knife."

Halifaco pressed his weight against her for a second but Isra held firm. Then he relaxed and Isra was able to take the knife from his hand.

Halifaco stepped back and strolled toward his chair, watching the Houston as if just waiting for another opportunity to strike. "If that is the case, come down from your shameful city. Quit pretending to be as gods and come to the refinery yourself and I swear by *Kompanio* you will see Earth before the next sunrise."

The Houston bowed his head, feigning great sadness. He still refused to look Halifaco in the face. "When *Kompanio* left this place and the evil ones came, did not your people help them? And now that they have come again, did your people not flock to their aid? It fills me with great sadness that you cannot see the many offenses your people have committed against *Kompanio*."

Halifaco stopped and glared at the Houston but did nothing. Isra watched his hands but neither of them went for another weapon. "I think that we are, again, off topic. Can we please return to the issue at hand?"

The Houston took a deep breath to puff himself up, going from despair to haughty condescension in an instant. He truly was the perfect politician, willing and able to display whatever emotions the situation called for while feeling none of them. He turned his head toward Halifaco. "This is the only discussion at hand. If they will atone, we will accept. If they will not, then we will use force. That is the will of *Kompanio* and the only law."

This time Halifaco made no attempt to hide his intentions. He glared at the Houston and marched toward around the table toward him. The Houston pushed his chair back, readying himself for a fight but Isra, again, stepped in front of Halifaco, stared directly into his eyes, and said, "Sit down."

He paused for a moment and took his seat on the other side of the table.

Isra sighed and left a pregnant pause in the room before she tried again. "The issue at hand..." She looked at The Houston, "Your city...," and then at Halifaco, "and your people are both under attack from an enemy you have not seen in a thousand years, if ever. Your only chance for survival is to work together. You must put away this ancient and archaic grudge and provide a unified force against the outsiders. It is the only way. If you do not do this, you will lose your city. And your freedom."

The Houston chuckled, "I have told you, there is no danger from outsiders. The sun will set and the *Venganto* will drive them away. You witnessed their power during a few minutes of darkness that the eclipse provided. That was but a blink of an eye. *Venganto* rule the dark night and when sun next arises there will be nothing left but ash."

"And we have the forest," said Halifaco. "We move through the trees without being noticed. Outsiders come, but they will die."

Isra shook her head, "You do not understand. Outsiders will come again. They have weapons that can level this city three times before the sun sets. And once the city falls, it is only a matter of time before the whole planet is under their control. The forests included. Please. I want to help you."

The Houston smirked. "We do not want your help."

"*Kompanio* has given us everything we need," added Halifaco.

Finally, thought Isra. *They agree on something.* In a weird way this was actually progress.

"And furthermore," Halifaco continued, "If the outsiders wish to tear the city down, then they are truly sent by the

Kompanio. If those gods of the past could see how this man and his people parade around their glorious city they would burn Titan to the ground."

The Houston snarled, "This city was given to us by *Kompanio*. It is their legacy and a gift to their chosen people. It was not us who turned against them!"

Halifaco jumped up grabbed the end of the table with both hands and, with a show of strength that was impressive even in Titan's gravity, flipped it so that it smashed against the ornate wood carvings on the wall. "We did not turn against them. You did! You soil everything they gave to us. This place, it is made filthy by your presence. I would rather see it all burn..."

For the first time, the Houston showed emotion that Isra believed was genuine. He jumped up with horror on his face and called at the door, "*Soldato! Venu ci!* Stop this man. Take him and throw him out!"

Three soldiers ran into the room and swarmed Halifaco. The leader of the forest people managed to repel one with an elbow to the face, but the other two were on him immediately and, after a short tussle and a fourth soldier running into the room, pulled his arms behind him and bound them with leather straps.

There was so much anger, so much hate in this room that Isra could feel it as a thousand tiny needlepoints on her skin. These two men would never come together. They wanted so much to see the other suffer that they would endure greater horrors to make it a reality.

Now bound, the soldiers marched Halifaco out of the room. The Houston stood up and held up his hand; the soldiers paused for a moment. "You cause me great pain Halifaco. I love you and your people. But you cannot see. You refuse to see. I will help you."

Halifaco steeled himself for a moment and spat in the Houston's face.

The Houston retrieved a small square of cloth from a pocket in his robe. "Put him with the others. When the *Venganto* drive the strangers from the refineries I expect

219

him to be among the workers. Take him."

Isra watched as the three soldiers started to walk Halifaco out of the ornate room. The two men were so alike. The only real divide was the fact that they held completely different and incompatible world views. In that way, they were perfect symbols for the people they represented. And that was the real tragedy. There was only one thing that kept the two people of Titan bent on destroying each other. Unfortunately, that thing was two very different perceptions of reality.

"Wait please," implored Isra just as the soldiers were a meter or so from the door, "The issue at hand here is the refineries. We can find a way—"

The Houston dismissed her with a wave. "There is no point. This man, he refuses to see reason."

"Then let us help," Isra insisted. "There is so much we don't know about how the refineries function. The truth is, neither of you know exactly how they work."

The Houston sniffed. "The *Kompanio* commands—"

"Yes, yes," Isra interrupted, "But do you know why? Our person researching the system is not entirely sure that they are refineries at all."

The Houston said nothing, but a twitch in his mouth said that, as annoyed as he was by it, he really had no clue.

Isra turned to Halifaco. "Your people have been sent there to die for generations, but do you know what they are sent there to do?"

Halifaco shook his head.

Isra walked to the head of the table. "Then I suggest we build some measure of cooperation based on that, if nothing else. Combine forces and drive away the outsiders together, and we will try to provide some answers for you both."

The Houston's face quickly became the definition of severe indignation, "You would give sacred knowledge to this man?"

Isra snapped back, "And why not? Was it not you who wanted to help him and his people see the truth? Did you not just claim to love them? If the wisdom of the *Kompanio* could help them, would you deny that to them?"

The Houston started to say something but Isra turned to Halifaco and spoke before he got the chance, "And you, will you help protect this city and this world in return for some real answers? Not just words passed down but real answers to questions you and your people have asked for generations?"

Halifaco, his hands still bound behind him, took a moment to look at the soldiers holding him captive as if he were weighing a personal vendetta against the good of the planet. He turned to Isra and nodded.

"Houston, will you accept Halifaco and his people's aid in return for the same?"

The Houston looked like he was chewing on something unpleasant but he bowed his head toward Isra.

"Order your men to unbind his hands and seal this agreement. The *Perfiduloi* and the Urbanoi will work together for their mutual survival and a greater understanding about their place in the plan of the *Kompanio*."

Cronus squinted at the hologram of Vince Laban's head floating over a projector near the keyboard of the Markee Supercomputer. "How much longer until the uplink is active?"

"We just need another hour to align the satellite. *Innovation* is on the other side of the moon at the moment. It just takes time."

Cronus checked over his shoulder and looked back at the hologram. "I'm trusting you Laban. No tricks."

"You have my word, Cronus. We won't even look at the data. Your work on the Fall of Civilization and its causes is very valuable. The Corporation would never dream of interfering. The only thing we are interested in is the refinery schematics. They are easy to read, right? Light on the Old Earth technicalities?"

"Extremely. The data I'm sending you can be used to

produce a holographic replica along with very specific readings about every piece and part in the whole facility. One could use this to teach a child to operate the refinery."

Laban smiled. "That's good to hear Cronus. As soon as the uplink is up, I authorize you to store as much data as you want on our servers."

"And what about the refineries?"

Laban nodded slightly. "You have my word. We will only take what we can. It is in our interest to keep Titan the lush, beautiful land it is now. And as production increases, we can dedicate more resources to the maintenance and expansion of the terraforming project on Titan."

Cronus touched a few icons in the air. "Send me notification as soon as the satellite is in range. Along with routing numbers and—"

Isra's voice echoed through the corridors. "Cronus?"

Cronus switched off the holographic projector just as Isra walked into the chamber. She stopped at the catwalk and gave Cronus a quizzical look. "Cronus, what were you doing?"

"Nothing," said Cronus, trying to keep the desperation out of his voice. "Just waiting for the data to compile. Taking another run at the complexities of the Code."

Isra started walking across the catwalk. "Who were you talking to?"

Cronus looked back up at the screens if only to avoid her gaze. "Talking? I must have been talking to myself. I do that when I am working. I don't even know it sometimes."

Isra stopped walking. "Cronus, look at me."

He did and immediately regretted it. Isra had the eyes of someone who could dismantle a person's soul to see how it worked.

He couldn't lie; she would be able to tell if he was lying. So he didn't. "I was trying to find a safe place for everything I have found here. So that when the war you create erupts, it won't be destroyed with the rest of the planet."

Isra straightened up. "And what have you found?"

"Something incredible," said Cronus.

"Tell me."

He could no more hold back information from Isra at that point than he could resist a black hole's gravity. "The Code. The quaternary set of numbers flowing between this computer and the refinery complexes. It's simple and yet brilliant. The basis of all life; why would you not encode the instructions for complex organic chemistry—"

"Cronus," Isra barked. "Please try to contain yourself and tell me exactly what you found."

"It's DNA," said Cronus, resisting the urge to add 'you ignoramus' at the end.

Isra blinked a few times. "I do not understand."

"That's what I was trying to explain," said Cronus on the edge of exasperation. "The Code is DNA written in numbers. Zero, one, two and three as opposed to A, T, G, and C. The essence of life is being transmitted at all times between these two locations."

Isra's mouth moved a little as she tried to understand what she had just had laid out for her. "But why?" she asked finally.

Cronus turned back to the screens. "Energy." Then he spun around. He was wearing the glove like two metal vines twisting on his hand. He raised it in the air and a hologram of Titan appeared between them and the image zoomed in close and broke through the clouds until it showed a fly-over view of Titan's forests. "We are nearly one and a half billion kilometers from the Sun. There is not enough energy to fuel a biosphere like this. But a thousand years ago, some genius figured out how to make Titan run on hydrocarbons."

Isra shook her head, "How is that even possible? How could you physically burn enough hydrocarbons to power the entire planet?"

Cronus grimaced as the hologram stopped over the refineries and circled there, "Such narrow minds. Energy is all things. One need not burn the hydrocarbons to release their power. Life itself makes a refinery flare look like a dying candle."

Isra peered at the hologram. "I still do not follow."

Cronus was losing his temper. These meat-world humans... these people who lived in the so-called 'real world', had the gall to accuse his kind of having minds trapped by technology. Even someone as brilliant as Isra couldn't free her mind to possibilities that the Universe presented.

Cronus got up and ran his hand through the holographic gas rising from the refineries, "What Viekko saw was not the gaseous waste product of refineries. It was the product. A gas thick with yeast, bacteria, and other microorganisms."

Cronus twisted his hand and the hologram started flying over the forests again. "These microorganisms provide basic nutrients for the plants. The plants feed the animals that feed on the leaves. The humans feed on the animals and the fruits of the forest. The chain of life in microcosm..."

Isra's eyes widened. "...with Titan's hydrocarbons at the base. I could not have conceived of anything like this."

Cronus closed his hand and the hologram disappeared. "Now you know. Everything on Titan depends on the refineries. By ejecting the Corporation, we may have made things worse."

Isra sighed. "No, the people of Titan maintained the system for a thousand years. They can once again. Can you create some way to ensure that the people of Titan have the ability to maintain the refineries themselves?"

Cronus thought for a moment. "The Transplanetary Energy tutorial. The one that I played for the Houston and his soldiers. It has everything." Cronus opened his hand and the complex schematic of the refineries appeared again, "Using AI voice translation, I can take the instructions left behind and produce a step-by-step guide. Instructions so complete and detailed that it would tell them what valve to open and when."

Cronus caught himself and closed his hand, causing the hologram to disappear. Of course he could do it, a hack and slicer with his skill. He had programs so advanced that the likes of Viekko could probably manage it. But he failed to see the obvious question. "Why do you need this, Isra?"

"I came here with the intention of giving the knowledge of this planet to the people of Titan. This information has hardened my resolve to do this. The people must be allowed to govern themselves."

Cronus's mind went back where he saw Carr cut and left to bleed out on that field of horrors. The sight of Halifaco and the Houston's faces were burned into his mind. There was not a single trace of shock, horror or even sympathy in their eyes. All they could see was death and they were comfortable with it. "Are they capable of that? Can they act beyond their own ignorance and hatred?"

Isra turned to leave. "I do not know. But it is no longer up to us. We can protect these people from the Corporation but we can never stop them from destroying themselves if that is what they intend to do."

Cronus stared at the screen until Isra's footsteps on the metal walkway faded. He waited a few more moments for complete silence. He reached over and activated the holographic transmitter and Laban's face appeared once again.

Laban looked bemused. "Everything all right?

Cronus typed a few lines of code, "Perfect. A perfect little world. It just needs a place to be safe. Tell me the minute the uplink is active, Laban. I'll make sure you get what you asked for."

He switched off the transmitter and sat for a while. He shouldn't feel guilty anymore; apparently Isra was willing to hand any and all dangerous information to every psychopath on the moon. Why couldn't he do the same?

Of course, if Isra ever found out...well, at least he wouldn't be alive long enough to appreciate to true horror of it all.

When the world morphed into focus, the first thing Viekko saw was Althea's face. At first, he was worried that it was just another dream, a fevered memory replayed by some demonic force in his own head to torture him. It had been an endless stream of them since he lost contact with reality near Halifaco's base camp. He was lost for so long in that world, he started to wonder if he would ever get back. But then, there was Althea, standing over him like a guiding light to take him home.

"You gave me a shard?" asked Viekko.

Althea turned away to put something back in her bag. "I did. I'm sorry. You should have gotten one sooner. You were well lost to us when I found you."

Viekko looked at his surroundings. By the plush, red wall coverings, he would guess he was in the palace. He started to get up but Althea rushed to stop him. "Don't. Let the dermal mending gel do its work. If you are active too soon, you'll just rip the wound open again."

"Where am I?"

Althea brought him a cold pack. "A bedroom in the palace. Here, put this on your eye. The swelling went down, but you still look bloody awful."

Viekko took the pack. He winced as it touched his swollen eye. "Hate to think I went and messed up my pretty face for ya. I was low on options at that point."

"So you decided to let that marine use your head as a speed bag?"

"It worked, didn't it? What happened to Carr anyway?"

Althea stopped what she was doing. The hand holding a syringe shook slightly. "He...he was killed by Halifaco...to prove he was ready to ally with The Houston."

"Damn. I'm sorry."

Althea laughed a little as she plugged the syringe it into a port on his medical regulator just below the shoulder. "No you are not. He was a bastard and you wanted him dead from the moment you met him. You're not sorry. If anything, it is me who should be sorry."

"Why do you say that?"

Althea removed the syringe and sat down. "I should have listened to you back on the wall before you jumped into the middle of the battle. You were right; you needed another treatment before all that happened. When I finally found you, there was almost no synoptic response. When I finally got one, you didn't know who I was. You were lucid for a short time before you dropped out entirely. To be perfectly honest, I wasn't sure you'd come back. Part of me knew that you shouldn't have gone out in that state, but I let you do it anyway."

Viekko took a deep breath and stared up at the ceiling. "Why did you?"

"I guess part of me wanted to punish you for putting me, putting us, in this situation in the first place. That was wrong. You have a disease, and we need to find a way to treat it."

"Fair 'nough. So where do you want to start?"

A warm smile crossed Althea's face. She got up and activated the screen on her EROS computer. "Glad you asked. That thing I just injected you with, it helps the medical regulator penetrate the blood-brain barrier so I can better analyze the damage to your pituitary gland. It's become clear to me now that it's reached the stage that the triple-T is interfering with your body's ability to produce endorphins. The good news is your body is still producing them. With the right medication I think I can encourage more production while weaning—"

Viekko interrupted, "Yeah, Althea. That all sounds just wonderful. Really, I can't wait. But can I get a glass of water or something first? The back of my throat feels like the backside of a sand mole."

Althea switched off the screen. "Of course. I'll be right back."

She walked out the door. Viekko's eyes went immediately to the black medical bag. There was no way she'd leave him in the room with the triple-T.

He got up as fast as the pain would allow and swung his feet over the bed. Everything seemed to hurt worse now than it did when he was walking around with a chunk of metal in his side. Of course he was so lost in the Haze, he couldn't have felt a two-by-four if someone slammed him in the face with it.

He got to his feet and hobbled over to Althea's black medical bag. *This is foolish*, he thought to himself. *What kind of sick junkie am I? So desperate for a fix I'd go rootin' around Althea's bag? Besides, there's no way—*

A quick search found the load of glass capsules in the side pocket. Viekko looked at them for a moment. It must be some kind of trap. Althea's way of seeing if he was trustworthy. If he had any brains, he'd close the bag and lay back down.

He took roughly half the pills and palmed them. He got back into bed and shoved the capsules under his pillow.

Althea, he said to himself, *I love you. I really do. But this thing ain't over yet. And this may be a terrible thing to do, but I've got to do it. I've got to stay sharp. It might be the only thing that gets us both out of here alive.*

CHAPTER TWENTY-ONE

The Global Revolution made allies of people across ethnic, religious, and national borders. Men and women fought shoulder-to-shoulder with ancient enemies against a much greater threat. It made for wonderful recruiting propaganda.

But in the sparse records from the era, one thing becomes clear. These alliances were ones of convenience. And as soon as the Corporate threat was extinguished, hatreds going back to time immemorial would flare up with renewed vigor.

-from The Fall: The Decline and Failure of 21st Century Civilization *by Martin Raffe.*

This was, without a doubt, the most fractured military force in the history of warfare. Viekko stood on a wooden platform in the middle of a kind of training camp for *Urbanoi* warriors. Each faction brought about a hundred fighters and they were segregated on opposite sides of the field with a wide space between them. Looking out over the crowd, Viekko felt like he was about to preside over a blood wedding. On the right, the *Urbanoi* warriors with their long brown coats, clubs, and snares stood in neat, ordered lines. On the left, the *Perfiduloi* with their roughly sewn cloaks of animal fur gathered in odd little clumps.

There were two translators standing by the stage waiting for Viekko to begin the briefing, each standing in front of their respective sides. Viekko nodded to each of them to indicate that he was ready to start.

Cronus sat on the far right of the stage, fiddling with the metal device wrapped around his arm. Viekko turned to him. "Cronus, bring up the map."

Cronus raised his arm in the air and a holographic map of the area appeared in front of the crowd. They gasped at the display for a moment before Viekko began.

He waved at the spot indicating the city. "Okay everyone. We are here. Our mission is to drive enemy forces away from the refineries, here."

Cronus closed his hand, adjusted the device on his arm and raised his hand again. A new map appeared showing a crooked line between the City and the refineries. Viekko continued, "We have discovered a set of maintenance tunnels that run in between Ligeia City and the refineries. Before the attack begins, Halifaco will lead *Perfiduloi* forces through those tunnels. They will enter the pyramid—"

Several people on the *Urbanoi* side started yelling over the translators. Viekko stopped. "What the hell are they sayin'?"

The translator turned and shrugged. "They say that pyramid is sacred. *Perfiduloi* defile it by being there."

Viekko removed his hat and rubbed his forehead. "Well, tell them that their sacred spot just happens to be right on top of a covert path to the refineries. This has got to happen to keep the outsiders from destroying the whole *kharaasan* world, so make peace with this now."

Viekko paused while the translator relayed the message. The people who spoke up didn't look pleased with the response, but they kept it to themselves for now.

Viekko continued. "Once the strike force is in position, the attack can commence." The holographic map zoomed in to show just the refinery and the debris field in front. "Myself and Isra will lead the *Urbanoi* attack. You will take up fortified positions in front of the refineries. You will use those guns the *Perfiduloi* got and use them to draw out—"

Viekko's words were lost in another uproar, this time from the *Perfiduloi* side. Viekko stopped and glared at the people shouting. "What is it now?"

The *Perfiduloi* translator looked up at Viekko. "They say those guns belong to them. They will not give them to those murdering—"

A pitched screaming match cut off the translator's words. Both sides yelled and made rude gestures across the strip of grass separating them. Before things got out of hand, Viekko interrupted with a loud, shrill whistle. "Hey! Let me go ahead and end this debate right now. Those guns that you're arguing about. They ain't anyone's. We brought them, they're ours." He pointed at the *Perfiduloi*. "You folk went and stole 'em from us. Now we ain't holdin' a grudge, but the fact is that we are takin' 'em back and usin' 'em as we see fit. If you want our help to fight these bastards, that will be the end of that discussion."

Both sides, again, looked temporarily mollified. Viekko uttered a few Martian curses under his breath and continued. "One more time. *Urbanoi* draw out the soldiers. Once that happens, the *Perfiduloi* begin their attack. All you got is spears and arrows right now, and that will have to do. But as soon as you can, you pick up a gun from the first body you happen on. This attack should create enough chaos in the ranks of the enemy that they will be forced to fall back. Once that happens, the *Urbanoi* move forward and join the assault. Y'all shoot everythin' wearin' blue until we drive them to the sea."

Cronus closed his hand and the hologram disappeared. Viekko took a breath and stood with his arms akimbo. "All right, any questions?"

The courtyard erupted in the cacophony of a hundred people trying to shout over each other. Viekko stood silent until the crowd quieted down enough for one of the translators, the one for the *Urbanoi*, to inform him on the general consensus. "My people want to know why the *Urbanoi* must attack from the front. It is dangerous and

231

more suited to the likes of *Perfiduloi*."

This created another uproar on the left. The translator jumped on stage. "See? See! This is why we should keep the weapons. What is to stop them from killing our people once they are no longer useful to them?"

The *Urbanoi* translator rebuked, "We never have need for low people like *Perfiduloi*. The *Venganto* will save us during the eclipse—"

At this point even the translators started screaming at each other in their native language. It was chaos; pure, distilled chaos. And Viekko had to lead it into battle.

Viekko unholstered one of his guns and fired it into the air. The shot silenced the entire crowd. "This is the reality of the thing. The plan is the plan and there ain't no arguin' it. Your leaders, The Houston and Halifaco, already signed off on it, so that's what is happenin'. Now y'all got some work to do, so I suggest you do it."

The translators finished their work and the crowd shuffled off with all the energy and enthusiasm of a child being sent to the corner.

Viekko passed Cronus on his way off the stage. Cronus removed the device from his arm and beamed at Viekko, "I think that went well."

"Jaysus, Cronus." groaned Viekko shaking his head, "I don't know what Universe you live in, but help a fella with directions. It seems nicer there. Excuse me."

The Martian warrior walked off the stage and left the training grounds as the soldiers prepared for battle. He walked down the city streets for a few meters before slipping into a narrow alley. When he was sure he was alone, he removed a capsule from his coat and stuck it between his molars. He bit down and breathed in, letting the triple-T flood his brain. This operation was going to be a disaster, but at least he'd be good and sharp so he could watch it fall apart in vivid detail.

Viekko crouched in the grass behind a massive boulder a

few meters from the refineries. The last of the *Urbanoi* warriors settled in position behind a slab of stone and awaited orders.

Isra crouched next to him, peering through the scope of a Peasant Gun. Viekko whispered, "See anyone?"

"Just one. He is standing on a catwalk a few hundred meters back. He does not appear to have seen our approach."

Viekko sighed. That was a small miracle in and of itself. One of many that would be needed to pull off this assault, but a necessary one. Viekko put his fist in the air; a ready signal for the other squads. One by one, the appointed team leaders assembled behind various pieces of cover raised their fists in the air in confirmation.

He dropped his fist and pulled up the sleeve on his jacket to activate the communicator on his EROS suit. Before they left, Cronus gave Halifaco a handset that linked into the network.

"Halifaco?" asked Viekko. "Are you in position?"

There was static and Halifaco's voice. "We are. We wait for attack signal."

"It looks like we're all ready. You got that guy in your sights?" whispered Viekko.

"I do," said Isra.

"Drop 'em."

Isra squeezed off a single shot. Somewhere far away there was a soft plop of a body hitting concrete from a long way up.

Isra reset. "That worked. Two more marines are on the ground investigating."

Here it goes, thought Viekko to himself. *No turnin' back now.* He took a deep breath. "Drop 'em."

Isra squeezed off two more shots.

Urgent yelling echoed off the metal inside the refinery. Isra squinted through the scope. "I see five of them now and more coming out every moment."

"Take down as many as you can," said Viekko. He looked in both directions at the groups of *Urbanoi* warriors armed with peasant guns crouching behind rocks and blocks of concrete. Every one of them gripped their weapons with white-knuckle intensity. Their eyes darted back and forth from Viekko to the battle just beginning in front of them. He called out, "Stay calm. Wait for my signal."

Isra unloaded a couple more shots and the marines started shooting back. Within a few seconds, the air crackled with the sound of rifles firing and the high-pitched whine of bullets ricocheting against concrete.

Isra knelt down against the block and switched the gun from sniper mode. She closed her eyes, took a couple deep breaths and said, "That did it. There are more than twenty now," she said talking much faster than normal.

Viekko nodded and waved his hat in the air. As soon as he did the air exploded with noise as every *Urbanoi* with a gun opened fire at once. The marines emerging from the refinery sought cover from the storm of bullets and several fell dead before they could find sense to react.

Given the rate of fire and time to reload, Viekko estimated that they could sustain this assault for only a couple minutes. He activated the radio. "Halifaco! Now! Attack now!"

Viekko turned off the transmitter and pulled his guns. Seconds ticked by. He peeked over a rock and fired a couple rounds. A marine crouching behind a pipe dropped backward. Nearby, an *Urbanoi* warrior fell backward howling in pain and clutching his collar bone.

Viekko dropped down and Isra inched up to unload a burst of automatic fire. Then, she dropped back to reload. "Got three of them."

Viekko paused for a moment and peeked up over the rock. There was no change in the rate of fire from the other side, no sign of disruption. Despite the heavy casualties they were inflicting, there were nearly twice the number of marines assembled now as there were just a few minutes ago. It seemed like, for every one that dropped, three ran up to take their place. Viekko squeezed off a few wild shots before ducking back down to safety.

Already, the battle was taking a distressing direction. *Urbanoi* fell at an alarming rate. A quarter or more were already dead or wounded. One position was already out of ammunition and cowering behind a boulder.

Viekko took a deep breath to steady his nerves. He inched up and emptied his guns. Three advancing marines fell dead.

Several more seconds went by and still nothing. Isra raised herself into a fire position, took a deep breath to steady her shaking hand and unloaded another burst of full-automatic fire. She dropped back down and ejected the magazine. "I am out of ammunition," she said, throwing it away.

Viekko looked at his EROS display. It had been a minute and a half and still no sign of Halifaco and the pincer attack.

Maybe he had been delayed. Maybe that force ran straight into a marine ambush. Most likely, Halifaco realized that both of his enemies were about to slaughter each other and all he had to do was wait and pick the bones. Either way, it was over. More and more squads fell silent as they ran out of ammo and were pinned down by the marines.

It was going to be a bloody retreat.

Then, something changed. The constant barrage from the marine's side dropped off and frantic yelling could be heard above the short bursts of gunfire.

Viekko reloaded and peeked his head up. It was hard to see exactly what was happening in the thick mass of pipes and steel that was the refinery, but he could see enough. The left side of the marine line was nothing but chaos. He could see flashes of savage brutality as the *Perfiduloi* warriors attacked. They used spears, arrows; hell, he caught a glimpse of a man in a dark grey fur cloak caving a marine's head in with a piece of pipe he found on the spot. As they picked up the fallen soldiers' guns, the firefight continued from a new direction.

Viekko got to his feet and waved his hat in the air. "This is it! Forward!"

He and Isra scrambled over the boulder and charged at

the refinery with the remaining *Urbanoi* force following close behind.

The next several minutes were a blur of blood, horror, and violence as the Corporation line crumbled like a sand castle in a hurricane. They drove them all the way back to the Ligeia Mare and fought until the last survivors retreated to their ships and disappeared over the horizon.

There was a celebration in the great hall of the palace. *Perfiduloi* and *Urbanoi* alike sat around large round tables eating mammoth meat and drinking fruit wines. There were so many packed so close together that servants with plates of food and drink had to squeeze between the chairs packed with veterans of the great battle. The Houston and Halifaco made a show of the newfound alliance between the two peoples at a small table in front of the ornate throne. Isra, Althea, Cronus, and Viekko sat around a slightly larger table off to the side; a place of honor in the victory celebration.

The two leaders took turns raising a glass to the newfound cooperation of the *Urbanoi* and the *Perfiduloi* and to the forgiveness of all previous wrongs. On the surface, the whole party had an amicable feel to it, if not joyous. One without Isra's sensitivity to emotions would see a pleasant gathering between two peoples who differed in almost every conceivable way. A tepid coming-together in the spirit of harmony, unity, or any other words that sound nice written in a speech and delivered by somebody with really good hair.

But Isra could see the truth. It was in the muted conversation all around her. It was in the physical distance the *Urbanoi* and *Perfiduloi* kept from each other. And, in particular, it was in the eyes of two of the Houston's soldiers in particular. Isra recognized them as Mikelo and Alisa, the two survivors of Viekko's first attempt to take the city. They watched the proceedings with a burning resentment. It vibrated in the air like millions of rubber bands stretched to the breaking point. There was anger in this room. It was so thick and stifling that it made it hard to breathe. The *Perfiduloi* were angry at the *Urbanoi* for centuries of murder and slavery. The *Urbanoi* were angry at the *Perfiduloi* for their very existence and the rebellion was the greatest insult of all. Waves of fear washed over Isra's skin and made her shiver. The rage made her bite down so hard her teeth hurt. The mistrust made her stomach turn so that she could barely get a bite of food down.

Viekko didn't have that trouble. He shoveled hunks of mammoth meat and roasted vegetables in his mouth at a rate that would choke most people. He was either oblivious to the mood in the room or, most likely, simply didn't care at this point. Not enough, at least, to put him off his appetite.

He stopped and wiped a smear of grease from his mouth. "What's he sayin' now?"

Isra turned to see the Houston standing at the table addressing the crowd in his signature ostentatious bravado.

"Nothing of any substance," said Isra. "Forgiveness. Strength in numbers. A new period in History for those willing to accept the will of the *Kompanio*."

"It won't last, will it?" said Althea absent-mindedly, pushing food around her plate. "As soon as we are gone, it will all go back to the way things were."

The Houston sat down and now it was Halifaco's turn. His speech was about strength in unity and giving thanks to the gifts of the *Kompanio* and rising against those who would take them away. Both from near and far away.

"Most likely," said Isra, still watching the speeches. "But we have got a chance now. They have known a common enemy. And we have found something."

"What did you find?" asked Viekko around a mouthful of meat. "The button that will blow this *kharaasan* moon into a new set of rings? 'Cause that's the only way these people are going to stop pickin' at each other."

Isra gestured at Cronus who was staring miserably into a ceramic mug of fruit wine. He had barely touched a bite of the meat on his plate, but he had already sunk three mugs of wine. He shook his head. "It means nothing. The truth now is the same as the truth then. This is not new knowledge. It was always there. Always visible for one who had desire to see."

Althea leaned forward. "What do you mean, Cronus? What did you see?"

Cronus sighed and slid his goggles over his eyes and held out his right hand with the metal apparatus wrapped around it. They both lit up and a series of holographic images appeared over the table, "There was not enough energy from the sun to make Titan habitable. So they used Titan itself as a source of energy. The refineries are not that at all. They are incubators. Giant machines that take the building blocks of life and assemble them into simple microorganisms that the plants can absorb and consume to produce energy."

Viekko stopped eating. "Which is why the forest turned to *baas* the minute Laban shut them down."

Cronus nodded. "It also explains my illness earlier. My body reacted poorly to the microorganisms in the atmosphere."

"But the refineries have been off for a long time, haven't they?" asked Althea. "And who knows what bloody idiocy Laban and his goons were up to there. Can they fix it in time?"

Isra watched as Halifaco sat down. "All the more reason we must be successful here. Cronus, are you ready?"

Cronus pulled the goggles off and looked at her with dead eyes. It was as if all the joy and purpose had been sucked out of his body and Isra was responsible.

"Are we going to have a problem?" Isra hissed.

Cronus shook his head. "No. No problem. You command. I follow. As you ask."

Isra looked back at The Houston and Halifaco's table. "He is wrapping up. Remember, just like we talked about."

Cronus nodded obediently. "Simple so everyone can understand. Explain the meaning of the thing, not just the function. The spirit behind the body."

"Close enough," said Isra, standing up. "It is time to go

now."

Isra walked to the table and shook hands with both Halifaco and the Houston. It was all mechanical and staged. On earth there would be photographers and holo-lenses capturing the moment so the entire world could watch and feel good about it. She walked in front of the table and nodded at Cronus. She could feel heavy resistance in his words and his actions but he did what he was told.

Cronus spoke and Isra translated for the room. "We have learned much from this world. Not only about its people and the creatures that roam the surface, but about the deep mysteries from a time long gone by. What you call the *Kompanio* created the world. Before them, Titan was a cold, barren moon. The life you see around you was made possible by those people and everything they built serves that balance.

"I have found the complete instructions of the *Kompanio*. A way to maintain and improve the refineries. It is all connected. The City, the refineries, the forest, and the people that live among them. Destroy one, you destroy each other, and you destroy yourselves."

Cronus bowed stiffly and went back to his table. He played his part well enough. Better than Isra expected.

She turned and walked back behind the table, stood in between the Houston and Halifaco, and held out two black disk-shaped objects. "We give this knowledge to both your people. In hopes that you will use it to learn and grow together. Revive your world, restore balance, and live together."

Halifaco and the Houston both stood to receive the gift from Isra. The room gradually erupted into a dull roar of half-hearted applause.

Althea rose and walked to where Isra was standing. She handed Isra two hand-sized communicators. Isra turned to the two rulers and held them out. "These connect to our communication network. If you should need or want to speak with us for any reason, you may."

Both men took the devices, clasping Isra's arm as they

did. Isra smiled and bowed to both the Houston and Halifaco, then returned to her seat. She sat hard, slumped down and knew that it was not enough. It was never going to be enough. At best they delayed the coming conflict.

Or maybe not. As Isra sat and watched the Houston and Halifaco embrace, she couldn't help but feel doubt pricking at the base of her spine. She couldn't help but think that, somehow, she had just made everything so much worse.

CHAPTER TWENTY-TWO

I can only imagine the pride the soldiers on the battle lines felt the day the Corporation was brought to its knees or the intense sense of patriotism as the old Earth governments rose from irrelevance to lead their people against global oppression. Young soldiers must have felt an immense sense of hope and accomplishment as they looked on a new world they helped build.

Likewise I can't begin to understand the despair of an entire world watching all that they had created dashed to pieces in only a few years.

-from The Fall: The Decline and Failure of 21st Century Civilization *by Martin Raffe.*

The team emerged one by one from the forest onto the pebbly beaches of the Ligeia Mare. They traveled on foot electing to leave all the supply crates behind except for one. Viekko and Althea lugged the green metal container containing most of the peasant guns between them. It was a small concession and useless in Viekko's mind. There were still a few unaccounted for and the dead marines had been stripped of their weapons. Firearm warfare had arrived on Titan and things were never going to be the same. The best they could hope for was that they'd use up all the ammunition and be forced back to hitting one another with sticks.

Still, when Viekko saw the waves lapping at the shore of the Titanian sea and breathed that foul-smelling chemical air, he felt a sense of relief. One might even call it joy. Okay, maybe it was the extra dose of 'T' he stole, but things were good in other ways too. Cronus no longer needed the breather and he marched beside the crate, chattering at the group about what he found in that archaic computer. Althea humored him with feigned interest. Even Isra marched at the head of the group with a peasant gun slung over her shoulder and a slight self-satisfied smile on her face. She didn't even tell Cronus to shut up once. They all walked along the beach together like a band of soldiers returning from assignment.

As Viekko continued to watch the landscape pass, he was reminded that they didn't succeed so much as they didn't fail as spectacularly as they could have. Viekko remembered being awestruck by the beauty of Titan when they first made their way to the City. The dense foliage was awash with dark greens accented by vibrant flowers of all colors. Now, everything was muted. The leaves high in the trees that once looked wide enough for Viekko to use as a hammock hung shriveled and low to the ground. Flowers were few and their color was nowhere near as vivid. Bright greens gave way to dull yellows and dark browns and the air was overwhelmed with decay and rot.

Viekko took some slight comfort in the fact that soon Titan would be just another speck in the vast blackness of space. And, yes, the people who lived here would most likely go back to their indiscriminate slaughter, but the land would recover to its former beauty and return to a magnificence that would last long after the last human drew breath. It wasn't exactly a happy ending, but it was one Viekko could live with.

They made good time without the extra equipment and were nearing the base camp within a few hours. Viekko set down the crate. "We should hold up a moment."

Isra stopped. "What is wrong?"

Viekko unholstered one of his guns, popped the clip out, and unloaded the chamber. "That camp is likely to be agitated. Don't wanna give them any reason to get the wrong impression about us."

Isra looked hard at the temporary buildings of the base camp just beyond the water. "They lost a significant portion of their military power, but a small group would not be a threat to them."

Viekko opened the crate and tossed the gun and clip in. It rattled on top of the peasant guns piled inside. "All the same, don't want to give those fellows a reason to shoot first and ponder their reasonin' later. Your gun please."

Isra unstrapped the rifle from her shoulder and handed it to Viekko.

Viekko placed it with the others. "Your med bag, Althea. And your pack Cronus."

Althea tossed her black medical bag in immediately, but Cronus hesitated. "There is so much left there. So much we do not know. When we return, if we return, it could be lost forever."

Isra touched his shoulder. "Let it go, Cronus. Have faith in people."

He unstrapped the large pack on his back and crammed it in with the guns.

When they were all disarmed and unencumbered, Viekko and Althea lifted the crate again while Isra and Cronus walked in front.

Viekko didn't know what to expect: a base in the grip of full evacuation or a small fortified compound holding onto the last sliver of land they yet controlled. Either would have made sense. But what he saw when they emerged into the clearing did not.

Every man and woman, whether they had signed up with the Corporate marines or not, was now in uniform. They stood in perfect formation while four or five officers walked in between the lines inspecting the troops. Engineers, scientists...hell, by the looks of things they even dragged the cooks out of the mess halls and gave them a gun. Everyone in the line stood at attention with the solemn face of the condemned.

The group's arrival set off the entire base like a hornet's nest kicked down the stairs. A few officers shouted orders and the entire formation dissolved. Every soldier ran to their position.

"Everyone just stay calm," said Viekko dropping his end of the crate. "Nothin' sudden."

Althea dropped hers and stood with her hands raised. "You weren't kidding when you said 'likely to be agitated'."

Viekko watched the whole formation of soldiers surround them with guns raised. "To be honest, this is just a touch more agitated than I was expectin'."

Once all the soldiers were in the circle surrounding them, an officer walked out of the ranks. "You all have a lot of guts coming back here. Make sure they are disarmed and bind their hands. All of them."

Soldiers broke from the circle and went to carry out the officer's orders. One tried to pull Isra's hands behind her but she shook out of his grasp. "This is uncalled for. We are not an assault force. We are representatives of the Ministry and we are here to see Vince Laban."

The officer sneered. "Don't you worry, he wants to see you too. It's the only reason we don't take you out to the forest, beat you with rods and leave you to feed the local wildlife."

"What the hell does Laban want with us?" demanded Viekko.

"Couldn't say. But he was very insistent."

Viekko stood defiant as a marine pulled the plastic piece that tightened the cuffs while another patted him down for weapons. He laughed. "I'd be careful if I was you. We ain't exactly under Corporation jurisdiction and you can get into a heap of trouble messin' with Ministry officials. Tell 'em Isra."

Isra winced as a marine tightened her own cuffs. "Titan is not recognized as settled territory which means it is neutral ground. If we are under arrest, then the charges must go through—"

The officer cut her off. "Perhaps you haven't heard. That's okay. Laban is waiting to fill you in." A couple of soldiers opened the crates and the officer examined the contents. "And with this kind of contraband, charges will come easy enough."

Viekko lunged forward. "Titan don't belong to you. Not as long as that city still stands."

The officer didn't budge. "Yes, well, that may be a temporary inconvenience. But that's for a conclave to decide. But if you are all smart, it won't get that far. Laban wants to make a deal." He spoke to his troops. "Take these people to Laban. And secure this contraband in the armory."

Laban's office was just one of the dozens of dome-shaped structures that dotted the base camp. Through the door, Viekko entered a strange, overpowering warmth. The EROS suit masked the perpetual cold of Titan, but any exposed skin tingled in the air. Viekko had grown used to that feeling and its absence felt unnatural. The structure was relatively large compared to the others but was so crammed with dark, expensive wooden furniture that it had a claustrophobic feel to it. There were several plush chairs, small tables, and bookshelves crammed with more books than one could read on a year's long expedition. Laban himself sat behind a desk large enough for Viekko to lay on and heavy enough that he would strain to lift it even in Titan's gravity. Whole cities on Earth could be powered for a decade with the energy it took to carry all this to Titan and back. But Vince Laban was a Corporate man and no expense was too great when it came to demonstrating superiority, wealth, and a genuine spirit of true excess. The fact that millions back on Earth starved and died in the cold was just another impressive line on the expense ledger.

Laban stood up with that same omnipresent smile as soldiers lead Viekko, Althea, Isra and Cronus into the room.

"Welcome. Please have a seat."

Viekko struggled against the bonds. "Some might find that difficult with their hands strapped behind 'em."

Laban sat in a chair that was just a little gilding away from being a throne. "Well I'm afraid we must have a rather difficult conversation. But if you wouldn't mind someone standing by to keep things civil, we can make you more comfortable."

Viekko glanced at Isra who nodded slightly. A marine walked behind them waving a small metal tab near the plastic cuffs. As he passed by, the bonds released and fell to the ground.

"Please, have a seat," said Laban, gesturing to the chairs lined up in front of the desk.

Two marines entered and stood by the door shouldering automatic weapons. A third gathered the shackles and took a place near Laban's desk. While they did, Laban pretended to busy himself on some kind of built-in screen. He tapped icons and swept his hand across it as if he were reading some document. Finally he looked up, steepled his hands and smiled. "I have to say, I'm a little surprised to see you."

Before Viekko could answer, Isra said exactly what he was thinking. "We heard you were doing something immensely stupid. We had no choice but to come see for ourselves."

Laban let a chuckle escape. "Charming as always, Miss Jicarrio. I'm assuming you are referring to the next step of our military campaign. Let me assure you that it isn't so foolish as you make it seem."

Isra cocked her head mimicking the same polite, condescending smile as Laban. "Well, maybe not immensely stupid. Perhaps just unfathomably idiotic."

"Perhaps we should discuss why I called you here in the first place." He tapped some keys just to the side of his desk and a hologram appeared.

Viekko recognized it instantly. He didn't understand it any better but he'd seen it enough times. "Hey Cronus, that looks a lot like the pictures of the refineries you found."

Cronus didn't say anything, he just sunk in his chair looking guiltier than an adulterer in church.

Isra glared at Laban with an awful hatred. "Where did you get that?"

Laban shrugged. "That is not the issue at the moment. Allow me to show you what is." He tapped a few keys and the hologram zoomed in through the pipes and machinery until it displayed eight tanks in a row. They were pulsing red in a way that could not signal anything good.

Cronus catapulted himself out of the chair with a speed and suddenness that Viekko didn't think the little man physically capable of. He leaned over the desk with his face so close to the hologram that pictures swirled around his head. "This... what have you done?"

"It is not what we have done," said Laban, his voice taking a slight annoyed edge. "Rather, if we were to blame anyone specifically, it would be you and the riot you incited against our people. We shut down the outlets to transfer the refined hydrocarbons within the complex so we could continue to extract pure, refined fuels, but we never got to finish the job. The pressure is building in these storage tanks and volatile chemicals are backing up all over the system. Not just these tanks specifically, but all over the complex. I'm afraid the whole refinery is becoming a bomb just waiting for a trigger. It is in no immediate danger but, given the explosive nature of the fuels being produced, it has become a top concern of the Corporation."

Viekko folded his arms. "They ain't yours anymore. We kicked your pasty white rump outta there."

Again, Laban chuckled. "The pallor of my posterior notwithstanding, as you might have assumed when you arrived, we have every intention of reclaiming the refineries. That is where you will prove useful. Your rather blunt description is not entirely incorrect, Viekko. The native people of this planet have been able to resist far more than we assumed they would be able to. I am confident that the Corporation marines will triumph, but I wish to bring this situation to a speedy conclusion. Therefore, I am asking that you share what you know of the people of Titan."

Althea snorted in a humorless laugh. "Why would we even consider helping you?"

Laban leaned back in his chair. "Why, it's the most logical choice for you to make at this point."

Viekko and Isra exchanged glances and he knew without speaking that the same question on his mind was also on hers. Laban's army was crushed. His mission was in complete disarray. So why did he act like he just won? Isra studied him a moment. "You will have to explain the logic behind that statement."

Laban steepled his fingers again. "My mistake. I assumed as a respected diplomat in the Ministry, you had a basic understanding of Corporation laws. Without going into too many details, your situation is this: We have proof that you not only allied with enemy combatants, but actively participated in armed terrorist actions. We have holo-vids of you both actually taking up arms and killing Corporation military personnel. Not to mention that little payload you brought into camp. Since you are all subject to Corporation rule that makes you all guilty of treason, which means you are all under arrest until you can be brought to Earth to stand trial.

Laban stood up and started pacing in front of his audience. His hand gestures accented the haughty tone in his voice, "But luckily, despite your egregious actions, I'm a forgiving man. Furthermore, I still support your mission at its core. I think I can convince a conclave that what you did was part of an overall covert action campaign. Of course, for that to work, you'll need to help us."

Isra leaned forward as he walked past. "Laban, Titan is not a Corporate colony, not yet. And even if it were, us four," she waved at Viekko, Cronus and Althea, "are not under Corporation rule. We are agents of the Ministry and protected by the treaties signed—"

Laban stopped and turned on his heels to face Isra. "Let me stop you there. First, those treaties became annulled the moment you brought weapons to Titan. Second, you have been disavowed. As of two hours ago, you are no longer acting agents or representatives of the Ministry."

Before Isra could begin to process that, Laban sat back at his desk and produced a sheet of electronic paper. He placed it on the desktop and slid it forward. In a dynamic interface, it displayed each of their faces, some general information about them, and the word 'disavowed' in bright, red, flashing letters.

As Isra started to read through the document, Viekko removed his hat. "We're both reasonable men, Laban. So let's cut the *nokhoi baas* and be reasonable. Ain't nothin' to be gained by charging back into those refineries. Just a lot more dead bodies and grieving families back home who will want a payout. Now I understand that you're good and fired up considerin' what we did. And if you wanna take a swing at me, I understand. But this? There ain't nothin' in it for you."

Laban nodded. "I must say you are remarkably well spoken for a Martian savage."

Viekko clenched his fist and reminded himself that punching this man's nose through the back of his head wouldn't be helpful.

Laban continued. "And there is too much at stake to simply walk away. The hydrocarbon deposits on Titan will give the Corporation leverage over the terrestrial energy supply not seen since before the Fall. And thanks to Cronus here, we have a way of using the existing structures."

Viekko slammed his hat back on his head and glared at Cronus who sat back down and looked like he was trying to disappear inside the cushions of the chair, "Cronus, what exactly is Laban talking about?"

"He betrayed us," said Isra, still reading the paper Laban gave her. "We have been disavowed for passing information to hostile Corporate entities."

Viekko got up and pulled Cronus out of the chair by the collar of the green vest he wore over his EROS suit. "You better start explainin' and explainin' fast!"

Cronus struggled in Viekko's grasp. "I didn't... I..."

Althea jumped out of her chair and took hold of Viekko's

arm holding Cronus by the collar, "Viekko! Let him talk. There's got to be-"

Before the little man writhing in Viekko's grasp could put a coherent thought together, or Althea could make him drop the traitor, Viekko felt a sharp pain just below the neck. He let go of Cronus who fell to the ground while two soldiers, one armed with an electric truncheon, pushed Althea aside and forced Viekko back into his chair.

Laban held up his hands. "Please, please. There is no reason for this. But now you understand your situation fully. Like I said before, you can help us or submit to Corporation rule and be brought to Earth for judgment."

Althea sat back in her chair hard and glared at him, "And if we do neither? If we refuse Corporation rule?"

Laban shrugged, "If you are not Corporate traitors, you are enemy combatants. Corporation bylaws are very loose regarding captured enemy forces and they are not well enforced." He motioned to the soldiers standing at the door, "They both lost friends in your little attack. So did most everyone here. Do you really want to take your chance with them?"

"So, help you dismantle the entire civilization on Titan or submit to Corporate rule?" said Isra with a far-away look.

Laban opened his arms. "Like I said. It's your best option."

Isra looked at Viekko and Althea and took a silent poll from their faces. Then she turned back to Laban, "We will submit. Call us traitors all you want, we will not help you destroy the people of Titan."

Laban shook his head. "That is disappointing, but not surprising considering your reputation. Just Cronus, then. I know you don't know as much about the people but your knowledge of the refineries themselves—"

Cronus got up and leaned over the hologram with the parts flashing in red. "Listen to me Laban. See past your own ambition and your myopic view of the Corporation. See past your petty struggle for control and greed. Titan is in danger. The forest, the air, the ground will be scoured clean by ambition and ignorance unless you listen to me.

Laban looked confused. "Is that an agreement to help us?"

"It is an assessment that you do understand the entirety of the situation. This is not about the Corporation anymore. You must let us go back. We must return to the City."

Laban shook his head, "Your friends have made their decision. If you help me put down the rebellion, I will consider your request. Either that, or you may join your friends in lock-up."

Cronus was wild with fear, bordering on panic. The soldiers stayed close to the door on the chance that Cronus would bolt. The way his eyes shifted made it likely he would attempt it. Then a calm washed over him. "No. You deceived me, Laban. I will not give you anything else."

Laban massaged his temples, "Then I'm afraid you can join the rest of them. Nothing in this world is simple, boy. Or free. There will always be someone waiting to collect and today, that person is me. Take them away. Put them in the brig."

CHAPTER TWENTY-THREE

Then came the Exodus. The exact nature of its beginning is unknown. All that is completely understood is that there was a period toward the end of The Fall when humans around the globe contributed unprecedented amounts of resources towards ships escaping Earth.

I have my own simple and private theory. If the Corporation did indeed turn the Earth into a complex prison of torture and pain, who among the survivors wouldn't try to escape?

-from The Fall: The Decline and Failure of 21st Century Civilization *by Martin Raffe.*

Well, this had to be a new record somewhere, thought Viekko as four marines lead him, Althea, Cronus, and Isra through the tight corridors of the shuttle. There were three opposing forces on Titan and Viekko had been imprisoned by all of them. He'd managed to annoy everyone on the planet so much that, at one time or another, they all threw him in a jail rather than deal with him. A perverted part of him was a little proud of that.

The brig aboard the shuttle was just a large steel cage set among the piles of crates and equipment; just another bit of cargo. On a hostile planet working around the clock, there was usually no need for a sophisticated jail. But human behavior being what it is, it never hurts to have a secure place where people can sober up and think about what they did.

Three marines armed with non-lethal electronic rifles led them to the brig. That was for the best since Cronus struggled, screamed and fought against the soldiers so much that it wouldn't be long before they were forced to use them. Viekko, Althea, and Isra walked silently with their hands bound.

Even with the brig in sight, Cronus tried to bolt again. It was about the fifth or sixth time and the marines were ready for it. One grabbed Cronus by his hand restraints while another aimed the electronic rifle, clearly dying to use it.

"You don't understand," said Cronus, struggling. "We must contact the City or we will lose it! We will lose it all. There will be nothing left. Nothing left to underst—"

The marine holding the rifle told Cronus to shut up and slammed the butt of the gun against the back of his head. He fell like a wheat sack, mumbling the same warnings.

The two marines picked him up, carried him to the brig, and threw him inside. Without a word, they motioned to Viekko and the rest to join the little man curled up on the ground which they all did without a sound.

There was a set of metal benches bolted to the floor along the parameter, so Viekko took a seat to wait for whatever came next. As far as he was concerned, he was quite happy waiting until Laban's nasty business was done.

But that wasn't going to be the way of things. As soon as the door to the little cage slammed shut and the marines walked away, the energy in the confined area reached a rolling boil. Cronus writhed on the floor clutching his head. "It's over. The last untouched history of the planet. Unedited. The Complete and Total History of the Fall. Wiped out."

Isra sat down at one of the benches, pulled up her sleeve and activated her EROS computer. "There will be much to talk about soon, Cronus," she said with an air of impatience. "But first I need you to help me fix this problem."

Cronus rolled over, still clutching his head. "These

people will not fix it. They barrel toward disaster and death. It is the only thing they know."

Viekko thought back to the mammoths being butchered near the city gates. All human endeavors were always at a constant sprint toward disaster with no way of stopping it.

"Figure out a way," Isra snapped. She activated the comm on her computer and sent a call to the Houston's communicator. She paused for a moment while it made a connection and said, "Houston, it is Isra. This is an emergency. You need to send people to the refinery. Something terrible—"

Isra paused as the Houston responded. Her face, normally a mask of neutrality and passivity, cracked. Her eyes widened and she let out a gasp. In Isra's reserved emotional lexicon, that was the equivalent of a thirty-minute cursing tirade.

Viekko leaned back, content to ride this out until the end. Althea, on the other hand, paced the room examining the bars that surrounded them and the electronics that kept them locked in. Looking for some kind of weakness that didn't exist.

Viekko removed his hat and pulled his queue in front of him. "Might as well relax, Althea. If the *Venganto* are fixin' to cleanse this planet when the sun sets, it will only be a couple of hours before Laban will be high-tailin' it out of this horror show of a moon."

Althea ignored him and kept examining the brig for weaknesses.

Isra closed her eyes. "I understand. Get your people to safety. We will try to help." With that, she shut off her computer and hung her head. "The Houston says that the alliance between the *Urbanoi* and *Perfiduloi* has broken down already. Halifaco and his men have already moved to occupy the refinery complex."

Viekko shook his head. "That don't make any sense. Why now? They still got Corporation dimwits chargin' forward. Why break off ties with the City so soon?"

Cronus rolled over onto his back and stared straight

ahead at the ceiling. "Because he intends to destroy the entire complex."

Isra leaned forward. "Foolish. But also impossible. The *Perfiduloi* do not have the munitions to accomplish such a task. Perhaps cause some damage, yes, but not destroy the entire complex."

Cronus spoke again but this time his voice had a distinct automated rhythm about it as if he were imitating a recorded computer voice. "Containment must be maintained. Back flow will cause catastrophic failure."

"What are you talking about?" asked Isra.

Cronus, still lying flat on the ground, closed his eyes and breathed hard as if he were holding back tears. "It's all in the program you made me give to Halifaco. I need my equipment. I could show you..."

Isra got up, reached down, and pulled Cronus to a sitting position by his arm, "Well you do not have it. So try. Tell us what is happening."

Cronus's eyes moved as if trying to work something out in his head then he dropped down to all fours. The floor of the shuttle was thinly coated with a yellowish dust, a product from when the refineries were still pumping out life to the moon. Cronus ran his finger through, drawing a crude diagram. Viekko leaned forward to see and Althea and Isra gathered close as well. When Cronus was done there was a picture—if one squinted at the right angle and added a decent helping of imagination—of the holding tanks that were flashing bright red in Laban's diagram.

Cronus again started talking in that mock-computerized voice imitating the instructions from the tutorial he built. "It is most critical to monitor the levels of refined products in the mid-sequence holding tanks. Disruptions can cause unsafe levels of volatile chemicals to build. In the event refined fuels build to critical levels, the first step is to isolate the tanks from all equipment involved in the first stages of the refining process and halt further production until the problem can be resolved." Cronus drew a line across the left side of his drawing, apparently indicating a shut-off.

"Containment must be maintained. Back flow will cause catastrophic failure."

"Catastrophic failure meaning what, exactly?" asked Viekko.

Cronus wiped away the crude diagram with one swipe. "All of it. Gone. The back flow could cause an explosion that will consume every piece of the refineries."

Althea took in a sharp breath. "Was that mentioned in the information you gave Halifaco?"

Cronus shook his head miserably. "Every word."

Althea started pacing their little cage again with a renewed sense of urgency. Isra, on the other hand, displayed a kind of preternatural calm as she sat back down and eyed Cronus with a predatory edge. "I understand why Halifaco and the Houston would know about this. But Laban...why did you betray that information to him?"

Cronus sat back. "It was the only way I could protect the data inside the city. A wealth of un-edited information from before the Fall. You have your mission, Isra. I have mine."

Viekko, still watching Althea pace around the cage, put his hat back on and stood up. "Not that it matters much. We're stuck here and I don't see that changin' anytime soon."

Althea walked back to the brig door and held up a key card. "Lifted it from one of the marines."

"That's great. Only problem is the panel is way over there," said Viekko, pointing to the console a good ten meters out of reach. "So what exactly do you have in mind?"

Althea looked up, tracing a set of wires back with her eyes. "These key cards are impossible to clone. They carry an encrypted code on a chip as well as a small power cell. Now these cheap electronic locks are often badly shielded." Her eyes followed the cabling back down to the electronic lock on the brig door. She shoved the card into a space in between the door and the frame. "If I find the right spot, the cell will cause a power surge and the door will spring open." Althea took several steps back. "There it is now. One good whack and that would do it."

Viekko folded his arms. "One good whack, huh? Then a burst of sparks and a loud slam? After that a pack of armed marines are bound to get really curious as to why we're not in our little cage."

Althea took a deep breath and looked at Viekko. Her glare felt strikingly similar to the one Isra was boring into Cronus's head. "And just what do you think we should do, then? Sit and wait for all of Laban's men to march into a suicide mission? Or wait for them to tear down the City and kill everyone in it. If we sit here, hundreds will die."

"Hundreds are going to die regardless of what we do. There ain't no sense in getting in the middle of—"

Viekko was cut short by Isra's voice. It had a sharp, sub-zero edge to it that commanded the attention of everyone in hearing distance. "Who are you, Cronus?"

Cronus stood up rubbing a growing bump on the back of his head. "What do you mean?"

"Who are you? Who are you working for?" Her voice, cold and dense as lead echoed through the cargo hold.

Cronus stood up, his eyes wide with fear. "I don't know —"

Before Cronus could even finish the thought Isra was up and across the small enclosure. She grabbed him by his vest and slammed him against the barred walls with a crash. "You are either a traitor to the Ministry or working for somebody else. So start talking or I swear by my father I will end you right here."

Althea made a slight movement towards Cronus and Isra as if she might do something to stop it. Viekko took her by the forearm and shook his head. This was one of those things that had to be worked out. No amount of understanding or seeing things from the other's point of view would help. It had to be out.

Isra slammed Cronus against the bars again. "Tell me who you are! Tell me what you are doing here."

Cronus groaned as the back of his head collided with the cell, "I am Cronus. I sliced into the Ministry via the Old Internets and recalled the original commands. I faked a request for a multi-spectrum communications and field operations technician and I copied it to all the appropriate data networks. I linked that to the shuttle registry. Too much paper to untangle. Too many orders. No one would ask questions when I turned up."

Isra pressed Cronus harder against the bars. "Who are you working for? What is your relationship with Vince Laban?"

Cronus struggled against Isra's grip and he croaked, "We are an organization of slicers. The Truth of the Fall has been denied to the people.... They must know.... We can't let it be destroyed! Somebody help!"

The commotion caught the attention of some marines nearby. Viekko heard shouts and footsteps heading their direction.

Isra pressed harder. "Liar. Why did you betray me to Laban?"

Cronus croaked. "Not...intentional. Your wars were going to destroy the mainframe. Laban gave me a safe place to upload it. I didn't...he turned on me."

The same four marines from earlier ran up to the door of the brig. They each cradled an electronic rifle in their arms and watched Isra and Cronus with a certain amount of bemusement.

Althea whipped around and hissed at the soldiers. "Don't just stand there, help! Before she kills him."

One of the soldiers laughed. That was as much help as he was prepared to offer.

Meanwhile, Cronus started to turn blue. Isra added more weight. "What can Laban do with the data you gave to him? What are you so afraid of?"

Cronus was past the point of answering. All he could do was gasp in pain.

In that moment, Althea tapped Viekko on the shoulder and tilted her head at the door of the brig. The key card was still in the space. All it needed was a good whack and the door should fly open... right into the marines standing on the other side.

He'd have to move fast. He pushed back and hit the card with a side kick. There was a flash of bright white sparks and the door flew open and, with Viekko's kick, did so with enough force to smash into two of the marines.

Before the other two could get any sense of what was happening, Viekko bolted out of the cage. One of the marines had his electric rifle charged but, before he could fire, Viekko grabbed the barrel and pulled it toward him. The marine stumbled forward and Viekko threw a crushing punch to the man's face. He staggered backward and released the rifle. Viekko spun around and fired a bolt of electricity at the other marine still standing. The man screamed as he crumpled backward, his muscles painfully contracting.

The marine he just punched in the face was up and getting ready to rush his position. The rifle needed several minutes to charge and was useless until then. Well... more or less. Viekko took it by the barrel and swung at the man's head. The butt of it connected and the whole thing exploded in a shower of sparks and plastic shards. The marine crumpled to the ground.

"Cheap Corporate *us uukh*," muttered Viekko, turning his attention to the two marines he smashed with the door. They both were coming to their senses now. One had a broken nose, the other a nasty gash in his head.

The one with the broken nose went for his weapon. Viekko ran forward and kicked the man in the stomach before he could reach it and dropped him to the ground with a jab across the jaw.

Viekko picked up the rifle himself. It was charged and ready. Viekko aimed it at the marine with the gash in his head and pulled the trigger. A flash of electricity and a scream and the last marine fell to the ground twitching.

Isra shook her head and let Cronus fall. "About time. What do I need to do, broadcast it for you?"

Viekko glanced at the aftermath. "You could have told me you were running a distraction."

"If I had the marines would have known it was a

distraction, and it wouldn't have worked would it?" She turned her attention to Cronus gasping on the bench. "How can we stop Halifaco from destroying the refineries?"

Cronus gasped, "Near the center...main junction system. He would need to open the right valves, send the volatiles back into the boilers."

Isra knelt beside him. "And how do we find that?"

Cronus got up. "The communicator. If he has it with him, it is linked to the satellite network. If he intends to destroy the refineries, he will be there. Find him, find the junction station. If he is not there, then there is nothing to fear."

"Then we will need to work fast," said Isra.

Viekko prodded one of the fallen soldiers with his foot to see if he was still stunned, "Fast would be good. We need to be gettin' ourselves out of here before these boys go and wake up."

"I will need my equipment," said Cronus, starting for the open door. "I can run scans of the refineries and..."

Cronus stopped short when Isra stepped into his path. "Not you, Cronus. You have done enough damage. When we get to Earth there is going to be a lot of talk about what you did. Falsifying official documents, illegal use of Neuvonet, interfering with official business, destruction of protected Ministry territory and anything else I can think of between now and then. When we get to Earth, I will make sure they put you in a dungeon so deep they will be shipping light to you in jars. Now get out of my way."

One of the marines on the ground started stirring. Viekko fired a blast from the electric rifle, causing the man to convulse and stop moving. "Not to belabor the point, but time is a factor."

Isra turned and lead the way out of the cargo bay followed by Viekko and Althea. Viekko glanced back over his shoulder to see Cronus standing alone among the fallen bodies.

CHAPTER TWENTY-FOUR

Once the Corporation was no longer a player on the world stage, people's hearts turned again to deep, ancient hatreds. They looked on their allies, not as new friends, but as old enemies.

In its signature flash of opportunism and ingenuity, the Corporation sold off their weapons to the highest bidder and stoked an inferno that made the Global Revolution look like a dying campfire by comparison.

-from The Fall: The Decline and Failure of 21st Century Civilization *by Martin Raffe.*

Viekko peeked his head out of the cargo bay door of the ship. The camp was all but deserted now as was the shuttle. A breeze blew off the Ligeia Mare with a strange, otherworldly whistle and blew dead leaves from the surrounding forest through the camp. A few uniformed runners scrambled through the temporary shelters on some mission or another, but it was abandoned otherwise. It was as if the humanity had just been swept away in the night and left the remains to be consumed by nature.

Once he was sure that they could move through the camp in relative safety, Viekko motioned for Isra and Althea to join him. Isra pressed against him—too close for his comfort—and said, "They most likely took that crate to the armory. It will not be hard to retrieve. I will grab our things. Althea, come with me, I will need your help collecting it all. Viekko, we need transportation."

The hovercrafts, troop transports and lifters parked by the sea were mostly gone, taken out to ship more men to some horrific fate on this moon. There were only a couple left, but one in particular caught Viekko's eye. It wasn't much, just a small loader with space for four passengers, a small cargo bed and a grabbing arm built on one corner.

Viekko made one more scan of the area. "Okay, I see somethin'. Do what you need to do and meet me by the coast."

With that, he bolted from the cargo bay at a dead run toward the vehicle he selected resting on a platform by the sea. It was an older model with a few patches of fading paint clinging to a rusted frame. The engine mounted on back was attached; that was all Viekko could say with certainty about it. Viekko plopped himself behind the controls and started the warm-up sequence. The engine whined and the hovercraft shuttered and rose a meter or so off the pad.

Some distance away, an irritated voice called, "Hey! What the hell do you think you are doing?"

A marine rushed toward the hovercraft pointing a rifle— a real one this time with real bullets—aimed at Viekko's head. "Sir, who are you? You are not authorized—"

Viekko flipped a switch to heat up the thrusters. "It's okay. Laban said I could borrow it. I'm with the Human Reconnection Project. We're helping each other. Just one big team. Haven't you heard?"

The marine stepped in front of the loader. "Sir, I cannot let you leave until I receive official verification."

Viekko flipped another switch to activate the stabilizers. "Well by all means, call him up and verify. Verify to your little procedure-filling heart's content, but I'm takin' this."

The marine continued to hold the gun on Viekko and flicked his arm to expose the screen on his own EROS suit. Viekko pretended to pay him no attention as he worked through the checklist but his eyes were already looking for a quick way out if needed.

The marine tried to use the radio when movement in Viekko's peripheral caught his eye and Isra's deadly serious voice said, "Nothing sudden, please. Lower your weapon and move out of our way."

Isra approached with a small arsenal of three automatic rifles and Viekko's shoulder holster slung over her shoulder. She held a fourth rifle trained on the marine. Althea ignored the gunplay and tossed her black medical bag in the back seat before climbing in herself. She sat low in the seat in case Isra and the marine started swapping slugs.

The marine bared his teeth at Isra while holding the rifle at Viekko. "I can't do that. That is Corporation property. Tell your man to stand down.

Viekko stood up in his seat with his hands in the air. "All right, let's just calm down. Nobody do nothin' permanent here."

They all stood in that silent standoff for a few moments,. The marine aimed a shaking rifle at Viekko while Isra stood ready to send a head-shot through the marine's brain. Another marine jogged up from the direction of the camp. His uniform, age and the brisk pace made Viekko think 'officer class'. As he approached, the unfortunate grunt nodded toward Isra. "Captain. These people are attempting to steal one of our vehicles."

The captain scowled at Viekko in the loader. "Who are you? Get out of there."

Viekko eased himself back in the seat and flicked a few switches on the control panel for dramatic effect. "Captain. Glad you're here. I need a quick word."

The Captain pulled a sidearm. "Get the hell out of that vehicle!"

Viekko examined the officer for a moment. Deep lines in the man's face and greying hair suggested a man in his fifties. If he had served his time in the Corporation marines, it meant that he might have some intelligence. Independent thought and common sense were a rare commodity in the marines, but there was just enough to keep the whole operation from falling apart. And it tended to be concentrated in a select few.

"Captain, listen to me," said Viekko leaning over the side. "That attack that Laban's got going? It's gonna to be a disaster. I'm talkin' a force five *baas* storm."

The Captain eyed Viekko for a moment and then the two women and back to Viekko. "What makes you say that?"

Viekko motioned out over the water. "By now you heard about the city on the other side of the sea and you've heard that the marines already got pushed out. What you haven't heard is that civilization is fixin' to self-destruct, and I ain't talkin' metaphorical. They are currently sitting on enough fuel to shoot a hundred ships off this moon and there's at least one man interested in blast off. Trust me, you don't wanna be here when that happens."

The captain looked at Isra as if for confirmation and said, "Go on."

Viekko continued, "We've got a narrow window to try and stop it. It's a long shot but I need this vehicle. Either way, I would spend less time worrying about us and more time worrying about an emergency evacuation. I'd say the chances are better than good that we don't come back from this."

The captain considered this. "Marine. Stand down. Report to the shuttle and order an evacuation sequence."

"Sir?" said the marine.

"Do it."

The soldier hesitated for a moment before running toward the shuttle.

Althea and Isra boarded the loader while the captain watched. "I couldn't say anything to Laban but the amphibious assault was as brash as it was ill-planned. How bad is it going to be?"

Isra handed Viekko his shoulder holster with his two guns and he took off his jacket. "You ever see what a proximity mine does to a squad? Well multiply the explosive by several million tons and see what it does to an entire

264

army."

"How much time would you estimate we have?" the officer asked.

Viekko slipped on the shoulder holsters. "Hard to say. Be on the safe side and get ready to hit sky five minutes ago."

"And if you're wrong?"

Viekko pulled his white khaki jacket back on. "If I'm wrong, there will be plenty lining up to take their piece of me. Tell you what, I'll make sure you get first in line. Avoid the rush, as they say."

Viekko gunned the engine and left the captain behind. Viekko steered the vehicle over the waves of the sea and in the direction of the City.

He pushed the throttle on the hovercraft as hard as it would go. The engines whined and shuttered like they could blow out the back at any minute. Droplets from the super-cooled water of the Ligeia Mare sprayed up and stung his face. He squinted at the sun just a few degrees above the Western horizon. He didn't even bother to inform the officer about the *Venganto*. Well, he was likely to find out in due time.

Isra sat next to Viekko in the passenger side using her EROS computer to hail Halifaco. She repeated the call, "Halifaco or any member of the *Perfiduloi*. This is Isra Jicarrio. If you or your people are in the refineries, you must fall back. A major Corporation force is descending on your position now. Repeat. This is Isra Jicarrio. Your position is not safe. The Outsiders are coming to force you out and the refineries are growing unstable. Repeat..."

The first indication that they were close was when the refinery smokestacks started popping up above the horizon obscuring the setting sun. When the rest of the complex started to come into view, Viekko could see the full magnitude of Laban's insanity. Virtually everything the Corporation had on Titan was parked just off the coast. At least ten troop transports, a few heavy cargo movers and several medium to light gunships all hovered above the water less than a kilometer from the beach.

Althea shielded her eyes from the spraying water. "Are we too late?"

Viekko turned the wheel to veer the hovercraft to the left. "For those poor bastards, yes."

They made a wide arc to avoid the Corporate fleet. Viekko throttled down and brought the loader onto dry ground. He drove along the coast for a kilometer or so and turned toward the refineries until he brought it alongside the grey wall surrounding the compound. He throttled down farther and moved just above a walking pace near the barrier.

Althea stood up and looked at the refineries beyond the wall through a set of binoculars. "I can't see anyone there."

Isra stopped transmitting. "There is no answer from Halifaco." She tapped some icons on her screen. "If he has his transmitter, it is linked to the satellite network. We can find his location inside the refineries...Yes, he is there."

Viekko jumped out of the loader and unholstered his gun. "Can we get to him before somethin' terrible happens?"

Isra stepped out and picked up an automatic rifle. "Depends on how long he has been in there. We need to confront him. Althea, stay here. If this ends poorly, there may be need for emergency medical care."

Althea took a seat in the driver's side and nodded. "Okay."

Viekko ran his hand along the wall. "Keep close to this. If the worst should happen, it will stop the worst of the shock wave. Isra. Let's go."

Viekko took a step back, jumped, and scrambled over the wall. Isra had more difficulty but she fell to the ground on the other side not long after him. They sprinted across the open ground into the tangled mix of steel and Viekko stopped to scan the area through the sights of his weapon. "Any clue where he might be?"

"Near the center of the complex," said Isra in between gasps of air.

"Okay, lead the way. But be careful. This place was a death trap when everyone thought it was working perfectly.

No tellin' what kind of hell it has become since."

Viekko felt even more unease walking between the tanks and through the maze of steel pipes. The entire apparatus groaned with increased strain. Pops and hisses became more frequent than they were in the past. Every time Viekko stepped next to or over a pipe or moving piece of machinery, he listened close for any sign that he would have to jump out of the way.

Isra crept forward with her rifle raised. She occasionally stopped to consult the readout on her arm computer. Viekko, meanwhile, watched for an attack on their flanks. Far away, beyond the straining, hissing and cracking machinery, he noticed the smell of hundreds of Corporation marines sweating in their EROS suits beneath Corporation Blue uniforms getting stronger with each passing moment.

They came to a spot where the narrow walkways opened up to a passage where Viekko and Isra could walk side-by-side with room to spare. They moved a few meters before Viekko heard voices through the constant mechanical cacophony. He raised his hand to indicate to Isra that they should pause.

Isra checked her EROS computer and nodded. They agreed without saying a word: Halifaco was just up ahead. Viekko unholstered his second handgun, Isra shouldered her rifle, and they continued with an added measure of caution.

They found Halifaco shouting orders to six *Perfiduloi* warriors. There were rows and rows of rusty metal wheels and the forest people ran back and forth turning them according to some order that was out of Viekko's understanding. It had been a while since these valves had been manipulated; it often took two or more warriors to turn the ancient valves. Halifaco watched and consulted the device Cronus gave him at the dinner. It projected a smaller version of the hologram, just a few centimeters from the leader's face.

Viekko came up behind him with both guns aimed at the small of his back and shouted, "Halifaco! Stop right there. Put that thing away, tell your people to stand down and come with us."

Halifaco, with his back to Viekko, didn't move or flinch. "Viekko. It is dangerous here. You should not have come."

"Stop! Everyone, stop!" yelled Isra waving her rifle at the *Perfiduloi* men and women executing Halifaco's orders. She released her grip and let the weapon hang by a strap around her shoulder. "Halifaco. Listen to me. There is another way."

Halifaco turned and smiled at her with the look of a condemned man who has accepted his fate and was looking forward to the next world. It was a strange, calm smile that made Viekko's trigger fingers twitch.

"There is no other way," said Halifaco. "The Houston and his people only see us as slaves. As animals to work and die. *Vi ciuj daurigi!*"

At the order from Halifaco, his people went back to opening and shutting valves. Isra raised her gun and held the barrel just a few centimeters from Halifaco's face. "Tell them to stop. I will kill you."

Halifaco looked down the barrel of the gun as if daring her to carry out her threat. "Do what you must."

That's where they stood for several seconds. Eye to eye, both people sizing each other up and measuring their resolve. But you didn't need to have Isra's preternatural ability to read people to see that Halifaco had a death wish and wasn't going to budge.

Isra lowered her gun. "Please. We can help your people."

The frantic activity among the others stopped and one of them shouted, "*Kompleta!*"

Halifaco's smile grew and he turned to walk away from Isra. "All promises. Endless promises." He reached a spot on a pipe with a ball valve lever as long as Halifaco's forearm. He stopped there and gripped the lever. "My people do not need promises. They need freedom."

Viekko, still keeping his guns trained on Halifaco for all the good it would do, said, "Don't do what I think you're gonna do. Didn't you hear Cronus earlier? Don't you understand that you will destroy all of Titan?"

Halifaco cocked his head. "That is what you say. That is

268

what the Houston says. How can I trust any of you?"

He paused, waiting for an answer. Viekko looked to Isra who seemed to be scanning the entire contents of her brain for a response. Halifaco shook his head and sighed as if he knew there was no answer she could give nor one he wanted.

"We have ships!" Isra blurted.

Halifaco stopped and looked at Isra, confused. Viekko lowered his weapons as well, waiting for an explanation for that outburst.

"We have ships," Isra repeated, "To take you to Earth. Or elsewhere. We have enough space for all *Perfiduloi*. We can take your people away from this place."

It was an act of desperation. Isra couldn't honestly believe there was a way to persuade Laban to shuttle every single *Perfiduloi* off this rock. But Halifaco paused as he considered it. It gave him some time and Viekko took in the entire situation. The rest of Halifaco's people watched now and a couple of them, Viekko noted, were cradling assault rifles taken from marines. In this place, a few stray bullets could be as disastrous as what Halifaco had in mind. He'd have to work fast to incapacitate the madman and get in a position where he could disable the ones carrying guns.

More shouting somewhere in the distance drew everyone's attention. It came from the direction of the Ligeia Mare. The invasion had begun.

Halifaco turned to glare at Isra. "I will not trade one slave master for another."

Before Isra could stop him, Halifaco opened the valve.

The rush of moving liquid made the pipes vibrate and a deadly silence was punctuated only by the hiss and whirr of the machines and the shouts of the Corporation marines getting closer and closer. For a moment, Viekko thought Cronus could have cooked up the story about 'catastrophic failure' as a means to deflect from his apparent treachery. Or, at the very least, it was an exaggerated product of an overactive mind.

Then every tank, pipe, condenser and boiler groaned and rumbled. The ground shook as if a sleeping giant from somewhere below had just woken up with a major hangover.

"*Iru! Kuri!*" yelled Halifaco, and he took off before either he or Isra could react. The five *Perfiduloi* sprinted after him.

There was a loud pop like a firecracker going off followed by the sound of crashing metal. Above, the tanks and smokestacks started swaying.

"What is happening?" asked Isra, turning her eyes upward to the shuddering towers.

"I don't know, but I don't think we wanna be the last folk here tryin' to figure it out. Go! Run! Now!"

Viekko turned and sprinted back the way he came. He leapt over banks of pipes and charged through whatever open areas he could. Behind him, the metallic screech of steel being torn apart seemed ever present and getting nearer. Somewhere above, the sky lit up as one of the smokestacks belched flame into the air. Viekko resisted the urge to look at the destruction behind him and kept his mind focused on the path ahead.

He left the tight confines of the refinery and paused. For a moment, he worried about Isra. He focused so much on getting himself out that he never stopped to check if she was still following. She was and she wasn't far behind him. She sprinted past him nearly taking flight across the open field. Viekko turned and ran after her. The EROS suit felt like it was ripping his muscles apart with every movement and the place where he took a scrap of shrapnel to the side flared up like he tore it open again. Even so, he pushed himself harder.

The first explosions from the refinery echoed off the wall. Viekko reached it in time to give Isra a boost over. When he scrambled up the side himself, the whole world was lost in a flash of bright white light. The force of the shock wave threw him the rest of the way over and he fell head-first into the soft ground on the other side.

When Viekko's eyes refocused, he saw the remains of a fireball form a mushroom cloud towering over the grey wall. Althea's face appeared over him and she yelled something he couldn't hear above the ringing in his ears. Gradually, his

270

hearing recovered enough to hear, "Viekko! Viekko! Are you okay? Can you hear me?"

Viekko coughed and sat up. The ground was covered in scraps of metal and clumps of earth. The shockwave pushed the hovercraft several meters back into a tree and the windshield was shattered. Isra was already in the driver's side trying to start the engines.

Halifaco and his people were clustered together against the wall a few meters away. The rebel leader of the *Perfiduloi* propped himself up on his elbows and gazed in absolute wonder at the destruction he created. Two of the warriors pulled him to his feet, but he never looked away from his apocalyptic handiwork. He patted both of his men on the back and spoke to them. Viekko didn't have to understand the words to realize that he was congratulating them on a job well done.

Viekko got up and brushed himself off. The light was fading but there was just enough to see something rising from the direction of the city. They were specks at the moment, but there were dozens of them and they rose as one like a swarm of wasps looking for the poor sod reckless enough to throw rocks at their nest.

Viekko pulled Halifaco back by his fur cloak, "You damn fool! You went and brought the *Venganto* down on you. They'll kill every single one of you."

Halifaco pulled himself away, "*Neniu!* My people will defeat those demons. They will not be able to hurt my people after this night. We will no longer be forced into slavery by fear."

Viekko grabbed Halifaco again and tried to pull him towards the hovercraft. "Althea! Come on, we've got to go before those things get here!"

Isra struggled with the controls when they arrived. "Come on you...you bastard! Work!" she yelled pounding the control panel.

Halifaco pulled himself away again, "I will not leave. I created this battle. I intend to fight it."

Viekko jumped into one of the back seats and leaned

forward, screaming above the roar of the explosions, "Ain't nothin' good gonna come out of staying here! Come with us or you will die."

Halifaco turned back to the burning refineries. "Then it is the will of the *Kompanio*."

Isra fired the engines and the hovercraft lifted off the ground.

"The Houston was right about outsiders after all," said Viekko. "Nothing comes from them except more death and destruction."

Isra throttled the engine and sped south, leaving Halifaco looking at the fire and clouds of smoke with an air of triumph. He and his men turned and ran into the trees as the throng of *Venganto* grew close.

Isra gunned the engines around the wall and the burning refineries and steered out into the open sea.

CHAPTER TWENTY-FIVE

The true genius of the Corporation lay in its precise, mechanical nature. It has no passion, no hate, no love, no sympathy. Any slight against it can be healed with enough money and it uses that to buy the hearts and minds of anyone they wish.

It is wealth that motivates it and wealth alone. Its entire goal is to own all that can be owned. Because of this single-minded drive, the world has known no conqueror more pure, focused and enduring.

-from The Fall: The Decline and Failure of 21st Century Civilization *by Martin Raffe.*

Viekko held on to the side of the loader as Isra maneuvered it into steep banks, rapidly accelerating over the Ligeia Mare and in between the wreckage of Laban's amphibious assault force. The shockwave from the blast created a tidal wave that sent the hovering troop transports and gunships slamming into each other. At least one of the transports was damaged completely and sunk beneath the black, frigid water, sending whole platoons to an icy death. A few others had just enough power to stay above the water but escape was impossible. Hoverships that could still move retreated. Isra had to weave and dodge between the larger craft to get out of the area.

And that drive became more pressing by the moment. Viekko looked behind him to see the last flicker of the sun's disk disappear behind the raging fires that were all that remained of the refineries. At that point, it was impossible to tell if the last flickers of light were from the final remains of the sun or the inferno. The light reflecting off the clouds of Titan revealed the *Venganto* soaring toward them, preparing to take their last revenge for the destruction of the planet.

In the back seat, Althea faced the rear and watched the fires through the scope of an assault rifle. "It's gone. All of it. The whole coast is burning."

Isra took a hard left turn and Viekko braced himself in his seat. Well, this was it. To hell with this frigid Eden and its higher-than-average collection of psychopaths. Maybe humans would return here someday, sift through the wreckage and wonder what happened to a settlement of this size. Civilizations vanish and nobody knows exactly why, but if Titan was any indication, unadulterated human stupidity and insanity were to blame.

Isra steered the loader out over open water just as the *Venganto* reached the remains of Laban's fleet and started dropping their first firebombs. They were so close already that Viekko could make out the wings against the shifting light reflecting on the clouds. So close that he could see their awful humanoid form.

Viekko shouted over his shoulder, "We gotta go faster, Isra. Those things are comin' and comin' on fast."

Isra jerked the controls to avoid an escaping equipment hauler and nearly sideswiped a group of marines on a smaller craft. "There are too many hovercraft on the water. We will hit one of them if we go any faster."

Viekko watched the fast-approaching horde through his own assault rifle. "That ain't gonna cut it. At this rate, we're gonna to be knee deep in a firefight in just a few moments."

Isra took a sharp turn to avoid running over the remains of a sunken troop transport and the bodies of dozens of marines frozen stiff in the sea. "Althea. Take the controls."

Althea made her way to the front of the loader. She

274

handed Isra the rifle and sat down in the driver's seat.

"Viekko!" yelled Isra, raising the assault rifle. "Four coming in fast. 7 o'clock high. Viekko!"

"*Omkhi baas!*" yelled Viekko turning in the direction Isra indicated.

Four *Venganto* flew in close behind them. Against the darkening orange haze of Titan's sky, they looked about as long as a man and had a wingspan to match. They had two legs, and two wings. Other than that, they were just dark, flapping shapes in the fog.

The creatures dove in formation toward the loader. Viekko fired first into the middle of the group, causing them to scatter in all directions. Isra aimed and fired next. If she tried to lead the flying creatures or aim in any way, it didn't help. She might as well have closed her eyes and pulled the trigger.

Viekko looked up just in time to see a *Venganto* dive close to the edge of the loader. It was so close that, for an instant, Viekko saw a snarling face and eyes that burned red like the fires they left behind. A sphere the size of a tennis ball shot from the creatures open mouth and plunged into the sea a few meters behind them. Light shone off the creature's black skin as it pulled up to avoid the blast that jolted the hovercraft and nearly sent Viekko into the water.

Viekko braced himself. "Keep it steady, Althea!"

"Well, keep the bloody bastards off of me!" she yelled back.

Yep, this was bad. Althea never swore.

Isra emptied the rest of her clip at the creatures circling overhead. "They move too fast. I cannot get a decent shot."

Viekko watched another creature break away from the group and start a dive. Viekko aimed and fired. The creature pulled up to avoid the bullets, but the deceleration gave Viekko a clear shot. He fired three more rounds and hit the creature at least twice in the chest. It tumbled over backward and fell into the sub-zero ocean.

"Isra!" yelled Viekko. "Watch for their attack dives. You'll get a window if they pull up."

Another Venganto dived at Isra. She fired several bursts but the creature never flinched and a bomb flew out of its mouth. Just as it fell into the sea, Isra yelled, "Althea, hard right!"

Althea jerked the controls just as a spray of water crested the sides of the loader.

"Try again" shouted Viekko wiping the stinging water from his face. "Aim just below their dive and open full automatic."

Another *Venganto* started toward the front of the craft and Isra raised her rifle. She waited a moment and then fired two short automatic bursts. The *Venganto* pulled out of the dive at the last moment but the bullets shredded the creature's wings. Althea throttled hard and the hovercraft passed beneath the creature as it dropped into the water, as if it was never meant to fly in the first place.

The last two *Venganto* gained altitude and started a gentle glide, letting the loader and its occupants go. Viekko dropped back into his seat while Isra scanned the sky through the scope on her weapon.

Once the two creatures were nothing but black dots in the distance, she sat down hard in the back seat. "Looks like they are giving up on us. The rest will be at base camp in a matter of minutes."

The last flicker of light and color in the clouds faded. One of the icy moons overhead bathed the planet in a dim, silver glow.

Viekko sighed. "I just hope that, for once in his life, Laban listens to reason and doesn't try to stop the evacuation. It's the only chance for any of us to get off this rock."

They arrived to find the evacuation in frenzied progress. Marines, engineers, and workers ran between the camp and the shuttles with boxes of equipment, cases of supplies, and anything else that could be moved in a hurry. The transports that escaped the carnage made directly for the holding bays.

The familiar computerized female voice echoed from the loudspeakers: "Attention all personnel. Shuttle lockdown in fifteen minutes. Any person not on board must proceed immediately to the shuttles and prepare for liftoff. Repeat, shuttle lockdown in fifteen minutes..."

Viekko jumped out of the loader just as Althea parked. "Just in time. The fireworks will be more fun in a high orbit."

Cronus ran up to the hovercraft nearly vibrating with excitement, "You guys are back! What happened? We heard the shockwave in the air and felt it in the ground. Even this far away. It was Halifaco, wasn't it? He started the war. What of the city? What of the pyramid?"

Viekko adjusted his hat. "The City is fine. The pyramid will likely outlive everyone else on this awful moon but I don't see much sense in hangin' around to find out. Let's get to the shuttle before things get out of hand."

"Out of hand?" asked Cronus.

"Relatively speakin', of course."

Viekko joined the mad rush of marines and other Corporation personnel towards the shuttles. He risked a look back to see Althea and Cronus running behind him. Isra was still back at the hovercraft looking in the direction of the City.

Viekko stopped. "Isra! We gotta go! We've got to get on board now!"

For a moment, he assumed she didn't hear him. She looked at the camp with a strange longing before she slung the assault rifle over her shoulder and walked away.

Viekko stopped Althea. "Hold up, I'll see to Isra." He ran back, knocking over a few crew members running the opposite direction and yelled, "Isra! Where the hell are you going?"

Isra kept walking. "I am staying."

Words failed him as he ran to keep up with her. He eventually settled with, "Have you completely lost your damn mind?"

"I cannot let this civilization self-destruct. I am going to put a stop to this before it is too late and there is nothing to do but sift through the ruins."

Viekko grabbed Isra, spun her around and pointed at the *Venganto* cresting the horizon. "Have you missed the entire series of events up to now? Titan is dead and its civilization with it. It's over. We have to go."

Isra turned and kept walking.

Viekko tried to keep close behind her. "The mission is over, Isra! This whole moon is going to be a damn killing field and I won't be a part of it."

"Nobody is asking you to."

"Fine, you crazy *gichii*! Get yourself killed." He waved her away and turned just in time to nearly run into Althea.

"And what are you doin'?" he asked.

She held up her black medical bag. "I'm going with her."

"Althea, listen hard. You see that mass of *Venganto*? Well, they aim to be showerin' us with badness in just a few minutes. They're gonna make this camp look like the refineries Halifaco just finished with." He glanced back at Isra. "She let her obsession overtake her good senses and it's going to destroy her. If you follow, you're heading for the same."

Althea smiled. "Take care of yourself, Viekko."

She stood on her toes, kissed him on the cheek and ran to catch up with Isra.

Viekko watched them leave. He felt someone lurking behind him and turned to see Cronus looking up at him with a sort of pleading in his eyes.

Viekko motioned to the shuttles. "This is your lucky day, kid. Ain't no one gonna be alive to put your ass in jail. You can go back home, get yourself plugged in and forget you ever saw this cursed rock."

Cronus started to say something but thought the better of it. Instead he just smiled and ran towards the shuttle.

Viekko turned to catch up with Isra and Althea. He always suspected Isra would be responsible for his death, he just assumed she'd be holding the knife.

Cronus sprinted as fast as he could for the shuttles. The computerized voice announced five minutes before lockdown just as he was strapping himself into one of the seats.

"Hey, you're part of that...Reconnection Project, right?" asked a marine sitting next to him.

"I am, or...I was." said Cronus.

"Where's the rest of your crew?"

"They decided to stay behind."

The marine's jaw dropped. "You've got to be kidding me! That's suicide. How they ever goin' to get off that rock?"

"They are going to try and stop the war."

The marine whistled. "Well if they got religion, they better pray their god shows up or they are screwed."

Cronus paused for a moment. "Say that again."

"I said they better pray a god shows up to help. That explosion, those flying...whatever they are. Ain't nobody going to survive down there without some divine intervention."

Cronus mouthed the words 'divine intervention' several times then mumbled, "If the people from Earth are like unto gods, who are we to disprove them?"

"What?" said the marine, uncomfortable with any thought that couldn't be expressed in monosyllabic words.

"Never mind. I must go."

Cronus undid his restraints and stumbled through the rows toward the back of the ship, shouting, "Wait! Wait! Hold the door!"

CHAPTER TWENTY-SIX

Global Revolution gave way to the Global War. Global War led to the Exodus. The intense fighting turned Earth into a Hell from which there was no escape on land. So people turned to the sky.

-from The Fall: The Decline and Failure of 21st Century Civilization *by Martin Raffe.*

Viekko rushed to catch up with Isra and Althea who were already running towards the shelter of the camp. Behind him, the shuttle's engines whined as they started the liftoff sequence. A few stragglers carrying armloads of expensive-looking equipment dashed for the open cargo bay but most were safely aboard the shuttle.

Viekko maneuvered his way through the rushing crowds to Isra. "So, did you have a plan, or are we relying on your winning personality?"

Isra risked a glance behind her. The *Venganto* were still fluttering dots over the sea but getting larger each second. "The marines' armory and equipment storage is on the southwest side of the base camp. It should be strong enough to keep us safe and have some supplies left behind."

Viekko looked behind him as well and was inspired to run harder. "And the plan after that?"

"If we survive...I might have to give personality a try," Isra confessed.

Viekko stopped. "If we're fixin' to do anything, we'll need transportation. I'll go commandeer that hovercraft again and I'll meet you two at the shelter."

Viekko turned on his heel and sprinted back towards the platform. He got behind the controls, fired up the machine and risked one more look over the Ligeia Mare. In that short time the *Venganto* went from specks to flapping figures so close he could almost make out their ghoulish faces.

Viekko swore, put the throttle down, and turned back to the camp.

He parked the vehicle along the side of the armory and slipped through the door. As soon as he was inside, Althea slammed and braced it with a metal pole about two meters long. Isra turned off lights, equipment, and anything else that made noise or light. Viekko crouched by the window to watch the fireworks. At this distance, the shuttles were nothing more than a series of tail fins poking up beyond the rows and rows of smaller shelters. Althea joined with the electronic binoculars from the hovercraft.

"Oh no..." she muttered.

The Venganto swarmed the shuttles just as the lift-off engines fired. The tail fins were now illuminated occasionally by bursts of flame as incendiary bombs burst on the surface.

Althea's grip on the binoculars was so tight her knuckles were white. "Can they lift off?"

"They'll be fine," said Viekko. "Those shuttles have a heat shield designed to protect it from re-entry."

On the bottom, he added in his own mind, *where it does no good from winged bastards attacking from above.*

The roar of the engines shook the shelter and three shuttles started their vertical lift. Most of the *Venganto* scattered. A few dove close to the ships to fire a few bombs at their hulls. The flames rolled off the side like glowing water.

The shuttles aligned themselves over the Ligeia Mare and, one by one, fired their primary engines. Althea and

Viekko turned their heads from the blinding flash. A few moments later, all three shuttles became just another point of light in the sky.

Althea took a breath for the first time in a couple of minutes. "They are away."

Viekko crouched down out of sight from the window. "Good for them. We'll give the *Venganto* a moment to ransack the camp and see nobody's home. After that, they'll go find themselves someone else to incinerate."

Viekko's arm tingled, indicating an alert from the EROS suit's computer system. He muttered a few curses and touched the side of his ear. "What?"

Cronus's voice came over the comm, "I've got a plan. A sort of theology hack. Belief turned inward into a slice for the mind."

"Cronus! This is not the time. We are deep in some heavy *sarmagchin omkhii baas uurkhain* and the last thing we need—" A thought fought into the center of Viekko's brain and demanded his attention. The shuttles were in the middle of a full burn to reach orbit. Never mind getting a signal out, it should be so loud in that tin can that Cronus would be screaming to be heard over it, but there was no background sound at all. "Cronus, where are you?"

"Mess hall I think. Large building. Darted inside to hide from those... things."

Viekko and Althea both found themselves at a loss for words but Isra was quick to fill in the gap. "This cannot be real! Are you part of some social experiment so see how much stress I can take before I snap and strangle someone with their own fiber optic wires?"

"Cronus!" Viekko added, "You better have a damn brilliant reason for not bein' on that ship."

"I figured it out. We can hack the very civilization. Get inside the people's heads. Bring them what they want. Stop the war. Save Titan."

Althea peeked out the window. "I think I know what shelter he's in, but there's no way to get to him without being seen."

Viekko tried to keep from yelling into the receiver. "Cronus! Wherever you are, stay put and shut up! Don't talk, don't move, don't even breathe too much. You got a whole mess of unpleasantness overhead and the only thing you can do right now is hope they don't find you. Understand?"

"Um...yes. I think—"

"No, you don't because you just failed. Don't move, don't speak or you are going to die. Do you understand?"

There was no response.

"Atta boy," said Viekko.

He sat back against the wall. The expressions on Althea's and Isra's faces were better than an opinion poll. Althea's hand shook and she made several glances at the door as if she might run out and try to save the kid. Isra's glare had already sentenced Cronus to a brutal death at the hands of the *Venganto*, or her own if the winged creatures couldn't manage enough cruelty.

Viekko, Althea and Isra waited and watched. The *Venganto* continued to circle the camp. Every swinging door, scrap of paper or other bit of debris carried by the wind caused one of the monsters to dive and fire one of their exploding balls of flame. After a while, however, they appeared to accept the camp was deserted. One by one, they flew off in search of more hapless fools to incinerate.

Viekko could barely breathe. His muscles started to ache from being frozen in position but, still, he didn't dare make a motion until only a select few continued to circle overhead. There was only a few. Maybe four or five and they showed not a single sign of leaving.

It was as good as it was going to get, thought Viekko. He got up and pulled the bar away from the door.

Isra watched with a mix of surprise and anger as if he had just said something unkind about her father. "What do you think you are doing?"

Viekko set the bar down without making a sound. "I'm gonna get up in the trees and guide Cronus to us. Assumin' I can do that without dyin'."

"I'll help," said Althea, standing.

Viekko considered this. "Grab the hovercraft. It's noisy, but you can use it to bolt if things get dicey. Get behind the wheel, but don't start her up until I give the go-ahead. Once I do, drive north until you see Cronus, yank him in, and get back."

"And what happens when she leads those things right here?" asked Isra.

"Then we find out if this here shelter is fireproof."

Viekko pulled the door open just enough for him and Althea to slip out. He scanned the skies and sprinted for the tree line while Althea ran for the hovercraft.

Viekko ran and scrambled up the side of a tree and found a perch among a growth of dense foliage. It was quite dark now, but one of Saturn's icy moons, Rhea, hung to the East half-illuminated by the sun. It, along with two or three smaller moons, provided light similar to a full moon on Earth. It wasn't much, but he could just make out two Venganto flying along the North side of the camp. They were far enough away that Althea could get in and out before they had time to cover the distance. There was a chance, if they were lucky, they could extract Cronus without any of the flying bastards noticing.

Viekko pulled one of his guns. His track history for being right had been shaky as of late. He reached into his jacket pocket and found the small cache of triple-T capsules. Bad things were afoot and he needed to be sharp.

He pulled one out, slid it between his teeth and bit down.

Spitting out the spent capsule and blood, he pulled up his sleeve. "Cronus? Are you there?"

There was no response.

"Fair enough, I asked for that. You can talk now, but do it quietly."

"It is safe?" asked Cronus.

Viekko glanced up at the *Venganto* flying slow circles around the camp. "As soon as I say 'go', you are going to run out the door and head south. Althea will pick you up en route. Got it?"

"I think so."

"Good. Althea?"

Althea's voice was shaky over the radio. "I'm ready."

"Good. On my mark."

Viekko watched as the *Venganto*'s constant lazy circle brought them out over the sea. It had to be now. "Go, go, go!"

The still silence of the night was pierced by the high-pitched whine of the hovercraft at the same time Cronus left the mess hall crouching low through the camp. There was a moment of relief until he saw a movement in the trees just a few meters away. A *Venganto* jumped into the air and started circling towards Cronus.

"Cronus! You got one on your tail, you got to move. Move now!" said Viekko.

Cronus jumped out of the crouch and started a mad sprint.

"No! No! That's west! Turn left you idiot!"

The sudden change in direction caused Cronus to slip and scramble in the mud, but he got up and continued the run. Althea was on her way, but the creature was already too close.

Viekko aimed his gun and waited. The moment the *Venganto* dove behind Cronus, Viekko fired a single shot.

The crackle of gunfire caused the thing to lift out of its dive. Viekko waited until it reached the top of its arch and fired again. It spun around in the air like he had hit it, but it recovered, picked up altitude and fled north. He relaxed for a moment until he saw that the crack of gunfire caught the attention of the two that had been flying over the sea.

"Viekko!" said Althea's voice on the radio. "Behind you!"

Viekko turned just in time to see yet another *Venganto* start its dive. He jumped off the top of the tree moments before it was engulfed in fire. The jump was awkward; he didn't have time to get his balance. He hit the ground hard and rolled in the mud. The wound in his side flared to life again and several bones voiced their dissatisfaction. He ended up on his back and glanced up to see something moving behind the flame and the smoke. Instinct and fear took over and he pulled his second gun and fired. He pulled the trigger again and again until the shadow shot straight up and he lost it in the dark.

Viekko got to his feet just as Althea called again. "Viekko! There's another one. It just flew over me and it's coming back around."

Viekko ran south towards the sound of the hovercraft. He rounded a corner and saw Althea stopped while Cronus struggled to jump into the passenger side. The *Venganto* hovered several meters above the canopy getting ready to start an attack. Viekko raised his guns and pulled the triggers.

Click.

He only had the briefest of moments to curse his rash stupidity. In a blind panic, after he had nearly been killed, he forgot to count bullets.

Althea hit the throttle on the left engine and used the thrust to slide the hovercraft back towards the armory. The *Venganto* started its dive. In the narrow path between the main camp and the armory, Viekko's ability to maneuver was limited by domed structures on either side. He sprinted as hard as he could for the trees.

He replaced his spent guns into his holsters and pressed harder. His muscles burned but his mind was sharp. Sharper than it had been in a long time. He watched the *Venganto* starting its decent just beyond the tree line. It would fry them both in an instant and there wasn't much he could do to stop it. At least, nothing that wasn't totally insane.

Viekko reached the nearest tree, and pushed hard as the momentum carried up the side. The light of Rhea shone through the leaves along with a shadow moving just above him. He closed his eyes and raised his fist as he broke through the canopy. Even he was surprised when it made contact with something rough and metallic. Two glowing red eyes flashed in front of him before it tumbled into the darkness of the forest below and him along with it.

"Get in! Get in! Hurry!" yelled Althea.

Cronus jumped into the passenger side and looked up. "Althea! One coming in. On top of us! Must go, must go!"

Althea gunned the left engine and spun the craft around so fast that they both had to hold tight to keep from being thrown from their seats. When they were facing in the direction of the armory, she opened the throttle as far as it would go.

Cronus tried to catch his breath. "Too close. Much too close."

Althea focused on the path ahead. "Where's Viekko?"

Cronus turned and perched on his seat. "He ran up the trees again. Althea, what are those flying things?"

"That's the *Venganto*. Avenging angels for the City," yelled Althea over the roar of the hovercraft.

"Viekko just punched one in the face."

"Any more of them?" asked Althea, ignoring that particular bit of information. Her psyche would need a less stressful time to deal with that image.

Cronus spun around and sat down. "Two more coming in! Two more, right behind us!"

"Calm down!" yelled Althea. "Viekko! Viekko! We're almost there. Two more behind us!"

Cronus peeked over his shoulder. "Uh...Althea? They are getting closer."

"Viekko? Viekko!" screamed Althea.

Isra's voice responded on the radio instead. "I see them."

Isra stood in the door of the armory and unloaded her assault rifle into the air. Althea jerked the controls to the left and killed the engine. The loader careened broadside towards the wall of the shelter. Off-world structures were built to handle thirty-meter-per-second windstorms on Mars, 100 millimeter-per-hour torrential rainstorms on Europa and, theoretically, even the fallout of a cryo-volcano. Althea hoped they conducted a crash test as well.

The hovercraft slammed into the side of the building hard enough to leave a dent and threw Althea into Cronus's lap. She picked herself up, pulled Cronus from his seat and ran for the door.

Isra reloaded as the two *Venganto* got close to the shelter. She fired several rounds and caused one to veer off while the other made the mistake of pulling straight up. Isra aimed for the chest and fired until it tumbled into the trees.

Althea pulled Cronus through the door and crouched for cover on the other side.

"Any more of them?" asked Althea.

Isra continued to scan the skies. "Got one of them. One of the others fled. Can't see any others."

"Where's Viekko?"

"I cannot see him...oh wait. There he is. And he's... oh no." said Isra.

"What's wrong?"

"He's chasing one of those things from treetop to treetop. I think he means to catch the stupid thing."

The last few minutes were a blur. When Viekko opened his eyes, everything on the right side of his body hurt, and his hand felt like he smashed it with a hammer. He rolled over and saw the light from Rhea reflecting off the *Venganto* lying less than a meter away. It didn't stir, breathe or do anything else that would make it appear alive. The eyes were still bright red points of light and he could see now that they protruded several centimeters from the creature's face that was frozen in a snarl with long incisors bared.

Viekko rolled over and grabbed the creature's wing. It was hard and smooth, not like flesh, sinew, or bone. It was cool and artificial like plastic or some polycarbonate alloy.

He sat up to get a better look. For a moment, the creature just lay there staring at him with those glowing red eyes. Then, as if the *Venganto* had come to as well, it twisted its limb away, rolled to its feet and started running through the trees back towards the camp. Its wings swept behind it like a bird, but every other way it moved was human, if not awkward. The way it stood up and ran was not smooth or natural but looked like a person trying to work around a cumbersome piece of equipment.

Viekko groaned as he got to his feet and stumbled in the direction the thing ran. The *Venganto* ran past the last of the trees, entered the clearing, and spread its wings. Viekko sprinted forward, jumped, grabbed it by the midsection, and tackled it before it could get off the ground. The creature turned in his grip, kicked and beat him with its wings, but he just tightened his grip. The creature's struggles became faster and more desperate. It continued to kick, twist and buck. Viekko's hand slipped and found a strange protrusion just behind the head. The creature twisted again and Viekko pulled.

There was a soft click followed by a whoosh of air and Viekko pulled something away from the *Venganto's face*. He held it up for a split second in the moonlight. The creature's face was still frozen like a snarl, except there was no head behind it. Viekko realized his hand held some kind of sophisticated mask. Below him, he could make out bright blue eyes in the moonlight and a feminine face staring at him in terror.

Before Viekko could process this information, the *Venganto* pulled a leg free and kicked. The blow connected hard with a particularly tender bit of Viekko's anatomy. The world swirled into a personal Universe of pain. He curled up to lay in the mud, only aware of his own exquisite agony and screaming.

Excitement, physical activity, and pleasure all release endorphins. So does pain. It's why they are so closely linked in the human mind. Viekko managed to keep control of himself up to this point. The triple-T never even got close to overwhelming his brain; just the opposite, it made him clearer and sharper. The world slowed down to give him time to respond. Triple-T gave him an edge, so long as he could control the Rage.

Unfortunately, he had never factored a minor testicular injury into the equation.

When Viekko's world came back into focus, the pain was

gone. The biting cold of Titan was gone. Even the sound of wind blowing through the trees and the perpetual stench of petroleum and ammonia were gone. His attention condensed to the silhouette of the *Venganto* flapping its... her wings in the moonlight.

Viekko sprang up and ran toward her with a single-minded intensity. She flapped her wings and caught sky just as Viekko closed in. He ran up the side of one of the small domed shelters and jumped. He got a grip on the *Venganto's* ankle and pulled them both back down to the ground. They fell face-first into the mud and rolled several meters. Viekko lifted his head, spitting dirt, and tried to pull his prey closer. She spun around and tried to kick him with her free leg.

At first, Viekko tried to get control of the other leg, but a strong, solid boot caught him along the side of his face and he lost his grip. Then, an instant later, the *Venganto* reared back and kicked with both feet. The blow caught Viekko under the chin and sent him sprawling backward.

He blacked out for a moment and, when he came to, he sat up and spat out some more mud and a little blood. The *Venganto* was already in the air and gaining altitude quickly.

Viekko's world was wobbly but he was still oblivious to any pain. He jumped to his feet and started sprinting again. This time, he ran back along the forest and scrambled up a tree to the canopy. Once at the top, he took a flying leap and landed on a branch. The momentum carried him farther. He jumped from one tree to another using his inertia each time until his strides carried him across the treetops. His mind focused on nothing but the flapping wings just ahead.

The flying bastard hadn't picked up a lot of altitude yet. Viekko could reach her if he got within range. He lengthened his stride. He got closer to the *Venganto* and, a moment later, he kept pace with her. The line of trees came to an end up ahead so he put extra force into his last strides. When there was nothing left to jump to, Viekko threw his body out as far as he could and reached out to grab her before she was out of his reach.

Even in the heat of the Rage, he realized two things:

First, he couldn't jump far enough to grab the *Venganto*. His hand brushed along her leg as she flew by, but there was nothing to grip.

The second thing he noticed was why there was no tree ahead. The white crescent of Rhea reflected in the sub-zero water below him.

Somewhere in the distance there was a voice like the sweetest angel calling his name before he splashed into the sea.

Althea gunned the engine of the hovercraft. "What is he doing now?"

Isra watched through the electronic binoculars. "The fool is still chasing the stupid thing. He's going to fall into the Ligeia Mare if he keeps going like he is."

Althea caught a glimpse of both figures in the dim light. She pushed the hovercraft harder as Viekko got closer to his victim. Althea muttered to herself, "Don't do it. Don't do what I think you're going to do."

"He is going for it," said Isra

Althea's hand hurt as she tried to twist the throttle past its mechanical limits and she shouted out loud, "No! Viekko! Don't!"

Viekko lunged forward to grab the *Venganto*, missed and fell into the Ligeia Mare. Althea pushed all her weight into the throttle but it still wouldn't go any faster.

Isra lowered the binoculars. "We have to hurry. The water-ammonia combination on this planet is well below freezing. He will not last long out there."

Althea clenched her teeth. "The EROS suit and medical regulator will keep him alive for a few minutes."

At that temperature it was closer to a few seconds, but Althea pushed that thought from her mind.

She slowed the hovercraft over the water and stood up in the seat. Her head turned every direction in a frantic attempt to see anything in the black water. "I can't see him! It's too dark!"

Isra stood up and looked at the sea through the night vision on her rifle. "He is over there, Althea. Get close. I will use the arm to pull him out."

Althea circled the hovercraft around the body and Isra lowered the grabbing arm. It wrapped around Viekko's leg and Isra shifted the controls to pull him out of the water. Althea reached out to help get him into the hovercraft. The water-ammonia solution was so cold that just touching Viekko's wet clothes felt like needles pressing into her hands.

When they laid him across the back seats, his whole body started shaking so hard it looked like a seizure. Althea put her hand on his forehead. Corpses weren't that cold.

"Viekko! Viekko! Can you hear me?" yelled Althea.

"Alth...Alth...Althea?" said Viekko in between his chattering teeth.

"Viekko! Stay with me!"

"The...the...they're human! Althea. Vvvvenganto. Huhuhuuman."

Isra scrambled to the controls while Althea tried to keep Viekko focused on her. "It's okay, Viekko. It's going to be okay. Just try not to go to sleep."

Viekko shook harder. "H...h...uman...They...just... " Then he closed his eyes.

Isra yelled over the rising whine of the hovercraft engines. "How is he?"

Althea shouted back, "I think he's going into shock. We need to get him medical attention, fast."

CHAPTER TWENTY-SEVEN

Just as people have managed to adapt to and settle in virtually every environment on Earth, they soon found their place on alien worlds. One thousand years later, one can only imagine what those people would look like to us. Who knows what generations outside our terrestrial Eden will do to the human body and mind? Whatever the consequence, I believe the human spark can endure.

-from The Fall: The Decline and Failure of 21st Century Civilization *by Martin Raffe.*

Isra kicked the door to the armory open and, with Althea's help, carried the unconscious body of Viekko Spade inside. They laid him on the ground and Isra yelled, "Close the door. And barricade it. Before those things find out where we are."

Cronus shut the door and started fumbling the metal bar to brace it while the two women took Viekko to a wooden bench that ran along a series of metal supply lockers.

He continued to thrash as they laid him down, although his movements were weak. He moaned, "No...hu...humans. Don't..."

Althea started unbuttoning his formerly white jacket now smeared with black mud. "He's in shock. Get these wet clothes off of him. Strip him down to the EROS suit."

Isra removed his boots and socks and unbuttoned his pants. The cloth was stiff, cold, and cracked when it moved. Isra's fingers hurt just touching it.

Within minutes, he was down to the tight fitting EROS suit and the medical regulator mounted on his shoulder. All the time, Viekko continued to mumble about the *Venganto*. Althea sat back, pulled up her sleeve and activated the diagnostics on her EROS computer.

Isra stood up. "What is he saying now?"

Althea shook her head. "He's delirious. Still talking about the *Venganto*. Keeps saying that they are human.

Isra sat back to watch Althea work. "Is he going to live?"

Althea scrolled through the data and shook her head. "I don't know. The medical regulator and the EROS suit used up almost all of their power trying to keep his core temperature up. Right now, he will die without them."

"All the power?" asked Isra, tapping her own regulator. "Both devices are powered by nano-porous electrodes. They can operate for months without a replacement."

Althea shook her head. "Water at freezing temperature can kill someone in a half an hour. And the Ligeia Mare has so much ammonia and other chemicals that it's significantly below that. It needed every bit of energy just to keep his body above ninety-five degrees."

"So what do we do?" asked Isra.

Althea looked around the lab. "I need a replacement battery for the RX5. Size NB-103. Usually used to power portable industrial devices. There might be something around here."

Isra got up and walked to the equipment storage. There were guns of every shape and size on the walls, crates full of ammunition, and work tables filled with all manner of unidentifiable equipment. Isra looked around helplessly. "I do not even know where to begin."

Cronus came up beside her and pulled an electronic rifle down off the rack, the same type the guards inside the shuttle were carrying earlier. Cronus turned it over in his hand. "One never appreciates the nature of things until they stop to think about it. Complete incapacitation at a distance, no lasting harm, no long term ill effects. In terms of crowd control, nothing like it has been developed before or since. A marvel of engineering." He took it by the front and smashed it as hard as he could on the side of the work table. Isra jumped back as shards of metal, glass and plastic flew in all directions. "It's too bad that the Corporation would rather sell a thousand of them than make the batteries rechargeable," he said, picking a small donut-shaped device out of the remains.

He brought the battery to Althea who ejected the spent one from the medical regulator. She put the new one in its place and sat back on her heels. There was a small, high-pitched whine from the device, then it went silent and Viekko went completely still.

Althea felt for a pulse, "Need to wait for the system to boot up. His core temperature is still in the toilet. Hopefully he doesn't suffer permanent damage.

"Will he live?" asked Isra.

Althea leaned back. "He's just passed out. We won't know until he comes out of this."

Viekko was Althea's problem now; time to move on to the next issue. Among the guns mounted on the wall were several knives of varying size and intimidation qualities. Isra selected something large and nasty-looking.

While that little saboteur Cronus watched Althea and beamed over his minor contribution, Isra spun him around and held the knife to his throat. "While we wait, perhaps we could discuss what you are doing back here."

"Isra..." Althea started.

"Please stay out of this, Althea. You deal with your patient, I will deal with mine. Once again, Cronus. What are you doing here?"

Cronus tried to look down at the knife pressing against his neck. He held his breath as if it would keep the blade from slicing it open. "I suppose this isn't another diversion, is it?"

Isra flicked her wrist. A dot of blood appeared. "It is not.

I need answers now and the knife should persuade you to be both honest and, most importantly, quick."

Cronus took a long, deep breath. "I...I had an idea. I know how you can stop the war. If you kill me, you will never figure it out. I came back to help. I just wanted to help you. Please don't kill me!"

"Isra. Just listen to him for a minute," said Althea.

Isra studied Cronus's face. He was tragically inept, his train of thought was on far too steep a grade, and his priorities were manic at the best of times, but every muscle twitch in his face radiated sincerity. Or maybe a deep desire to not be bled like a pig. She let Cronus go and paced around the armory for a few moments to set her own mind right.

Finally, and as much for effect as anything else, she jabbed the knife hard into a wooden work table. "Okay, Cronus. I will listen to what you have to say."

Cronus gulped. "Okay, it's like this. The people on this planet, they worship the corporation. Well, not *the* Corporation, but a corporation. But see, the corporation has become the Corporation. So what we do is we get the head of the Corporation to speak to them as the head of the corporation. The two sides see that their corporation is now the Corporation and maybe they work together for the good will of the Corporation."

Isra and Althea sat blinking in a sort of bewildered silence. Isra pulled the knife from the workbench. "That is it. I am killing him."

"No, no, wait," said Althea. "I think it's a bit brilliant in a way."

Isra blinked, glancing from Althea to Cronus. "Then clearly you heard something that I did not."

Althea leaned back. "This planet has developed a kind of bizarre cult around the old Transplanetary Energy Corporation, yes? So we use that. The people will surely listen if the *Kompanio* tells them to stop the war."

Isra threw the knife away. "Well, that is all well and good in theory, but these people are not stupid. We have no credibility left with the Houston or Halifaco. They have no reason to listen to us anymore."

Cronus relaxed just enough to breathe normally, "The *Kompanio* have contacted the City before. The giant screen in the city center. The screens at the spaceport. There was a time when this colony was in constant contact with Earth. All we need to do is re-establish that connection through the old channels."

Isra paused a moment. He was right. He was a pedantic little turd, but he was right. She imagined screens all over the city lighting up for the first time in a millennia. If that sight didn't inspire awe and pause in the city, then it was a lost cause.

Viekko's medical regulator finished rebooting and Althea replaced the reader into the port and checked the readout. "He's fine for now. The medical regulator will keep his blood moving, but just barely. It will take some time for his core temperature to get back to normal. And I gave him some medication to mitigate any organ damage but he's going to be out for a while."

Isra looked down and shook her head. "Damn it, Viekko. What could have possessed him to do something like this?"

Althea went to grab something in her medical bag and then stopped. Every part of her face showed shock and fear. Whatever she found, she wouldn't pull it out and she avoided looking Isra in the face.

Isra knelt down beside her. "Althea, what is wrong?"

Althea shook her head still avoiding Isra's gaze. "Nothing...it's nothing."

Isra's gaze hardened. "Althea..."

The medic sighed and pulled her hand from her bag with something clenched in her fist. She opened it up to show Isra five shiny blue capsules.

Isra examined them for a moment. "What exactly are those?"

Althea gulped and breathed hard to try and keep from breaking down. "Trihydroxide. Thiosulfate. Tretraoxide."

Nobody said anything for several minutes. Those three words had been repeated over and over across all parts of the Neuvonet so often that the chemical names were no longer a term reserved for those with specialized knowledge. It was a household name associated with horrible, senseless atrocities committed on all corners of the Earth. Murder, rape, suicide; violent crime of all kinds had been on the rise over the last several years with one drug to blame.

"Triple-T!" said Cronus, looking at Viekko. "Viekko Spade is on triple-T?"

Althea nodded. This time she could not stop a few tears creeping down her face.

Isra didn't say anything at first. She wandered off to some corner of the armory. Triple-T. Viekko Spade was raged out on Triple-T and Althea not only knew about it, but facilitated it. Deep down, Isra knew it too. Maybe not the specifics, but she knew there was a secret that had the potential to leave everything she worked for smoldering in their wake.

"How long?" asked Isra, not looking at Althea. "How long have you known?"

Althea looked down at Viekko. "Since that first day when he started lapsing into a dissociative state. I suspected something immediately but couldn't prove it until—"

Althea kept talking but Isra didn't hear her. At that moment, Isra realized she didn't care what Althea was about to say. Althea, Viekko, Cronus—they were all operating according to their own whims and, as a result, her mission was completely tanked. She felt a surge of anger rush through her and, instead of repressing it, she decided to let it work for her.

While Althea was still talking, Isra grabbed a tool chest and threw it to the ground. Equipment and supplies spilled across the floor with a crash. She grabbed an upright supply chest and slammed it to the floor. A whole rack of tools next. After that, things were just a blur of destruction. Every piece of equipment smashed to bits just drove her on. There was something liberating about letting go and letting her emotions take over. But she soon ran out of objects in her immediate vicinity to destroy. She took a few deep breaths to collect herself. Althea and Cronus were staring at her as if she'd completely lost her sense. That was good because there was a fair chance that she had.

She grabbed a chair and pulled it over to Cronus. He backed up against the wall, putting as much distance between her and him as possible.

Isra sat down, put her head in her hands and muttered for a few seconds, then looked up at Cronus and said, "You have no idea how sad this statement makes me, but you are the only human I can trust on this moon."

Cronus's mouth gaped open.

Isra shook her head. "Do not get excited; my options are poor at best. But before we go any farther: truth time. Right here, right now. Convince me that this plan of yours can work. How are we supposed to activate the screens? I doubt very much that we can just set up a signal here and be done with it."

Cronus kept his back pinned against the wall. "You would be correct. The Transplanetary Energy Corporation was extremely concerned about outside interference. You need the right modulation. A code in the waves. Fortunately, people are creatures of habit. The modulation the Corporation uses is similar. It will only require a minor alteration for the system to accept it as genuine."

"And how does that help us?" said Isra slowly. She had a feeling she wasn't going to like the answer.

"The same way I hid information aboard *Innovation*. I take control of their relay station and use it to rebroadcast."

Isra tensed. "You mean the same way Laban got his hands on the refinery plans in the first place. What's to keep him from finding out what we are doing?"

Cronus's face twisted in thought. "He won't be expecting it. He is not tuned to the Signal. We can move like shadows through the data."

Isra got up and paced. "It is not good, but it is a start. So what do we need for that to happen? Can we find the needed equipment here?"

Cronus looked at his shoes. "That's where the plan gets

complicated. I will need to be in the pyramid to route the signal to the proper sources. It will take time and I will need to remain undisturbed."

Isra clenched her teeth. "And not easy with the Houston's army patrolling the city looking for anything threatening. To say nothing of the *Venganto*. We will die six times before we get anywhere near the city."

Althea stood. "Those screens in the city are ancient, installed before the Fall over a thousand years ago. How do you know they will even work?"

Cronus's eyes flashed back and forth between the two women and he kept his back to the wall. "The screens in the city are fine. Graphene-based alloys with sub-molecular transistors built into the material itself. Their durability made them a popular choice when Earth civilization expanded to the planets and moons. Most will still work so long as they have power. That will be the difficult part. The power systems in the city are a disaster."

Isra raised her head. "Disaster? How so? Can it be fixed?"

Cronus glanced at Althea. "Some paths are better than others. We must route the power through a specific path. There's a substation not far and some energy left in various capacitors around the city. They are unused at the moment, but I can reroute it as I need to."

Isra looked at her team, or what remained of it. It would be a challenge to complete Cronus's tasks if everyone was at peak performance. Exhausted and one person down, it struck Isra as impossible. She shook her head. "Not going to happen. We would never even get into the city much less the pyramid and we could not hold it if we did. There has got to be another way to get the message into the cities."

Cronus closed his eyes in thought, but the answer came from the other direction.

"Halifaco," said Althea. "He's the only person left on the planet who's got enough people. He could draw out the Houston's army long enough for us to do what Cronus wants."

Isra stood. "I do not know if he will help us. But he still has a radio. We could ask."

Cronus pulled up the sleeve and started tapping on the screen. "Halifaco. Halifaco, this is Cronus. If you can hear me, respond. It is an emergency."

Isra paced as she watched Cronus. "Not picking up?"

Cronus looked down at the screen. "He is not. And no signal on the satellite locator. He either can't hear us or does not wish to be found."

"The derelict," said Althea. "It's a fair bet he would go there and, even if he didn't, someone there might know where he is. Besides, we need the *Perfiduloi*, not Halifaco per se. That is where the center of their society is."

Isra sat back in a chair and shook her head. "There is sixty kilos of jungle and flying death from above between us and him. How do we get there?"

The room fell silent as the realization of what was in between them and Halifaco's derelict ship sunk into their minds.

Cronus was the first to speak. "Viekko said the *Venganto* were human."

Althea shook her head. "He was delirious. Who knows why he was saying that."

"But let's assume that he saw something that proves that. It is the most logical explanation after all," said Cronus. "What is the alternative? That some alien race was either found or developed here that has the ability to fly, spit fire, and see in the dark?"

"But how could they be human?" asked Althea. "If you could fly by just strapping wings to your arms and flapping away, we'd not need to develop the machines to carry us through the sky."

Cronus started to answer but Isra cut in. "You cannot on Earth, but on Titan..."

Cronus beamed like a teacher whose students just grasped an important concept. "Exactly right. Titan has lower gravity, a thicker atmosphere, and more oxygen for strenuous activity. Humans cannot fly under their own

301

power on Earth. But Titan is different for many reasons."

Isra sat down and squinted at Cronus, "Okay, so how does that help us?"

"If they are human, then they are using technology to accomplish their superhuman feats. Technology can be exploited. For example..." Cronus got up and went to the work bench. He found a gun about as long as his arms and designed to fire some sort of large cartridge. "Night vision can be easily compromised by sudden, bright lights. They cannot compensate as well as the human eye."

Isra got up and took the gun from Cronus, "A flare gun?"

"It should be enough," said Cronus matter-of-factly. "It will disorient them and make us harder to track."

"What if you're wrong?" asked Althea. "What if they are using something else or have some innate ability to see in the dark?"

Isra loaded a flare cartridge into the chamber. "Only one way to find out."

She crept to the door of the shelter and opened it a crack. There were four *Venganto* circling overhead, possibly waiting for some helpless person to try and escape. She stepped out into the open and, sure enough, the flying creatures stopped their slow circle and started to converge on her position.

She aimed the flare gun into the air and fired. The cartridge flew high into the air where it burst into a brilliant white light. For a couple seconds the sky was so bright, she could clearly make out the bark on the trees and the footprints in the mud. Isra had to look away from the blast itself.

When the sky was dark again, the *Venganto* were nowhere to be seen.

Isra went back into the armory, "Grab all the cartridges you can and find some way to carry Viekko. If this is going to work, we have got to move while we have the chance."

CHAPTER TWENTY-EIGHT

The Alliances that allowed the governments of Earth to beat back the encroaching Corporate armies dissolved in a few years. New friendships gave way to ancient hatreds and hundreds of wars over the smoldering ruins of Earth were fought. A battered and desperate Corporation found new hope for life. Deals could be made. Allies could be turned on each other.

One by one formerly independent territories were brought to heel, not with bullets and bombs, but with one backroom deal after another.

-from The Fall: The Decline and Failure of 21st Century Civilization *by Martin Raffe.*

Isra crouched behind a fallen tree just at the edge of the clearing that contained the derelict ship the *Perfiduloi* used as a base. Her hands sweated around the grip of the assault rifle she carried. The duffle bag and flare gun slung over her shoulder made muscles in her back ache. Overhead, shadows of the *Venganto* streaked across the sky lit by the small icy moons and the ringed gas giant. Every few seconds, one of the *Venganto* dove towards the ship and let a bomb fly. The bombs burst, spilling fire on the hull of the ship or on the ground, but did no real damage. Still, they had a clear effect. Those holed up inside were now a besieged army.

Cronus squatted in the mud just a few meters away and watched the skies with Isra. Althea, carrying Viekko on a makeshift A-frame stretcher, lagged behind. She stopped in a dark patch of forest, set Viekko down, and whispered, "Even in microgravity he's bloody heavy. How does it look?"

"Not good," said Cronus. "*Venganto* watch every move. Every step. And out in the open, we don't stand a chance. Run, flash, fire, burn, die. That's it."

Isra set the assault rifle against the log and pulled the flare gun from her shoulder and cracked open the chamber. "One flare left."

"Will that be enough?" asked Cronus. "The duration of the average flare is 15.5 seconds. In that time we will need to cross the field get to the ship—"

Isra closed the flare gun. "And hope that there is somebody inside who has the slightest inclination to let us in. Considering that, sooner would be better. Are you ready?"

Cronus stood up and braced himself against the log as if he were intending to vault over it in the most awkward way possible. "Ready."

Althea steeled herself and picked up the end of Viekko's stretcher again. "As am I."

Isra adjusted the bag on her back and raised the flare gun. It was better to go now. Less time for Althea and Cronus to dwell on the possibility that they will get stuck in the field or outside the ship with no means of escaping.

She pulled the trigger. The last cartridge flew and, a couple seconds later, bathed the field in a brilliant white light.

Isra dropped the flare gun and picked up the assault rifle. "Go! Run now!"

Isra vaulted over the fallen log and sprinted across the empty field. She didn't look back at Althea or Cronus but kept her mind focused on the ruined, ancient spacecraft. As she got closer, she could see a door and she doubled her efforts to reach it. The low gravity combined with her desperation allowed her to clear the distance in a matter of seconds but, by the time she got to the door, the light had started to flicker.

She ran full force into the hatch, banging on the metal and screaming with every breath left in her, "Open up! *Malfermita! Dangero! Dangero! Ni en!* Let us in!"

Just as quickly as it appeared, the light died. Isra risked a look behind her. Althea was close with Viekko's stretcher bouncing on the uneven ground so much it was a minor miracle he wasn't thrown. Cronus was just behind her stumbling and falling with every other step.

The skies were clear but that would be short-lived. Isra resumed banging on the ancient airlock. "*Ni en! Ni en!* Somebody let us in!"

Fear swept across Isra's consciousness. Nobody was here. Or, at least, nobody would let them in. Her mind started racing to figure out how they could escape before the *Venganto* recovered and descended. Then she heard the scrape of metal on metal as somebody on the other side started opening the door.

Overhead, the first shadows of the *Venganto* appeared. They were close; so close that Isra saw the red light in their eyes. She raised the assault rifle and held down the trigger. It erupted in full-automatic, spraying bullets into the sky.

The door opened just as Althea and Cronus rushed past her and into the safety of the derelict. She continued to fire into the air to buy a few more seconds.

Whoever opened the door screamed words in his native language, "*Get in, you will kill us all!*"

As the last bullets fired, there was a sharp burst and a flash of heat. A fire bomb exploded on the hull just a couple meters from where she stood. Isra turned and leapt through the open door. The *Perfiduloi* man slammed it shut as more bombs hit the hull and the hatch.

Isra dropped the bag of weapons, leaned hard against the wall, and slid to the floor, taking the precious few moments to catch her breath. For a few seconds, all anyone did was sit on the floor and collect themselves and listen to the bombs against the hull. Even the man who opened the door for them just stood staring off into space.

The moment of peace ended with heavy footsteps on the metal floor. Isra stood up just as Halifaco appeared around a corner. He was accompanied now by a whole cadre of *Perfiduloi* warriors carrying Marine assault rifles and an air of cool death. Somehow, against all logic, it looked like he had aged a few years in the hours since Isra had last seen him. At the same time, his face and every muscle had a new intensity. Isra pictured him as a human ballistic missile; unstoppable until he reached his target where he would obliterate everyone including himself.

When he spoke, his voice was monotone and dispassionate. "Why have you returned?"

Isra brushed herself off and adjusted her posture. She spoke his Titanian language. "*Halifaco. This thing you plan to do, you need to stop. We can save you and your people, but we will need your help.*"

The Perfiduloi around him laughed softly, but Halifaco didn't even raise an eyebrow, "*You help? My people are about to save themselves. Even as we speak, Perfiduloi gather here for the final battle. We will crush the Urbanoi.*"

"*Please,*" Isra pled in his language, "*You must listen—*"

Halifaco cut her off, "*I have listened to outsiders. It has done nothing but lead my people to death. I will not listen again. You have wasted your time coming here.*" Halifaco noticed Viekko laying on the ground and spoke in English. "What is wrong with him?"

Althea stood up. "He was hurt fighting the *Venganto*. He needs a place to lay down. Can we bring him somewhere?"

The *Perfiduloi* leader sighed. "Come with me."

Halifaco led them through the tight corridors of the derelict until they arrived in a dark, open space. Judging from the layout and remains, Isra guessed this to be the ship's med bay appropriately enough. There were three tables side-by-side in the center of the room. Each table had metal loops for straps although those had long since either rotted away or been removed. Metal shelves and cabinets lined the walls but all of them were empty. The only light came from a couple of wooden torches soaked in Titan's hydrocarbon mixture.

There were a few Perfiduloi in the room sitting on the tables. They sharpened stone knives and spearpoints, chatted or stitched their own wounds. They got up to make way as Althea and Isra brought Viekko in and set him on a table.

Althea place her bag at Viekko's feet. "I'll need some more light to work."

Cronus rooted around in his bag and produced a small white dome. He touched it and it glowed bright enough that they all squinted at the light. He held it up over Viekko, let go and it stayed suspended just above him.

While Althea began her work, Isra set the bag of weapons on a table and went back to stand near Halifaco. He stood watching with the same resolute expression he had when he entered the hallway. Isra started to wonder why he hadn't just tossed them back out the door or let them stay but left them to their own business. Why did he feel the need to be here himself?

Then Isra caught something in the way Halifaco watched Althea work on Viekko. It was subtle but it was there. Respect, maybe. Admiration. Maybe a touch of longing.

"What do you plan to do?" asked Isra eventually.

Halifaco breathed hard. "We have but one path open to us now. The *Venganto* will not stop until every one of my people are killed or enslaved. The power of the *Urbanoi* and the demons lies in the pyramid. I must lead my people into the final battle to destroy it."

Cronus nearly fell over himself scurrying over. "You... you can't. You don't know what you are doing. The last records of The Fall... the voices of the past. There will be nothing left..."

Halifaco regarded the hacker for a moment, "*Kompanio* demands it. I see that now. It is the only way to free my people."

"Your people will die," said Isra.

"*Then we will die free,*" he said with his voice raising in

307

his native language, *"All of us here are prepared. We will finally join our ancestors on Earth, not as slaves but as free men and women."*

The armed militia standing around the room raised their weapons in a salute and shouted 'Al la morto!' which Isra translated as 'To the Death.'

"There is another way," said Isra. "We can show you how to fight the *Venganto* without destroying the rest of your people."

There was a slight twitch in Halifaco's eye, but he persisted. "I have listened to outsiders enough. The *Venganto* are immortal. This is the only way to defeat them."

"And yet," said Isra with a sly tone in her voice, "You call the *Venganto* demons. The *Urbanoi* call them avenging angels of the *Kompanio*. They clearly have an agenda. Strange that it seems to be the same as the Houston's."

Viekko groaned and stirred on the table.

Halifaco indicated Viekko. "When he is better, it is best you go. Go back where you came from and leave us in peace."

He turned to leave but Isra chased him, "What if I were to tell you that there is nothing powerful or special about the *Venganto*? They are people like you, under the control of the Houston. They enforce his will."

Halifaco stopped and turned, "What you say cannot be true. The *Venganto* use the skies. They rain fire on their enemies."

"Only because they use technology that you have forgotten. Technology they have preserved since the time of the *Kompanio*, but they are just people."

Halifaco stepped close. So close that Isra looked up his nose. He made a fist as if he might try to hit her. "I have heard enough of these things. My mind is made up. It is best if you leave before the battle."

Halifaco turned again to leave and this time Isra let him go.

From the direction of the table, Viekko's deep voice

slurred, "She's right you know."

Halifaco looked in shock at the table where Viekko still laid. In truth, Isra was surprised as well.

Viekko started to sit up with Althea's help.

"Careful, Viekko," she said, taking his arm to steady him. "You've been out for the last several hours."

Viekko rubbed his head. "Did I miss anything?" He took a moment to take in his surroundings and added, "Where in hell am I?"

"We took you to the *Perfiduloi* lair," said Isra.

"Ah...well then hell was a lucky guess wasn't it?" mumbled Viekko. "What're we doing here?"

Isra glanced back at Halifaco, "Trying to convince him that the *Venganto* are just people like them."

Halifaco ranted in his own language, "*You will not lead us away from the Kompanio. Our path is clear. Leave us.*"

Before Isra could translate Viekko added, "Just going to take that as a 'not too well'. Am I right?"

Isra nodded. "Perceptive. Any ideas?"

Viekko got to his feet with some effort. Althea helped steady him and kept him from falling. Even standing upright, he was still disoriented and bewildered. Then he patted himself, down feeling his jacket. "My guns, where are they?"

Isra motioned to the duffle bag she carried from the armory. Althea held him while he staggered toward it. He steadied himself on the edge, opened the bag, and searched until he produced two pistols and holstered them. "Okay... where is the door?"

Isra pointed the way and Viekko, still wobbling, staggered back out into the hallway. He wandered down the halls at Isra's direction. To her barely concealed amusement, Halifaco and a group of his people followed with weapons in hand. It had to be out of sheer curiosity. Isra had to admit she admired that about Viekko. He had a certain audacity and a reckless spirit that drew people to him if only to see what might happen next.

They came to the door and Viekko leaned his head

against the metal. It was quieter now although the occasional burst shook the room and caused rust to flake off the ceiling. Satisfied that there must be something still out there, he tried the door. He strained at the wheel that would draw the steel bolts back but he didn't have the strength yet.

He took a step back, annoyed. "Little help here?"

Two *Perfiduloi* warriors went to the door and turned the wheel to unlock the thick steel door. Viekko pushed it to the side and peered out into the dark gloom. He unholstered his gun and waited.

"What is he doing?" hissed Halifaco in his own language and craning his neck to see better.

Isra smiled slightly, "Proving to you that they are just people."

As Halifaco watched Viekko hanging out the door, his expression remained passive but the tension and the sweat forming on his face showed Isra that it was an act. The leader swallowed and and spat at Viekko in English, "The *Venganto* are invincible. You will do nothing but make things worse for us."

There was a burst by the door, so close that Isra could feel the heat, but Viekko stood still. "Aren't you already set to go out and die? I fail to see how this can possibly make the situation worse."

For a moment, Halifaco looked like he was ready to bolt over to where Viekko stood and do something drastic to stop him, but he didn't. Isra could feel the conflict in his mind. The intense belief she saw earlier collided head-on with everything he knew to be true and, until one or the other gave, it paralyzed him.

Viekko took a deep breath and held it for a few seconds. There was another burst by the door and Viekko fired a single shot. Everyone standing in the hallway held their breath until something hard clanged on the steel hull. Viekko holstered his gun and disappeared into the dark. He returned dragging a *Venganto* by the arms.

The anger that rose from the assembled *Perfiduloi* was matched only with the confusion as to what they were seeing. It was right there in front of them, an immortal being limp as a puppet without strings. Blood seeped through a wound in the chest and left a trail across the floor where Viekko dragged it.

He knelt down beside the creature, gripped the mask and pulled. Isra smiled at the collective gasp. It was a young man with the round face and short, curly hair reminiscent of the *Urbanoi*.

Word got around fast and more *Perfiduloi* came running in to see what he noise was about. Viekko stood up to watch the crowd's reaction. "So...are we good? Put that to rest then?"

Isra took her seat in the great hall while Viekko hauled the dead *Venganto* in front of Halifaco and dumped the body on a table. *Perfiduloi* emerged from all directions to see the aberration laid bare in front of them. As they did, they all argued at once about what it could mean. There was too much crosstalk in native language for Isra to pick up any one argument over another, but Halifaco somehow took it all in. He sat motionless and resolute like the last beacon of law and order.

Althea and Cronus sat on one side of Isra. She could hear their fear in their silence and feel the tension in their nervous movements; Althea pulling her long red hair over her shoulders and Cronus fidgeting with the wiry metal glove wrapped around his arm.

"There used to be others," said Viekko, sitting down on Isra's other side.

Viekko referred to the empty chairs on either side of Halifaco. Isra sensed a power vacuum within the *Perfiduloi* society. It tugged on her mind in the same way it must tug on the minds of other ambitious members of this culture. The way Halifaco sat with his back straight, his shoulders back and his arms spread across the table with his hands resting on the adjacent space broadcast his intent to fill it himself without any help from potential upstarts in the room.

"How many people were there?" asked Isra. "And do you know what happened to them?"

"Five. And my guess is Halifaco went and made them obsolete. Possibly even biologically."

"What's happens now?" asked Althea.

"It's hard to say," said Viekko, watching the crowd pressing around the table and the dead *Venganto*. "Don't believe there is a history of this. It's all up to Halifaco and he's got murder in his eye. Ain't nothing gonna satisfy him until this whole planet burns down."

The crowd around the *Venganto* continued to chatter until Halifaco had heard enough. He raised his right hand, a simple gesture that had everyone in the room heading for a seat at one of the tables spanning the room.

Viekko leaned over again. "Last time I was here, this room was packed. Now look at them, ain't hardly nobody left."

That was an exaggeration, thought Isra, but even a generous estimate would put this room at about half-full.

Halifaco gestured to the crowd of *Perfiduloi* in the room. "Many have died since your arrival and the arrival of the other Outsiders. This is our last, best chance to raise an attack. After this, there will not be enough of us."

Isra stood to address Halifaco. "Please...if you will allow me to explain."

"However," Halifaco added holding his hand up, "You have brought us proof that the Houston and the *Urbanoi* have used our faith and love of the *Kompanio* to keep us subject to their will. And, for that, we will all hear what you propose."

Isra dropped her head in a slight bow. "Thank you. If you will permit me, my associate here can better illustrate our plan."

She motioned to Cronus who hopped out of his chair and sidled over to the table where the *Venganto* lay dead. He set one of his little black disks next to the body and performed a complex series of motions with the device wrapped around his arm. The disk activated and lights swirled around the room. Even though this wasn't the first time these people had seen such a spectacle, the whole room still gasped in amazement.

The lights swirled around for a while until they condensed into an image of the land in-between the two Titanian seas.

Isra began, "This plan requires exquisite timing. Besides the *Venganto* who will make movement outside the city dangerous, there are soldiers inside the city that must be dealt with in order for us to accomplish our goal. We require the *Perfiduloi*'s help in two areas.

The map zoomed in to the center of the city focusing on the courtyard and the pyramid, "First we need to get inside the city without being noticed. From there, we will proceed to the center of the city and retake the pyramid. Cronus will have free reign of their computer system once again. With what he has learned, he will be able to use it to draw the *Venganto* away from this place. However, the soldiers in the city will still be a problem for us. We need you and your people to rally a force and create a distraction at the city walls."

Halifaco sat and listened with mild interest. When Isra was done, he motioned to the map, "Do you intend for our people to run against the city walls again. We have not the numbers anymore nor any weapons."

Viekko jumped up from the bench and yelled, "Don't give me that. I know for a fact you folk are loaded to the gills with guns you took off the other Outsiders."

Isra shot Viekko a glare. He adjusted his jacket and sat back down hard.

"It is not enough," Halifaco added. "They have more guns and more people. It would be suicide."

Isra had to admit this stumped her. How could she ask these people to attack the city again? Especially an attack that was only meant as a distraction. More would die but would they see any value in their sacrifice?

"How exactly were you going to destroy the pyramid?"

313

asked Viekko. Then he looked at Isra with a smug look. "Sorry, did I speak out of turn again?"

Halifaco responded coolly, "We found a way."

The cryptic and evasive nature of Halifaco's answer was not like him. He was an audacious man. The type who assigned as much value to his mistakes as he did to his triumphs. For him to waver on this issue, it had to be something so bold and dangerous that even he was not sure of himself.

Isra fixed a look on him and said, "What did you find?"

Halifaco waved his hand in a dismissive gesture. "It is something we recovered after the first battle. We intended to keep it a secret until all the Outsiders left."

"Show me," said Isra.

The *Perfiduloi* leader paused again as if weighing the ramifications and then gestured to the crowd. A few soldiers hurried out while the rest waited in muted anticipation. Not for what would come through the door, Isra sensed, but for how the team and she in particular would react.

Two doors at the other end of the room opened and the last railgun was wheeled into the room.

Viekko jumped up, rattling the table as he did. "The rail gun? The *khoyor mogoin khuked* rail gun? You must be out of your mind if—"

"That is acceptable," said Isra coldly.

"Isra, do you have any idea what that thing can do—"

"It is acceptable," Isra repeated firmly. "If they are willing to put their people at risk again for us, they will need a show of power."

Viekko growled, "Isra, if you let them keep that *kharaasan* gun, there ain't gonna be nothin' left of this rock 'cept a smoldering hole."

Isra addressed Halifaco. "That is why, after this is over, we will insist that this gun be returned to us so it can be destroyed. Is that clear?"

Halifaco sat forward in his chair. "You will not tell us what to do with it. We recovered it—"

"And it's only a matter of time before the *Urbanoi*

314

recover it from you. That is, unless you intend to keep it locked up forever, but how much good will it do you then?"

Halifaco sat back, considering this. "How long will we be required to keep the *Urbanoi* occupied?"

"Ten minutes, max," said Isra.

"What happens then?"

Isra let a small, sly smile break across her face. "If all goes well, you will be able to see a message from the *Kompanio* itself."

Halifaco thought on this for a moment before he stood to address his people. With sweeping gestures and a grand speech in the native language, he filled the crowd in on the proceedings. When he reached the word '*Kompanio*', the room erupted in gasps and yelling. Isra stood serenely as Halifaco raised his hand to command order again. This time it took more than a few seconds.

"*What trick is this?*" one of the *Perfiduloi* soldiers hissed in Titanian.

"*No trick*," said Isra, responding in the same language. "*The Kompanio has yearned to speak to its people for a long time; the Houston has managed to prevent it. If you can distract the City soldiers long enough, we can change that.*"

More debate and more yelling in Titanian. Isra felt an energy in the room like something powerful contained in a vessel too small. Halifaco stood resolute leaning slightly on the table in front of him, but the way his eyes darted back and forth and the way he clenched and unclenched his hands revealed a measure of anxiety. He was worried about being able to control the crowd if this did not go as planned.

"Very well," said Halifaco eventually. "We will consent to those who want to go. We are trusting you for the last time. But know this, if I get the hint that things are not going as planned, I will order my people to breach the city walls and I will destroy the pyramid myself."

Isra bowed again. "That is fair."

Althea stood up. "But how? We cannot leave this place for all the *Venganto* waiting to attack. How will you even get there?"

Halifaco smiled and paced behind the table, "There are tunnels. They lead into the forest. They provide a way for our people to escape the *Urbanoi* and their slave chains. But the entrance to them is far away. It will be difficult to reach them from here without being spotted."

"What the hell good does that do?" asked Viekko, leaning his chair back. "Gettin' halfway don't help none. How are we going to get to the city?"

Somewhere in the distance, a mammoth bellowed. Halifaco's face spread into a mischievous grin. "We have ways."

CHAPTER TWENTY-NINE

It is possible that Earth Civilization could have survived the Global Revolution. By this time, the great megacities were ruins and war, famine, disease, and a host of other atrocities left smaller cities all but abandoned.

But a second storm was brewing, one that would sweep away any remains of the greatest civilization humans had ever assembled.

-from The Fall: The Decline and Failure of 21st Century Civilization *by Martin Raffe.*

Viekko squatted in the mud and looked through the scope of the assault rifle. A few *Venganto* shot across the moonlit sky, but they didn't stop or show any signs of interest in the people crawling out of the tunnel among the mammoths.

"I don't believe it," said Viekko, lowering his gun. "It's like they can't see us."

Nearby, Cronus climbed a muddy embankment. "Of course they cannot see us," he said with an angry, harsh tone. "Just because there is no light we can see, does not mean there is no light. They use the light from all living things to see. But many things live. Not just us but—"

Cronus was cut off when the ground underneath him

317

gave way and he slid into a pile of something unspeakable. "Let me be clear, that does not mean I endorse this plan!"

Viekko turned his attention back to the sky. "What the hell is he babbling about?"

Althea ran her hands down the side of one of the mammoths. "Body heat," she said. "The *Venganto* must have some means of using infrared radiation as night vision." She stopped and shook her head. "These mammoths are sick. They are so thin and they seem to have some form of diarrhea."

Viekko had noticed the ground around the mammoths was squishier than anywhere else on the moon and the powerful odor could be the other reason the *Venganto* were keeping their distance. Any breath too deep brought a tear to his eye.

It also didn't take a lot of imagination to guess at why. The Titanian ecosystem was failing and, with the destruction of the refineries, was on a death spiral. Against the moonlight the leaves hung like wilted flower petals. The brush under his feet crackled with every step.

Halifaco surveyed the *Perfiduloi* army hiding between the mammoths. Behind him, ten soldiers pushed the railgun through the sludge.

"How close are we?" asked Viekko.

Halifaco walked up to him in slow, easy strides. "That should be the last of them."

Viekko slung the rifle over his shoulder. "About damn time. So what happens now? Are we just here to wade through the mammoth *baas* or have we got a plan?"

"The horn from the city goes off at regular intervals," said Halifaco. "Then the herd moves to a new location. It will stop near the river where my men can show you to a place where water from the city drains. My people will stay with the herd. They will travel close to the city next."

Viekko adjusted his hat. "Oh thank the gods. And here I was worried that I wouldn't get to stomp through more *omkhii baas*."

Althea stepped beside Viekko. "That will be fine. Once

we are in the tunnels we can find our way, right Cronus?"

Cronus extricated himself from the pile and looked down at his EROS suit. "My files contain a thorough explanation of the city systems. Much has changed in the many years, but it should be enough to get us close. Though I fear I may never smell the same again."

Viekko shielded his nose. "I smelled you coming off the shuttle, Cronus. I can't say this is appreciably worse."

Althea shushed the both of them and cocked her head. Somewhere in the distance, the horn blew from the city. Just as a flock of birds moves as one, the mammoths all started walking together. The team kept close together in the dark to keep from falling beneath one of the gigantic feet. Above, the *Venganto* continued their patrol oblivious to the army moving beneath them.

Viekko waved goodbye to the *Perfiduloi* soldiers as they darted back into the forest for the safety of the mammoth herd a few meters away. The light from Saturn's many moons provided enough to cast shadow, but the whole area was bathed in a dense fog rising from the running water.

Viekko shouldered his rifle and took a quick look at the sky. "We're clear for now, but I don't like the idea of bein' out here in the open. Cronus, got a lock on that sewer entrance?"

Cronus pulled up his sleeve. "Just a few meters ahead. And I have found a path that should lead us to the pyramid."

"Great," said Viekko, sliding down an icy embankment. He hit the ground next to the river and stumbled, and the world spun around him.

Althea dropped beside him. "Are you okay, Viekko?"

Viekko coughed. "My stomach feels like it's in free fall and I think I can feel my toe rattling around in my boot."

Althea stopped him and made him look her in the eye. "Anything else?"

Viekko wanted to push her away and he did in the gentlest, most polite way possible. "We're exposed, Althea. I'll be fine, we can't stay here long."

319

Viekko helped Cronus down the embankment and they moved on. All the time, the withdrawal effects of the triple-T made itself known. His mind started to wander and it was hard to stay focused. And it was all made worse given that his body was still recovering from an overdose. It had been years since he took enough 'T to rage out and it made his brain feel like he'd just come out of a month-long bender. Nothing felt real; it was all shapes and shadows like from a dream.

They came to a block of concrete sticking out of the embankment. A slow stream ran out of a metal grate and emptied into the ammonia-laced water of the river. Viekko had to maneuver carefully to keep his feet out of the sub-zero liquid. The grate had been forgotten for an extended length of time as evidenced by the fact the metal bars were rusted all the way through in some cases. It only took a quick jerk to pull the metal away from the concrete.

Viekko knelt beside it, took a flashlight from Althea and peered inside. It was long, dark and reeked of the worst of humanity.

Viekko put the flashlight away. "Okay, Cronus, you're leading the way."

The hacker had a disgusted look on his face but he did as he was told. He disappeared into the darkness until, deep inside, there was a splash and Cronus cursed the world.

Viekko suppressed a laugh. "All right, Althea, you next."

Althea paused. "Are you sure you are up for this? You look a little...you don't look well."

Viekko shook his head to try and clear it. "I'm fine. I'll maintain. Enough to get us through this. But quicker is better so if you please—"

"Do you need a dose of triple-T?"

The words ignited a powerful hunger somewhere in Viekko's mind. He did. More than anything. He wanted to bite the shard and clear his mind. He wanted the Haze to lift and to see this horrible world in color and in high definition. He wanted to feel all his senses operating at their highest level. He wanted...

Viekko swallowed the urge. "No, I'm fine. I just need—"

Althea reached into her bag, "Now's not the time to be brave, Viekko. Do you need it?"

She held out a small handful of blue capsules, around ten by Viekko's count, which probably represented the last of his stash.

Viekko reached out to take one. He placed it between his teeth and bit down. This wasn't a great place to come out of a Haze. The smell was so thick as to be asphyxiating. There was nothing to see but gloom and fog. They weren't far from the burning remains of the refineries here and he could almost taste the charred petrochemicals and steel in the air.

Althea kept a close eye on him as his mind came around to normal. She watched him close, waiting for that tell-tale sign that he was no longer lost. She smiled. "Feel better?"

Viekko nodded.

In one swift motion, Althea threw the rest of the blue capsules somewhere in the distance. It happened so fast...if he were to see it coming maybe he could have made a dive for them. Maybe he could have caught a precious few before they smashed against the rocks or dropped to the bottom of the frigid creek. But all he could do was watch dumbfounded as the last of his stash disappeared forever.

Althea brushed her hands together. "That's it then. Enjoy that last dose. When we get back to Earth, you'll be going into a program. You are going to get yourself cleaned up and I never want to hear of you messing with that dreadful stuff again, are we clear?"

Viekko still stared in the direction that Althea threw the shards of triple-T. He wanted to push her away and go digging through the mud. Even if he found just one, one remaining shard of -T intact, it would be worth it.

"Yeah, Althea," he muttered. "I get it."

"Good," said Althea. "Now stay close."

She climbed into the tunnel and started crawling into the darkness. Viekko risked one more look back at the debris where Althea tossed the last of the drugs, then he followed.

The derelict felt empty. A few of the wounded stayed behind but most everyone who was able volunteered for the battle. Aside from the occasional moans or the faint footsteps on metal, the ship was completely silent and it made the ancient freighter feel like a crypt.

Isra sat on a bench arranging some equipment Cronus left behind for her. They consisted of a portable computer as thin as a scrap of sheet metal that was operated by a holographic interface that floated just above it, a couple of spherical camera drones and, by far the largest piece, a portable microwave transmitter as large as a suitcase.

She set the thin computer flat on her lap and waved her hand over it's surface to activate it. Several shining spheres with labels orbiting their axes appeared and she selected one that would sync the computer to her EROS suit computer. Cronus assured her that it would be easy to hack into the Corporation's signal. Time to see if it was worth keeping the miserable little hacker alive or if she would be better off ordering Viekko to dump him in the Ligeia Mare.

She opened the case and unfolded the transmitter dish. As soon as she did, the hologram over the portable computer took on a life of its own. The spheres disappeared and were replaced by a rapid series of diagrams, numbers and shapes until a window popped up announcing that the signal was locked.

Isra allowed herself a smile. Maybe he wasn't completely worthless.

She sat back down and picked up one of the camera drones. It activated in her hand and she watched as the hologram over the portable computer changed into an image of her. She raised the drone up, released it and let it hang in the air. She did the same with the second one. She synced both of those with her EROS computer and moved them into position by waving her hand. She adjusted their positions and their built-in lights until the display on the portable computer showed that she was just a barely visible dark figure against a black background. Isra felt it was a little ominous and on the nose, but it would have to work.

One final step. She patched her radio through the portable computer and started speaking. She used the computer to modulate her voice until it had a low, resonating tone to it. Isra was aware of how the whole production looked. Shadowy figure, deep, booming voice...it sounded good when they discussed it earlier. But, now that she saw it, she wondered how anyone could take it seriously.

She sat back and closed her eyes, forcing herself to relax. It didn't matter now. The plan was in progress and it did no good to worry about the semantics. She touched her EROS computer and activated the radio. "Viekko, Althea, Cronus. I am ready to begin the transmission. Let me know when you are in place."

Viekko crawled out of the tunnel, keeping low to the ground behind some brush. He surveyed his surroundings and noticed, with no small amount of irritation, that they were not inside the pyramid. They weren't far, only fifty or so meters, but Viekko felt that it was a small but important distinction given the nature of their operation.

"Viekko pulled up his sleeve and whispered, "Roger Isra. Just moving now." He tapped the display on his EROS suit and whispered, "Halifaco, are you in position?"

There was a pause before Halifaco's voice came over the radio. "We are. The weapon is in position and ready to fire."

Viekko looked around again. There was an air of calm here in the courtyard. There was only one group of soldiers that Viekko could see and they were walking through the grass with a certain relaxed stride.

"Then fire," said Viekko. "We're ready."

The radio went to static for a moment. "Very well. Firing the weapon."

Viekko was far enough away that when the rail gun went off, all he could hear was a strange high-pitched wail followed by the rumble of stone and concrete collapsing. The soldiers casually patrolling the grassy area stopped and then moved at double-time toward the source of the commotion.

He helped Althea and Cronus out of the tunnel and activated the screen on his EROS suit. "How much time do we need, Cronus?"

Cronus glanced at the pyramid. "Once you get the power on, about five minutes."

Viekko checked the map on his screen. "And we've got to make the substation, four kilos away from here. Halifaco agreed to give us ten minutes. Let's make 'em count."

Viekko took off running toward the pyramid with Althea and Cronus following.

The first obstacle was the guards in front of the steel door. Even with the city in crisis, the relic inside was important enough to the City that they would never leave it unattended. But the guards wouldn't be armed with anything more impressive than their standard issue clubs and snares. The new weaponry confiscated off of dead marines would be used in battle.

Viekko made short work of them. He crept around the side of the pyramid and caught them unaware and at gunpoint. He made them lay down and Althea bound their hands with some plastic shackles she took from the armory. It took a short few seconds for Althea and Cronus to bypass the ancient keypad, and then the door was open.

After that, they moved through the empty halls of the pyramid toward the center and the supercomputer. The acolytes were missing, a fact that didn't cause Viekko much distress at the moment. Fewer people to have to secure and watch. Within five minutes Cronus was back in the chair of the Markee 8700 with his own equipment scattered around him, typing away furiously on the keyboard.

"You good here, Cronus?" asked Viekko, finishing one last sweep of the area.

Cronus didn't answer; he was far too absorbed in what he was doing, and that was a good enough answer for Viekko.

He and Althea bolted for the exit.

Althea stopped at the door, bashed open a panel with the

butt of her gun, and twisted some wires together. Before Viekko could ask what she was doing, she grabbed and pulled him through the doorway before the metal door slammed shut, damn near catching his white coat in the process.

Althea observed her handiwork. "I felt it prudent to rig the door closed. Give Cronus more time to work."

"We're gonna to be able to get him out again, right?" said Viekko.

A smile crept across Althea's face. "Assuming you want him out, yes, most likely. One way or another."

Viekko felt somehow obligated to try and pull the door open. Even if he could find a decent handhold on the solid steel, it wouldn't budge. "Good enough. Right, just a few minutes left. We need to get to the transformer."

They both sprinted through the courtyard and into the city. The soldiers were all moving at a run toward the conflict outside the gates and didn't notice Viekko and Althea creeping through the shadows.

Soon, they were in position at the substation. Viekko shut and barricaded the door with some scattered debris inside while Althea followed Cronus's instructions to warm up the equipment.

The timing was perfect. Viekko finished his work and stood next to a lever as long as his arm.

"Cronus, are you ready?" asked Viekko.

Over the sound of typing, Cronus said, "Do it now."

Viekko nodded to Althea. She flipped a series of switches and Viekko pulled hard on the lever. It resisted at first but, with some effort, he was able to jam it into place. Somewhere in the bowels of the substation, machinery started spitting, sputtering and finally roaring to life. A red light above the panel flipped to green.

"That did it," said Cronus over the radio. "Power back up fifty percent. Diverting to screens now."

Viekko ran his hand down the length of his queue. "Okay, Isra, we're ready."

Silence on the other end. Althea and Viekko exchanged

worried glances.

Viekko tried again. "Isra, come in. Are you ready?"

Still nothing.

There was static and Halifaco's voice came in from the field against the background of machine gun fire: "We got soldiers on us. Hundreds. We cannot hold them for very long."

"Isra, damn it, we've got to do this now!" yelled Viekko.

Isra's voice finally came in. "There is a problem."

CHAPTER THIRTY

The Corporation that emerged from the fire of global warfare was even stronger than before, fearless and without remorse.

Before, people were just casualties in the Corporation's grab for power and resources. But now, the Corporation actively sought to punish those who stood in its way.

-from The Fall: The Decline and Failure of 21st Century Civilization *by Martin Raffe.*

The system was locked. No matter what she did, the holographic interface did not respond. She touched every icon floating in front of her. She tried reaching out and grabbing them. As desperation set in, she started to frantically wave her arms through the interface with no improvement. Then she paused, centered herself and said with her voice straining against the calm she imposed on it, "There is a problem. Cronus, I need help—the transmitter is no longer functioning."

"That's impossible," snapped Cronus against the background noise of his typing.

"It is possible, Cronus," said Isra trying, to contain her growing irritation. "It is happening. How do we fix it?"

"Does the transmitter have power?"

"Do you believe I would call you if I was not sure there was power?" she asked, stealing a surreptitious look at the transmitter for a tell-tale green light.

"Did you knock or disturb the dish?"

"I have not touched it," said Isra, her voice cracking.

"Perhaps I can be of some assistance," said an oil-slick voice.

It didn't take Isra more than an instant to recognize who was on the channel with them. She could taste the bile rising from her stomach, "Laban! What do you want?"

"Well, to put it simply," he said in a smooth, soothing tone, "I would like you and your people off my private channel. It is a confidential Corporate channel and I'm sure I don't have to tell you—"

"Laban," said Isra, her voice carrying as much violence as she could manage, "You do not know what you are doing —"

"Well, I know what you're doing. You're piggybacking on a Corporation signal in order to speak directly to the Titanian people posing as the Corporation. Maybe deliver a plea to stop fighting before they all destroy one another?" Isra sat trying to figure out how he could have known all that when he added, "A few of our technicians came up with the theory after they dug your signal out of our system. Were they close?"

Isra ran a hand through her short, black hair. She wanted it tear it out while screaming curses at the Universe. She wanted to be aboard *Innovation* where she could rip those stupid office knick-knacks off Laban's desk and beat him with them. She wanted to smash every piece of equipment in front of her until they were nothing but dust and walk away. But, again, she closed her eyes to center herself and spoke in a plain, clear voice, "Laban, listen to me. This is the only way to save the city."

"Well, that is a shame. Seeing how it is a Corporate signal you are using, we have more claim to the technology on the planet than you do and, if you will forgive me Isra, I've seen more convincing performances from children with nothing but a light and a bed sheet."

The earbud crackled to life and Viekko's half-mad voice sounded, "Isra, damn it! We've got to do this now."

"Oh dear," said Laban. "It appears that you are running

out of time. If it helps, I am all set up in the office and I would be willing to speak on behalf of the Corporation."

Isra growled, "Laban, I would never even consider such a thing."

Halifaco's voice bellowed in her ear. "We cannot hold. More are coming. What is happening?"

"It seems to me, since we control the signal, you have no choice," said Laban. "What is to stop me from doing what I want regardless of you?"

"You need Cronus on the ground to patch the signal to the screens. Without him you might as well be screaming into space."

Laban paused. The only sound was machine guns from Halifaco's open channel.

Finally Laban said, "Then we are at a stalemate."

Viekko yelled over the radio. "Isra! Where are you? This needs to happen now!"

"Or maybe not. Just say the words," Laban continued, "And I will do what I can to help save your people."

Screw it, thought Isra, she would rather watch all of Titan burn then let the likes of Vince Laban have control of it. She activated her transmitter, "Halifaco. Carry out your plan. Move to take the city and destroy the pyramid. Viekko, Althea. Get Cronus out before that happens."

"Are you sure?" asked Laban. "Who knows what kind of damage that will cause to the civilization."

"You have your orders. Carry them out," said Isra, "Cronus, see what you can do about the signal."

"Roger," said Viekko keeping his voice low in the small room. "Althea what does it look like out there?"

Althea cracked open the door to the substation and peeked out. "It's clear for now. I think we can make the pyramid if we hurry."

Viekko activated his radio. "That only means something if Halifaco can break through." He touched the screen and said, "Halifaco? Halifaco! Come in."

Althea crept over to stand near Viekko while they waited for a response. She placed a hand on his shoulder and, only then, did he notice a tremble in her fingers. For a moment, there was only static until the warrior's voice broke in between the rattle of assault rifles. "Overrun...we have no choice...retreat. We have...we must retreat."

Althea broke away and went back to the heavy steel door for another peek. "More bad news," she said after watching for a moment. "They must know something is going on in the pyramid. Several squads just ran in that direction."

Viekko took off his hat and ran his fingers through his hair. He knew the red flags of a military operation that was about to become explosive and this situation had all of them. Victory would mean survival and survival meant retreat. He muttered, "Bi buutsad khurekhiig khusch baina. It's possible they are just running in that direction. But that ain't likely given our luck. All right, we call this off. Call Cronus and tell him to strip everything down and that we are coming to get him."

Cronus, wearing his immersion goggles and controller glove, searched through *Innovation*'s systems. There were hundreds of receiving channels and even more transmitting channels. But getting a signal through one and out the other with the same Corporation encryption...that was the difficult part. It was like trying to pass a message telephone-style through a room of a hundred people who spoke dozens of languages and trying to make sure the language going in was the same as the one coming out.

But he found it. He could patch through an emergency back-channel system, through satellite communications and relay them through drone transponders.

He clenched his fist, finalizing the final connection and said, "Isra, there is a path. Prepare to—"

He stopped as he saw the signal strength drop to nothing. He moved the connection protocol aside and opened the satellite operating system and examined the code.

"Cronus," said Isra's voice in his ear, "Talk to me, tell me what is going on?"

Cronus turned his head left and right, watching the numbers swirl around him. They were different from the last time he was here and changing even as he watched them.

"Isra. I think Laban's people are onto me. Somebody severed the connection and blocked the path."

"Get out of there. We are out of time. Viekko and Althea are coming for you."

Cronus clapped his hands together and the numbers disappeared. He reached up and touched an icon for *Innovation's* core systems. He waved his hand, moving icons that represented the ship's computer systems, as fast as he could see and understand them. As he cycled through another series of pathways, he heard a faint banging on the metal door. At first, Cronus wasn't sure he heard anything at all. But it soon became more insistent.

But he could ignore it. Althea locked the door. Sealed it. There was no way anyone could get in. He was alone. Alone with the servers and the precious, precious data. More banging on the door. This time it did sound like someone could break it down. He forced himself to focus on the numbers and the code. He had to find another patch before it was too late.

Then he found an opening. He could reroute the signal through the atmosphere monitoring system. It was perfect; it was always on and it was wired through the entire ship. He touched the icon and sliced into the code.

More banging and more shouting.

Cronus shook his head. They can't get through. Viekko saw to that. He was safe—no matter how hard they banged on the door, they would not get through.

He focused his attention on the numbers floating and swirling around him. The banging got even louder. Now it could be heard clearly and could nearly be felt through the floors of the pyramid. This wasn't somebody just pounding or kicking the door, this was someone on the other end using a ram to try and knock it out of the walls.

Cronus activated the radio. "Isra. Get ready. I have found a way to route the signal but their technicians will try to stop me again. So get ready to transmit on my mark."

"One more try, then you need to leave," said Isra in a resigned tone.

Cronus opened his hand and a blinking blue icon appeared. The numbers swirled around it as if they were caught in its gravitational field.

"Stand by," said Cronus.

He reached up to touch the icon but as he did, it flashed red and disappeared.

"This...there is no way..."

"Cronus, what happened?" asked Isra.

Cronus clenched his teeth. "They are tailing my signal. I'll have to find a way to hide my signature..."

"Ain't gonna happen kid," said Viekko's voice in between gasps for air as if he were running. "We're out of time. The Houston's got every soldier he has surrounding the pyramid. We need to get you out of there."

Cronus waved his arms and went back to the ship's core systems. "No. This can work, I just need a little more—"

There was a high-pitched whine and a sound like a cork from a bottle. An instant later, the ceiling and the sloping sides all around him shattered. Cronus fell under the supercomputer's console as steel, plastic, and concrete rained down on him, smashed against the console and fell onto the servers below.

Viekko grabbed Althea and dove behind a crumbling brick wall to avoid the spray of rock and dust that shot from the top of the pyramid. One moment he was sprinting toward the gleaming golden structure and the next the apex of the monument was gone. Just... gone. He didn't have time to do anything but rely on instinct to protect himself and Althea.

"Where the hell did that shot come from?" he asked

peeking over the wall.

Althea pulled herself out from under him and poked her head just above the wall, "That had to have been the rail gun. Halifaco must be close."

Viekko checked his rifle and peeked over the wall again. The hundreds of soldiers in the courtyard took off running leaving only a handful.

"The good news," said Viekko sitting with his back against the wall and setting the rifle in his lap, "Looks like most of them folk suddenly found themselves with more pressing problems than Cronus. Bad news, them that are still there are armed and I ain't talkin' sticks and stones."

Althea spun around and sat next to him. She leaned back banging her head lightly on the wall and took several deep breaths. She was never trained for combat and was not as accustomed to its stresses as Viekko. Still, she held it together remarkably well, Viekko thought.

Once she had taken a moment, she fixed her bright green eyes on him that were, for the moment, as hard a steel and said, "So what do we do?"

Viekko handed her the assault rifle. "Take this and move a few hundred meters away. Find a spot behind that rubble. Stay low and just fire a few shots. No need to raise hell, just draw their attention."

Althea took the weapon. "And you?"

Viekko peeked over the wall and drew one of his handguns. "I hope to be relievin' one of them nice people of one of theirs, but we'll work the specifics later. Go! Now!"

Althea peeked up again to make sure her way was clear and then ran. While she was on the move, Viekko watched the men clustered around the pyramid door. Until the railgun took off the top of the building, they appeared to be trying to bust their way in with a makeshift wooden ram. Viekko doubted whether they could break into a sophisticated old-Earth colony complex with a bit of lumber, but the remaining soldiers looked to have their mind set on that idea.

Althea moved from rubble pile to trash heap, staying low

and mostly out of sight to anyone not paying attention. She moved with a timing and grace that someone working behind a computer or, in her case, in a hospital couldn't muster. Viekko had to laugh to himself. If Isra was mad about the triple-T, just wait until she found out what Althea did in her spare time. Or at least, what she used to do.

The medic reached a spot behind the remains of another stone wall. She ducked behind it for a moment, then raised up and let loose a burst of fire in the general direction of the group of soldiers. She didn't hit anything but air, but it got the soldier's attention in a big hurry.

While they were looking around for the source of the gunfire, Viekko rose up and fired three precise shots. One hit a soldier in the neck. The other two hit another in the lower spine and the back of the head. Both of them crumpled to the ground.

Althea rose and fired again. There still was not an ounce of precision to it but, all the same, the soldiers in the middle of the killing became unhinged. Those with guns fired them in all directions unsure of where the attack was coming from. Others found cover any place they could, even behind each other.

This was about the best chance he had. There were maybe ten soldiers left and they didn't know which way was up. He'd need to be quick, precise, and above all, lucky.

"Althea, I'm going in!" Viekko yelled over the radio, "I'll take down who I can. After that, it's up to you. Get Cronus out and get outta here."

Althea paused and ducked behind the wall to reply. Viekko took the opportunity to fire a few more shots while Althea called back, "Viekko, what about you?"

Viekko ducked back down and reloaded his guns, "You and Cronus get to safety. I'll find my own way. Count to three in your head and then hit 'em with everything you got."

Viekko turned off his radio and counted slow. On three he jumped and sprinted toward the soldiers. At the same time Althea started firing at full automatic. Bullets whizzed above and around him but they didn't hit any of the soldiers.

Still, she hadn't accidentally shot him either, so that was a plus.

He was only a few meters away when one of the soldiers, unarmed and lying prone on the ground, saw Viekko coming. He jumped to his feet to stop the martian but he didn't even break his stride. Viekko plowed through the man like he wasn't even there.

Another soldier saw him coming and this one had a rifle taken from the marines. He raised the gun but Viekko slid past, ripped it from the man's grasp and shoved the butt of it in the soldier's face before he even had a chance to react.

There was another. This one appeared out of nowhere. He swung a club and connected with Viekko's temple. Viekko raised the gun and fired a few shots blind. The bullets didn't faze the soldier who brought his club smashing against Viekko's gun and again across his head. The blow caused lights to go off behind the martian's eyes and his vision got blurry.

Viekko swung the butt of the gun around but, again, didn't hit anything. Then there was a sharp, crushing pain in his side.

Another soldier was on him. He grabbed the gun in Viekko's hand and tried to wrestle it away. Another clubbed Viekko in the back of the head. Soon, he couldn't tell one blow from another. In the frenzy, he might as well have been fighting a thousand people. Everything was just clubs, boots and fists banging at every corner of his body. He pressed forward, trying to propel himself through the crowd.

Finally, his body gave out. The pain was too great even for the triple-T to mask. The shrapnel wound in his side flared up. The exhaustion was even worse. The last group of muscles keeping him upright and fighting gave out and he collapsed face first to the ground.

In a feeling that was becoming far too familiar, a soldier pulled his hands behind him and tied his wrists.

CHAPTER THIRTY-ONE

Even as the Corporation consolidated control of the entire planet, something more destructive than anything ever seen gained strength. Records only hint about a growing problem somewhere in the heart of the Corporation in the form of destabilizing economic trends, supply shortages, and massive inflation. The root cause of all of this is a mystery. All records that might contain that information have been either redacted or destroyed.

For the historian, this is where evidence ends and pure speculation takes over. What event could have been big enough to deliver the death blow to a civilization that existed since before the ancient World Wars? Theories are as wild as they are varied and few can be discounted out of hand.

-from The Fall: The Decline and Failure of 21st Century Civilization *by Martin Raffe.*

More gunfire, more screams, this time closer than ever. It was all just beyond the door, somewhere in that clearing around the pyramid. Then as fast as it started, silence.

Cronus poked his head out from under the control console. The first rays of the sun emerged from behind Saturn and shone through a gaping hole at the top of the pyramid. All around him, metal, glass, concrete and assorted polycarbonate alloys scattered on the catwalk. Above, the wind blew shards of glass and bits of plastic loose that fell and clattered on the floor below.

A fear gripped him as he slid out from under the desk and creeped to the edge of the catwalk to see the rows and rows of servers.

To his relief, the damage was minimal. The worst of it was a metal beam about twice as long as a man that fell across several rows of servers, crushing at least three or four individual units. In the vast storage capacity of a Markee 8700 with its hundreds of units, three or four servers meant less than one percent of the total storage capacity.

But for Cronus, looking at the smoking mess below, he felt a sorrow that he'd never encountered before. It was like the death of a close friend. No, it was something worse than that. It was the death of a person he'd never met but who possessed a wealth of knowledge that he would never have access to. Knowledge that, because it was gone forever, was more valuable than anything Cronus could conceive of.

A whistle of air drew Cronus's attention back to the hole in the top of the pyramid. The orange clouds swirled faster. The sides of the walls, now unsupported by the strength of a completed pyramid, swayed just enough for Cronus to perceive the movement. They would never be repaired. Not before they collapsed. Not before the whole structure came down and the last server units to survive would be exposed to the Titanian environment. Petabytes. Maybe even exabytes of data. Messages from an ancient golden age before the Fall would be gone forever.

Someone outside banged on the door again. More people trying to get through. More people who would destroy everything.

He pulled up his sleeve and tested the radio. Nobody responded. Not Viekko. Not Althea. Not even Isra.

More banging. The impacts came once every few seconds and they were strong enough to rattle the floors and walls.

He was alone now. He was alone and, like the data he came to save, he was going to die.

337

He grabbed his equipment that he managed to get under the console with him and pulled it onto his back. He was going to die and so would most of the data. But he could still save some of it within the computers aboard Innovation. He would save something even if it wasn't himself.

He followed the catwalk to the opposite end of the pyramid where two metal ladders allowed him to descend into the spaces between the rows of servers. The space where the acolytes in their white robes once tended to them for a thousand years.

Once on the ground, he darted from server to server looking for something very particular. To get as much data as he could, he needed a central location. Somewhere where he could connect to the most available units. A place where he could access more data. He also needed a newer unit. Something they may have replaced more recently with the right ports. And he needed it as fast as possible.

He ran along the rows with his hand outstretched letting the tips of his fingers brush against panels. His fingers traced the shapes faster than any human eye, the entire history of computer connectors passed under his touch. He stopped at a server panel underneath the catwalk when he touched a connection from the mid-twenty-first-century. He slipped the controller glove over his right hand and lowered his immersion goggles. He selected a flat, hexagon-shaped, silver device from his bag -a portable microwave transmitter- and set it on the floor just beyond the catwalk where it had a clear view of the sky. The six panels opened to form a dish as wide as a serving platter.

One last thing, he had to find a physical data port on the machine itself. This one was newer than some of the others, but the connections were still archaic. It took some modification with his equipment, it always did with ancient connections, but he found a way to plug in.

The immersion goggles flickered on and his world was filled with billions of little yellow dots. They swirled around him like a galaxy of stars. He could reach out and touch any one of them and see the data they contained, and he longed to. He wanted to see the data with his own eyes before it was all gone. Old voice messages and texts. Spreadsheets and covert love letters. Company memos and family news. Corporate training holograms and small video files of children taking their first steps off a transport ship and onto an alien world.

He pushed it all away with a wave of his hand. He would never live to see any of it, but if he worked fast, maybe a tiny section would survive for someone else.

He accessed the long range transmitter, sliced into Innovation's system and used the security codes that Laban gave him earlier. The same codes that allowed him to unknowingly betray Isra and her mission.

He had to put that thought out of his head. He did what he did, and he couldn't change that. Maybe Isra would forgive him someday, maybe not. Either way, he wouldn't be around to notice.

Inside the information centers of the ship, he found an unused sector. It was part of the auxiliary nav system. Not something most ship engineers would notice, not without a complete system scan and, if they ever performed such a process on the ship, it wouldn't happen until they were docked in Earth orbit.

He established a connection and waved the galaxy of lights back. The uplink was live. Now it was just a matter of deciding which of the little stars of information to send.

While he looked at the points of yellow light, he noticed something. There were people outside the pyramid. Lots of them. But there was no pounding, no yelling, no gunfire; just a lot of frenzied discussion and then an expectant silence.

And, finally, a high-pitched whine just on the edge of hearing.

Cronus fell to the floor as the railgun fired again. This time the projectile hit the metal door, ripped it out of place and sent it screaming across the room and into the opposite wall above. The whole structure groaned and more pieces rained down. Several more crashes followed by an electric hiss signaled the death of more server units. Cronus lay face down on the ground and watched as thousands of little lights winked out of existence forever.

Pieces continued to fall. They slammed on the catwalk overhead but, by some luck, the steel structure held. Cronus crawled through the shower of debris through the rows of whirring servers. Around him, metal cases collapsed under the weight of steel and concrete, electrical systems shorted out and showered him with sparks, and more yellow dots winked out of existence. He crawled until he came to the edge where there was a metal door cracked open. Odd that he had not noticed it before, but it was tucked deep within the server room underneath the catwalk.

Soldiers shouted and their boots slammed on the metal surface as they ran. Cronus darted through the door, being careful to make no sound, and shut it behind him.

Dim lights lit a metal stairway. Cronus followed it down, hoping that it might lead to a tunnel system where he could escape. Escape and leave these wretched people to their fates.

The stairway twisted back on itself and ended in a circular room. The first thing Cronus noticed, with some despair, was that there was only one way in or out. At least there was now. The silver cylinder that stretched the entire height of the pyramid was in the center here as well. Sliding doors were torn open and the crumpled remains of some sort of machine spilled out. It confirmed Cronus's suspicion of an elevator that ran—or rather, used to run—from the base of the pyramid to the top. The Acolytes at the bottom became the *Venganto* on top. To the people of the city, they defended the faith, but the smoldering remains here told Cronus that the only thing the *Venganto* defended was the status quo according to the Houston.

Cronus stepped the rest of the way down the stairs. Fifty or more nooks in the circular wall contained metal racks in the shape of a stick figure. Every nook was empty and every rack stripped bare, except for one. The metal arms still held the shiny black suit which was topped with a helmet that featured a ghoulish face, like a gargoyle snarling at eternity.

Back up the stairs, soldiers shouted in Titanian. Cronus couldn't understand what they were saying, but he was sure they were looking for him. They would drag him away and leave the data to be destroyed in this place.

He eyed the *Venganto* suit again. It was a perfect tool for controlling people. It was technology just advanced enough to inspire awe in those who didn't have the means to understand it. The wrath of the gods made flesh and bone and able to burn the unbelievers in holy fire. It seemed uniquely compatible with human beliefs.

Cronus smiled as an idea entered his head.

The suit barely fit. The *Urbanoi* were shorter on average with stubby limbs so Cronus fit in surprisingly well. Still, there was some pinching and pulling in some new and unique places. But Cronus decided that it was good enough. Especially since there weren't a great many alternatives.

He crept back up the stairs, trying to keep the metal of the suit as quiet as he could. He pushed the door to the server room open with a careful ease so as not to alert anyone to his presence. There was nobody nearby, so he slid inside and closed the door behind him. Shadows and sounds on the catwalk above indicated that there was a great deal of activity overhead. Among the servers, only a few soldiers patrolled.

He walked out into the open, a place where the area was clear overhead. He would need an entrance. Something that would inspire the desired respect and, failing that, a hefty dose of fear.

It had long been theorized that humans could fly on Titan, Cronus knew that. But he also knew that it wouldn't be as simple as flapping one's arms. For example, they would need a touch of propulsion.

He raised his arms. As if he'd tripped some sort of automatic mechanism, the armor jerked up and locked into place with the wings extended. He pushed his arms back down in a flapping motion. He felt a burst of air on his ankles and, to his slight dismay, he was airborne.

He wasn't ready for it and his stomach rebelled at the

341

idea. The pyramid left little room to maneuver and he did not have any practical idea of how to control the suit at this point. As he reached the apex of his arc, however, he found he could position his wings to control the descent. He aimed for the catwalk.

It was hardly the most graceful landing in the history of avionics. In fact it was little more than a slow, barely controlled crash. But it did have the desired effect. The soldiers on the catwalk all watched him with mouths and eyes wide open. A few of them gripped the handles of their clubs but they were shaking so much that they would just as likely drop them and run if it came to it.

Cronus felt like he should say something. "You must all leave now. You desecrate this place! Leave and never come back!"

It sounded good to him, but the soldiers just looked confused. They talked to each other in their language but none of them made any motion to leave.

The problem was, Cronus was still stuck with his arms straight out. That was no way to intimidate people. He already knew what would happen if he tried to push his arms down. He tried pushing them forward but the suit resisted. He twisted his left wrist. As he did something shot out from the front of his mask at such a force it would have broken his neck if it weren't braced by the suit.

A small orb sailed over the catwalk, hit the side of the pyramid and burst into a shower of flame.

There was a universal language there. Seeing the fire, all the soldiers ran for the exit. Even the few in the server room below practically ran on top of each other to climb the ladder and disappear down the long hallway that led outside.

Cronus rolled his shoulders back and the mechanism that held his arms out disengaged.

He took off the suit and stashed it in between the servers back down the ladder. He retrieved his immersion goggles and control glove and slipped them on. He had a few precious moments. He might die, but he could still save some of the data.

342

Ten soldiers led Viekko and Althea through the streets of the ruined city while the citizens gathered on the sides to gawk or shout obscenities. The soldiers marched in perfect lock step and looked ready to move them the minute either Viekko or Althea got any ideas. One of them, Viekko recognized.

"Hey," said Viekko to the soldier leading the way, "Mikelo. It's you ain't it?"

The soldier turned his head so that just the edge of his face was visible from behind the high collar, "*Silento.*"

"It's you ain't it? I know it's you. Hey, where the hell are we goin'?"

Mikelo didn't turn his head again. He didn't answer but just kept the steady pace toward whatever destination lie in front of them.

Being captured, bound in chains, and forced to walk down the middle of the street was becoming a leitmotif on this trip. Viekko's wrists were starting to chafe, but that was the worst of it. The *Urbanoi* that gathered on the side of the road shouting and jeering at him didn't cause him much worry. The soldiers didn't scare him; they were just glorified slavers in brown coats. Even the Houston didn't put much of the fear in him. Viekko walked down the street, hands bound but his head high.

He tried to share this confidence with Althea who was being marched behind him. She kept her head down as if trying avoid looking at the crowds of people who turned up to see them paraded down the street.

"It's okay," he tried to say multiple times, "They ain't gonna do nothing brash."

"They need us and they know it. They just don't know which side we are on."

"Isra's probably working the Houston right now. This ain't a problem yet. She'll talk sense into him."

But Viekko's assurances didn't have any effect on Althea. She wouldn't look at him or anyone else, but kept her head down as the soldiers prodded her forward.

They turned a corner and the big city square was in sight. What he saw put the first bit of fear in Viekko's mind. The place was packed by a vicious, screaming mob. It was like every person in the city had gathered to watch something happen. Just from the mood, it didn't look like these people would be satisfied with anything less than blood.

The real fear hit when the soldiers marched them to the stage. Kneeling in a row before a line of *Urbanoi* soldiers was Halifaco and several of his officers. Out in the crowd, he noticed a hundred or more *Perfiduloi* men and women gathered tight in the center being watched by a circle of soldiers. All around them, the people of the city yelled through the line, threw rocks, bits of dirt or anything else they could get their hands on. The soldiers looked like they intended to keep the crowd back, but that was it. They had no intention of stopping any of the abuse the people of the city were heaping on its prisoners

The soldiers marched Viekko and Althea onto the stage and clubbed them in the back of their legs, forcing them to kneel. They set Viekko next to Halifaco who leaned over and whispered, "You needed a better plan."

Viekko shifted in his leather bonds. "I'm sorry it lacked the subtlety of genocide and civilizational destruction."

One of the soldiers stopped in front of him. It was definitely Mikelo, the soldier's old and scarred face was not one Viekko would forget in a hurry. He just looked down at Viekko and, with a touch of pity in his voice said, *"Pardonu Viekko."*

That was as good as a death sentence in his book. He shifted again to try and activate the screen on his EROS suit.

"What are you doing?" whispered Halifaco.

"Calling for help," said Viekko, "Or what might pass for it on this cursed moon."

The *Perfiduloi* leader glanced around as if worried that someone might spot him. "How will you do that?"

Viekko winced as he wrenched his arm in an

uncomfortable position to work the touch screen, "Luckily, they ain't figured out we gots computers attached to us at all times. Hell, I only know just enough to get in trouble."

He shifted one more time and he heard the radio pop on.

"Cronus. Isra," Viekko whispered. "Somebody's gotta be on this line, answer me! Cronus, are you alright?"

There was a burst of static and Cronus's voice came through. "I'm okay."

"Where are you?"

"I'm in the pyramid...Set against the ruins...Lost to history."

The roaring of the crowd went quiet. Viekko looked over to see the Houston climbing the stairs of the platform in all of his splendor. "Cronus, we don't have a lot of time. Get with Isra and figure out how to play the message. Do anything. We're out of options."

There was a pause on the other end. "Not enough time...And yet infinite time soon...One transitions to the other like..."

The Houston stood in front of the crowd who greeted him with a roar of cheers.

"Cronus, cut the *nokhoi baas*. Listen to me Cronus, something bad is about to happen—"

Viekko stopped when the Houston motioned behind him. The soldiers brought one of Halifaco's men forward and laid him across a wooden block at center stage. An *Urbanoi* soldier appeared from the other end to another roar of crowd approval. He was dressed in the same high-collared brown coat as the other soldiers, except his coat had a collar so high that Viekko could only see a few strands of hair and a touch of scalp. He was also carrying a large axe, the kind that wasn't used for chopping trees. That detail stood out particularly well in Viekko's mind.

The man approached the wooden block and the man lying on it. The soldier hoisted the axe with one quick swing. Less than a second, that was it. The crowd cheered as Halifaco's man had his head unceremoniously removed from the rest of his body.

345

Halifaco yelled in his native language and struggled to get to his feet. It was just rage of course. There wasn't much he could do with his hands tied behind him.

The soldiers removed the body which was still spurting blood from the stump of its neck and flung it off the front of the stage. The crowd below parted to let it fall and swarmed over it like a pack of starving animals.

The Houston took his place again at the front and continued to harangue the crowd.

"What's happening?" said Cronus's voice in Viekko's ear.

"They are executing them, Cronus. *Tamyn kharaal*, they are killing them. We're next Cronus. We're going to die if you don't do something."

Cronus paused again and sighed as if he were being terribly put upon. "If I stop my work now, all the data in the pyramid will be destroyed—

Viekko fought to keep his voice at a whisper. "Don't care about the pyramid, Cronus. You wanna know why? Because any minute these *minii etsguudiin yas, tuunii bukh mori ni* are going to cut off our heads."

Another pause. "I will see what I can do."

"That's good. Hurry. And where the hell is Isra?"

Her voice snapped in his ear. "I am here. You need to buy me some time."

"They just grabbed another one of Halifaco's men. Isra, we don't got much time," said Viekko's voice in Isra's ear.

Isra closed her eyes and took a deep breath. She wanted to tell Viekko that she was perfectly aware of his predicament, and the yelling wasn't helping. She couldn't let Laban knew that anything was wrong. It was bad enough that she was the one walking back to the negotiation table.

On the other hand, Viekko would be the one with his head literally on the chopping block, so she decided to excuse the attitude for now.

"I hear you Viekko. Laban. Are you listening? I am ready to talk."

Vince Laban's smug voice sounded in her ear. "Isra Jicarrio. I must say I'm surprised. You seem like the type that would sacrifice her entire crew rather than admit wrongdoing.

Over her earpiece she heard the faint clang of metal and Viekko say, "Hurry up, Isra. Damn it, hurry..."

Isra shook her head ignoring Laban's shot, "Help me save my people and I will be willing to negotiate an agreement for research extraction."

Laban just laughed, "You really are a fascinating woman. Your mission is at the brink of failure and your people are in mortal danger. And you wish to negotiate? Well, go on...I'm listening.

Isra breathed deep. "The city is to remain untouched as are the people. We can designate a drilling area on the far Eastern shore of the Ligeia Mare—"

Laban interrupted. "Unacceptable. All our data shows the richest deposits are near the city."

Viekko's voice came over the headset again. "Laban. If you let me die out here, I'll haunt you. You won't be able to *belgiin moljlogiig guitsetgekh* without me crawling up your ass."

Isra slammed her fist on the table and immediately regretted it. It showed frustration. "Viekko, quiet. Laban. Meet me halfway."

"The Ministry renounces all claims to Titan," said Laban, "The whole moon including the city and its people become official Corporate territory. That is my condition."

"Oh hells," said Viekko. "Isra, Cronus. You need to do something right now. They just took Althea. It looks like she's next on the block."

Isra felt her stomach drop. It twisted her gut and if there had been anyone nearby to see, they would have noticed her eyes become shiny with tears. In her mind, she wanted to scream, cry, burn and destroy until the empty husk of *Innovation* orbited a blackened, cratered rock around Saturn. Until this moment, she could have stalled. Maybe let Laban think that she might be able to accomplish the mission without him. But he knew she would never compromise her people.

"Cronus," she said flatly, "Patch Laban through to the screens. You win, Laban. Titan is yours."

CHAPTER THIRTY-TWO

It was during that dark period in history that 21st century civilization ceased to be a force on the planet. All recorded history vanished. Given the evidence, one might believe that, on New Year's Day 2155, the people of the world decided to pull an elaborate prank on the people of the future and moved the date forward.

Or, more realistically, history was erased by persons who wanted to keep the exact cause of the Fall a secret.

In the age of information saturation that was the mid-twenty-first century, that should have been impossible. An event big enough to end civilization must have been recorded and written about a million times and only one such record would have to survive to tell the world what happened. Yet one can walk to the edge of the gaping hole in our knowledge of human history, stare at it and declare that it doesn't exist. Those words will also disappear into the abyss.

-from The Fall: The Decline and Failure of 21st Century Civilization *by Martin Raffe.*

Viekko heard Isra surrender over the radio but it gave him little comfort as soldiers surrounded and pinned him to the ground as two others pulled Althea to her feet. He wanted to tear the throat out of every bastard that touched her, but Althea walked with silent dignity to the blood-soaked chopping block. Meanwhile, the Houston kept the theater going as good as any showman who had ever lived. He ran his hand along the wooden block, held up a fist of blood and shouted some words of triumph. The crowd responded with a roar like a pack of hungry hounds teased with meat.

Viekko struggled some more against his bonds and the soldiers holding him to the ground but there was nothing he could do. "Cronus..." he said with a kind of pleading.

Cronus's voice came through among the clatter of manic typing. "I've almost got it."

The two soldiers forced Althea's head down on the block and the soldier with the axe approached. In that moment, Althea glanced back at Viekko. It was strange, there was no fear in her face, no pleading, just a kind of sadness like the end of a long goodbye.

"Cronus, we're out of time. Do it now!"

"I need a little more time! Stall them!"

The executioner raised his axe.

More time. Fine. He could do that.

Viekko stopped struggling. A few soldiers relaxed their hold just enough for Viekko to lunge to his feet before the soldiers behind him could react, and he charged at the executioner. He lowered his head as they collided.

The impact sent Viekko sprawling backwards onto the stage and sent the executioner flying off. The crowd just beneath the stage spread out in an instant and the executioner's axe clattered on the concrete below along with the executioner.

The crowd gasped and roared as Althea rushed to help him up. She got him to his feet and said, "Viekko we have to get out of here!"

The world was spinning. The screaming crowd and Althea's voice all coalesced into a confusing mass. The only thought that formed in Viekko's mind was the intense urge to flee. But it was Althea who grabbed him by the coat and pulled him toward the edge of the stage. She had, in the confusion, managed to pull her arms around so that her bound hands were now in front of her. A trick she no doubt perfected dealing with law enforcement on Earth.

They stumbled forward a few meters but didn't get far before soldiers surrounded them. A couple pulled Althea screaming, struggling and kicking away from him. Two more took him by either arm while a third smashed in him the face with his fist. He crumpled to the ground and moaned in pain as another soldier kicked him in the area around the healing shrapnel wound.

He heard Althea yell his name somewhere behind him as more soldiers came to hold Viekko in place. He glanced back to see the soldiers holding her on her knees pressing her hands painfully behind her head. She still made a valiant effort to struggle but she could barely move. The Houston approached, looking at Viekko as if he were something disgusting that he would have to scrape off his fancy red shoes. He jammed a finger in Viekko's face. "I've tolerated your disturbances too much. I will not do it—"

"I demand the right to speak!" The words shocked Viekko as much as it did the Houston.

He backed up and looked at Viekko with surprise. "What did you say to me?"

Viekko wasn't sure. The words just seemed to come from nowhere. But they were out now and he thought it best to just roll with it. "I said I demand the right to speak."

"You have no such—"

"On Earth those condemned to die are allowed to speak some last words. But you have never spoken to the Kompanio, so I don't expect you to—"

The Houston moved fast for an older man. Before Viekko even saw him move, he felt the sting of his palm against his cheek. The Houston stood back, his face red with rage. And then, as fast as it came on, the Houston relaxed. A small smile even materialized. It was like someone pulled a stopper and let all the anger drop out.

He held out an open hand motioning to the crowd. "Very well, outsider. Go. Speak to them."

Viekko hesitated. Maybe the Houston had a notion that Viekko had no idea what to say. If he did, it was accurate.

351

The Houston blinked in anticipation. "Come on then. They await your words."

The crowd, silenced by the commotion on stage, waited for something. Viekko's mind reeled for something to grasp. "A translator. I need someone to tell 'em what I'm saying."

The Houston shook his head. "That was not—"

One of Halifaco's generals stood up despite the soldiers next to him. "I will. I will speak his words to the people."

There was a flash of disgust in the Houston's face. Viekko added, "He's got rights to last words too. Might as well be mine. Kinda two-for-one thing."

The Houston smiled and bent in a small bow.

Viekko stepped forward with his hands still bound behind him. Althea, still held on her knees by two *Urbanoi* soldiers looked at Viekko with eyes that said, in no uncertain terms, *I need you to do something spectacular right now.*

Viekko cleared his throat. "Er...People of Titan, I bring you a message. A message of peace. A message of hope. You are two people divided by a common belief. You need not fight anymore."

He paused while Halifaco's general finished translating. There were some stirrings in the crowd. A kind of low mumble that could become a frenzied, bloody riot at any moment. It held the same foreboding as the first thunder before a martian sandstorm. "The *Kompanio* has been calling to its people for years, desperate to reach those left behind so long ago. He wants to bring you all back home, but your leaders have denied that to you." He motioned at the Houston. "They have blocked the voice of the *Kompanio* from its people so that they could maintain supreme power."

The Houston folded his arms and remained silent.

"I can prove it!" said Viekko with a touch of desperation.

"Just a little longer..." said Cronus's voice over the radio.

Viekko swore under his breath and continued, "But before I do...I have just one more thing to say..."

"I think you have said quite enough, prisoner," said the Houston, motioning for soldiers to put an end to this.

"Just one more thing. The people you hold as slaves. The

352

people you have captured. They ain't your enemy. You share this moon together. The fate of one...well, that's what's gonna happen to the other. You can't destroy one without destroying yourselves."

As Halifaco's general finished translating, the crowd got more and more riled up, especially around the center where the *Perfiduloi* warriors were held.

"How are we coming?" asked Viekko, taking advantage of the momentary reprieve.

"Just a few more seconds," said Cronus

The Houston bowed again, although this time it was little more than a slight bend at the waist and an impatient head nod. "Are you finished?"

Viekko looked around desperately. "Not yet. Don't be mistakin' me. The *Kompanio* is coming and it's coming right now. You kill me...you kill her," he said nodding his head toward Althea, "and you ain't never going to see the end of its wrath."

The Houston held out his hand. "The *Kompanio* comes here? Where are they? Show it to us."

Cronus's voice came over the earbud. "Another second."

"... I just. Need. A couple. More. Seconds," whispered Viekko, mentally strangling Cronus with every word.

The Houston smiled, "The *Kompanio* speaks to its people already. They speak to me and they say to kill the enemies of Titan. *Mortigi la eksteruloi. Restarigi ekvilibron!*"

Those words kicked off a frenzied response from the crowd. Viekko tried to keep talking but anything he said was drowned out. Not that he had anything more to say anyway. One of the soldiers pulled Althea away and another kicked Viekko behind the knee. He fell forward and the soldier shoved him onto the chopping block.

"Cronus! ..." said Viekko.

"One more second..."

"*Li parolas mensogon,*" bellowed the Houston to the delight of the crowd and pointed a bony finger at Viekko being held on the block, "*Li moros unua!*"

There was a particular dark emphasis on the word 'moros' that associated it with, in no uncertain terms, death. He tried to move but a soldier shoved Viekko's face onto the bloody block. "Cronus!"

"Viekko!" screamed Althea struggling against the soldiers.

The executioner walked up from wherever he fell, gripping the axe with a sort of intense determination. Blood trickled down from the top of his head.

Cronus's voice crackled over the radio, "Just one more... there. I got it!"

The executioner raised the axe. Just as he brought it down, Viekko rolled off the block and the blade came down and embedded itself into the wood. Viekko fell onto the stage and two guards ran to jerk him back onto the block.

The Houston roared in anger. "*Akiri lin. Tenu lin malsupren!*"

The soldiers tried to force Viekko's head down, but he twisted his body so he could kick one in the kneecap. Then he turned and head-butted the other in the face.

"Laban!" yelled Cronus over the radio. "You must begin now!"

More soldiers surged forward. Viekko yelled as they grabbed him. "Stop! In the name of the *Kompanio* stop!" Maybe it was the look on Viekko's face. Or maybe because he invoked the name *Kompanio*. But they stopped as if gripped by a spell. Viekko stared up at the black screen towering over them. "You wanna see your gods. Here they come."

In that moment, the crowd became unnaturally silent. Nobody breathed, the soldiers didn't twitch a muscle and even the Houston stared up at the screen with a kind of wide-eyed fear like a child who's just been caught in their parent's dresser drawer.

And then, nothing happened. The screen stayed black and still.

"Well, shit," muttered Viekko.

The soldiers jerked Viekko back and slammed him down on the block. His head bounced hard off the wood, scrambling his marbles. One of the soldiers planted his boot firmly into the small of Viekko's back so that he couldn't move.

The executioner raised his axe.

Viekko closed his eyes and waited for the thump of the blade into the wood. Would he be able to hear it? Or would the lights simply go out like someone flipping a switch? Viekko released his last breath. At the moment of death, he heard trumpets. Viekko's thoughts flashed to the preacher of his martian colony talking about Hell and Heaven and the choir of angels.

Viekko always discounted it as arcane superstition, but was that preacher right all along?

Was this the afterlife?

Viekko opened his eyes. The screaming masses hushed themselves and focused on the space far above his head. The trumpet fanfare blared even louder. The guard relaxed his leg so that Viekko could turn over and see the screen for himself. The Corporation logo, a letter 'C' encapsulating an image of the globe, spun above him as large as the ringed orb of Saturn in the sky. The logo for the Corporation was rarely associated with anything but unfettered greed and an insatiable lust for power. But, right now, on that screen in front of all these people, it was more beautiful than anything Viekko had ever seen.

The image changed to a man in a suit sitting at a desk. The banners of the various Corporation consortiums flanked him on either side. Little holograms of the Corporation logo floated above the otherwise antique desk. Everything about the man was perfect. Perfect smile, perfectly pressed suit, perfectly styled golden hair. It took the resources of an entire planet to make someone look that good, but the CEO could afford that and more.

The leader of the Global Corporation clasped his hands together. "People of Titan. Allow me to introduce myself. I am Malcolm Moore, CEO of the Transplanetary Corporation of Earth. I speak to the..."

The man looked down at sheet of notes in front of him.

"The *per-fine-doo-loi* and the *urban-oi*. Just as the various energy companies of Earth's past came together to form the mighty Energy Consortium, just as those Consortiums now band together as the Corporation, I appear before you today to unite the people of Titan under one banner."

The CEO paused and the crowd cheered.

"The CEO..." said Viekko as he stood up. "How?"

The man on the screen continued, "Our people have been separated for far too long. Much has changed on Earth as I am sure much has changed for the far-flung world of Titan. To help with the process of bringing the people back to the Corporation, I have appointed Vince Laban as my official representative on your planet..."

Althea bent, with her hands free to help Viekko to his feet. She used a knife she no doubt lifted from a soldier to cut Viekko's bonds. "It takes more than two hours to get a signal from Earth. Laban...he must have known."

"He will be arriving tomorrow," the CEO continued. "Until then, let's talk about getting you people home."

The people of Titan cheered.

"Viekko, what is your status?" called Isra over the radio.

Viekko shook his hands as he watched Althea moved down the line of Halifaco's men cutting their bonds as well while the soldiers and the rest of the people were totally entranced by the spectacle in front of them, "We're alive. Wasn't by much, but enough."

"And Cronus?" asked Isra.

Viekko looked around as a slow, terrible realization formed in his mind. He called out, "Althea...you seen the Houston take off?"

Her face went white as she helped the *Perfiduloi* leader to his feet. "Halifaco, where did you leave the railgun?"

Halifaco stood up. "We made it to the pyramid before the Houston's army stopped us. The weapon is still there."

"*Burkhdyn omkhii baas khamt.* And I'll bet he's in a mood to rip down the entire *Kompanio.* Let's go. Quick, before he does."

356

Viekko had no idea how the pyramid still stood at this point. The top had been blasted off and the four walls, still reflecting the light from the moons, crumbled as they approached. At the edge of the courtyard, just on the other side of the short, dilapidated wall, Viekko saw where Halifaco left the rail gun. The bodies of both *Urbanoi* and *Perfiduloi* warriors littered the ground around it, a grim monument to a mad drive for power. And there was the Houston in full ceremonial regalia, working the controls and looking like a man who had long since sprinted past sanity and was deep in the dark recesses of madness.

Isra yelled over the radio, "Viekko! What is happening?"

Althea activated her radio as she ran alongside Viekko, "Isra... we might have a situation."

Viekko left Althea and sprinted to the rail gun. The Houston's face, lit by the screen on the gun, split into an insane grin as he flipped switches and pressed buttons at random. He didn't know how to work the technology but, given its high pitched whine, he had figured out enough.

The martian ran full force across the field when, as much to the Houston's surprise as his own, the weapon fired. He ran into the Houston at full speed, knocking that ridiculous spiked hat off his head. They tumbled and rolled in the grass and mud as the sound of the shot echoed off the buildings around them. He pinned the old man down and sat up to watch. The projectile hit its target and the remaining walls of the pyramid collapsed into itself. It was only a few seconds before the pyramid in the center of the courtyard disappeared into a pile of dark rubble, dust and smoke.

The Houston laughed, *"Mizera mensogo!* I am the *Kompanio!* Those false voices will never—"

Viekko's fist struck the Houston just below the jaw. His eyes rolled up in his head and he laid still. Viekko got up and staggered over to the railgun, pulled away a maintenance panel, and grabbed a handful of wires and a few metal pieces and pulled. White hot sparks erupted and burned his hand,

357

but it was done.

Viekko looked up at the smoldering ruins of the pyramid.

Althea ran up and stopped next to Viekko, panting, "Oh Lord...Cronus!"

Viekko activated his radio. "Cronus, come in!"

No response.

"Cronus, damn it! If you are there—"

Althea touched his shoulder and shook her head. A few tears streamed down her face.

"Viekko, what is happening? Where is Cronus?" said Isra's voice.

Viekko swallowed hard, "The Houston managed to fire the railgun and destroy the pyramid. Looks likely that Cronus was inside."

Smoke rose gently from the smoldering wreckage as Viekko watched. Althea approached and put her arm around his shoulder, "We couldn't....I mean we tried, but—"

"Yeah," Viekko murmured. Then he activated his radio, "Isra we're gonna check out the wreckage. As much as we can. See what's left."

There was a long pause and Isra said in a firm, clear voice, "I understand."

Isra shut down the system and walked through the derelict. She wandered through the halls of the ancient ship until she came to the airlock. She twisted the wheel and pushed the thick, steel door open. The moonlit skies were clear of *Venganto* now. And it left a kind of dreadful peace in the air.

She leaned against the hull and looked at Saturn's largest icy moon, Rhea shining like a great silver jewel. A stiff breeze kicked up and the air filled with leaves. She pulled her coat around herself. It reminded her of a brisk autumn day on Earth. But here, she had the desperate feeling that spring would never follow a winter. Even now the giant trees looked bare like mere skeletons of themselves. The once all-pervasive hum and screech of insects, birds and animals was gone replaced by a silence that was as cold as the wind.

Titan was lost. And the worst part about it was that she'd lost a man in the process. Not that she'd feel better if her mission succeeded but at least he would have died for something. This was nothing. Nothing but a catastrophic failure.

She felt a white-hot anger rise inside her. He had no business on a mission like this. He lied, cheated and bluffed his way into a situation that he had no control over and no training for. He was like a child wandering into the woods with no sense of the danger that surrounded him. If he would have just stayed on Earth. If he would have—

A chilling breeze blew her hair. She brushed it out of her face and wiped away a tear. If he would have stayed on Earth, Viekko would be dead. Althea too, most likely. But there was no point in rehashing what was done. Titan was lost. Cronus was dead.

Isra activated her radio. "Finish what you need to and make your way to the city gates. We will rendezvous there before we meet up with Corporation transports.

"Isra," said Viekko, "You might want to delay that for a moment. Somethin' weird is happening.

Viekko and Althea both watched a *Venganto* circling overhead. Viekko, trying not to make any sudden movements, picked up a gun off a fallen *Urbanoi* soldier.

"When I say go," said Viekko raising the gun, "You bolt for cover. It don't matter what it is, you just—"

"Wait," said Althea, watching the winged soldier circling overhead, "There's something wrong with it. I...don't think it means to harm us."

Viekko kept the rifle trained on the threat, but she was right. *Venganto* were graceful, elegant and deadly. This *Venganto* had all the grace and elegance of an overweight, drunken gerbil. It didn't make any fast moves but just circled overhead getting lower and lower.

Finally, the creature swooped toward the ground. Not in the sharp descent that usually preceded an attack, but more of a long shallow dive as if coming in for a landing. Although 'landing' was a generous term for what it did. It would be more accurate to say that it careened into the ground and rolled a few times.

Viekko rushed over and held it at gunpoint. "Okay there, buddy. You just stand up real slow now."

The *Venganto* did as it was told. A high-pitched voice behind the mask said, "In such a series of events, it would be a shame to fall to the gun of one's own comrade, do you not agree?"

"Cronus?" said Althea with a bit of excitement.

Cronus removed the *Venganto* mask. The bald little man beamed at the both of them. "A daring escape. Worthy of a martian warrior you might say."

"I might. With enough to drink," said Viekko. "How did you get out?"

"It was the acolytes in the pyramid. They had a secret in the basement. It was them who became the *Venganto*." Cronus looked mournfully at the wreckage. "I suppose they are gone now. Along with everything else. More history lost forever."

Althea went to him and clasped his hands in hers. "Cronus...I'm...so sorry. I can't understand what that data meant to you or how hard it must have been to leave."

Cronus stared off in the direction of the wreckage. His look was far away as if he were looking past the debris to the bright silver moons in the distance. "The mainframe, my equipment...there will be others, but a seeker is rare. And only a seeker knows what he is looking for. If I allowed myself to die, I don't know if there would be someone who could listen to the data and hear the secrets it contains." He paused for a moment, his eyes narrowing as he thought about what he just said. "Is that presumptive of me?"

Viekko slapped him on the back. "Maybe, but ain't no shame in thinkin' you're the only one who can do the job proper. Hell, I'm not even sure I know what you do."

"It's very simple. See, when Civilization fell—"

Viekko stopped him. "And we ain't got time to find out now. Come on, Cronus, let's go find Isra and see about gettin' off this frigid rock."

They started walking. Althea, always the person who filled any silence, asked, "Did you manage to find anything at all?"

"The data needs to be processed," said Cronus. "But yes. I found something. Time will dictate its value. But I believe it will show itself worthy."

The long night on Titan stretched on. Seventy-two hours later, darkness still covered the moon with only a dim red glow on the eastern horizon signaling the beginning to another long day. And when the sun finally did rise, it wouldn't recognize the world it left only a few hundred hours ago. Less than a week on a more civilized planet.

For a start, what amounted to a second city had risen in and around the Corporation camp. It still consisted of simple, temporary dome structures but there were more of them and those that existed had to be expanded. The mess hall, especially, grew two or three times and now served as the center of this growing society.

The old, decaying city and the forests surrounding it were all but devoid of human life as its citizens streamed to the Corporation camp to be closer to the return of the *Kompanio*. The parameter grew as more and more people set up simple shelters, some made with nothing but branches and leaves from the dying forests surrounding the camp.

Hundreds of *Perfinduoi, Urbanoi* and Corporation soldiers flooded the mess hall filling it to beyond capacity. Whatever Titan was going to become when the sun rose was going to be decided and nobody wanted to be left out.

Even with twice or three times the extra space, Viekko still felt claustrophobic sitting on a bench in that mess hall.

The small, round folding tables the Corporation used to furnish the area had been replaced by long, heavy wooden ones not unlike those at the communal gathering place of the *Perfiduloi* in the ancient spaceship. In fact, Viekko couldn't be totally sure they had not been brought from there.

It was standing room only as every survivor from the *Urbanoi* and the *Perfiduloi* crammed together drinking, eating, and conversing. This time, it didn't feel as forced as it did in the Houston's palace. A few people kept to their own kind, but everyone else mingled in a kind of kinship that hadn't been seen on this planet in a millennium.

Viekko was seated at a table with Isra, Althea, Cronus, and five other *Urbanoi* who more or less ignored them. Wine flowed through the whole hall, which did a lot to explain the sudden camaraderie. Viekko preferred to drink alone and in quiet, letting the booze sooth his battered body.

Althea sat next to him with a mug of wine in her hand, although she only took a couple sips from it. She mostly just turned it around and around in her hands while watching the people of Titan moving from table to table, chatting and laughing as if they hadn't just spent generations trying to enslave and slaughter each other. She sighed and said, "The forests are deteriorating faster than any of the scientists anticipated. They say that most plant life will be dead within a month. Maybe less."

Viekko took a drink. "Nothin' we could do about that, Althea. We weren't the ones who blew up the refineries."

Althea cast an evil eye at Halifaco who was sitting at the front of the room with the Houston and Laban. "What do you think will happen to them now?"

Viekko leaned back. "They'll survive. People have a way of doin' that."

Laban tapped his mug on the table until the conversations around the room ceased. Backed up by two interpreters, Laban began speaking. "Honored guests! I welcome you to the grand opening of Titan Outpost One. What we build on this foundation will ensure the safety and prosperity of all people of Titan, *Urbanoi* and *Perfiduloi* alike."

The *Urbanoi* clapped while the *Perfiduloi* raised glasses of the imported Corporation wine in the air.

Isra was sitting across from Viekko, looking down at a mug of wine as if trying to discern the individual molecules that made it up. But when Laban began his speech, Isra started mumbling to herself loud enough for Viekko to hear, but he doubted anyone who wasn't listening could. "First step, he will make sure the people know that the resources of the moon belong to the native people..."

Laban waited smiling until the room was quiet again. "I am so pleased to be sitting down with Halifaco of the *Perfiduloi* and the Great Houston of the *Urbanoi*. There have been troubles on this planet in the past, I know this is true, but those will be repaired. To help heal this amazing planet, we want the people of Titan to know that their resources belong to them and nobody else."

"Next," said Isra, not looking up, "Make the population dependent on the Corporation by putting them deep in debt."

"Even as we speak," Laban continued, "A ship is being loaded with new equipment to maximize the extraction of the great wealth of hydrocarbons. A small investment by both peoples of Titan that will guarantee prosperity for every living person."

Viekko and Althea exchanged glances. They started to recognize the Corporation playbook even as Isra recited it.

"The third part is tricky," Isra continued, "You need an element of self-interest so that people in a position of power will continue to work in their own best interests rather than for the good of the people."

Laban walked in front of the table. "I would also like to announce an exciting new opportunity for the people of Titan. You are not just a proud Titanian race, but you are children of Earth. Your ancestors found themselves alone here after the Fall, but they created a grand society and it is a society that you all should be proud of. However, as

363

children of Earth, you are entitled to return to your ancestral home. And, in exchange for some of the hydrocarbons extracted, we can make that happen."

The crowd cheered, louder and longer than ever. Isra gave a single, solemn nod and said, "Well played. All you need now is the consent of the current ruling class so that it doesn't feel like a hostile takeover and that is it..."

Laban motioned back to Halifaco and the Houston who both stood up and joined Laban in front of the table. "This deal will not only bring an end to the division between the *Perfiduloi* and *Urbanoi*, but will ensure a peaceful and prosperous future for all of Titan."

Isra looked up just as the Houston and Halifaco took a step forward to shake each other's hands and then embraced each other. The show was over and everyone went back to their conversations.

Althea sat up slightly, "And that's it? All is forgiven and forgotten? The slavery? The cruelty? The senseless killing? Can the Corporation really erase all that so easily?"

"Of course not," said Isra taking a drink, "It is still there. It is just hidden now. Look at Halifaco."

Viekko watched Halifaco and the Houston pull away from their embrace as continue shaking hands.

"Look at his eyes," Isra continued, "The ambition is still there. He will play by the rules for now because he still believes in *Kompanio*. But he will grow tired of it and seek a way to power again. Look at that group over there."

Viekko and Althea both turned to see where Isra pointed. It was a group of five or six *Perfiduloi* men and women gathered around an *Urbanoi* couple listening to them talk.

"The woman on the far right," said Isra, "She knows that couple. One of them at any rate. Something happened to her. She can't look them in the face. Her smile is forced. She laughs a half-second later than everyone else. She is trying to fit in. She knows that the thing to do now is pretend that the past is the past, but one cannot pretend forever. She will slip up and the truth will be known. Now look over there."

Isra motioned to two *Urbanoi* men sitting close to each other at an adjacent table, "They have not talked to a single *Perfiduloi*. You can see the concealed disgust in their faces when one stops to chat. They see this gathering as an abomination and they will act accordingly someday."

"What are you saying?" asked Althea with a touch of admiration in her voice.

Isra smiled and even laughed just slightly, "I am saying that the children all behave when the parents are watching. The parents, in this case, being the cult of the *Kompanio*. Religion is the ultimate parental figure. It may cause them to change their behavior, but it will not change who they are at heart. The hatred is still there. And that is good."

"How do you figure?" said Viekko finishing his drink.

"Hatred leads to violence. Violence leads to suppression. Suppression leads to revolution. The Corporation requires complete domination but they cannot something as energetic as hatred. It only gets stronger the more it is contained." Isra got up. "Come with me, Viekko. You need to see something."

Viekko set his mug down on the table and followed Isra. She marched up to Laban and extended her hand. "I suppose congratulations are in order."

Laban smiled wide and said, "I must say, I am surprised. You never did strike me as one who would be magnanimous in defeat."

"Oh, I am not," said Isra. She flashed Viekko a fast smile and added, "I know you knew about the city and I can prove it. You had thousands of feet of hose and almost no drilling rigs. Your plan from the start was to take over the refineries that you knew were there."

Laban pulled back. "Hardly a violation. Besides, you still can't prove it. The shipping manifests will prove that we took advantage of a situation."

"And the fact that you had a message from the CEO ready? It takes over two hours to get a signal to and from Earth. You made it earlier and intended to use it to subjugate the people."

Laban waved his hand. "That is your interpretation. The Corporation will have theirs."

Isra smiled. "Indeed. And the legal battle will be long and drawn out. And there is you, Laban. I suspect as the leader of this expedition, you will spend a lot of time arguing for the Corporation." She grabbed him by the arm. "You are a rare Corporation man, Laban. Enterprising, resourceful, a free thinker with a taste for adventure."

Laban forced a smile and, with awkward tact, pulled his arm away. "So nice of you to notice."

Isra continued, "I suspect spending all your time in and out of Ministry courts and Corporation tribunals would crush a man like you."

Viekko saw a slight glint of horror in Laban's face as his future flashed in front of his eyes.

"There is not much satisfaction in pyrrhic victories," said Isra, "But one has to take what they can."

She turned and started to walk away. "Nothing in this world is simple, Laban. Or free. There will always be those waiting to collect."

She went back to her seat across from Althea and sat back down. Viekko stood behind her. "So what exactly did I need to see there?"

With a serene smile, Isra picked up her mug of wine and held up toward Althea. "To another mission complete."

Althea hesitated but clinked her mug against Isra's.

In that moment, Viekko realized that maybe it wasn't that *he* needed to see it, but that Isra needed him to see it. In his experience, a general who no longer seeks the approval of his army has given up. But so long as he—or she—is willing to put up a semblance of strength there's still some fight left.

CHAPTER THIRTY-THREE

In the end, the only hope to discovering the truth might lie in the planets and moons of our solar system. The real story could still exist somewhere out of reach of those who worked so hard to hide the truth of the Fall. There are many reasons to venture from our home planet. Discovering the truth about our own past is arguably the most important.

-from The Fall: The Decline and Failure of 21st Century Civilization *by Martin Raffe.*

Viekko floated near his locker in the hibernation pod aboard *Innovation*. He pressed his thumb to the black pad to unlock it and retrieved a small silver-colored metal container. It was about the size of his palm and a few inches thick. He unscrewed the top and brought it to his lips. The action opened a valve in the neck and released the liquid inside. A splash of sweet, warming whiskey burst in his mouth. He held it for a moment, savoring the flavor before he swallowed. It was a small celebration worthy of such a small victory.

He let his body relax in zero gravity. Constant free-fall was soothing in an odd way. Without gravity exerting force on his aching, bruised muscles he could fully relax. He could lay back suspended in air and let the tension drain out of him. He brought the flask to his lips again.

The hatch hissed and creaked open. Viekko winced as he quickly spun around to stash the flask back in his locker. Contraband like whiskey was a minor issue, certainly nothing close to several days' supply of triple-T. But he had troubles enough for one trip and listening to Althea or Isra chew his ear off was more than his tattered psyche could handle.

So it was a strange relief when it was Cronus who floated through the door feet first with the immersion goggles still on his head.

He pulled the goggles off and grinned with great excitement. "Viekko. I thought I would find you in here."

Viekko reached into his locker for the flask again. "Ah, what made you think I would be in here?"

Cronus cocked his head. "You seem like a man who celebrates a victory on his own. I am as well. But this time...I had a strange desire...I thought it would be good to share the moment with another person."

Viekko smiled and tossed the flask from hand to hand watching it spin slowly in the air. "Celebratin' alone ain't healthy anyway. Here."

He tossed the flask toward Cronus. It flew in a straight line for several seconds before it got close enough for the little net baby to grab it out of the air. He twisted open the cap and sniffed it. "What is it?"

Viekko folded his arms. "Just a little somethin' they make on the farm."

Cronus arched an eyebrow, took a drink and immediately launched into a coughing fit. "That is not a drink for humans. That is fuel. That is something you burn to keep warm or maybe escape the gravitational pull of a small body."

He tossed it back to Viekko who smiled. "It takes some gettin' used to." He raised the flask and said, "Here's to a successful mission. To nobody gettin' killed and...to a new member of the Human Reconnection Project."

Cronus blinked. "You mean it? What about Isra?"

"She has a way about her, but she don't always mean what she says. Besides, you did good at the end. She can be reasoned with."

"Viekko!" yelled Isra through the open hatch of the hibernation chamber.

"In the same way one might reason with a sandstorm," said Viekko. He took another drink since being caught was inevitable.

Isra shot through the hatch and caught herself on a handle attached near the door. "Viekko, are you in here?"

Viekko raised the flask. "Isra, good to see you. Hell of a mission, eh? Join us for a drink?"

Isra glared at the little metal container as if it had personally insulted her. "No, thank you. I do not want to know where you got that. Anyway, I am here to give you an order."

Viekko ran his hand down the length of his queue. "Oh good. I was floating here worried that—"

"Viekko Spade, I hereby order you enroll in and complete a triple-T rehabilitation program upon your return to Earth. What happened down there was unacceptable and I will not have a man I brought on for security running around strung out on some super-drug. You will enroll, you will complete it and you will submit to a complete screening and physical assessment before you are cleared for another mission. Is that clear?"

"As a brilliant, starry night."

Isra floated forward until she was too close to his face. "I mean it, Viekko. Clean up your act or I will toss you out and leave you to die in some gutter on Earth. You have the occasional ability to make situations slightly less dangerous and that is the only reason I did not shoot you myself."

Despite Isra's proximity, he managed to get the flask to his lips. "Understood."

Isra spun around to face Cronus. "As for you, once we get back to Earth, I want you to report immediately to Ministry security for clearance and a background scan. You will also schedule a medical examination as quickly as possible. We will be scheduling a new mission soon and I expect you to be better prepared than you were for this one."

Cronus nodded so fast that his head was in danger of disconnecting from the rest of his body.

Isra looked both men over and, satisfied with her work, spun around and launched herself toward the hatch.

She grabbed the handle at the door. "Cronus, one more thing."

Cronus gulped.

Isra spent a moment looking at the little man floating in front of her. "You are not entirely useless."

Cronus relaxed.

"But if you ever cross me or otherwise undermine my work again, I will throw you out an airlock and see how long you can hold your breath."

Cronus's entire posture again had the tension of a guitar string. "Yes...yes. I'm sorry. Absolutely."

With that, she pulled herself out of the hibernation chamber and went about her business of terrorizing some other hapless victim.

Viekko shook his head. "Coming from Isra Jicarillo, that was a hell of a compliment. It was beautiful. Seriously, I might cry a little."

Cronus watched the hatch close behind Isra. "I suspect that is the nicest thing she will say to me. But that is okay. I should go; I should retrieve the data I saved from the pyramid in case someone stumbles across it."

Viekko raised the flask as Cronus left. "What are the chances they find it?"

Cronus smiled. "Almost zero. But why take a chance if no chance is necessary? Besides, if I can download what I have now, I can start the processors on it during hibernation. I should have results before I wake. See you on Earth, Viekko Spade."

Viekko watched the man open the hatch and pull himself through. As he did, Althea came from the other direction.

She pulled herself inside and looked at the flask. "Oh

you've got to be bloody kidding me Viekko."

Viekko tried to relax again. "That's why I'm in here. Didn't think anyone would come lookin'. Turns out I might as well have posted a *kharaasan* sign outside. Care for a drink?"

Althea sighed. "Sure. Why not?"

Viekko tossed her the flask. She took a couple hefty swallows from it.

"Something on your mind, Althea?" asked Viekko, watching her.

She screwed the top back on and coughed a little. "Nothing much. I just...I wonder if we did the right thing."

Althea tossed the flask back to him. He started to unscrew it. "Couldn't say what the right thing is. We completed our mission, that's all that matters."

"Come on, Viekko. You heard what Laban said, so don't play dense. Trading labor for passage back to Earth? You know as well as I do what is going to happen. They will demand thousands of tons of methane, ethane and propane for a single ride. People like Halifaco and the Houston will secure their own freedom first. A few leaders will follow. Meanwhile, the Corporation will import more desperate people onto the moon and force them into indentured servitude that they will never pay off. When we arrived, roughly half the population of Titan were slaves. Now that we are leaving, almost all of them are. Bloody good job if I do say so myself."

Viekko shrugged and took a drink. "They worship the Corporation. I understand that being a servant to a god is one of the great pleasures in life."

Althea had to laugh as Viekko tossed the flask back to her. "I knew you were cynical, but...this is not the same thing at all, and you know it."

"I suppose that's a matter of theological debate. I wouldn't worry about it, Althea. The Titanians drove off the last invaders before the Fall. The Corporation knows that or they will know it soon enough. The Ministry wants to conduct their own operations there as well, and that means

371

that the Corporation will be on their best behavior for a few years. Just until the money can find the right pockets, at least."

Althea took a drink. "You know what I love about you, Viekko? Your sunny disposition."

He smiled, "There will be another Halifaco someday. Some upstart kid will gather a force and fight the Corporation. They'll win too. Nobody has figured out how to fight a war over a billion kilometers away, regardless of how powerful they are. If there is one thing history shows, humans have the powerful urge to misbehave."

Althea smiled. "There is that."

"There's always hope Althea."

She raised the flask. "Here's to hope."

Viekko raised his empty hand. "Here's to the rebels and maniacs that keep it alive."

While Althea took another drink, Viekko added, "And, depending on how megalomaniacal those rebels get, who knows what exciting new oppressive regimes await this world?"

Althea sighed and tossed the empty flask. "Good night Viekko."

For Viekko, home was an apartment in the Ipanema neighborhood of Rio de Janeiro. At least it was for one more night. Viekko packed a bag in the darkened room while the bright lights and sounds of perpetual celebration floated through the open window. Rio might not be the city that doesn't sleep, but it's definitely a city that's gonna have to sleep off what they did the night before.

Part of him wanted to go out one more time. Say goodbye to the hustlers and bartenders and the daughters of the wealthy upper class. They would be sad to see him go and they would express their grief through gallons of alcohol and no small amount of illicit substances. It was how they expressed most every emotion, come to think of it. He opened a drawer and dumped everything into a canvas bag.

What he wanted was one more shard of triple-T. So he stayed upstairs.

He just finished removing all his fine clothes from the closet when a ringing drew his attention from the bedroom into the main room. He walked out and stood in front of a screen embedded in the wall. He waved his hand in front of it and called, "Hello?"

The screen in the main room was a couple meters wide by a meter tall, and Cronus's face filled every millimeter in rather horrifying detail. From that distance, he could see every one of the little hairs still hanging on Cronus's balding head. His eyes were hidden behind his glowing goggles. He had a manic grin on his face, but that was nothing new for him.

Viekko sighed. "Cronus, good to see you. I see you got back to...wherever it is you live."

"I live in the Signal. The code is my senses. I hear everything, I see—"

Viekko stopped him. "That's great, Cronus. Really. Great. Listen, I don't have a lot of time to talk. I've got to pack what I can and catch a sub-orbital in the morning, so if you could just make this quick—"

"Have you ever heard of the Hereclese Project?"

"Nope. Can't say that I have. Good talk Cronus, now—"

"It's some kind of obscure project from the mid-twenty-first century. There's only one mention of it in any document on the Neuvonet."

Viekko took off his hat and ran his fingers down the length of the queue. "So?"

Cronus cocked his head and leaned closer to the camera. "I have a small sample of communications from that time period from Titan. It's mentioned in almost every single one. Talked about constantly on Titan, but nothing on Earth."

"I don't understand," said Viekko getting impatient, "What's a project on Titan got to do—"

"No. It was a project somewhere else. A big one. But there is no mention of what it was. Only people wanting to leave Titan time for Hereclese. Others spoke of jobs related

373

to the project. No details, but it's big."

Viekko rolled his eyes. "Right, a big project that nobody knows nothin' about it. Cronus, what has all of this got to do with me?"

Cronus paused and looked around a moment as if to make sure they were alone. "How long have you known Isra Jicarrio?"

Viekko sighed again. "She was on the crew of the first expedition to Mars. She wasn't in charge then, just a Ministry wonk getting her feet wet in interplanetary relations. Cronus, is this going somewhere because I've got a lot to—"

Cronus's face disappeared and was replaced by a document of some kind. "There are no records of Isra Jicarrio of any kind anywhere before she was twelve years old. This document is the first record of her existing at all."

Viekko peered at the document on the screen closely. "Where did you get this?"

"Leaked documents. Part of a deep Ministry slice. Highly classified knowledge. The kind of thing where if you know about it, they kill you."

"Then could you please take it off my screen?"

"Don't worry. My communications are secure. Bounced through the old Internet cables so nobody could track it. Now pay attention. Remember how I said there is only one mention of Hereclese anywhere on Earth? It's right here."

The document zoomed in and a particular passage was highlighted. Viekko leaned forward and read out loud. "Isra's origins before her recovery are unknown. Several hypotheses have been proposed, however. From her testimonial and the advanced nature of the technology she arrived with, it is possible that she is a product of the Hereclese project."

The document disappeared and was replaced with Cronus looking more manic than normal, an effect enhanced by the shapes and numbers moving across this goggles. "The only record of the Hereclese project on Earth is directly related to Isra Jicarrio. What...what does that mean?"

Viekko stared at the screen for a few moments. Isra never talked about her past. In fact, he couldn't pinpoint a single moment when she brought up life before the Reconnection Project. So what did this mean? Probably a whole mess of trouble.

Viekko stepped back. "It don't mean nothin', Cronus. Not yet, anyway. Take care of yourself. I'll see you on the next mission."

Cronus started to say something but Viekko waved his arm and the strange little hacker vanished.

There was too much to do right now. An apartment to pack up, a life to put back in order. As he went back to the bedroom to put away the last of his things, the nagging thought still echoed in his head.

Isra Jicarrio and the Hereclese project. It probably made sense in some way, but nothing that would be apparent. And nothing that Isra would talk about.

The past should remain the past. Best to focus his mind on the here and now. Outside the window, the perpetual party of Rio de Janeiro screamed on. He stuck his head out of the open window and breathed in the air. The space above the streets was filled with strange glowing shapes; holograms that turned the warm Brazilian night into a constant light show along with laughter, shouts, and music. Down below, a group of women dressed in their shortest, tight-fitting clothing looked up at Viekko and waved. He recognized one. She reached into her pocket and held up something small. Even this far away and with that many bright lights, he recognized the little blue capsule.

The past is only the past when one decides to make a change. Otherwise, tomorrow just becomes another today.

Viekko waved back and closed the window.

ACKNOWLEDGMENTS

The dirty little secret about self-publishing a book is that there is nothing 'self' about it. The only reason that this book exists and is looks as good as it does is because of the help of a small group of extremely generous individuals.

Particular thanks to Shaun Vincent for producing and editing the Ruins of Empire Podcast thus far. Not only was he the first to listen to me read this book all the way through, but he had to listen to the hundreds, if not, thousands of screw ups along the way. Also to Tyler Murphy for lending his voice to the project as well. They both have, in one form or another, been partners in crime with me for years and it was awesome to hammer this project out together.

To Madison Hansen for taking on this project and helping me turn about 120,000 words splattered onto a Word document into something that actually looks like a book.

And to Nick Martin for lending his artistic skills for the cover art. I don't know what I would have done without them, but it would have been messy and unsatisfying.

And, finally, to everyone who was nice enough, during this whole process, to saddle up next to me at the bar and ask, 'Hows the book going?' Having so many friends engaged during this publishing process meant a lot and I hope this book was everything you thought it would be.

JEREMY L. JONES

Writer. Brewer. Traveler. Slightly crazed human-person.

He is the author of the Ruins of Empire Series along with hundreds of other books that, for the moment, only exist in his own head. He lives in Boise, Idaho with his wife, a cat named Mist and an office where he can lock himself away and write the crazy stories he dreams up. He can be found wandering the craft beer scene sampling the fermented arts created in his home town, or in his garage making his own.

Seek him out online at www.sagaofinsanity.blogspot.com

83736058R00234

Made in the USA
San Bernardino, CA
30 July 2018